KU-738-881

GOLD

ABOUT THE AUTHOR

Raven Kennedy is a California girl born and raised,
whose love for books pushed her into creating her own worlds.

Her debut series was a rom-com fantasy about a cupid looking
for love. She has since gone on to write in a range of genres,
including the adult dark fantasy: The Plated Prisoner Series,
which has become an international bestseller.

Whether she makes you laugh or cry, or whether the series
is about a cupid or a gold-touched woman, she hopes to
create characters that readers can root for.

When Raven isn't writing, she's reading and
spending time with her husband and daughters.

You can connect with Raven on her social media sites,
and visit www.ravenkennedybooks.com

GOLD

THE PLATED PRISONER SERIES

V

INTERNATIONAL BESTSELLING AUTHOR
RAVEN KENNEDY

MICHAEL  JOSEPH

PENGUIN MICHAEL JOSEPH

UK | USA | Canada | Ireland | Australia
India | New Zealand | South Africa

Penguin Michael Joseph is part of the Penguin Random House group of companies
whose addresses can be found at global.penguinrandomhouse.com

First published in the United States of America by Raven Kennedy 2023
First published in Great Britain by Penguin Michael Joseph 2023
001

Copyright © Raven Kennedy, 2023

The moral right of the author has been asserted

Cover Design by A.T. Cover Designs
Formatting by Imagine Ink Designs
Bridge by Bex Creations
Crowns Illustration by Bex Creations
Rip Illustration by Aude Ziegelmeyer
Editing by Polished Perfection
Map by Fictive Designs
Printed and bound in Great Britain by Clays Ltd, Elcograf S.p.A.

The authorized representative in the EEA is Penguin Random House Ireland,
Morrison Chambers, 32 Nassau Street, Dublin D02 YH68

A CIP catalogue record for this book is available from the British Library

HARDBACK ISBN: 978–0–241–69012–3
TRADE PAPERBACK ISBN: 978–0–241–62162–2

www.greenpenguin.co.uk

MIX
Paper | Supporting
responsible forestry
FSC® C018179

Penguin Random House is committed to a
sustainable future for our business, our readers
and our planet. This book is made from Forest
Stewardship Council® certified paper.

About The Book

Please note: This book contains explicit content and dark elements that may be triggering to some. It includes explicit romance, mature language, violence, death, animal cruelty, past trauma, and grief. It is not intended for anyone under 18 years of age.
This is book five in a series.

When you feel swallowed by the dark,

may you become your own light.

CHAPTER 1

AUREN

I go loudly.
Loudly, loudly into the void.
The blaring rattle of a solitary fall.

I don't close my eyes against the strange dark. My grief wails like thunder, clapping past a broken chest, while echoed teardrops stream down my cheeks like rain.

The world ripped, and I was ripped from *him.*

It feels wrong. So wrong to be rent apart. Like fingers curled around my ribs, yanking me open. Hollowing me out.

Thick wind peels at my skin. Rushing air plugs my nose and condenses on my tongue. A howling clatter drowns my ears. The flash of lightning and stars surrounds me in the yawning dark.

Through it all, I can see the rip.

I can see the jagged edges of the torn sky above me, a betraying Orean air gaping like a wound in the dark. Liquid gold bleeds through, falling like gelatinous droplets, glinting as they drip down into the nothing. But that rip gets further and further away from me, my body plunging deeper into the starry unknown with unstoppable force.

I'm alone. Alone in this dark, endless void, torn away from Slade.

I keep falling and falling, further and further away from that rip. Further away from him. And as if that weren't terrifying enough, my senses are suddenly stripped away.

My sight. Sound. Feeling. Taste. Scent. All of it—*gone*.

The scream tearing from my throat is no more either. Or if it is, I can't feel it. Can't hear it pierce my ears.

Without my senses, without any way to experience what's happening, my grief and fear condenses. Time stretches and snaps.

I don't know what will happen to me in this void. I don't know if this is what it feels like to die. Though I do know one thing.

This

       is

           what

               it

                  feels

                  like

                    to

f

a

l

l

CHAPTER 2

SAIRA TURLEY

In the beginning, there was a bridge.
A bridge to nowhere, they said.
A bridge that existed into non-existence. A bridge where people went and didn't come back.

Where cold and color warred. The former winning, the latter drained.

And I...I went.

I walked that bridge that didn't want to end. I slogged through the barren gray, scraping through time that ceased to exist with goose bumps pebbled on my thin arms.

I was just a girl, but I went. Because my father had been forced to go, and he never came back.

None of them did.

So I snuck onto it, determined to find him. I told myself I

wasn't going to fail. I wasn't going to turn around.

Now, when the story is told, people think I kept going because I was brave. But really, it was because I was scared of falling.

So I walked.

For days and years. Through memories and moments.

I soon found that it wasn't just a path. It was an all-consuming void of my own bleakness. It had me believe I'd never make it to the other side of the bridge itself any more than I'd ever make it to the other side of my soul's grief. They went hand in hand. They became one and the same—the journey on the bridge and the path of my own desolation. Because my mother had died, and my father had gone, and I was so utterly alone even before I started the long, solitary trek.

I became hungry and thirsty on that path, and so very tired. The cold air did strange things, playing sounds that came out of the foggy nothing. There was the voice of my father, telling me to keep going. The sound of my mother, crying, urging me to come back.

But that earthen, colorless ground was steady and perpetual, so I kept dragging my tired soles on and on and on, letting the land guide me through the forever. Because I had nothing to go back to. I had nothing to lose by going forward. And the way down looked such a long way to fall.

So I kept walking.

Until I was so exhausted I thought I might just finally have to give in and lie down to die. Forlorn body and forsaken spirit drained out into the voided path.

But then, it...ended.

It's funny, I kept going because I was terrified of tipping off the edge. But that endless bridge did have a limit. The rough path of earth was there step after step, until suddenly, it wasn't.

GOLD

After all of that, I ended up falling, anyway.

It was a strange sort of falling, though. I didn't fall down, I fell through.

My scraped and blistered feet slipped through the shade of the earth, tearing a scream from my throat. I plummeted down, down, down, through dirt and rock, past grime and rubble. Where my breaths were just dust and the sand had no purchase.

I thought I was going to fall forever through the ground, but then I was spat out like a bitter taste, and I crashed through the clouds in an amethyst sky.

Whereas the ground had felt intangible, the sky felt liquid. Its dense weight shoved at me while cotton-bloomed clouds tossed me left and right. The ground was up and the sky was down, and I flipped so many times that my clothes tore to shreds. Thick strips of my dress cascaded out behind me like tattered wings while my arms flapped uselessly in the air, trying to gain control, trying to fly when all I could do was fall.

Until, suddenly, I wasn't falling anymore.

Like gravity was just a breeze, and I was lighter than the grass. The tips of my toes bounced lightly before my heels met the earth, the frayed strips of my dress billowing down around me like wings tucking back in.

As soon as both of my feet were planted, a shockwave poured over the earth like a ripple through the water, and out of it spread a sea of glowing blue flowers that burst from the soil. The ground was now as solid as it should be, the air bursting with the perfume of blooms, and the sky no longer felt like a current wanting to whisk me away.

I was...here.

I'd crossed the bridge to nowhere, and I reached somewhere new. I didn't know much—I'd never left my city in Seventh Kingdom—but I knew I wasn't in Orea anymore.

I wasn't alone, either.

People were around, staring at me wide-eyed, looking up at the clouds I'd jostled through. I could feel the magic in the air even then, though I didn't know what the feeling was. I didn't know what those bystanders would be to me. Didn't know what those pointed ears meant.

But I would soon.

Years would pass, and this magical world would become my home, but I never forgot that endless trudge on the bridge. In turn, the fae never forgot the way I burst through the sky like a broken-winged bird, and that is what they always called me.

So, yes, I was scared to fall. But without falling, I never would have landed.

And what a beautiful thing it was to land.

CHAPTER 3

AUREN

T*hump.*

Fragments of awareness nudge against me.

They thud against the barrier of my mind, like a log thumping on a shoreline rock. It's a hollow, steady sound that reminds me of dead, washed-way things. Some pieces have edges sharp with pain, and others are dulled by watered-down memories long ago lost.

Thump

The first lugging piece that knocks against my consciousness with a forceful thump is a *taste*. Like the void took my senses away only to slowly offer them back.

I taste the sweet and woodsy relish of a sugarcane against my tongue. I can fathom the split stalk, of peeling back its edges to lap up the goodness inside. I remember being a little girl, remember popping it into my mouth and sucking out its sugar. It's so real that I can even feel the sunshine warming the reed. It's like I'm back there, in Annwyn, tasting it all over again. My mouth waters as the saccharine slurp explodes on my tongue.

Thump

Suddenly, scent surrounds me.

A flower. Though, I can't remember its name—not even what it looks like. But the moment the smell invades me, a memory of my nose buried against my mother's coat becomes a fragment in my prismatic mind. The perfume is rich and deep, heady in its floral crispness that makes me want to crawl inside the smell and breathe its air forever. But not just because of the scent—because of my mother. Because of the comforting way it clung to her the same way I did.

With that scent, my nose seems to work again, the claggy air of the void replacing my mother's perfume with something deeper and far more riotous. Like some untouched cavern in the earth that hasn't been disturbed by light or breath in thousands of years.

Thump

Thump

Incessant, the next sensation knocks against my skin, announcing its return. It sparks life down my limbs, reigniting my nerves to touch and feel.

The catalyst is a hand holding mine. The memory so real that my fingers flex, even as the sensation of falling returns, my stomach plummeting right alongside the rest of me. But that palm, that callused, warm grip… I can't see his face, can't hear his voice, but I recognize the feel of my father's hand. Strong and sure. *Safe*. So long as I kept hold of it, I knew nothing scary or painful could ever touch me.

Thump

Thump

Next, my hearing abruptly returns with a rounded piece that fits into the slats of my mind, twisting the lock.

"Auren!"

I hear a young boy calling my name.

"*A-Auren!*" His voice is so full of laughter, the excitement making him stutter slightly. It makes my name sound like bubbles and bumps, up and down for every letter, rising to a pop at the end. The joy, the pure effervescent happiness of childhood, accompanies that single word called into the echoes.

It makes my heart hurt.

When the voice fades away, I once more hear the wind rushing past my ears, the thunder spitting in the void.

And then, my last sense returns, like a gift. Wrapped paper peeling open from the dark. It's the memory of an Annwyn morning, soft yellow beams of sunlight reaching out to caress the world like a kiss against the horizon.

It's as if my eyes snap open to the light, though they were never closed.

My vision returns, and I blink up at the rip. It's far, far above me now, looking like a piece of black fabric that was cut through with a dagger. It stays stagnant, unreachable, while liquid gold continues to leak from it like a gleaming waterfall, coating the stars.

Lightning flares and fumes in the darkness alongside me, making my skin glow, leaving streaks behind in the dark ether. I forget for a moment to feel afraid, because of how beautiful it is—this light in the dark.

But then, those frayed edges of the rip slowly start to close.

My throat closes with it.

Thump

Thump

Thump goes my heart.

I watch helplessly as the split melts back together, fingers of wax stretching to clasp me in its grip. I plunge down the gullet of this gap between worlds, while the fibrous jaw bites hard.

And I feel real fear.

Even with childhood memories of Annwyn flooding my senses, terror clomps over me until I'm trodden down with it. I'm still falling, and maybe I'll be stuck in this in-between place with these jagged memories and that's all I'll have. Maybe that's all I deserve.

The rip is threading back together, which means Slade won't be able to follow me through. Reality hits me in the chest like a punch. The rip is closing, and I'm drained of my power, and I have no idea what to do, and I'm alone, and I'm *falling*—

Don't fall. Fly.

Slade's voice cuts through my kaleidoscope mind. Like the scrape of solder melting together all the scattered pieces, bringing me back together again.

He's grounding me, even when I have nothing beneath me but air.

You have to go into it, baby. You have to. I can't get to you.

I watch as the last of the opening inches shut more and more, faster and faster. Tattered strips of void clump together like ink bleeding over the final inch of paper to absorb the rip that was made—made for *me*.

I didn't want to go. I didn't want to go alone.

Look at me.

My eyes snap to the stitching seam as if his gaze will still be there. As if he weren't already closed off from me.

I will find you. I will find you in that life.

Now, my senses flood with him.

I remember the taste of his skin as I licked up his neck. His scent when my cheek was pressed against his chest. The feel of his arms around me. Steady. Solid. Safe. His heartbeat, thumping for *me*.

The sound of his voice when he called me *Goldfinch*.

I remember the sight of him coming down from the sky

like a vision. A fierce, raging warrior come to rot the world to keep me safe. Those variegated eyes going from green to black, boring into me, telling me a thousand things all at once.

I'll find you, Goldfinch. I swear to you.

Now fly.

Fly.

There's an echoing crash, like ocean waves slamming together. Then, with one final stitch, the rip cinches shut.

Totally. Completely.

There isn't even a gap for my gold to drip through anymore. I can't tell a rip was ever there to begin with, and the bleak emptiness of the black void settles around me like a suffocating cloak.

The way back is closed. Orea, the world I've grown to know, is gone, and all that's left is the stark unknown.

And I...I have Annwyn on my mind and Slade in my ears.

Reassuring me. Reminding me.

Don't fall.

y

l

F

Can I?

I close my eyes for a breath. I shut down my dread. Shove down my weakness. Replay that strong, steady voice of his to fortify me. So that when I open my eyes again, I can turn and face my plummet head-on.

So that strength can rise out of the fear.

All the gold that spilled down the rip alongside me starts gathering. It wraps around my body in shining rivulets like it's answering some unspoken call. Even the void itself changes with my mood. The lightning starts to spark in gilt splinters. The stars begin to pulsate with golden thrums that match the beat of my heart.

I smile in the glinting dark. Because once I force myself to stop being afraid, I realize that somehow, this feels...*right*.

When another flash of lightning juts through the air, it brings my attention down, and I notice one star that's brighter than the rest. I feel it pulling me closer, until I'm squinting at its light.

Until I'm close enough to reach for it.

My fingertip grazes along its dazzling flare, searing me with warmth. As soon as I touch it, it cracks against the black and hatches like an egg, its radiance spilling from the burst shell. The insides pour out like a flood, and I fall into it, letting it sweep me away into its starshine river.

And I am not afraid.

Because now, I'm no longer falling. I'm soaring toward the unknown, guiding myself to be swept away, no longer screaming or fighting or fearing.

The glimmering river of light that sweeps me away feels a bit like falling in love. Fast and gripping, blatant and blazing. It's a resplendent comfort, as it keeps me caught in its current, crackling against my skin and filling me with shivers.

I fall back in its flow, like floating in a sunshine ocean. I don't know how long I stay in the flux and the ebb, but I drift with its pulsing magic for ages, and it warms me up from the inside out.

Then, I'm poured into an earth.

Each speck of sparkle is now a grain of dirt, fertile soil clogging my nose and filling my mouth. I'm in quicksand, except instead of pulling me down to the core, it's pushing me up up up until—

I'm spilled out into a wayward sky.

The dark is gone. The starshine is too. Even the grains scrubbing against my skin disappear. In their place is soft buttermilk light and tufted clouds of silk, bright with the shine of a sun that feels so very different from Orea's.

The air is both new and familiar all at once. As soon as I breathe it in, I feel that wild beast, that effervescent *fae* inside of me, open her eyes. That part of me basks in the inhale and croons in my chest.

Because *this*. This is what it feels like to *breathe*.

With eyes wide open, with my mouth pressed in determination, and embraced by the sky's current electrifying my veins, I spread my arms, and my beast spreads right alongside me.

I feel my *faeness* viscerally, as in tune with me as ever, and in this perfect bond, this fulfilling moment, something *surges* out.

Like feathers sprouting from skin, or petals unfurling from a stem. Like cutting teeth from empty gums, or light spilling from a splintered horizon.

The pain that accompanies it is consuming, yet freeing. It's a whirlwind of sensation hacked from loss and reborn with change.

I'm diving through the spongy clouds as if I'm a fish swimming through water, until suddenly, land appears beneath me, beckoning.

Welcoming.

And as I curl into its open embrace, something else curls with me—*around* me. The pain is gone and all that's left is this strange, ecstatic comfort that yanks free from the very center of my spirit.

Just before I land, I feel something flow behind me. As if I really did stop falling. As if I really did learn to fly.

It wraps around my body like threads of the sun.

Like bands of steel.

Like rays of warmth.

Like streams of light.

Like…

Ribbons.

CHAPTER 4

AUREN

I land the way a skipping rock grazes over the water. There is no crash, no pain. I simply glide into the landing, sinking into a blanket of a glowing, blue-blossomed field.

When my body stops, I lie there on my back, staring up at the soft sky dotted with dandelion clouds. My ears are ringing like I breached the surface after diving too deep.

Where am I?

It feels as if there's a gentle tide buoying my body, but instead of water, there are plush blossoms holding me up. When I turn my head, I see my gold-touch has kissed the blooms nearby, creating a perfect circle of gilt flowers all around me, gleaming daintily in the light and sinking into the soil.

The blossom tide ebbs, my heartbeat flows, and with quickened breaths pulling in the perfumed air, I push myself up to a sitting position, the golden flowers grazing my arms.

But that's not all that's brushing up against me.

At first, I don't really register it. I don't connect the layers of gold wrapped around my arms with reality. It's not until the breeze shifts one of them that my mind confirms what my eyes are seeing.

My breath catches.

My heart does too.

I sit here amidst the incandescent flowers, beneath a lavender sky, and all I can think is, *am I dreaming, or am I dead?*

My trembling hands lift the ribbons beside me, and I *feel* them. Not just with my fingertips, but through the lengths themselves. When I slip my hand between a few, my eyes instantly well with tears, relishing in the silky feel.

Great Divine…

I count them, like a new mother counts a babe's fingers and toes. I curl all two dozen strips into my fists like I'm holding the hands of a friend. I pull lightly, feeling the answering tug coming from my back, all up and down either side of my spine. They feel satiny and sun-kissed.

A sob breaks through my mouth. Tears slip past my lids.

My ribbons are *real*.

They aren't in tatters at my feet. They aren't shredded from my skin. They aren't plucked from me like feathers off a bird, lying in deadened heaps on the floor.

They're back.

The pain and trauma of what I felt when they were taken from me comes rushing up, and I tremble all over. They're here, given back to me like some divine gift, and I feel their loss, their absence, and their return all at once.

"They're back," I whisper to myself, as more tears glide down my face, landing in gilt dots on their silky soft strips. "They're back."

I'm back.

Because without them, I wasn't fully me.

I feel like I could cry forever, that I could weep out my soul's wrenching relief. But I simply tug them again. Just to keep feeling. And they're still here. Still real.

A smile—a true, heart-deep smile—treads up my face even as my tears keep tracking down because *they're back.*

But that smile suddenly freezes when I realize something else.

They aren't moving.

I try to strain the muscles in my back, try to get them to move, but nothing happens. My smile morphs into a frown as I tug at them again, as if I can wake them up, shaking them back and forth to stir them. Pulling each length, flexing the muscles along my spine.

Nothing works.

They're here, they're real, but they don't stir. Not even an inch. Like the hair on my head, they simply hang down, immobile, instead of me being able to shift them at will. Instead of them seeming to move with a mind of their own.

They're just…*still.*

My heart jolts, and I let out a shaky breath. More tears pool in my eyes, but I don't let them fall. Don't let myself get caught into panic.

My ribbons are back. That's what matters, and that's what I need to focus on now. By some miracle, they've returned to me. Even if I can never move them again, I'll be thankful, because it's like a missing piece of myself being returned.

Maybe, after some time, they'll move again. Maybe they just need time.

I wipe my eyes as I gather the ribbons and hold them in my lap to admire them. They're so…*bright.* A new, shiny sheen to them that wasn't there before. They feel just as soft as they used to, but they also feel stronger. As if beneath their satiny exterior, they've come back reinforced to their very core.

But then, maybe that makes perfect sense. After all, I'm stronger too. I'm not the same woman I was before I lost them, so it makes sense that they wouldn't be the same ribbons they were before they were severed.

I wrap one strip around my hand and then lift my eyes to look around. Tall flowers surround me. Still reeling, I push myself to my feet so I can get a better look. But as soon as I do, I cry out in pain. I look down at my burnt, mottled feet, trembling as I try to stay upright.

Ouch.

At least I know now that I can't be dead. I'm certain death would be kind enough to take pain away. Which means everything that happened at the Conflux is still imprinted on me.

The Conflux...

Reality and memories make my adrenaline surge, sending my body into a heavy shock. It crushes me with the weight of its landing, all of my joy and disbelief replaced with pain and exhaustion. The forced drain of my power that I endured makes itself known, tearing into my body with snapping teeth. My breath wobbles, shaken like a bottle of liquid, and I sway on my feet as a wave of dizziness rams itself into me headfirst.

But then I hear a collection of whispers and gasps ring through the air.

I whirl in surprise, ribbons tangling around my waist. About thirty feet away, there's a group of two dozen people staring at me. The field of flowers stretches around us further than I can see, the blooms giving off a soft blue glow as they gape at me with pure awe in their eyes.

Awe...and *fear*.

My mouth opens, but instead of managing to say something,

all that comes out is a gulp of pain. My legs tremble beneath me. Voices tremble in front of me.

"She's...*gold.*"

"Did you see the sky? Did you see how she fell from it?"

"Just like the broken-winged bird!"

"Look at her back!"

"Come away! We can't be here!"

"But look! She's *gold*! How can she be *gold*, unless—"

My gaze swings like a pendulum, while dizziness makes my focus sway and twist. "I..."

Words fail my mouth, but I see one person come forward. While I try to keep my feet under me, she eats up half the distance between us, only stopping when I try to step back and nearly collapse from the agony coursing up my burnt heels.

She has wisps for hair, like strings of silken spiderwebs have grown from her scalp, gathered into a puff that sits atop her head. She halts in front of me, aged gray eyes wide and searching as she stares at me like she's seeing a ghost.

"*Lyäri Ulvêre,*" she utters, a hand flying up to cover her lined, pinched mouth as her watery gaze falls to my ribbons trailing down from my back.

"What?" My voice feels far away, barely able to be heard by my own ears.

Behind her, the murmurs get louder, the same words being repeated. I can feel the palpable wonder resonating through the small crowd.

"You've come, just as she came—the broken-winged bird."

I don't know about a bird, but I certainly feel a bit broken right now.

"You're the Lyäri Ulvêre," she says again, her voice choking up.

My own voice pants out, my temples throbbing as my

dizziness begins to tunnel through my spiraling mind. "I don't understand…"

A tear falls down her cheek, even as a smile tugs at her thin lips. "It means it's alright, Lady Auren. Because you're *home*."

The shock of her answer is the last straw to take me tumbling down.

I hit the ground, knees buckled, feet fuming.

My mouth is unable to work. Mind far too shaken to process. I'm drained. So, so drained. Not just my power, but *me*. From what happened at the Conflux to the long, lonely fall to the shock of her words. Crippling debility creeps in, while my vision sputters out.

But her voice circles my mind like a spool of thread constricting around my chest.

Because she said I'm home.

Because she said my *name*.

Her words ring loudly, loudly into the unconscious dark.

CHAPTER 5

SLADE

I go silently.

The wind whips with thunderous noise, my blood pounds in my ears, and beneath my ribs, a rage roars, deafening and endless.

But I am silent.

Silent as I grip the reins of the timberwing. Silent as the roots of rot pulse beneath my skin, trying to split through me in angry tremors. Silent, even, as right there at the center of my heart, something beats with agony. With wrongness. Like an artery was ripped right out of my chest, leaving poison free to leak through my body. Because *she* was ripped away from me.

Silence is the only way to contain it.

So when there's a break in the clouds, when I see Third Kingdom laid below me, I direct the drop without making a single sound.

The air whistles with our descent, the beast beneath me

brays, and I watch with mute focus as Gallenreef Castle comes into view. It's standing proudly atop a rocky cliffside a hundred feet up from the water. There's a tall sea wall at its back, the stone stained from decades of protecting the castle against the invasion of high tide and perilous waves.

The ocean is calm right now though, where ships bob gently, teal crystalline water sparkling brightly in contrast to the castle's sandy-white walls and its coral roofs pitched sharply toward the sky. The shore at its feet leads up in a steady slope that feeds into the capital city. It's spread out far and wide amongst the chaparral of greenery. Buildings two and three stories tall mixed in with the lush plants.

It looks scenic. The epitome of an opulent, picturesque kingdom, bustling in its peace. A peace I want to obliterate.

The quiet rage inside of me bides its time. A cut-off ribbon in my pocket lies lifeless and still.

It's been two weeks since the Conflux. Many of those days were lost in my race to reach Deadwell. But Drollard Village, my secret haven in the mountains within Fifth Kingdom, now lies empty, caught in a frozen tomb. The rip in the cave is gone without a trace, right along with everyone there.

Including my mother.

Ryatt erupted in panic. Went out into a blizzard to search for her and the other villagers. But we both knew he wouldn't find them. We both knew deep down where they went.

Back through the rip. Back into Annwyn…or dead.

I've been trying every day to open another rip.

And every day, I have *failed*.

Ryatt's desperation is almost as intense as mine. I saw the panicked disappointment in his face every time I couldn't do it, though he never said a thing. He didn't have to, because his own emotions were mirrored in my chest.

No matter how many times I attempt to tear a hole through

the world and find the villagers and my mother, to get to Auren, *I can't do it.*

My rot has come back full force, but the raw power it takes to create a rip in the world hasn't returned.

I poured everything I could into the rip at the Conflux. It was the first time I'd ever made a rip on my own, without the clash of my father's power against mine. And when that happened, when all of my magic went into tearing that cleft in the air to save Auren, it must've done something to the rip in Drollard. It must've made it implode, absorbing everything that came with it. One rip opened, one rip closed.

Now, I'm helpless to open another. Helpless to find my mother or follow Auren.

And it's Queen Kaila's fault.

My hands tighten on the reins.

All of this—Auren propagated into a villain and dubbed *Lady Cheat* who stole powers and seduced kings—it was all Queen Kaila's words spinning a narrative. It was she who alerted the other monarchs, she who instigated the Conflux. It was she who sent her brother and soldiers to kidnap Auren from my own damn castle.

If she hadn't done all of this, Auren would still be here, safe. Instead, she's now a world away, and *I can't fucking get to her.*

Every day, every minute, my rage grows.

Into a fathomless, sinister thing. It's poisoned the already fetid rot within my veins. It's made everything else go eerily quiet. Made the fae instincts inside of me sharpen into the edge of a silently slicing blade.

And I will use it.

Because they tried to punish Auren. Tried to *execute her.*

Queen Kaila went against me—all of the other monarchs did. It's time I remind her and everyone else exactly why you don't fuck with me and mine.

My borrowed timberwing descends. Crest, I call him, since the youngling has a spot on his chest that looks like the crest of a noble house. Despite these beasts being naturally aggressive and distrustful, they've always seemed to have a sort of kinship with me—just like messenger hawks. I found Crest in Drollard's timberwing Perch, and although I've never ridden him before, he has no problem with me. He's even learned to anticipate my moves and pick up on my moods. Right now, his head feathers ruffle up with an intimidating flare as we fly further down.

The front of Third's castle casts a shadow over the sandy courtyard below. There's a pair of turret towers on either side of its giant front doors that are trimmed in bright coral, and the front steps leading to those doors rise up out of drifts of soft sand, as if they were simply swept into existence.

On either side of the front doors are matching statues of their kingdom's sigil—a carving of rolling waves, with the fin of a predatory shark jutting up between them. Guards are gathered in a show of force at the outer steps, double-ended spears strapped to their backs. They were no doubt alerted by the watchers who must've spotted me as soon as I broke through the clouds in their sky.

Gaze snatched upward, I count five more guards up in the towers at the protective outer wall, though not a single one of them makes a move to descend the stairs. Their silver armor gleams, sigils bared on their chests, bows in their hands, tunics almost as bright blue as the sea. Their wariness reveals itself in the way they shift on their feet and back up closer to the towers, watching me from above but refusing to move toward the stairs as guards *should* do when someone approaches a castle.

Especially when it's someone like me.

Movement in the front windows catches my eye, and I see even more guards watching me, grim faces bared behind the glass.

Crest lands inside the defensive wall with a screech, beach sand spraying up around his taloned feet. I jump down, ignoring the guards standing at attention as I stare down the front doors of the castle. My hands curl around my mouth before I let out a roaring call.

"QUEEN KAILA!"

It's the first crack in my silence. The first splintering line leading from all that roiling, raucous rage I'd contained during the entire flight from Deadwell. I want Kaila to come to me. I want her to have to walk out of her pretty castle and meet my ugly fury face-to-face.

My gait is determined as I cross the sandy courtyard and step onto the first slate step that leads up to the doors. Just as I do, I hear the telltale noise of arrows being nocked in their bows from the towers above me, and more from the defensive wall behind me. It's good to know that even with filthy clothes and an absent crown, I'm easily recognized.

"Halt, King Ravinger! State your business!"

I turn, my eyes lifting to the one brave enough to call down, landing on an older soldier at the right tower. There are two other guards standing behind him, their arrows pointed in my direction.

"You pull back those bowstrings, and I'll rot you all before you can release." Though I didn't shout, I know they've heard me based on the nervous glances they exchange.

Just give me a reason.

No one moves. No one makes a single sound. In fact, they stay very, very still. I turn away. Let out another roar.

"QUEEN KAILA!"

My voice rings out against the castle's outer walls, reverberating through the open air. The hate, the violence, and the need for retribution burns through me. Rot starts to bleed into the sand beneath my feet. Thick, black limbs that spread a sour stench into the oceanic air.

Tension thickens, killing roots coiling through the ground, twisting sinisterly. I can sense the strain in the guards, the anxiousness pouring off their rigid stances. Still, the castle's front doors don't open. The guards don't move.

My call is even louder the third time, and behind me, Crest rumbles like thunder.

The guards inside who watch from the windows stare out at me with wide eyes, hands on the hilt of their weapons. They think, by not coming out, that they're safe? The ones in the towers think the height keeps them secure?

Wrong.

They could cower behind the thickest steel at the bottom of their precious sea, and I would still be able to rot their muscles from their bones and let their skin peel from their corpses.

Just as I start to call for Kaila again, the massive doors open. The shadowed entryway reveals a silhouette, and then out comes a round man with spectacles balanced on the tip of his bulbous nose, sigil pinned to his vest.

"King Ravinger." He gives me a low bow, though the customary greeting of respect is subverted by the line of guards that file out to stand behind him, spears in hand.

"Sonnil," I reply coolly, watching as a flash of surprise crosses his face. If he doesn't think I'm aware of who every advisor is in every kingdom, then he's sorely mistaken.

"We weren't expecting you."

I arch a brow. "Weren't you?"

Hesitation spreads out like a heavy rug for him to trip on. I watch him squirm on it, watch the drip of nervous sweat that gets stuck against his graying mustache. I have to hand it to him, at least he's got the balls to stand here in front of me, even if he does have a dozen guards at his back.

"King Ra—"

"Bring your queen out, Sonnil."

His throat bobs. "I'm afraid I can't do that, Your Majesty."

I click my tongue. "Wrong answer."

More rot seeps from the soles of my shoes, aiming to spread its poison. It slithers like sand snakes, viperous streaks ready to lash out, to sink its teeth in the soil and inject it with venom.

Sonnil's eyes drop, face paling as rot creeps up like seeking vines. Step by step, the stone stairs begin to crack and crumble, the sand behind me staining brown. When it reaches the step beneath his feet, he stumbles in surprise, making a strangled noise in his throat. The guards behind him step back, watching with unrestrained fear as the roots encroach toward their feet.

"King Ravinger, you cannot...this would be an act of war!" Sonnil gasps, turning in a circle as the rot begins to surround the stairs.

"The first act of war was instigated by *your* queen. Now bring her *out*."

He makes the mistake of flicking his finger instead. A signal that he thinks I won't notice. My head jerks to the right, ears attuned to the sound of the archers who let loose their arrows.

Time slows.

I hear the bowstrings snap, the arrows cutting through the air with faint whistles. My fae instincts surge.

In a split second, I turn, plucking the first arrow out of the air like a feather caught in the wind. I dodge the other three, two of them slicing past me and hitting one of the guards instead, the last lodging into a crack of the castle wall.

By the time I turn back to Sonnil, the guard with the arrows in his chest lurches over and collapses, making the rotten step crumble beneath his weight. The other guards scramble back, some of them knocked off their feet as the stairs disintegrate.

I tsk, wagging the arrow in my hand. "Bad idea."

When Sonnil's eyes flash over my shoulder, he flinches, and I watch as he tracks movement that goes down, down, down.

Thud.

The rotted bodies of archers who shot at me now lie at the bottom of the castle's defensive wall, caught in the spoiling courtyard.

When the advisor's eyes come back to me, they're unblinking, his hands visibly shaking, but the idiot opens his mouth. "Attack!"

Another bad idea.

Every single guard behind him drops with barely a thought before they can do more than grip the hilt of their weapons. Rot wraps around their throats like choking collars, spears forgotten as they writhe on the ground, scrabbling at their decaying necks. The ones in the towers collapse.

Sonnil jerks around. "Stop! Stop this!"

"Bring. Her. Out."

The poor bastard starts blubbering. "I can't!"

I raise the arrow in my hand and point it right at his jugular. His gaze locks on it, and he watches wide-eyed as the wood shaft crawls with rot—rot that's heading straight for *his* throat. I pierce the sharp tip against his skin, watch as a bead of blood drips down.

He jerks backward, his heel making the stone crack so that he goes falling, nearly landing on his ass when he trips over the struggling guards, the smell of piss filling the air.

"Please!"

Just as I'm ready to infect the blood in his veins, movement catches my eye, and someone comes running out.

"King Ravinger, stop!"

My eyes narrow at the voice, and I see Queen Kaila's brother rush from the castle's front doors.

Manu Ioana.

With his long black hair pulled back and his bright blue vest and dark pants, he looks as polished and refined as always. Just like he looked when he came to my castle. When he took Auren from me and sat in the audience of the Conflux. Like some spectator to watch her execution as entertainment.

My lips curl up in rage, like ends of burning paper caught in a flame.

I turn to him, the advisor forgotten as Manu steps over the guards to meet me.

"*You.*"

His hands raise to ward me off. "I know you're angry—"

"*Angry?*" A cold, dark laugh slithers from my throat. "I am not angry. I am *incensed.*" I take a step forward, letting my rot curdle the stairs. "Tell her to come out here right now, or I'll rot her whole castle through."

His dark eyes flash. "I can't," he grits out. "She's not here."

I pause. "Where is she?"

He doesn't answer, and I shake my head in disgust. "She's in Sixth, isn't she?"

The flare of his nostrils is all the confirmation I need. I should've guessed that she'd fly straight there to continue stretching her power and influence. But she had to have known I'd come seeking retribution, yet she left everyone to face me in her stead.

Coward.

I tilt my head, looking him over, noting the dark circles beneath his eyes. "What's wrong, Manu, did lying and kidnapping make you lose sleep?"

I see his throat bob, see a flash of contrition in his

expression before he wipes it away. "I was following orders. I am loyal to my sister. Just as you have your own loyalties. I was doing my duty," he bites out.

I can feel the veins at my neck snapping against my jaw like they want to rip through my skin and attack him.

"What happened at the Conflux—"

My hand flashes out before he can finish his sentence, my grip choking off his words. More guards have come slinking out to surround my back, and the windows of the castle have been pushed open as more of them point their arrows in my direction.

I pay them no mind.

All my focus is on holding Manu's throat in my hand, in the pulse that beats against my thumb as I squeeze ever so slightly.

"What happened at the Conflux was your sister's most fatal mistake."

He chokes, face turning color from lack of air, eyes bugging out. It would be so easy to rot his eyes from his skull, to corrode his heart in his chest.

"I'd tell them to stand down if I were you."

Manu holds up his hand to stop the guards, and I have to give it to him, he doesn't even try to fight me off. He just lets me squeeze his airway, lets me lift him straight off his feet, my fae strength surging as much as my magic.

I lean in close, making him flinch as I speak through gritted teeth. "Your sister harassed Auren. Spread lies about her. Ordered that she be *taken from me*. And *you* carried out the order."

The fear in his eyes isn't nearly enough to satisfy me.

In an instant, I pulse out my rot, making the ground fracture behind me, swallowing up the dozens of guards who'd lined up. Their surprised screams burst out as the poisoned ground collapses in on itself, sucking them in like quicksand. The archers at the windows fall too, rot wrapping around them like ropes and yanking them to the floor, nerves dying, limbs failing.

Sonnil tries and fails to scramble back on his hands and feet, but the stairs keep giving way. A spoiled stench clings to the air, the once picturesque castle now a churning mess of destruction as my power spreads up its walls, piercing through its coral roofs and decaying the wooden doors. The sound of the ocean is drowned out by choking screams.

Too bad Kaila isn't here to see me give her the castle she deserves.

All the while, I keep my hold on Manu, let him see, let him hear. Let him *know* that I could end him and everyone else so fucking easily, and I see that realization in his expression. See the terrified resignation in his dark eyes.

He struggles, rasping out a struggle of words. "Kill me...then, Ravinger. Have your...revenge."

"No, Lord Manu!" Sonnil cries.

But I chuckle darkly and put my mouth to Manu's ear, my voice dropping even lower. "Oh, Manu, I'm not going to kill you."

I lean back just in time to see the flash of confused fear on his face.

"Death isn't enough. I want you and your sister to *suffer*," I say darkly. "Kaila ordered for the most important person in my life to be kidnapped, so I'll do the same. It's just a happy coincidence that you came out to face me today, Manu, because the most important person to Kaila is...*you*."

All he has time for is the widening of his eyes before I send a surge of rot to the nerve in his neck, making him instantly pass out.

I toss his unmoving body over my shoulder before turning on my heel and walking back the way I came on the narrow path I left unspoiled. The noise of choking guards behind me accompanies the sound of my steps as I pass the others still trying to claw through the infected sand.

Crest stands apart from the decaying ground, his maw snapping at the soldiers as if he wants to take a bite out of them. I tie down an unconscious Manu on the back of the saddle before climbing up and taking the reins.

Silence once more settles over my blaring rage as I look out at the carnage. I watch the castle's doors deteriorate and the hinges corrode. Watch the glass windows shatter and the lines through the beach sand spread like infected blood while bodies become embalmed in its poisoned grit.

But it's not enough.

I leave them all gasping, choking, staring up at the sky, trying to claw at life as my magic leeches it from them. Then I see Keon, Manu's husband, suddenly run out of the castle. His expression fills with terror when he realizes who I have flung on the saddle, but before he can take another step, the disintegrating doors collapse on top of him.

I snap the reins. Crest spreads his wings and takes flight. I leave behind a crumbling castle and a toxic ground, turning my back on dozens of corpses that will curdle in the spoiled sand.

A message.

The only thing I regret is that I won't see Queen Kaila's face when she finds out I've stolen her brother, killed her guards, and rotted her castle.

People should remember to heed my words. I warned them not to loose their arrows. I warned them not to fuck with me or Auren.

Crest lets out a roar, wings outstretched as we climb higher into the air, cutting up through the clouds just as quickly as we descended. Ryatt will be on his way toward Fourth Kingdom by now.

But me? I'm not returning to Brackhill yet.

GOLD

Because the seething rot still thumps beneath my skin. The raging wind thunders in my ears, and my fury clamors in a deafening roar.

Because I can't get to her.

So I'll take vengeance instead.

CHAPTER 6

QUEEN MALINA

I look between the bars on the window, gaze holding the path between the jagged clefts in the ground. From up here in the tallest tower of Cauval Castle, I can see the way the army moves like a snake winding its way through the snow. A sneaking plunderer hollowing out a path of hostility.

An army of fae.

It shouldn't be possible. Fae have been gone for hundreds of years. The way our worlds connected was broken. Permanently. They all left. Wanted nothing to do with Orea because they wanted nothing to do with us. They thought themselves superior, all because they brought magic to our world, and we had none without them. That broken connection should've been the end of it.

It *was* the end of it.

Until now.

My eyes skate to the left. It's nearly out of view from my window's vantage point, but just there, I can see its entrance—the bridge of Lemuria.

Where the droves of fae keep marching in.

I curl my hands into fists at my sides, but a twinge of hurt has me opening my fingers and glancing down at the slice across both palms. Instead of the gashes being red and angry, the skin along the cuts has gone blue. Little layers of frost pecked into the unhealing lines.

"I am Queen Malina Colier of the Colier royal bloodline, and I willingly give my blood to restore what was lost and to gain what is new."

My voice echoes in my own ears, and I feel my chest stiffen. The layers of that night float down, page after page, listing out a clear account of what actually transpired, because it felt as if I woke up from a flowery dream, and the nightmare was the reality.

The fae twins lied to me. Tricked me. Manipulated me and used some sort of magic to make me see what was not here. Until I gave them my blood and that broken bridge became *un*broken.

The first fae soldiers to cross over dragged me straight into Cauval Castle and locked me in here under Pruinn's orders. I haven't seen him nor Fassa and Friano ever since, and it's been days, maybe weeks. I can't tell. Perhaps time passes differently so close to the edge of the world.

I have raged and paced and cursed endlessly, but none of it was heard. None of it seen. None of it mattered.

That's always been the way of things. Once I serve my purpose to the men who need me, I am pushed aside, because I have only had one worth to them.

My blood.

In one shard of jagged glass that still clings to the broken window, I can see my ghostly reflection. My white hair is tangled and loose, hanging limp upon my shoulders. No oils or soaps to wash it, much like my clothes hanging wrinkled and dirty. My face looks almost hollow, the sharp bones of my cheeks beneath my deathly pale skin only contrasted by the dark circles under my icy blue eyes.

I look like a ruin, much like this castle.

The restoration was a farce. This room is intact, but barely. There's no wallpaper, no paint, no carpeted floors or warm chandeliers. It's all been stripped away with time and cold, leaving this place barren.

Like me.

The bed, which I thought was a grand, comfortable thing? It's actually crooked, two legs missing, with a threadbare cover over it and a stained mattress. The tub is nothing but a tin basin for washing clothes in, and the air itself reeks of decades' worth of dust.

There is no scent of crystalline flowers anymore. No sound of lyrical music. To think, I was under some sort of fae enchantment all along, thinking this a beautiful space. I bet the fae twins had a great laugh at my expense.

My fingers curl into fists again, and they instantly surge with cold. I gasp, looking down as flakes of white start drifting down from my hands. The snowfall oozes out of the cuts in my palms like pus from an infection, dribbling down and leaving tufts of snow on the floor.

Magic.

Frigid, foreign magic that somehow was born in me the moment the fae twins did their ritual.

"My brother and I have very unique magic, my queen. They work only in tandem. I can instill something new…"

"And I can restore something old."

"The blood of a pure Orean royal that is willingly offered to restore this Orean kingdom…"

"By offering this to us, I believe my brother's magic will instill magic into you, giving you exactly what you need to rule."

Lies and truth, woven together.

They didn't believe in my right to rule. They only needed my blood to restore the bridge, which I gave. Willingly.

It seems Friano was right. His brother's power *did* give me magic in return. Ice and snow that either pours out of me uncontrollably or lies in frigid dormancy.

Useless.

Behind me, the sound of a clink resounds, and I jolt. All I've heard are the sounds of my own thoughts and the wind moaning through the window, so anything else is jarring.

I look over my shoulder at the tray that's suddenly appeared on the broken table out of thin air. It pops up irregularly, but it always contains the same thing. One piece of bread. One bowl of stew. One cup of tea.

Prisoner's rations.

I glance away, utterly disinterested.

Lifting my hands, I grip the bars on the window and stare out. The cold breeze coming in from outside doesn't bother me, nor does the chill inside the room. The pile of firewood left inside the chimney remains unlit because I don't need it. Don't want it.

I watch as more regiments of soldiers wind their way forward through the snowy landscape. I know the rest of the castle has become a base of sorts, though I've only been able to catch glimpses of fae going in and out, only been able to hear shouts or voices rumbling up from the ruined walls when the wind didn't strip the noises away.

Yet I don't need to eavesdrop. I don't need to see the massive amounts of soldiers and weapons being smuggled into Orea to know what they plan. The twins spelled it out for me. The fae have returned to take over Orea. And that winding, continuous regiment? They're heading right for Highbell.

My kingdom.

GOLD

The bars beneath my grip go icy cold. I watch blue-tinged frost spread up the rusted metal, and I snatch my hands away to stare at my palms. At the slices across them. The frost recedes, the bluish white tinge creeping back down into the cuts. I quickly grasp the bars again. Urge the frost to come back, but it doesn't.

Just like every other time I try to control it.

It keeps creeping up without warning, but every time I *try* to use it, it's gone.

"Fancy trick."

The voice has me whirling around, and I find none other than the assassin before me, the shadows clinging to him like steam. His very presence screams threat, because even though he hasn't killed me yet, I can't forget that's the sole reason he followed me here. Can't forget the way he killed my guards and plunged a blade through Jeo's chest.

As always, he's in his black cloak with the hood pulled down low. All I can see is the bottom half of his face, his dark brown skin giving way to the patch of light pigment that surrounds his mouth. His lips curl up into a sneer, and although I can't see his eyes, I can feel them boring into me.

"Is that why you did it?" he asks, leaning against the wall, arms crossed in front of him.

His smug, overly comfortable pose irks me. I don't know how his magic works, but he seems to be able to materialize wherever he wants. The thought that he can simply appear in my room fills me with a shiver of fear.

"Is that why I did what?"

Though his hood is pulled low and his shadows are keeping him bathed in ink, I can see his eyes flash with anger. "Don't play dumb, Queenie," he says, his voice deep and grating, always with that roughness to it like he hasn't spoken in a long time. "It's common knowledge that Malina Colier was born without power. So is that why you betrayed your world? Because the fae assholes promised you'd be able to do some magic tricks after?"

Anger spikes in me, stabbing up through my tongue so I spit out the shards. "I didn't betray my world, the fae betrayed *me*! *They* did this!"

He shoves away from the wall so quickly I flinch back before I can catch myself. I can't let myself forget, even for an instant, that he's an assassin.

"*You* did this," he snarls in my face. His shadows are erratic with his anger, coiling like smoke that rises from a pyre, embodying death and destruction. Yet from this close, I can also see more of his face. See the dark eyes that bleed with enmity. "Because of your selfishness. Your own self-importance. Your own filthy ego."

"How dare—"

He grabs my throat. I'm so shocked at his daring that my words rip away. Not because he's pressing hard enough to cut off my air—because he isn't—but because of the warmth of him. It's a shock, a flare of heat that emanates from his touch that's almost painful, making me realize just how freezing my skin is.

"How dare *you*. It's because of you that the fae are now invading Orea. Wake the fuck up and do something!"

I reach up and tear his arm away, and he lets me. "What do you expect me to do?"

"How about take some fucking responsibility for starters?" he growls.

"I told you. They were the ones that did this. They manipulated me."

"And you were just so quick to believe them, weren't you? While they whispered about all these grand things you *deserve*. You never once stopped to question it, because that's really how you think. You think the world owes you, because you are a proud, entitled bitch."

My teeth gnash together. Tiny chips of ice crunching between them.

"*Don't* call me a bitch."

"Don't act like one," he bites back.

"This is the fae's doing."

"There you go again," he retorts, hatred swimming in his gaze. "It's always someone else's fault. Someone else's problem. When the truth is, you enabled everything that's ever happened around you."

My spine stiffens with ire. "You know nothing."

"And it seems you feel nothing. Do you even care that those soldiers are marching toward Sixth Kingdom?"

"Of course I care," I snap.

He looks me up and down with disgust. Like I'm repellant to him. "Doesn't look like it, Cold Queen. Maybe you really do have no heart like the people say."

Rage feels like slivers of ice gashing through my chest. "*Get out.*"

"No. I don't think I will," he says, stepping even closer to me, pressing until we're chest to chest and freezing me in place. The heat coming off of him is so startling that I suck in a breath. It soaks into my ribs, wanting to spark against them like flint on a stone. "I think I'll stay right here and stab you through the chest and see if my blade hits a chunk of ice instead of muscle and flesh."

"It's my kingdom they're marching toward!" I scream in his face, the shrill sound of my voice biting into the air. "Don't presume to know what I'm feeling."

"Fine," he says, his shadowed face tilting down just enough for me to see his dark eyes glinting with menace. "Then say what you *are* feeling, Cold Queen. About all of it. The way your kingdom rejected you. The way your husband did the same. The way your people revolted against you. The way your father barely tolerated you because you had no magic." He leans in to say the last part right into the cold shell of my ear. "The way I killed your lover."

My mouth goes dry.

He pulls back slightly to watch me, his eyes skating over my face as I heave in a shattering breath. The space between us grows thick, layered with something beyond tension. Our breaths seem to be at war. We inhale at the same time, chests pushing against one another like we're battling for dominance. For space. Both wanting the other to concede.

Or perhaps…both wanting to continue to fight.

To *feel*.

Even though all I've felt is a smooth, comfortable cold for so many days, the heat from his body and the exhale from his lips seems to scrape against me with the smallest hint of warmth. To thaw away the numb I've been stuck to, and I don't…dislike it.

Which makes me furious.

I wrench away from him, backing up, forcing the warmth away until we're no longer touching. His shadows coil around him as he watches me.

"Sneak me out," I abruptly demand.

The assassin cocks a black brow. "Excuse me?"

I draw myself up, shove away whatever reaction I just had and pretend it wasn't there at all. "I know your shadow magic will allow it. You wouldn't have been able to get in here otherwise. So get me out."

"And why would I do that?"

"Because contrary to what you believe, I do care about what happens to Highbell. That's my kingdom they're marching toward," I say, pointing toward the window. "I need to warn my people."

"You want to warn them," he repeats in a deadpan tone. "The kingdom who overthrew you, rejected your presence, and denounced you as queen? *You* want to warn *them*?"

Anger laces across my ribs, pulling tight like a corset. I feel his words cinching in, making it hard for me to breathe. Because those painful, infuriating words, the reminder of my rejections…they are far too raw. Far too biting. They've taken chunks out of me and left me to bleed.

"Are you going to help me get out or not?"

He stares at me for a long moment, the only sound coming from the gust of wind flowing in through the window. I wait. Unable to draw in an inhale until I hear his answer. Knowing this is madness. He's an assassin who was sent after me to kill me, and yet, there is no one else in the world I can ask for help, because I *have* no one.

I never did.

Finally, he says, "No."

His denial makes my mouth drop open. "*No*?"

"No," he repeats.

"Why not?"

"Because I don't believe you."

I rear back in surprise. "Believe me? About what?"

He turns, and his shadows drift around him like a long train hanging down from the folds of his cloak, scraping against the floor as he starts to walk away from me. From my request.

"Excuse me! I asked you a question!" I call after him, trying to drag him back and wondering why I even want to.

He stops at the door and looks at me over his shoulder. "And I gave you an answer, Queenie. Make me believe that you want to get out of here for the right reasons, and then we'll talk."

The assassin pulls the shadows toward him, like thick smoke billowing around flames. More and more, until it's a swarm of darkness and flashes of bent light. Then, he's gone, somehow disappearing from the room, taking all of his bulging shadows with him.

Taking my hope.

The devastation that starts picking apart my soul is clawing. Twin nails that scrape down my ribs and embed into my chest, because those accusations he threw at me...they were true.

Here I am, left alone with the toll of those truths. Left alone with the cold. Yet my chest still feels warm. Right where we'd touched.

And I don't...dislike it.

CHAPTER 7

AUREN

Consciousness comes with a breeze.

There's the strangest rush of air that wafts over my feet, both of which are still throbbing in pain though not as intensely as before. I'm frowning before I'm able to drag open an eye, and when one lid peels back, I see someone standing over me where I lie, her lips pursed as she blows air across my toes.

I stay perfectly still, trying to gain my bearings while I watch her continue to exhale over my feet from all angles, and I realize that her breath is what's soothing me. It feels like a balm spreading over the burns that are pulsating through both soles and each one of my toes.

As I fully drag myself away from the heavy tide of unconsciousness, I realize that the woman's breath isn't just soothing my feet. It's *healing* them.

Both of my eyes snap all the way open, and I jerk upward to balance on my elbows. At my sudden movement, she lurches back, hands coming to rest over her yellow dress.

"Oh, I'm so sorry! I didn't mean to wake you," she says soothingly. "I'm Estelia."

She has dark brown skin with tight black curls that hang down to her shoulders. Bright orange streaks swoop along both of her cheeks, but it's not from rouge. It's as if her skin just took on a gloss of color that goes from the apples of her cheekbones and curves up to the edges of her pretty arched brows. It makes the amber color of her eyes pop. "I'm so glad you're awake, though. Is it alright if I give you a few more healing breaths? I'm just about done."

I look around the room, unsure of what to say or do. She takes my silence for acceptance, leaning over me again as she purses her lips. The second I feel her exhale upon my skin, I have to hold in a groan from the instant relief.

After a few more breaths, she straightens back up. "There," she says with a kind smile.

Eyes flicking down, I see that my burnished and bloodied feet now look like they've had at least a week to heal. I sit up, bending my knees to get a better look. No more gilt blood drips from my raw heels, no more blistered arches. My toes aren't burnt anymore either, and even though the skin around the sides of my feet seems to have peeled away, a new layer has already come in.

"How—" My dry voice cracks. "How did you do that?"

Estelia reaches up, grabbing a brass pin from where it was tucked into her collar and uses it to clasp back an errant curl from her face. "Does it feel better?" she asks.

"Much." The pain has dropped to a low twinge, like a sunburn. It's tolerable now, even something I could ignore, instead of the scorching agony it was before.

"Good," she says with a satisfied nod as she places her hands on her hips. "I've done what I can. Your feet were in a very bad way. But they should be feeling better now, at least.

I'm only a fledgling healer, so I can't heal them fully, I'm afraid." Her hand lifts to swipe at a bead of sweat gathered on her forehead. "That's what I get for not getting any sort of formal training—not that I would've wanted any. They would've carted me straight off to the capital if they knew, and *no thank you*. I have my own life, not to mention the family business to run. I don't want anything to do with the monarchy. That's no life to live. Anyway, I can't heal more serious wounds, but I do plenty of minor hurts when the need arises. And believe me, in a farming town, there's *always* a need."

I blink at her, not knowing what to say, my gaze switching from my feet to her face. But I didn't miss what she said—*fledgling healer*.

Healer. Not mender.

My eyes flick to her ears, just barely poking out from her hair. Ears with very obvious pointed tips.

I feel my heart thump hard in my chest.

"Oh, but look at me, already chattering on. Let me go get you some food and something to drink. Just relax. You should stay off those feet until tomorrow, but I can bring up something for you to wash with." She hesitates for a moment, a tentative, almost shy smile coming on her face. "I'm so glad you're here, Lady Auren. It's an honor to heal you."

Before I can reply, Estelia turns and walks to the back of the room and pulls up a door set into the floor. It swings up and she steps down, pulling the panel shut behind her so that it's once more flush with the wooden floorboards.

As soon as I'm alone, I take a moment to look around. I seem to be in a cobwebbed attic. The shape of the roof has pitched the ceiling low, so it's quite short where I'm lying down but tall enough for me to stand up in the middle of the room, though the space itself is cramped.

There are stacked crates filled with trunks of fabric and

jarred foodstuffs, a couple of locked chests, and a damaged chair with a missing leg. I'm lying on a narrow bed in the corner, though it's soft and comfortable. There are half a dozen mismatched pillows behind me, with loose peonies scattered around them.

To my right is a small table with a lantern, and at the far wall, there's a single round window to light up the space, but only shards of sunlight show through because it's been boarded up. Seeing the boards nailed to the walls fills me with unease. I don't like that the sky is blocked from me. It reminds me too much of Highbell. Of not being able to see the sun.

Where am I?

In the silence, the back-to-back memories of what happened paint a picture in my head. I see each brushstroke as it depicts what occurred at the Conflux. The splash of color as my gold was forced out of me in unnatural rivulets, the black rot that laid waste to hundreds of people. The red blood that scattered over the ground.

Slade…

The attic door shoves open again, startling me out of my thoughts as it slaps against the floor. The spiderweb-haired female I remember from before comes climbing into the room. Her arms are laden with a tray as she pushes her way up, a smile perched on her slightly lined face once she stands.

"Glad to see you awake," she says with a grin as she comes over, tray filled with a plate of cheeses and breads that she sets on the bedside table. "Estelia got a snack for you."

I look from the tray to her, at a loss.

"Is the plate not to your liking? I can see if she has something else. Unfortunately, it's past supper, so the servette's stock is out until they get their supplies replenished, but I can walk down the road and see if the inn has something to spare. Though, I'll need to be discreet."

I have no idea why she'd need to be discreet, but I shake

my head. "The plate is fine, really. I just—I don't know where I am, or who you are, or…"

"I'm Nenet," she says, hands smoothing over the pockets of her dress. Even in the lantern light, I can see that the hem is stained brown, thick streaks of dirt covering the tan fabric as if she's often kneeling on the ground. Age spots dot her pale skin over lines of blue veins, but even so, there's a youthfulness to her in the way she carries herself. "Apologies, I should've introduced myself sooner."

"And…" My tongue feels thick in my mouth, gaze moving to the sharp tips of her ears budding from the silky strands of her silver hair. "Where am I?"

"You're in Geisel."

"And that's in…"

Her head tilts at my question, but when I continue to wait, her gray eyes go sharp as she leans forward. "You're in Annwyn."

Annwyn.

I think I already knew, but my mind needed the confirmation. My ears needed to hear it voiced. If I truly think about it, the truth was snapped into my skin the second I dropped to the earth, cradled in a field of glowing flowers. My body knew I was home the second I felt the sun against my face.

A sort of stunned melancholy washes over me.

Nenet's voice softens. "You're alright now, Lady Auren."

The back of my neck prickles. "How do you know my name?"

"Oh, everyone in Geisel will know your name." Her hand lifts as if she's going to touch my arm, but she stops herself when I stiffen. "Those who live here remember the lost gilded girl. It could only be you," she says, gaze sweeping over my skin, my hair, my eyes.

My brow furrows.

"I knew what was happening right away," she says with pride. "You flared like the dawn, spilling from a fracture, and then you fell from the sky and dropped into that field. Just like she did, so long ago."

I swallow hard. "Like who did?"

"Why, Saira Turley, of course."

That name sends chills down my arms, and my pulse pounds in my ears.

I used to beg my mother to tell me the story of Saira Turley over and over again. I loved hearing about the Orean girl who walked the bridge to nowhere and fell into a world of magic. How she grew into a woman and won the heart of the fae prince. She was the one who united Annwyn and Orea as sister realms and made the bridge of Lemuria our road to each other. It was a true fairytale.

Her story always stuck with me, even when so many other memories did not.

I clear my throat. "But I didn't come here like she did. Saira Turley walked on a bridge and came to Annwyn. I…fell out of the sky."

"Not just any sky. *This* sky. Here in *Geisel*," she presses, the wrinkles around her eyes crinkling as she smiles, finger raised toward the ceiling. "You fell through the clouds and landed in the *exact same* field as she, with broken wings streaming behind you like sunrays."

Both of our eyes drop to the ribbons wrapped around my waist. I grab hold of them protectively, reminding myself that they're still here, letting them steady me on this uneven ground.

"They're not wings, they're…" I shake my head, overwhelmed. "I don't understand."

She takes a step forward, creaky knees bending down to the floor until she's kneeling beside my pallet. Her callused fingers gently curl around my sweat-slicked palm, her grip surprisingly strong.

I have to work not to flinch.

It's still so new—being able to touch people freely. I always had to be so aware of it, always had to cover my skin and stay away. If only I'd learned how to use my power without gold-touching uncontrollably during the day sooner. If only I'd learned I wasn't helpless at night and could call to whatever gold was near.

"You don't know who you are to us, do you?" Concern coats her tone, and her eyes have gone sad. "We loyalists call you the *Lyäri Ulvêre*—the golden one gone. The gilded girl who was lost in the night."

Chills roll over my skin and scatter like ants.

"Why…?" Every question is voiced in that one croaked word.

Why does everyone in Geisel know me? Why is she calling herself a loyalist? Why is she looking at me with something close to pitying awe?

"We have prayed to the goddesses for a very long time, and they finally answered us," she says, squeezing my hand. "People tried to say you were dead long ago. Tried to make everyone forget all about you. But we remembered, and now, here you are. You came as she came, Lady Auren. And look at you…" Her gleaming eyes search me over, lingering on my back, at the strips that hang down. "*You* are the new broken-winged bird, just as Saira Turley was. You fell like a piece of light spilled out, here to bring us the dawn of peace."

My mind spins. My heart pounds.

"But *why* do you know me?"

Her eyes are so bright with hope that the gray shines like forged silver, but with her next words, it's me who feels molten.

"We know you, Lady Auren, because we've been praying that one day, you would return. We know you, because you are the Turleys' last-birthed heir."

CHAPTER 8

AUREN

Nenet's declaration buckles me.

If I'd been standing, I think my knees would've given out.

"I'm not…I can't…"

Words fail me, caught in a froth of white noise that churns like a whirlpool in the middle of a sea.

A Turley?

I can't keep sitting. Not with her proclamation. Not with her still kneeling on the floor as if I'm some kind of altar and she's come to pay homage.

I pull away from her and clamber to my feet, but the half-tossed blanket gets caught around my legs, making me stumble. Nenet lurches up to catch me, but I back away and hold out my hands to ward her off. She jolts to a stop, watching me with worry.

My feet are sore but bearable, and I have to stoop slightly so my head doesn't hit the ceiling. I look around the tiny attic, suddenly feeling claustrophobic. My mind is still caught in that condensing vortex, the foamy undercurrent of her words making me dizzy, though my tongue manages to drag across the barm enough to speak. "I don't have anything to do with Saira Turley. I share no bloodline with her."

A frown draws a line between her brows. "But of course you do."

I'm shaking my head before she even finishes, pacing back and forth. "No. I don't. I would've known…"

Right?

I remember my mother telling me the story about the bridge of Lemuria so many times. I remember the tale always staying with me, even when I forgot nearly everything else. But that was just because I liked the story. It doesn't mean we're related. I'm sure many fae children were told Saira's story.

"There must be some kind of misunderstanding," I tell her, pinching my fingertips, feeling dried smears of gold still stuck to my skin.

"Misunderstanding?" She shakes her head, as if that's preposterous. "Is your name Auren?"

I scratch a flake of gold off my thumb. "Yes…"

"And was there a battle on the night you were lost?"

My heart skips, fingers scraping down past the knuckle. "Yes," I whisper.

"Then it is you. I promise you that."

"But—"

"I assure you, there are no others with gilded skin, shining like the sun," she says with a lilting laugh. "There's even a song of the battle that happened the night you went missing—a verse that has mention of you, though we're the only ones to sing it."

I suck in a breath, brow caught in a furrow as she clears a crick in her throat. She begins to sing, the low timbre of her voice drifting through the air like a midnight sonnet meant only for the stars.

...Then Darkness fell onto Bryol,
but it wasn't just night that came.
A scourge came to beat, an army to rout.
The city rubbled and maimed.

And though due morning, dawn came,
A terrible truth arose too.
Our little sun couldn't be found.
Gilded girl Turley, gone with the blue.

The lyrics catch in my head as the last verse echoes into silence, my beating heart filling up the void. "Bryol..." I hear myself say, though my voice sounds so far away, like it's echoing in my own skull. "That was the city where we lived."

That was my home.

She nods, and the delicate strands of her hair catch slightly in the air, as if they'd float away if not attached to her scalp. "You were very young when the battle happened and you went missing, Lyäri. What do you remember?"

"Not much," I admit, voice thick, fingers still picking and peeling. "But I remember that."

There were cobbled streets stained with the black of night. Cracks littered with debris and stumbling footsteps. Smashed windows and glass scattered along the ground like glittering stars. Flames caught on thatched roofs like hair on fire, spreading down the straw and licking down walls.

I remember the screaming. Bangs and bursts igniting down the street as rubble poured from the sky like sparking rain. I remember being huddled with the other children from the street, the taste of fear and magic prickling in the air so thickly that it made me choke. My throat closes up now as it did then, and I swear, I can even taste bark-soaked leather and smoke.

Nenet's eyes still hold that same sadness as she gently says, "You *are* the golden one gone…who has finally returned to us."

I dig my fingernails deep into my palms. Grind and grate away clumps of tacky gold and squeeze them in my fist to ground me.

"So…where were you?" she asks, and although she's trying to play it off, I can see she's desperate to know.

My hands drop down to my side, sending tiny gold flecks falling to the floor. "Orea," I reply, my voice hoarse. "I was in Orea."

Her own eyes widen. For a beat, all she can do is stare at me with incredulous disbelief. "*Orea?* But…*how?*"

I shake my head. I've asked myself that question so many times it doesn't feel like something that can even have an answer anymore. That's what happens to some questions— to those unattainable truths. Sometimes, we ask and we ask, but there is no answer, no satisfaction. It leaves gaping holes that will forever drain us with its unsolvable query, and that's all we'll ever have. The ask.

"I don't know."

"Many searched for you. You were gone without a trace. Declared dead."

My throat feels like someone's heel is digging into it, trying to cut off my air. "And my family…?"

I can't say it. I can't say it all. But Nenet seems to know exactly what I'm asking. When her expression sprouts with more pity, when her head shakes, it's confirmation for what I've always thought, though for some reason, I still feel my eyes fill.

I was declared dead, but they truly *are* dead.

My parents died that night in Bryol, and all I'll ever have

of them are poor memories and those draining, unanswerable questions.

Sadness clangs in the cave of my chest, reverberating all the way through and filling me with its clamor. I'm an orphan, and I've had to live with the resonance of that for my entire life. But now that I know for sure that I truly have no family, that none of my childhood fantasies of being reunited with my parents can ever come true... It leaves a lonely sound to echo through every hollowed part of me.

I don't hear her move, but Nenet is suddenly gripping my hand, the dried gold on my skin buffering against her palm.

"You're here now, Lady Auren. Our new broken-winged bird has flown back home." Her gaze skims to my ribbons where they drape behind my back. "The last-birthed Turley returned to us like a golden dawn."

I don't feel like the dawn. I feel like my horizon has gone bleak.

I'm separated from Slade. My family is dead. I'm in an unfamiliar place, and I'm surrounded by people I don't know.

"So you're really fae," I say, my swimming mind needing to hear it all aloud. "You're fae, and this is *truly* Annwyn?"

She laughs, like that's the silliest question she's ever been asked. "Well, of course I'm fae, and of course it's Annwyn. You fell from the sky. Where did you think the goddesses would bring you?"

I swallow hard. Blink even harder. The dizziness comes back full force, and I sway on my feet. "I think I need to lie down again..."

Nenet's expression sobers instantly. "Oh, look at me. I'm just an old fae who's far too excited to be speaking to the Lyäri." She pats my hand. "Have another nice long nap to catch your bearings. Rest is best when sleep is deep," she recites as she starts walking away. "You'll feel much better when you've recovered from your journey. Rest now, Lady Auren."

She sends me one last smile before lifting the skirt of her dress and stepping through the opening in the floor to descend the steps. Her hand comes up to close the hatch behind her, and then I'm alone again.

I fall back onto the bed, my head spinning. Sinking down into the mattress, I cover myself beneath the blanket as if it can contain me. As if it can contain my rioting thoughts.

I'm in Annwyn.

Finally, after over twenty years, I'm here. I've started to get answers to the questions that have tormented me for decades, and I'm not sure how to feel. How to process. Learning who you are from someone else is disconcerting. I have to somehow reconcile who I thought I was with who they think I am, and figure out how to align the two.

If Slade were here, I wouldn't feel so uneasy. So untethered. He always had a way of reminding me of who I am at my core. Of centering me. Or maybe *he's* my center. Maybe that's why, without him, I'm unsteady.

I feel the separation from him like I've been sieved out. Holes poked through me, left to drain, left to empty, when all I want to do is wade in him. To let his presence buoy me.

I thought I was going to die at the Conflux. Thought I'd never see him again. And then, he came. He came for me like he always promised he would, being the villain I needed him to be. Killing for me, tearing through Orea for me, doing whatever it took to keep me safe.

All I want is to get back to him. Annwyn has been calling to me since I was stolen from it, but now that I'm back, I feel as lost as ever. Because I found myself with Slade, and only with him will I ever truly be home.

I love him with a fierceness that goes beyond the heart, and so I will ache and leak and grieve until he finds me.

And he *will* find me.

For now, I shut my eyes and think of him, letting my subconscious reach out with gentle fingers. Maybe somewhere in Orea, his eyes will close too. Maybe he'll feel my pull, and we can meet in our dreams while we sleep. And maybe there, we can be home, for just a little while.

Because my new home, I've realized…is *him*.

When I wake next, I can tell by the gaps in the boarded window that it's dark out. I must've slept hard and for quite some time, because the food tray is gone, and in its stead is a set of folded clothing on the table. There's also a bucket of water on the floor, with two rags neatly rolled over its lip, and a scrap of soap tucked against the base.

When I get to my feet, my ribbons drift down behind me.

It's jarring to see them. As if I'd only dreamt their return, expecting them to be gone again when I woke. But here they are, a comforting, familiar weight at my back.

I reach around to feel them, letting my fingers sift through their soft lengths. I might not be able to move them, but just having their presence sprouted along my spine and feeling them whisper against my skin…it's something that I never thought I'd have again.

I'm filled with shame when I think about how I loathed them before, how I was embarrassed about their presence. They're a part of me—they *are* me—and now that I have a second chance with them, with being *whole* again, I'm not going to take them for granted. And who knows, maybe the goddesses are finally listening. Maybe they'll breathe life and movement into them once more, if only I'm patient.

I strip out of the gray cowled dress—glad to be rid of the scratchy Conflux garb. I grab the rag with the bucket and soap and wash myself as best I can, shivering from the cold water as I scrub my skin free of the grime and gilt blood.

Once I'm clean, I pat myself dry with the second rag. The set of clothes left for me is a dress that's softer than any fabric I've ever known in Orea. It feels like both velvet and satin, though it's neither. It's the barest of gray colors, just a hint of blue sewn in dainty threads along the hem and bodice, slightly worn at the bottom and just a few inches too short for me. But the dress is loose and low enough in the back that my ribbons can feed through comfortably, so I let them hang down, relishing in the way I can feel them skate across the floor.

There are no shoes, but I prefer to let my feet breathe anyway. They're still tender, the edges peeling slightly, but they're so much better than they were before. I spot a hairbrush on the table too, so I comb through my tangled tresses before tying them into a loose braid.

But even going through these motions can't ease the anxiousness rising in my gut. I don't like being in this attic, with the cobwebs and the clutter and the boarded window. I don't like not knowing exactly where I am or who I'm with. And to make matters worse, I still feel drained from the Conflux, my sapped magic making me sluggish and vulnerable.

My body is buzzing with the need to hurry and leave. I want to go back to where I landed, as soon as possible. I need to see if Slade has opened another rip and come to find me. Everything in me pushes to go—to reunite with him. Everything in me misses him with the fiercest longing.

What if he's there in that field, and he doesn't know where I am? Who knows how many hours it's been since I collapsed? What if he's hurt? What if he reopened the rip, and it drained him of so much power that he needs me?

I have to get to him.

With hurry skittering through my feet, I rush to the hatch

in the floor and haul it open. Peering down, all I see are a set of narrow ladder-like steps in the dim light. I start to descend, feeling my way out of the attic.

Once I hit the bottom step, I turn around and see that I'm in a small closet with a rack of coats and clothing directly in front of me. I have to shove them aside in order to get through, and as soon as I do, the clothes settle back in place, hiding the attic entrance again.

I trip over a few big boots lined up on the floor, but I catch myself on the door just ahead. When I open it, I walk into a short hallway and follow the light I can see peeking from around the corner. I step into what looks like a living room, where dim sconces are alight, revealing a pretty pale blue on the walls and cozy furniture set up around an unlit fireplace.

It's a small space but clean, the windows at the front all closed off with heavy curtains. I spot a doorway into a washroom, and I bolt for it, quickly doing my business. After I'm finished, I catch my reflection in the mirror, noting the stress strained around my eyes.

When I get back into the living room, I freeze at the sound of muffled voices coming from across the room, through a door just to the right of the fireplace. Tiptoeing my way across, I pass the cushioned chairs and veer around the table, coming to a stop just outside the door. Carefully, I tip my ear against it, trying to listen. Yet try as I might, I can't make out any words. All I hear is a low hum of voices, though I can tell that they're female.

I hesitate, but my pause is interrupted when the door suddenly swings open with a rush of air, making me flinch back as the healer stops short in front of me.

"Oh!" Estelia exclaims, pressing a hand to her heart. "Lady Auren. I didn't expect you to be up and about at this hour."

I peer over her shoulder, where I can see a big kitchen behind her. Wooden cabinets and shelves line the yellow walls, a neat pile of dishes are stacked near the sink, and there seems to be just about every type of herb jar lined up along the countertop. Just like the living room, the window over the sink is shut, with thick flowery curtains covering every inch of glass so that not even a sliver of the outside is visible.

A wide countertop takes up the middle of the room, lit up by a pitcher-full of the same blue flowers that were at that field. They give off their subtle glow, helping to illuminate the space and casting off their calming color. There's a male sitting next to Nenet, drinks clutched between both of their hands that have swirls of orange steam rising out of them.

When Nenet sees me, she practically jumps to her feet. "My lady, you're up early! Dawnlight isn't for another half hour. Did you sleep enough?"

My gaze lingers on the unfamiliar person. He has shorn hair that looks blue from the flowers but I suspect is probably a dull blond. There's a dishrag tossed over his shoulder and an apron around his robust waist, but his face seems kind, his eyes curious.

"I feel very rested," I tell Nenet, glancing back at her.

The three of them share a look, and I get the distinct impression that those mumbled words they were exchanging had to do with me.

"You must be hungry," Estelia says, cutting through the awkward pause. "Come in, let's feed you."

The male takes this as his cue to stand while I'm ushered inside. "I'm Thursil. Nenet is my grandmother," he says, introducing himself as he pulls out a tall chair for me at the counter. Now that he said it, I can see a little family resemblance. He has the same gray eyes. "It's an honor, Lady Auren."

I'm not sure what to say to that. Their collective

veneration makes me feel awkward and wary. I'm also antsy to get back to the field, but I'll feel more confident going out in this unfamiliar place once the sun is up and I can see if my gold-touch has replenished.

As I sit in the offered chair with a nod, I make a mental note to wrap myself in as much gold as I can, so that I have plenty of it on me at all times. Just in case I need to call to it when the sun is down. I tap my foot against the bottom rung of the chair, trying not to show my anxiousness.

"What can I get for you?" the male fae asks. "We got fully stocked an hour ago, so we have just about everything in our kitchen."

"It's *my* kitchen, Thursil," Estelia drawls.

He shoots her a smile. "Sure, but we both know I'm in here more than you, love. You do the baking and dealing with the customers, but I'm the one standing over that stove for all the cooking."

She rolls her eyes, looking to me. "Only because he came into *my* servette one day and told me my stew was awful and swore he could make a better one. So I made him prove it."

"And?" he prompts with a smirk.

She sniffs. "And it was…marginally passable."

He looks to me with a laugh. "Better. The word she's looking for is *better*. She had to hire me on."

Despite my inner tension, I find myself smiling. It's impossible not to—their banter and obvious care for one another is contagious.

"Now look at us," he tells her, wagging his blond brows at her with a grin on his face. "I got into your kitchen *and* your knickers."

Her eyes pinch at the sides and she slams a pointed finger his way. "Watch your mouth, Thursil Tern, or I'll make sure you don't get into *either* of those again anytime soon."

He chuckles good-naturedly, showing off dimples that make him look boyish before he places a kiss on the orange swoop of her cheek. "Sure, love."

Nenet rolls her eyes and looks at me. "Listen to the pair of them. Ridiculously in love. It's a bit obnoxious, isn't it?"

I laugh lightly, but it makes me a little sad too. Makes me miss Slade like a sharp jab to the ribs. "You don't like love?" I ask.

"I prefer lust," the old fae replies matter-of-factly.

A snort escapes me.

"Ignore my grandmother," Thursil says before clapping his hands together. "Now. Let's get you full. What's your preference, my lady? There's a fresh loaf of bread from yesterday, or if you prefer, I can cut up some fruit or scrounge up a tart..."

I shake my head. "I appreciate it, but I really need to get back to the field where I...landed."

All three of them look at me with wide eyes, with hints of that same fear I saw in fae gathered at the field. An uncomfortable silence cuts between us like jagged strips left to hang.

When no one says anything, I push on. "Can one of you show me the way?"

"Oh, Lady Auren, you don't understand," Estelia says as she shakes her head, her expression almost mournful. "That field is the *last* place you can go."

CHAPTER 9

AUREN

A frown creases my brow and worry starts to wrap around me. My body tenses, muscles poised to bolt. I'm unsteady. Unsure. Not certain whether I can trust these people at all.

"Why can't I go to the field?" I ask warily.

"She doesn't understand," Thursil murmurs, darting a glance to Nenet. "She doesn't know anything…"

My back stiffens. "Know *what*?"

"You can't go out," Estelia tells me. "It's not safe."

Can't go out.

Not safe.

A jarring echo of Midas's words that rings in my head and instantly has my hackles raising. Has me reaching back to grasp my ribbons and pull them into my lap. Reminding me of who I am now. Of who I am not.

My eyes go hard. "I spent years being told that very same thing. Kept in a cage for my supposed safety, when really, it was about control. So know this—I'll *never* allow anyone to keep me trapped again, no matter the reason."

Estelia's amber eyes widen with surprise and immediately fill with apology. "I'm sorry, Lady Auren. I didn't mean...I only want you to be careful. If they find out who you are, they'll take you."

My hackles rise. "What are you talking about?"

"Geisel is Saira Turley's city. This is where she first came and where she lived before becoming a princess. That's why most of us who live here are still loyalists, why you can trust us—because having you here truly is an answer to our prayers."

"Okay..."

She tucks a thick black curl behind her pointed ear, looking at me with worry. "But when you fell from the sky, it flared. It sort of...tore open. It looked *strange*. The truth of your arrival will be protected by most of us, but it's possible that you were seen by more than just those in the field or that someone will talk in front of someone who *isn't* a loyalist, and that wouldn't be a good thing."

"Why not?"

Her amber eyes sink into me with a weighty hold. "Because while we are loyal to the Turleys, many more throughout Annwyn are *not*."

The way she says that makes stones scrape down the walls of my stomach and bleed out worry.

"Some fae don't like Turleys?" I ask slowly, trying to grasp what she's implying.

"Some will *hate* you. Think of you as an enemy to be snuffed out because they were fed lies about your family. While others have forgotten about you completely. The monarchy has made sure to help erase your family from our histories, painting your line with unimportance. But Annwyn is divided." She crosses her arms in front of her as she leans against the large kitchen sink, its faucet bracketed with crystal knobs. "It's been hundreds of years since a Turley sat on the throne, but we loyalists remember. We believe in the way things were back then. All of Annwyn was at peace, our land and magic was prosperous. When Saira came, she ended a war. Brought fae together. Many of us remember the golden age that came when she wore a crown."

I frown. That sounds good, so I don't know why some people would be against Turleys. Don't understand why I might be hated.

"But that succession changed in Annwyn centuries ago, when one Turley didn't want to rule," Thursil says, bringing my gaze toward him where he props up his elbows on the countertop across from me. "It was a shock to all of Annwyn when a new successor was coronated in their stead. The Carricks have sat on the throne ever since."

That name niggles in the back of my mind like a loose thread on a sleeve, tickling my skin.

"And with every new Carrick crowned, Annwyn slips further away from how things should be," Nenet tells me as she sits down beside me and picks up her cup again, bitterness lacing her tone.

"The worst of it was when Tyminnor Carrick ruled," Estelia says.

Thursil shakes his head. "I don't know. His grandson Tyec is a fucking menace."

"What makes them so bad?" I ask cautiously.

"They tax the hell out of everyone," Thursil says. "Bleed us dry every year, making it so more and more of us struggle to survive. They force magicked fae into the monarchy's service. Fill our cities with royal guards."

"But what Tyminnor did was worse," Estelia argues. "He was the one who spread the hate for Oreans. Called for all fae to return to Annwyn, tearing families apart in the process. He made some of us hate them and think of them as lesser. But he truly ruined Annwyn when he ordered that bridge to be broken."

My eyes go wide. "The bridge of Lemuria?"

"The very one," she says with a nod. "And ever since then, Annwyn has been languishing."

"How do you mean?"

"The land where the bridge was is now dead."

I frown. "What do you mean *dead*?"

She shrugs a shoulder. "I've never seen it myself, but I've heard plenty. They say the ground cracked open and death spilled out. Nothing grows there. It's covered in ash, no matter how much rain tries to wash it away."

I knew Seventh Kingdom was wiped out once the bridge was destroyed, but I had no idea that Annwyn's land suffered too.

"The dead land spreads a little bit more every year," she says. "And with it so close to our kingdom's capital, it's been making the king nervous."

"It's Annwyn's way of punishing us," Nenet cuts in before taking another sip from her steaming cup. "We were never supposed to break that bridge. Idiots. All of them."

All of this information spins in my head.

"The Carrick monarchs have always hated the Oreans, but they hated the Turleys even *worse*," Nenet goes on. "They think that when Saira had the bridge connect permanently to Orea and allowed our realms to unite, she weakened our land and our blood. Diluted it with non-magicks. Let our world be polluted with their presence. Bah," she exclaims, waving her hand dismissively. "Like I said, idiots."

"But really," Thursil begins. "The Carricks hate Turleys because they're a threat to their rule. So long as a Turley lives, they're the true heir to the throne and could overthrow the Carricks' claim. Meaning you, Lady Auren, are now their biggest threat. Now that you've returned, everyone will think that you'll be vying for the throne. Loyalists everywhere will support you and the promise of change."

Great Divine.

I stare at him in shock, his words dripping like ice cold rain that plops onto my head and soaks through my skin with startling discomfort. The way they watch me with almost hopeful anticipation makes my gut twist.

"Let's get one thing clear right away," I tell them. "I'm not here to overthrow anybody. I'm not here to change Annwyn or sit on a throne. I'm no queen."

"The gold on your skin says otherwise."

His words make frustration buckle around my waist, pulling uncomfortably tight. "I'm just here because I fell through the sky. That's it."

"So did Saira," Nenet counters. "And look what she did. You can bring a lot of good too, Lyäri. You're here for a reason."

I shake my head, trying to break free from their expectations. Their watchful eyes dim with disappointment. "I'm here because the air ripped open."

I'm here because Slade saved my life and gave me the courage to take the leap.

Just thinking about him makes my eyes burn. Makes my whole body cave in on itself, as if trying to fill the space where he should be. I press a hand to my chest, right there in the middle where something twinges. It feels stretched, like a too-taut rope, and I want to grip it and pull. I want to tug him back to me.

Desperation knots my veins, makes me lump up my ribbons on my lap. They always reached for him. Touched and danced and played.

Flirted.

Then they were gone, and now *he's* gone.

So I'm whole...but I'm not.

I'm yanked out of my dismal thoughts as Estelia sets a cup of tea in front of me. "We're not trying to pressure you, Lyäri, but to tell you how people will view your return."

Thursil nods. "It's true. Annwyn needs changing. The open hatred for Oreans who still live here, the encouragement of division and fighting between fae, of rewarding nobles and punishing the workers, our dying land…it has all systematically ruined what used to be good," he says. "But we fae who believe in the old monarchy do what we can for the Oreans still here, and we encourage our fellow loyalists. When your parents were killed and you were lost, it was considered a tragedy for us. But the Carricks were *happy* you were all gone."

"They facilitated it, more like," Nenet grumbles under her breath.

My stomach churns, and I squeeze my ribbons tight. "You mean…you think my parents were killed on purpose because of *political* reasons?"

"It's what we've always believed," Thursil says. "The Carricks knew damn well where the Turley family lived, no matter how much they tried to pretend your line no longer mattered. So long as a Turley lived, they were threatened. The battle that came to Bryol? Never should've happened. The war was long over. It was all too convenient that the city was sacked. That you went missing and your death was announced with your parents', though your body was never found. Many were convinced that you were taken. Some hoped that you were rescued, but as time went on, more believed that you were truly dead."

My heart contorts in my chest. After so long of knowing nothing, hearing these things makes my throat fill with bile. Were my parents killed, not as unwitting casualties of a war, but as a purposeful political scheme because some king felt threatened by their existence? By mine?

"Even with the Turley line wiped out, or perhaps *because* of it, us loyalists have only strengthened over time," Estelia says. "But so has the hate against the Turleys. If the wrong people find out that you're alive, that you're back..."

"You'd go missing all over again," Thursil finishes. "This time, permanently."

My stomach drops.

"*Thursil*," she admonishes sharply.

He shrugs. "What? She needs to know." His gray eyes lock onto me. "We are celebrating your return, my lady, more than you can probably fathom. But just being here means you're in danger."

I loop a ribbon around my finger again and again. "And you're sure that I'm actually a Turley? Because—"

"*Yes*." All three of them answer vehemently at the same time.

Great Divine.

I blow out a breath, eyes dropped down to the counter as I try to take everything in.

It makes sense now—why I'm up in that attic room. Why all the windows are closed off. Why some of the people in the field seemed both in awe of me...and terrified.

Coming to this town full of secret Turley loyalists means I'm putting them all in danger just by being here, and yet, I'm seen as some kind of ghost come back to life, with the promise of change.

"We remember every Turley, but you were especially beloved for your golden skin. But did you know that *every* Turley ever born had some part of them that was gold?"

Shock widens my eyes as my gaze snaps back up to Estelia. "Really?"

She nods. "Oh, yes. Your mother had golden eyes, just like yours. Her mother had lips that looked like she kissed liquid gold. And it's said that Saira Turley herself had flaxen hair with gilt strands that gleamed in the sunlight."

"And you have the Turley rounded ears," Nenet says, nodding at me.

My hand immediately lifts to my ear where it pokes through from my hair. "You're saying all Turleys have rounded ears?"

She bobs her head. "Every single one. Part of your Orean heritage."

"Rounded ears are dangerous here," Estelia says. "Not every part-Orean has them like the Turleys, but the ones that do…they have to be careful. Luckily, most know how to hide them. There are a lot of fae with Orean blood who live in Geisel. Some of them were unlucky enough to get that particular stubbed ear gene passed down, but fabricated tips are easy enough to come by if you know who to ask, and I happen to know a source." She turns to look at Nenet with a smile.

"Not that it matters for you," Nenet says with a chortle. "Your golden appearance will give you away far faster than your ears. Not everyone in Annwyn will remember the golden one gone, but when word spreads, they'll figure it out soon enough and everyone will then know you're a Turley."

"That's why you need to stay hidden," Estelia adds.

I stare at each of them, their gazes earnest and kind. I don't know what to make of it. I'm so used to seeing eyes filled with suspicion, fear, envy, anger. Yet these fae look at me with hope. It's both consolatory…and a bit overwhelming.

"I understand what you're saying, and I appreciate the warning, but I can't hide forever. I won't let that be my life again. I'm grateful that you're letting me stay here, but I need to return to the field. It's important."

"But we just explained how dangerous it is!" she exclaims.

"I know, but I'm looking for someone—the person who

helped me get here."

Nenet makes a noise in her throat, and there's a look of pity in her aged gray eyes. "Saira Turley came here looking for someone too. But she never found him."

For some reason, that irks me, and my gaze sharpens. "I'm not Saira."

I *will* find him. Even if I have to figure out how to slash open the world myself.

"Nenet told us you were in Orea," Estelia says, expression carrying slight disbelief. "*How?*"

"I don't know," I answer, telling her the same thing I told Nenet. I pull the ribbon away from my finger so I can rub my temples. This flood of information is boiling over and sloshing around my neck in overwhelming waves. "But now I'm suddenly back here, and you're telling me I'm a Turley heir that the monarchy wants dead, and that Annwyn is a mess I'm supposed to somehow fix, but I'm just trying to find someone. *He* is my priority. So I need to go back to that field and try to find him."

"But you could be seen. Caught," Estelia exclaims with distress, her twisting hands burying into her blue skirt. "They could imprison you or worse."

I pin her with an unwavering gaze. "I'd love to see them try."

She rears back, like my fierce words took her by surprise. Even Thursil looks a bit shocked.

Not Nenet. She suddenly slaps a hand across her thigh and *cackles*. "There's the fierce Turley I was waiting for! Heart of gold and spoken bold," she recites in singsong before looking at the others, teeth flashing in her grin. "She's a true Turley, isn't she?" Jumping down from her seat, suddenly seeming far more sprightly, she says, "Well. It's decided then. Lady Auren says she needs to get to the field, so we have to listen to her. This could be part of what the goddesses want.

It's not yet dawn. I'll sneak her into one of the harvest carts, just like I did when we got her here, and take her to the field myself."

"It's too dangerous. She *can't*—Thursil," Estelia exclaims, turning toward him like she's looking for help. "Say something."

He comes over and cups her elbow, looking at her tenderly, and just that one look shows me how much they care for one another. "She knows the danger now, love. We're here to help the Lyäri, not keep her locked up. My grandmother is right. Maybe this is what the goddesses want. If she says she needs to get to the field, then we need to help get her to the field."

Estelia pinches her lips together, and the orange streaks across her cheeks grow darker, like fall leaves just before they go brown and snap off their branches. "Fine," she relents with a sigh before she glances at me. "But you need to eat at least. I can't have an underfed guest staying in the best servette in Geisel, even if you are here in secret."

I almost protest, but her glare is very convincing, so I nod instead. "Alright. Just something simple. I've already been enough trouble for you two."

Thursil chuckles as Estelia whirls around and starts digging through the cupboards in the kitchen and pulling things down. "Trouble? My Stel's favorite thing to do is make food that people love, and I love to help her with that."

"I only wish we could serve you in the dining room properly," Estelia says over her shoulder as she starts putting together some food. "But there are too many windows, and the servette will be opening soon. We can't risk you going out there and being seen."

"Speaking of," Thursil begins. "I'd best go out back. Get a look at who's there. If I can find Keff, I'll get him to bring his cart right at the road. His is covered."

"Good idea," Nenet nods. "I'll go with you."

They disappear through a swinging door on the opposite side of the kitchen, while Estelia comes over with a plate and sets it down in front of me. "Here you are. Eat every crumb. You need your strength."

Her genuine concern makes my heart squeeze. She doesn't even really know me, and yet she's worrying for my safety and comfort. "Thank you, Estelia."

Her face softens at my words, amber eyes shining with concern. "Of course. It's an honor to have you in our home. We're just so thankful that our Lyäri Ulvêre has returned. We want the best for you."

I don't know what to say to that, because I've done nothing to deserve that kind of devotion and acceptance. I've never come across a group of people who instantly trust and support me, and I'm not sure how to navigate it. How to trust it.

At my smile, she points to the plate. "Eat."

I pick up the sandwich stuffed with meats that I don't recognize, though they're full of delicate spices. While I chew, I watch her curiously as she moves through the kitchen. I wonder at her life, her healing magic, this servette. "How long have you and Thursil been together?"

She gives me a smile over her shoulder. "Not as long as we should've."

My eyes drop to my plate, my bite suddenly hard to swallow. I chew in silence, listening to her flit around the kitchen, humming softly beneath her breath.

Just as I finish my sandwich, she speaks up again. "This *him* you're looking for… How long have you been together?"

My gaze flicks up and I give a sad smile. "Not as long as we should've."

"Thought so. You have that look about you."

"What look?"

"Homesick. Lovesick." She sets a plate of beautiful, dainty-looking cakes in front of me. They're four layers high yet still bite-sized, with the prettiest decorations on top of glossy icing and different syrups oozing over the naked sides. "I hope you find him," she says gently.

"I will."

I reach forward and pop the chocolate cake into my mouth. Except, it's not chocolate. The flavor is smoky and sweet, somehow both airy and dense at the same time. At the center, there's a bit that crackles with heat against my tongue. "Great Divine," I say around a moan. "These are delicious."

She beams. "These are my specialty. Puff cakes."

After I'm finished eating, I down my water, just as Thursil comes back in.

"I talked to Keff. He's got his cart ready."

"And you're sure he knows to be utterly discreet?" Estelia asks him.

"Keff knows to keep his mouth shut," Nenet says, coming in from the storage room. "His ears weren't always that pointy."

My brows lift in surprise. "He's Orean?"

"Quarter one," Nenet tells me. "And a bit bitter about it to be honest."

"It's nearly sunup," Thursil says, looking to me. "If you want to go today, you should head out."

"Or you could rest for another day or two…" Estelia offers hopefully.

"I'll be fine. Trust me."

"Wait," she says, holding up a finger as she disappears into the living room. She comes back just a few seconds later with a long cloak. "Here." She drapes the thick brown fabric over my shoulders and hooks it at my collar. "At least wear this. It might not do much to hide you, but it's better than nothing. We don't want too many tongues wagging."

I pull the oversized hood over my head and wrap my ribbons loosely around my waist so they won't drag. She nods, but when her gaze drops down to my feet, her lips pull into a frown. "I don't have a spare set of shoes that will fit you yet, but I'll get some today. Maybe you can wear socks? I don't like you being on them so soon after your healing. Are they hurting?"

"They're much better," I assure her. "And barefoot is fine."

She wrings her hands. "I'm sorry I'm not more powerful, but my magic runs out quite quickly. I wish I could've completely healed them…"

Thursil gives her a look of admonishment. "Love, you're one of the precious few who still have a lick of magic at all. I'd say that makes you plenty powerful."

I blink in surprise. "What do you mean?"

"Remember what I told you about the land dying when the bridge was broken?" Estelia says. "Well, that's where it started. At the same time, fae started giving birth to children with no magic. It's gotten worse ever since."

"And yet the king blamed that on the Oreans too," Thursil says. "Even though there'd been plenty of Orean and fae joinings that produced powerful children. He never claimed it had anything to do with the bridge at all. Said our sudden lack of power was brought on by diluted bloodlines. Just more propagated hate toward the Oreans. Some still believe those lies."

"Our betrayal of Orea poisoned our land. Mark my words," Nenet says as she pulls on her own cloak, buttoning it at the neck.

Thursil wraps an arm around Estelia. "That's why my Stel is so special. Magic is rare nowadays. If the monarchy knew she had it, she'd have been shipped off to serve them years ago."

"Another reason we need a new monarchy," Nenet says pointedly to me.

I give her a look. "Like I said before, I want nothing to do with any throne."

She sighs. "How unrevolutionary."

"Hush, Nenet," Estelia chastises. "You're going to scare her off with that talk."

"Bah," the old fae says, waving her hand. "Youth is wasted on the youthful. In my day, I would've marched right up to the king's castle and tossed him on his arse if I had a gilded face."

Thursil snorts. "I was told you used up all your youth flirting with every male who came through Geisel, tossing them on their arses in a *very* different way."

"Ah, the good old days," she laughs, showing off her sharp canines. Then she turns to me, her gray eyes alight with mischief. "This is the most excitement I've had since. So let's get you to your field, Lyäri, and help you find who you're looking for."

CHAPTER 10

AUREN

The pre-dawn air is dark and crisp, holding the sharper edges of a world not yet warmed up by the sun.

Nenet guides me, her wispy head a foot shorter than my own, hands clutching her skirts as she hurries me out of the back door. We pass through a small walled-in area that appears to hold more of the servette's storage barrels and supplies, and then we exit out of a gate and turn a corner into a narrow alleyway. Water drips from the downspouts of the gutters, forming little puddles that we pass. The whole area smells like the wet rock of the cobblestone street just ahead, but the air has a freshness to it—a sweetness that never existed in Orea.

"Stay here," Nenet tells me, just before she hurries forward to the end of the alley and reaches the street.

I see her give someone out of sight a nod, and within moments, a horse clops forward, pulling a cart. It doesn't look like Orea's horses, though. This one is white with swirls of pastel purples that strike through its hair and hooves. Its tail and mane are the same lavender, with delicate flower vines braided through it.

The cart itself is different too—more *fae* than I'm used to. Instead of normal wood and tarp, the walls appear to be made from some kind of metal with blue and copper specks. Even the wheels are made from that same material, shining with its smooth, speckled spokes. At the top of the walls is a taut stretch of arcing blue fabric that covers the whole thing, with a small bit bending up to shade the driver sitting behind the horse. The cart stops, cutting off the alley's entrance, the back hatch already open and waiting.

Nenet waves me over, and I follow her cue, hurrying down the alley and getting up into it. Inside, the space is stacked with empty crates, but there's a small spot for Nenet and me to squeeze past to get to the very back. As soon as we're settled, Nenet drags the crates in front of us and knocks, and within seconds, we're jolted forward.

I open my mouth to speak, but she shakes her head, placing a finger to her wrinkled lips, eyes darting to the end of the cart. There's a spot where the metal hatch and the fabric have a slight gap between. Her attention stays focused there, eyes trained on the speck of street. I watch it too, though I can't see much. Just the slivered view of buildings and other carriages that we pass by, accompanied by the sound of hooves clomping over the road and noises of people rousing before the sun.

It's not until the wheels beneath us finally hit dirt that Nenet seems to relax. Fresh air feeds into my lungs, and the dawn pours out, the noises of the street ebbing away. As soon as I feel the prickle of the sun, I let out a sigh.

Making sure Nenet's still focusing on the gap, I surreptitiously call to my gold-touch. Tentatively at first, making sure my power has replenished since being so dangerously drained. Relief spreads through me when my magic easily drifts out.

With my eyes up and my hands inside the cloak, I form gold pieces by feel. I first make a solid gold belt to wrap around my waist, fitting in neatly beneath my ribbons and hidden from view. Next, I make a cuff for each arm, wrapped securely around my biceps in thin swirls like coiled snakes tucked underneath my sleeves.

"It's safe to talk now," Nenet says, and I nearly jump, my focus snapping. I make my magic dry up, letting it soak into my palms, satisfied that I at least have a little bit of gold on me, at my disposal and ready for nightfall. "But it's better to be cautious when we're in town."

"Where are we now?"

"The road that leads to the fields. Geisel is part of the flower district, and our land here has the most harvested flowers out of all of Annwyn. Only our farmers are out here at this time, and Geisel farmers have lived and worked this land for generations." She leans forward conspiratorially and winks. "We're on your side, my lady."

"But this is dangerous for you, isn't it?"

"Danger," she scoffs. "What's life without a bit of that?"

"I don't want you getting in trouble for being with me. I'll be okay on my own."

She looks offended. "I would never allow you to simply fend for yourself. Can you imagine?" she adds with a laugh. "Waving the Lyäri out the door while I have a cup of tea? I think *not*."

My lips tilt up. "Don't worry, Nenet. I can handle myself."

"I have no doubt. But Turley loyalists will always stand by your side." She looks down at her lap. "Or sit, at the very least."

My smile grows wider. "So, tell me about Geisel. You

seem to really love it here."

"Oh, I do. Geisel is one of the last decent places. My family has lived and worked on this land for hundreds of years." I can hear the pride in her voice. "The town itself used to be much smaller, but our soil has become the richest in all of Annwyn, which is coveted even more because of the deathlands that have spread from the bridge. We also grow the rarest, most coveted bloom." Her gray eyes delve into mine. "It doesn't grow anywhere else but in Geisel. They sprouted when Saira came."

I feel my brows lift. "Those glowing blue flowers?"

"The very ones," Nenet nods. "It's the only thing of the Turleys that our monarchy hasn't destroyed. Too profitable for them, I suppose. Of course, once everyone realized how functional they turned out to be, Geisel grew, and with that growth came more attention. With attention, comes policing. The Stone Swords are very prevalent here—because of the fields *and* the Turley history."

"Stone Swords?"

"It's the royal guard. They police the cities, and they're under strict law of the throne. Every single one of their regiment trains in Annwyn's kingdom capital before they're sent off."

"And these Stone Swords…do you think they know I'm here?"

The corners of her eyes tighten. "I'm not sure, my lady. But I will say this—even some of the folk who weren't in the field that day mentioned seeing something strange in the sky. A sort of flare or a…a…"

"Rip?"

She snaps her slightly crooked fingers. "Exactly. There was a noise, and when I looked up, I saw the sky tear open. You drifted down like a bird in a breeze, with silken wings shredded into strips streaming down behind you. I saw the ground welcome your fall so that you did not crash, but instead *settled* into it like one settles back on the calm surface of a sea. Everyone in the field saw, and some in the city know *something* was in the sky that day. I got you out of there as fast as I could. I don't know what the whispers are saying yet, but they will be saying something."

Whispers. I've come to know all too well how dangerous whispers can be.

"And these Stone Swords...they'll recognize me?"

"They might, they might not. It isn't just loyalists who followed your bloodline. Some will remember the gilded girl who disappeared during the Hundredflame Battle and was declared dead. If they realize who you are..."

"I won't get a welcome party."

"Not the kind you'd want."

My eyes shift to the back gap of the cart, the horizon brightening while my thoughts cast shadows in my head.

If I'm recognizable, at least to some fae, does that mean...that Slade knew I was a Turley? Or if he doesn't, what will he think once he finds out? What do *I* even think about being a Turley? I haven't really had time to begin to process it.

"I'm sorry you're not returning home under better circumstances," Nenet tells me. "There should be celebrations throughout Annwyn. Parades in the streets. Not this sneaking around."

"I'm used to having to sneak around," I say, giving her a wry look. "It's funny—all I ever wanted for a long time was to get back here. When I was little, I used to dream of waking up in Annwyn again because my life in Orea was...uncertain. Dangerous. I never imagined that it would feel the same here."

"People have a way of ruining things," she replies, gray eyes far too pointed. "But other people have a way of setting things right again."

I shake my head at her insinuation. "I didn't even know I was a Turley."

"Saira didn't know who she would be to Annwyn either."

"Great Divine, you're persistent."

Nenet grins. "A goddess blessing, I'm sure."

"Mm-hmm," I say sardonically before switching the subject. "Are there many Oreans still in Annwyn?"

"Yes, though it's not a good life for them. Since the bridge was broken, the Oreans trapped here have lived a long life of oppression. Forced to work. Punished if they hold any fae power in their blood. Most live as servants to noble houses. Others have been imprisoned or worse."

"That's terrible."

"We hide and protect those we can."

"You're good people."

She gives a humorless laugh. "Some would say we are the scourge of Annwyn, weakening it with our wrongful sympathies. *Idiots*."

I laugh. "Maybe you should be the one challenging the king for his throne. I don't know how he could possibly stand up against you."

"He couldn't," she says with a confident nod. "The Stone King would shake in his marble boots."

"Stone King?"

"His power. He can control stone and rock. It's why his guard are called Stone Swords. He outfits them with magical stone weapons and armor."

"Sounds heavy."

"Not as heavy as gold, I daresay," she says cheekily.

My eyes sharpen on her and I go still, hand wanting to reach for the gold belt at my waist.

"Ha!" she says with a knowing grin when she takes in my expression. "That *was* your magic at the field, wasn't it?

The goddesses truly have a hand on you, Lady Auren."

Maybe a hand that shoved me down face-first into the ground over and over again. But I don't say that.

The cart jolts to a stop just then, and there's a soft knock against the wall. Nenet peers between the gap. "We're here. Keff just gave us the signal that it's safe, but let me go first, just in case."

I watch as she shifts aside some crates before scooting her way down. She pushes the back open and gets out, and then I hear murmured voices. I start to sweat nervously as the minutes drag on. Finally, she calls for me to follow. With trepidation sewing through the seams of my stomach, I make my way out of the cart, my bare feet hitting lush grass.

I look down, suddenly jolted with my past. It used to feel like a farfetched dream that I could be in control of my power and have *this*—the ability to walk barefoot in the sunlit grass. To no longer have to fear what my skin might brush up against during daylight. I can eat and drink and touch and *live* when the sun is up, and not have to cover, or hide, or live in terror of accidentally killing everyone and everything in my path.

I've come so far.

And now, I'm even further than I ever thought I'd be.

In Annwyn.

When I look around, all I can do is stand and stare. I didn't get a chance to truly take it all in before, but these fields are *beautiful*.

"We call this field *Eëdleth Bire*," Nenet says beside me. "Loosely translated into *her waterless blue*. These flowers bloomed when Saira fell here. Before, it was nothing but parched grass and patches of dirt."

Waterless blue is the perfect name for it. As far as my eyes can see, the subtle sloping of the hills looks like crests of gentle waves, every inch covered in the glowing blue blooms, lapping lightly in the morning's breeze as the plants sway.

"It's blue everywhere. Except for one spot now."

My eyes immediately drift to where Nenet is motioning, and I see the gilded circle right there in the middle, where the blue stemmed flowers now gleam gold.

"That's where you landed, my lady."

I turn to reply, but my eyes catch on to the dozens of fae standing around the field. Some of them have clearly been working out here, their clothes splotched with stains of soil as they hold their tools, but there are others here who aren't working.

There's a group of them near the golden circle of flowers, gathered around and staring at me openly, including children. They all watch me with intent eyes and pointed ears, and my nerves jump at the attention.

"Don't worry," Nenet murmurs reassuringly. "Everyone here is loyal to the Turleys."

Nodding, I slowly push the hood off my head, letting the sunlight lap against my face. My feet carry me forward through the soft grass until I'm walking between the neat rows of flowers. The stems are dark blue, the petals lighter, peeling open like a plume of feathers and emitting their soft glow. The blooms sway in the breeze like they could simply unfurl and take flight.

"The flowers are named after her too, of course," Nenet tells me as I let my fingers lightly drift over the soft petals at my waist. "Though, even that was banned. So instead of calling them Saira's Sea, now they're known more commonly as Blue Bird's Plume."

"They're beautiful," I say, watching as some of the farmers continue to work, carefully pruning the plants and placing them into crates and sacks. "What do you use them for?"

"They're one of the most potent medicinal plants in all of Annwyn. They aid in even the worst sicknesses and can also be used to make serums for some injuries. Lots of people use them for their glow too, until it fades as they wilt." She leans in and breathes. "Plus, they smell quite nice too."

She straightens up and then nods toward the circle of gold that's taken over the field several feet away. "But it's those golden flowers that brought the crowd here today."

I continue forward down the perfect row, not stopping until my toes are just an inch away from the gilt flowers. They've taken up the space like a golden eye in the middle of the sea, just waiting to blink. It's formed a perfect circle, left to glint in the sunlight. I can see where a cluster of them have been crushed, the space of grass molded to where my body must have landed at the center.

My gaze then lifts to the lavender sky, to the fluff of clouds that rumple like a billowing curtain. The air is sweet and the breeze is peaceful. When I take in a breath, it's like I'm breathing for the first time after so many stagnant, stale years. The sun is softer here, painting the world in a pastel light, and something in me settles down and sighs in familiarity.

But even with this sense of home, threads in my stomach begin to knot, because there is no torn line in the sky. There is no crack in the void.

The rip is truly gone.

I knew it was. I saw it close when I fell, but I'd hoped that it would reopen—that Slade would be here by now. But he'll find me, just as he promised. He'll reopen the rip. I just have to be patient.

And yet…there's a little voice in my head spewing doubts. Erupting unease. Making more and more knots tangle in my stomach. Because I saw how drained he was—saw how much power he used. That takes a toll, even on someone as strong as him.

What if something happened to him?

My body tenses, writing with worry, my chest pricking with needling hurt. What if he was so weakened at the Conflux, that the other monarchs hurt him? What if all that power he expelled made him so drained that he…

I yank off that thread of thought before it can unspool any further.

No. He's okay. He *has* to be.

A spot in the center of my chest pinches sharply. I twist my hands through my ribbons and squeeze just to keep from crying.

Forcing myself to take a breath and swallow down my distress, I ask, "Has anyone noticed anything else in the sky?"

She shakes her head. "I asked around, but there's been nothing, and believe me, plenty of people have been here since you came."

I try not to let the tightening ache in my stomach show on my face. Looking back down, I notice that the fae circled around seemed to have moved closer, like they want to be nearer to me, their attention rapt on my face.

"But I daresay if someone *does* come searching for you, they'll know you were here," Nenet murmurs, motioning toward the metal coursing over the petals and dripping down the stems.

I could pull the gold back, but like Nenet said, I want to leave it so that when Slade comes, he'll know I was here. And…one glance at the people gathered gives me the impression that they wouldn't want me to remove it. Like it's become as important to them as the flowers themselves.

"Is it…real gold?" Nenet asks.

The crowd leans in, as if straining to hear my answer. The farmers stop working.

I decide to go with the truth. "Yes."

The fae murmur, a soft sort of excitement billowing through them. One, a pretty fae with long black hair, steps forward and smiles at me. "Lyäri Ulvêre," she says and then makes a gesture, pressing her thumb to her ear, chin, and chest, before she bows her head slightly. As if she's set off everyone else, the rest of the group starts doing the same thing, all of them murmuring Lyäri, all of them looking at me with awe, some even with tears in their eyes.

"Nenet…" I murmur.

"They heard the whispers, Lady Auren. Came to see for themselves if it was true. Your presence is a gift they can't believe they're witnessing."

"But isn't this dangerous?" I ask. "For them to be here? To see me?"

"It's a blessing to see you with our own eyes," a young male fae calls out. "And we true Geisels would never betray the Lady Lyäri."

Nenet nods. "This might not be Bryol, but Geisel is still your home."

My eyes automatically lift to the sky, to the pristine expanse of pastel light and tufts of feathered clouds. Now that I'm here, under this sun, all I want to do is get back to him.

Because I'm looking up, it must hint at the direction of my thoughts, because Nenet says, "Do you truly think he's coming?"

"He is. I just have to be patient," I reply, resolve thickening my tone. Though I think I'm assuring her as much as myself.

She eyes me dubiously but lets the matter drop. "Let me show you something."

I follow her, careful to step around golden flowers as we walk around the circle, passing more people until we reach the other side. There on the ground, nearly hidden between the blooms, is a heaping basket full of feathers of every color and size.

"What's all this?"

"Offerings," she says, plucking up one of the feathers

and handing it to me. It's black, the length of my hand, and right at the end, there's a yellow thread tied to it. "We used to leave offerings here all the time for Saira, but that had to stop long ago for fear of getting caught. These ones though, these have been left for you."

"Yes," someone else says, harsh voice cutting across the field. "Because you're the golden girl we all thought was lost forever."

CHAPTER 11

AUREN

I turn around.

The fae who spoke stands just several feet away, but the distance seems to be eaten up by his pure presence. By the way the others in the field watch him with respectful familiarity.

He's wearing similar garb to what the other farmers have on—a simple long-sleeved tunic and woolen pants tucked into boots. And yet, he looks out of place. The shirt is just a little too tight, the boots just a bit too clean. One glance at his fingernails reveals the crescents are free of any dirt or grime, although he looks strong, used to working his muscles. His skin holds a russet hue, eyes as dark as the soil beneath our feet.

"Who are you?" I ask, keeping my attention rapt on him.

"My name is Wick, Lady Auren."

I glance at Nenet, but she's looking at him with familiarity too, and maybe even a bit of excitement. "Wick! I didn't hear you were back in Geisel."

"Just passing through. It was pure luck I was here," he says as he comes forward.

He stops and places a feather in the basket at my feet. When he raises to his full height again, he stands close enough that I can see a couple faint scars nicked into his forehead. His sleek black hair is swept back in a tousled line down the center of his head, while the rest of it is shaved short against his scalp.

He looks me up and down like he's analyzing every inch of me. I want to take a step back just to put some distance between us, but I dig in my heels instead.

"You really are her," he breathes, almost like he's talking more to himself than me. "You're Auren Turley."

"So I've been told."

His brown eyes flick between mine. "You didn't know?"

"That I'm a Turley?" I glance at Nenet. "Not until recently."

"How is that possible?" His expression and tone are coated in suspicion. Like he doesn't quite believe me. "How could you not know who you are?"

Irritation fills me, dumping down my stiffening spine. "Long story."

"I'd like to hear it."

The fact that he's pushing makes me uneasy. "Forgive me, but I don't know you."

"Well, I know *you,* Lady Auren," he says before waving a hand at all the bystanders, who are still and silent around me. "We all know you."

"You know *of* me. That's not the same thing."

The two of us stare at each other, and there's this awkward strain between us that I don't quite understand. I haven't known Nenet for long, but I found myself trusting her pretty quickly for some reason. Estelia and Thursil too. This fae, however, is making me wary. There's an ambitious

94

arrogance to him that I want to get to the root of. The crowd looks on with nervous energy that crackles like dried grass beneath booted feet.

Luckily, he relents, blowing out a breath that pops the intensity. "You're right," he says, posture loosening its tension like steady hands smoothing out bumps in a blanket. "I apologize. I didn't mean to get off on the wrong foot. It was just a shock to hear that the Lyäri Ulvêre had returned. Even though I heard the whispers, I didn't actually expect to find you, real and alive and standing right in this field. It's…inconceivable."

He keeps looking at me, so I keep looking at him too. He's trying to blend in, to seem like everyone else, but I have a feeling he's not a farmer.

"Who exactly are you?" I ask. "Do you live in Geisel too?"

Wick hesitates, but then he lifts his hand, knuckles bent to show me a small golden ring on his forefinger with the mark of a bird stamped onto the metal. "Do you know what this is?"

I shake my head.

"There are loyalists who have been working behind the scenes to undermine our current monarchy. We are called the *Vulmin Dyrūnia*—Dawn's bird. This is the Turley symbol. And now, it seems, it's yours."

"*Vulmin Dyrūnia*. So you're rebels?"

"Loyalists," he says again, gesturing around to the crowd. "The Vulmin help other sympathizers and the oppressed Oreans, while also doing what we can to uphold the old Turley principles and legacies. We have been working underground for a very long time."

"And you're…what? One of the Vulmin leaders?"

"*The* Vulmin leader," Nenet tells me.

"I see."

"I don't think you do," he counters. "Your return—it's a sign."

My brows pull together in both confusion and suspicion.

"A sign for what?"

"For us to step out of the shadows and rise up. For the Vulmin—for Turley loyalists everywhere—to finally take back Annwyn and undo the wrongs that the Carricks have facilitated and inflicted. And we can do that with your help, Lady Auren. You—"

"No."

My interruption severed his words, but he picks them back up with a cutting edge.

"What do you mean, *no*? You're not even going to listen to what I have to say?"

I bristle. This male has barely had one conversation with me, and he's already trying to *use* me.

Being gold is exhausting.

"I did listen," I tell him. "But I'm not interested."

His gaze flicks to the crowd for a second, like he doesn't want them to hear, and his tone lowers. "You are *exactly* what we need to mobilize our cause—to finally come out in the open and demand change. If more people see you, it will give everyone a reason to take action in a real way, which Annwyn needs now more than ever. You are the Lyäri Ulvêre, our *gilded one gone*, and you've come home. With you as our symbol, we can inspire *thousands* to stand with us."

Inspire thousands?

"I've only just returned," I tell him incredulously. "Just found out who I am, who I'm related to. I have no firsthand knowledge of Annwyn's politics. I'm not in a position to do anything. I don't know enough about it."

"So let us teach you." Vehemence bleeds through his face, his tone. "Come with me. Join us. Be the face of our cause so we may finally rise up against the monarchy. There's trouble brewing in the kingdom's capital. Soldiers have been conscripted, the army is on the move—it doesn't bode well for Annwyn. We need to face them, to force change. We *need* it to happen."

Seems to be a steep ask when I've been in Annwyn for a whole two minutes.

I take him in, really focus on the urgent gleam in his eye, the fist of his hands, the way he's homed in on me. I empathize with what he's saying and with what the others have told me, but at least they don't make me feel like I owe them something. This fae is acting like the purpose of my sole existence and arrival here is to help his cause.

"Again, I don't know you. I respect your plight, but I'm not a face to be used," I tell him. "I'm not a symbol, I'm a person. I've been gone for years, and I need to get my bearings and figure out where to go from here, not be pushed into doing something just because you say so."

Frustration digs through his tone, making it deeper. "You can trust us. The Vulmin always fought to protect the Turleys. That was always the main priority."

"Yeah? Well, the Vulmin failed at protecting my parents, didn't they?" I grit out, losing my temper. "At protecting me. I wouldn't have been missing for twenty years otherwise."

I can't be sure, but I think shame might flicker through his expression. "Then let us right the wrongs. We can protect you now if you join us."

My shoulders snap back. "I can protect myself."

If I thought the crowd felt inundated with the tension between Wick and me before, it's nothing compared to now. All I want to do is leave. To get away from everyone's watchful eyes and weighty expectations so I can process.

I turn to Nenet. "I'd like to go now."

Nenet looks hesitant, but she nods. "Of course, my lady."

Together, the two of us walk away from the gold circlet of flowers, away from the crowd, away from Wick.

I can feel his eyes boring into my back.

"What's his story?" I murmur beneath my breath.

"He's led the Vulmin for a long time," she tells me. "He's a good male, if a bit on the blunt side. But he believes in the cause and for righting the wrongs of the monarchy, that I can assure you."

I can't help but steal a look over my shoulder. When I do, I see him still staring after me, arms crossed in front of him, disappointment thick in his muddied eyes. I whip my head back around.

"I'm surprised he's even in Geisel. He's usually off on some mission or another. It's interesting that he's here," Nenet goes on, side-eyeing me. "Interesting timing, indeed. Some might even say...fated by the goddesses."

"Or a coincidence," I reply tartly as we reach the cart.

She snorts. "Coincidence is just the excuse people use when they don't want to acknowledge fate."

"Or maybe fate simply steals the credit from coincidence."

"The only thief around here is the monarchy," she replies seriously. "They've stolen the very heart of Annwyn."

A small sigh escapes me. "If you knew what I've been through in the last twenty years, you wouldn't ask this of me. I've been a pawn, a token, a tool. Now, I just want to be *me*. Nothing more, nothing less. And that means I'm going to make my own decisions for my own reasons."

She studies me for a moment, and I can see the questions building up, stacking against the creases of her face. Thankfully, she doesn't unearth them, because I'm too worn out to answer anyway.

At the cart, the one who must be Keff is sitting up on the driver's seat with a book propped in his lap. The gangly fae is all knees and elbows, his brown hair windblown from the ride and a piece of straw stuck between his sharp teeth. He gives me a nod and tucks the book beneath his leg before gathering up the reins.

Nenet reaches up and plucks a pin from her hair, passing

it over to me. It sits in my palm, feeling far heavier than it truly weighs, and I blink down at it in surprise. It has the same exact bird symbol that was stamped on Wick's ring. What I didn't notice on his, however, was that the wing on the bird is skewed. Broken.

"Maybe, by simply being here, you've already started change by tossing the first rock. Maybe it's up to us to make sure the ripple spreads."

Her gaze shifts to the flower fields around us. *Her waterless blue.*

"After all, out of all the places in Annwyn, the rip opened up *right here*," she muses, giving me a sidelong glance. "The Turleys' last-birthed heir, the first to land in the water."

She's ever persistent.

But so am I.

Which is why I turn back one more time, not to Wick or the crowd. Not to the gold or even the flowers. No, I look at the sky. At the uncut, untorn, pastel-stained sky.

At the place where I came down, and he did not.

"You *should* make your own decisions," she says, pulling my gaze back to her. "Trust yourself, Lady Auren, because we trust you too."

My heart tightens.

Nenet pats my arm with a smile. "If fate has taught me anything, it's to not ever lose hope."

"I won't," I reply, and I mean it.

Because he's the only thing in this world and the next that keeps my hope alive. Because he promised to find me, so he will.

Or I'll find him.

And *that* is the fate I believe in. That is the cause I'm willing to fight for.

The fate of him and me.

CHAPTER 12

SLADE

The shoreline is dark with browned foam.

At the slumping tide, there's a reek of rotting fish, their gills gaping open while their glossy, scaled bodies float on the surface. In the morning, the fishermen won't be dropping their nets. Sailors won't be dropping their anchors, either.

Off in the deeper water, the shadows of several ships sit, nobody yet aware that they're slowly sinking. Running out of time as they bob in the sea, keels disintegrating into sodden splinters while water slowly fills their hulls. Empty flesh trader ships, and all of them will be rotted and sunk to the bottom of the ocean by daybreak.

I walk through the cystic puddles pocking the beachside street, my steps seeming to echo. It was loud and raucous when I first arrived here a few hours ago, but everyone has since scattered, slunk away to hide. West End was full of every kind of depraved and debauched activity you can think of, but now, it's silent. The kind of stillness that only comes from death and fear.

When I turn the corner, I see shops lined up on the right. The faces of the buildings are stained from the briny air, scabs of moss caught on their dripping rooftops while scrapes of white skid down from the eaves.

A rat scuttles past me, hiding behind a barrel, and ahead, I see someone stagger out of a pub before he turns and starts pissing, completely oblivious to the carnage just down the way. When he turns bloodshot eyes toward me, his flaccid dick still in hand, he does a double take that nearly has him toppling over.

He quickly shoves himself back in his pants midstream and falls against the wall. "*King Rot.*"

My power hisses inside my blood, crawling through every vein. The salt of the air makes my skin feel tight.

Or maybe that's the rage that wants to burst out of me.

I stop in front of him, and I see his attention go to the black roots writhing up my neck. Then his glossy gaze drifts behind me to the putrid street corner. If he walked down there, he'd see the rotted buildings, the swollen corpses hanging out windows and wedged in doorways, caught in their attempt to escape.

No one was able to get away, though. Not from me.

Not from my rage.

The men involved in the flesh trade and their forced employment of saddles has ended.

I found out Midas killed his own rival and Auren's owner, Zakir West, long ago. He also ended everyone in his employ who came into contact with her. It was his attempt to cover his tracks and his previous life, but also to erase Auren's existence from here as well. He bought up all the saddle houses with his new wealth...and created *the painted saddles* of Derfort. They're the most notorious and popular brothels in

Third Kingdom. Famed for the saddles who paint their skin in different colors, and animal prints, and designs, making everyone forget all about the girl with golden skin.

Zakir West might be long gone, Midas might be gone, but that doesn't mean the wrongdoings were eradicated here. It wasn't long before new people took up the gauntlets of the crime rows, and Kaila is ignorant of it either by chance or by choice.

For her brother's sake, I hope it's the former.

But these new lords of East and West now lie in their own poisoned skin, where they'll be left to bloat like beached whales.

I lean toward the man, smelling the alcohol wafting off of him, noting the piss stain spreading through the front of his pants. He's probably lived in Derfort his whole life, based on the sun-scarred tinge of his skin. Probably partook in the exploits of the saddles who were forced to work these rows. If I had proof of it, I'd rot him where he stands.

The only reason I don't, and the only reason I'm not destroying it all and letting this entire harbor city wash up with those rotted fish, is because Auren wouldn't want me to.

She'd want me to spare the innocents. For now, I have to assume he is one.

So instead of letting my sizzling magic release on him, I lean forward and whisper in a cruel taunt. *"Run."*

Flinching, the man chokes on his spit and then turns and takes off, zigzagging in his mad rush to get away from me. Even with instincts drowning in booze, he's aware enough to realize the threat. The same can't be said for the others I dealt with. East's and West's crime lords had too many stupid men working for them. Too cocky, too relaxed, too certain in thinking they were at the top of the threat tier.

They were wrong.

Tomorrow, Derfort will wake up and see the ends obliterated.

People and buildings rotted through and left as a warning. If anyone takes up the trafficking torch again, I'll make sure they meet their deaths too, whether by my hand or my Wrath's.

Speaking of…

I veer off the street, boots sinking into the beachy sand as I make my way back to the figures on the shore. My chest shoots with a stab of pain, and I falter slightly, looking down where the rotted veins at my hands pulse.

Wither.

I bury my hand into my pocket. Fist the strip of gold ribbon inside of it.

When I get nearer, I ask, "You handle the middle?"

Judd deftly catches the dagger he'd been tossing up into the air before he sheathes it and straightens up from leaning against the side of his timberwing. The wind keeps knocking his bright blond hair into his eyes, but he looks as jovial as ever. Despite the long travel time he's had, which is evident in the patchy hair on his normally clean-shaven face, he's in a good mood.

Might be all the maiming.

His sharp eyes give me a once-over, probably to determine my mental state. "Of course," he says. "I made sure your message was *very* clear to those in the neutral zone. None of them seem eager to take over East or West side anytime soon."

"Good."

"But there will always be others."

I nod as I approach Crest. The beast isn't nearly as fast as Argo, and he's smaller, but for one so young, he's handled himself really well with the long distances. "And when there are…"

I see Judd's grin flash in the dark. "I'll gladly pay another visit."

Satisfaction slithers through me. Judd may seem like the

most easygoing of all of us, but he's my Wrath for a reason.

He had stopped in Third Kingdom to rest his timberwing on his flight back home from First, but he caught news of what I did to Gallenreef. So he tracked me down, somehow knowing I'd go to Derfort, and found me right before I reached the shore earlier tonight.

Anyone other than my Wrath would have taken one look at me and flown away in the other direction. But not Judd. He saw the fury in me, and the first thing he said was, "So, who are we killing?"

He hadn't yet heard about the Conflux. About Auren. About how King Thold, who he'd *just* finished renegotiating with, flew right to the Conflux and was a participant in Auren's trial.

After I filled him in, Judd was more than happy to join me in my objective. To help destroy the streets that used Auren and ruined her childhood, making her believe that her worth lay in pleasing others.

The thought that she was here, scared and subjected to endure terrible things, makes my fury spiral so tightly that every vein in my body twists.

We both mount our timberwings, and Judd looks to me as I grip the reins, tightening my thighs around the beast, flinching from the steady pain that's ratcheting through my chest.

"You alright?"

I grit my teeth. Shove the pain away.

"No."

And I won't be. Not until I can get to her. Not until I can find her and my mother.

He studies me. "You're not going back to Fourth yet, are you?"

I shake my head. "You go." I motion toward the lump of a body now draped over the back of his timberwing. "Take our package. It'll be a nice gift for Os."

On cue, Manu, tied and flopped over the saddle, starts to flail. He works to lift his head, and his furious brown eyes lock on to me. There's pale beach sand crusting his tawny cheek and sticking to the ends of his loose black hair as he hangs there like a sack of supplies.

I yanked out the rot I'd put inside him as I flew from Gallenreef Castle so it wouldn't kill him. No one pursued me. I don't know if it's because Kaila took all of her timberwings with her, so they couldn't...or if Keon and the soldiers were too nervous to follow me in fear that I *would* kill Manu.

Without the rot, without being poisoned or knocked out, he's been forced to live through every second of his kidnapping. Screaming at me until his throat went hoarse and I shoved a cloth in his mouth, tying it securely around his head, while also binding his wrists and ankles. Forced to watch as Judd and I killed people from his very own kingdom.

Judd glances back at Manu, who's trying to yell at us through the gag. "Don't talk with your mouth full," he says with a tsk.

Manu glares at him.

Judd turns back to me and lowers his voice. "And...what about a rip?"

I give a terse shake of my head. No matter how far down I dig, how hard I try to reach that void inside of me and shovel up some of the raw power that's always been there, it's still empty.

I'm still empty.

"It'll come back," he says, offering me reassurance. Just as Ryatt tried to do. Just as I've tried to reassure myself too.

"Of course," I reply.

I wonder when it started feeling like a lie.

With a parting nod and a snap of leather, Judd directs his beast into the air and disappears into the night sky, flying in the direction of Fourth Kingdom.

I glance behind me at Derfort, and once again, I frown, wondering how *the fuck* they smuggled Auren here in the first place. No child should be taken from her family, but to also be taken from her world?

How did they get her from Annwyn to Orea?

That question has been tormenting me since I first saw her. Since I first heard her story.

I wish Midas hadn't killed Zakir West. If the bastard were still alive, I'd be able to find out just who he purchased Auren from and then have some sort of trail to follow. But there's nothing. No matter how many inquiries I've made, the trail goes cold. I've asked Auren as many questions about it as she would answer, gone over every small detail, and I've come up with absolutely nothing.

Anger twists like a knife, that spot at the center of my heart searing. Spreading out in painful rivulets like acid streams slicking through my skin.

I don't know how Auren got here, but I know she's gone now. Until I can reopen another rip to get to her, this is all I have. This mission to hunt down everyone who hurt her, everyone who made her feel small.

And while tonight, I swept through the crime streets and decayed every piece of shit involved in the flesh trade, not even this has settled my churning call for vengeance.

I need more.

My separation from her is a smoldering rage that will burst from my skin and leave me to fume until I'm nothing but poisoned ash. Judd could tell that my rot power was riding me hard, but he doesn't know the half of it. Doesn't know what happened when I felt that rip slam shut. When I felt her leave me.

With a snap of the reins, I direct Crest to lift up into the air, cutting through the sky. We fight our way through the humid clouds while I steer us in the right direction, and I settle in, letting my spikes unleash, allowing them to burst through my skin like painful piercings. Blood soaks into my shirt and rolls down my brow, but I barely feel it, because the other pain I'm in is far, far worse.

It's like my heart—my fucking *soul*—has been torn from my chest, leaving me to gape. I'm hollow with nothing but the echo of her and the reverberation of fury. I imagine my aura must be a pit of malevolence churning in the deepest shade of black, because this rage...it will consume me wholly.

And I'll let it.

CHAPTER 13

QUEEN MALINA

I haven't seen the assassin in days.

He's left me here without a word, and I suspect he's doing it on purpose to get back at me. To prove his point.

"Make me believe that you want to get out of here for the right reasons."

What an absolute pompous ass. Who does he think he is? He's an *assassin*. His life's trade is to do nothing but murder people, and yet he dares to judge me?

My ire is a living thing, sharp and weighted, like a thick chunk of ice held in the pit of my stomach that grows each day I'm forced to stay locked in this room and watch more fae infest my realm.

I glare out the open window, the frigid air gusting straight into my face. More troops are marching onward, through the jagged remains of Seventh Kingdom. Toward Orea. Toward *Highbell*.

Ice congeals on my lashes. Heavy, frozen fragments gathering along my lids, flaking away with every angry blink and leaving a dust of snow on my cheeks.

My anger is frozen. Unchanging. Arctic. Hardened in its frigid ferocity. I'm frozen in place too. Stuck in here and made to watch the invasion through ice-hewn eyes.

A clank sounds behind me, and I turn to see the new tray of food has appeared, the old one gone in its place. I stare at the crooked metal tray, and anger chisels into my ribs.

Wrenching away from the window, I stomp over to the tray, and in one sweep of my arm, I send it crashing to the ground. The tin teapot clangs on the stone floor, the bread goes flying, and the metal tray clatters where it lands. I heave, puffs of air condensing like a cloud as I charge toward the locked door.

I grab the handle and wrench it, but of course, the lock stops it from turning. "Let me out!" I yell at the wood. At the lock. At the fae. At *him*.

Again and again, I shake and wrench at the knob, but it holds steady beneath my anger, anger that leaps up my throat and pours from my mouth in a furious, wordless yell. It tears free from my lips at the same time that it seems to explode from my palms, and then, the doorknob suddenly *shatters*.

Not breaks, not comes loose. The metal knob froze so thoroughly that one wrench of my hand made it break beneath my grip and fall into a million pieces on the floor.

I stare at the frozen fragments, my heart thumping, pounding with a permeating chill. My eyes go down to my palm, to the icy line across it. Magic buzzes through the shards of flurries gathered upon my skin, each one pulsing. Alive.

I hurry and fling open the door, only to jolt to a stop.

Fassa and Friano stand in front of me. Their thick hair hangs from their heads like heavy drapes, dark eyes peering out at me through the gaps. They're so identical it's eerie.

Those moles on their cheeks are their only distinction. Friano's is on the left, Fassa's on the right.

Their assessing gazes flick down to the hole in the door where the doorknob used to be before glancing back at me.

"You've got some nerve," I snarl as I step in front of the door, blocking their view of the remnants of the knob. "Locking me in there like some kind of animal."

"Oreans are really just a step above a pet," Fassa says smoothly before looking to his twin. "Don't you think, Friano?"

"Indeed. Though, good pets know better than to let themselves out."

My hands curl into fists. I feel the crunch of snow crushing between my fingers.

"At any rate, we were coming to fetch you," Fassa goes on, completely unaffected. "Come."

My nostrils flare.

The fae turn on their polished heels and descend the stairs, expecting me to follow behind dutifully. I open my fists, willing the ice to spread, to freeze them solid so I can shatter *them* to pieces next, but nothing happens.

I want to scream in frustration. This magic that's filled me with cold, this power that crusts ice at my palms, it's faulty. Dysfunctional. Or perhaps…it's me. Unable to create life, though I have a womb. Unable to create magic, though I now have power. Unable to rule, even when I wore a crown.

I hesitate a moment, but my only other option is to go back inside the room, and after being stuck inside, that's the last place I want to be. Turning, I start to follow, though it burns me to trail them. I keep my steps unhurried, clinging to the illusion that I'm choosing to follow them rather than obeying their order.

Fassa looks back and smirks as if he knows what I'm doing, and I wish I could smack the look right off his face.

Down we go, the spiral stairs split and broken, the walls cut through with holes that blare out bleak peeks of the drab sky. I suppose it's lucky the walls of this tower stand at all, because most of the castle has been wrenched open and left to hollow out.

There's no longer any carpet on this spiral, making every step slick with ice. The banister and railing are gone too, so there's no way to catch myself if I slip. Yet my feet stay stable, even when the brothers struggle, shoes sliding every so often. I want to raise my hands and shove, let the frozen floor crack open their twin skulls. Maybe I would dare, if there were only one of them.

At the base of the tower, there's a destroyed corridor open to the elements, walls cut off into a crumble just above my head where the blustery wind whistles in. There's old doorways leading to hundred- foot drops, entire rooms tumbled by time, piles of snow gathered at thresholds.

Then we reach a wide stairwell, the stones left with crooked clefts in the steps like gapped teeth. I stop short at the top of it, breath catching as I look below.

The ruined castle is filled with fae.

This once grand hall is now nothing but fallen walls and a tall, split-open ceiling showing slivers of sky through the stone chasms. Frosty ash clings to every surface of the raw bricks, making it feel like a gutted-out skeleton left to decay in its arctic grave.

The walls that are still standing have been expunged of all embellishment except for a couple lone candelabra sconces hanging bent and rusted. The faintest swatch of faded wallpaper is slashed across one corner at the back of the room, and there's an old pillar that's fallen like the cracked trunk of a tree.

And all of it, every inch, is taken up by snowfall and tents. Fae stream in and out of them, heading all throughout the castle, stations having been set up with tables of food and piles of weapons. It's all out of place—the tents, the food, the weapons, but especially the fae.

Their features are sharper. Particularly the pointed tips of their ears, the sight of which makes the ice in my body grind against muscle and bone. Their bodies move with a honed gracefulness, and even the way they speak carries an edged lilt.

Their eyes are sharp too, like hawks in the sky, and some have strange colored hair that's unnatural—too bright, too colorful—cutting through the blandness of their armor. Colorless pebbles cover their chests like cobblestones, and heavy swords that swirl like marble are tucked at their backs, ready to strike.

"Magicks, with me!"

I jump at the shouted order, my gaze flying across the broken hall to a huge fae standing in front of the downed main entryway. The doors are long gone, but the rubble was cleared enough to make an easy access to the outdoors.

Fae head toward him, lining up in perfect formation as his assessing eyes travel over them all. "Land fae, at the front. I want this snow shifted before the next regiment hits. We're behind schedule," he growls, and then he turns on his heel and leads them out into the storm.

"Queen Malina."

My head whips to the right where the twins have reappeared at my side. The word *queen* seems to have echoed around us with reedy sarcasm that drips off their tones.

All the fae below turn to look, and aggression fills the air. Vibrant eyes land on me like heated pokers, as their hostility gathers through the devastation of the castle. Some of them turn their full bodies toward me, and others grip the hilt of their weapons in a clear move to intimidate me.

I won't be cowed.

The twins each hold out a hand, smirking. "This way, Majesty."

I lift my chin, holding my back straight, and I descend and then make my way across the hall, ignoring each and every fae I pass. One of them spits on the snowfall at my feet, and I stop, brow arched as I glare at him. He stares back at me, clearly pleased with himself as he chews at his cheek. I feel the cold burrow deeper into me, making my bones go stiff with the freeze, though it's *his* bones I wish I could snap like a shard of ice.

Turning away, I walk the snowy path out of the hall and into a room that has lost its ceiling completely. Piles of snow are gathered at the corners, and the walls are only half-standing. One wall to my right has the bones of an old fireplace, its mouth empty and yawning, its chimney streaking up like a scar and left to stab at the sky.

Past this, the twins lead me through a gaping entryway, and then I find myself in a room that's been completely built anew.

Solid walls gleam in neat rows of bricks, as if someone plucked up pieces from the rubble and carved off their jagged edges, polishing them to a shine. The ceiling is closed, arcing up like a dome, and the floor is a swirl of trimmed stonework. With this room rebuilt, it's shut away from the cold air outside, but I'm still chilled through.

Because at the center of the room sits a man—a fae—propped up in a throne made of solid rock, its curved edges ending at least a foot above his head. The stone table in front of him is in the shape of a triangle, except the top point is slashed off, his hands braced on the smooth line.

There's a potency about him. Something powerful and deadly that makes the hair on my arms lift and puts me on edge, but his appearance does that too. His eyes are like granite. Speckles for pupils, mottled with browns and grays throughout his irises and masking the white of his eyes completely. He blinks, and it's like watching a statue come to life.

He has thick muscles chiseled into his form, his taupe skin nearly the same color as his gray-brown eyes and just as hard. His lips are thin, his nose is large, and rocky nails grow from his fingers like claws. On his head rests a gray crown that looks like it was lifted from the depths of a boulder and chiseled into gleaming spires before resting on his head.

I try not to shake where I stand, but my every instinct is yelling at me to turn and run. I've been around plenty of kings with magic. It's to be expected when you're born into a royal line. Yet I have never felt this innate fear of any of them like I do now. I have never felt such inherent threat. He is different. Other. And that otherness burns off his body like noxious fumes, forcing me to choke on it.

He glances up at me from a map on the table, then his eyes flick to his right. I look over to find Pruinn standing there. I bristle while his silver eyes take me in. I should have known right away that something was wrong about him. He's too magnetic. Too strange. He promised to lead me to my heart's desire, tricking me like a fool with the scroll in his merchant's cart and his charlatan's words.

I hate him.

As if he can sense the thoughts in my head, he grins, flashing too-bright teeth, his blond hair short, his face clean-shaven. "Allow me to introduce you," he says smoothly. "This is King Tyec Carrick."

The fae king looks me over like I'm a lowly bug crawling on his floor. "Hmm. Malina, was it?"

"*Queen* Malina Colier," I answer, thankful that I manage to keep the tremble from my tone.

"Indeed," he says, his voice just as stony as his visage. "So, you are the pure Orean queen whose given blood allowed us to remake the bridge." He pauses. "Born powerless, isn't that right? Pruinn here tells me you weren't allowed to sit on your own family's throne because of it. That your people hate you."

My molars snap together and grind.

"Some rulers think you need to be loved," the king goes on, rising from his throne. His steps sound heavy, like his boots are filled with rocks. "But this is a misconception. You need loyalty, not love. Allegiance, not adoration. That is the way to rule."

I don't say anything in reply, and he cocks his head and studies me.

"Pity that you're Orean. You might be considered a great beauty in Annwyn if it weren't for the inferior blood in your veins."

Outrage stabs through me, making my palms burn cold. "That *inferior blood* was what you needed to get here," I snap back. "Maybe it's your species who's inferior to us."

He laughs, as if my insult was ridiculous and ineffectual. Then that laugh abruptly cuts off, and the table in front of him jolts. I barely have time to realize it's streaking through the air until it slams into my stomach, sending me sprawling to the ground.

I cry out at the onslaught of sudden pain, so stunned that I don't notice for a moment that the stone tabletop is now on top of me, crushing me beneath its staggering weight. I gasp, mouth opening and closing like a fish out of water, limbs too pinned down to flail.

King Carrick walks over, steps unhurried. He looks down at me, hard gaze taking me in with apathy. "Cold Queen they call you, is that right?"

I can't answer. Buried beneath the rough weight, I'm caught, barely able to draw breath.

"Fassa and Friano tell me that they believe their restoration ritual imbued some magic into you. A gift, of sorts, from their give and take powers." He speaks as if he's not crushing me to death.

With his careless gaze, he watches me struggling, the granite specks glinting in the drab light. "Use it. Use this gifted power that you only have because a *fae* gave it to you."

I shake and sputter, feeling like my ribs are about to crack, my chest about to collapse. The pressure is seizing. Horrifying. Every second that I can't get free spikes my panic even more. My bones are pinned, my ribs trapped. This weight is pure threat, like even a single grain of sand added on top would make me split open. Pop like a grape.

I want to freeze this horrible fae where he stands, because I know that he *will* kill me. I can see it in his face. He doesn't care. He will let this slab of stone pulverize me into a puddle of flesh and blood without batting an eye.

So I try to concentrate through my panic, try to use this sputtering magic that seems to come and go without any control, but it does *nothing*. Black dots invade my vision, and my lungs feel like they're about to burst along with my consciousness.

He laughs. At my struggle, at my gasping breaths. Then he leans in, until I can smell the scent of wet rock feeding from his breath. "See? Inferior. Unable to even use the magic that fae power bestowed upon you. Proof that Oreans don't deserve magic *or* this realm," he spits. "So we will take back both."

He turns away, and the weight instantly lifts as the stone is removed from me with the flick of his finger. Air shoots into me, and I flip onto my side, coughing and sputtering with ragged breaths. Deep humiliation fills me, and rage at my own impotency makes my entire body shake.

"Bring her back to her room," he says dismissively, as the slab settles back onto the table's legs just in time for him to sit down again and give me a cruel smile. "It has the best view up in that tower, don't you think, Cold Queen?"

Fassa and Friano pull me to my feet, but I wrench my arms out of their grip and stare hard at the king. I'm not terrified of him anymore. He's a bully—trying to humiliate me into submission. It doesn't matter if he's a fae or an Orean or a god or a devil. He's just another arrogant man wearing a crown, and I've dealt with plenty of those.

"Do you know what the cold does to stone, King Carrick?" I ask.

He pauses and tilts his head as he looks at me.

I gesture through the doorway, to the crumbling stone walls that are worn and abraded. "Stone has rifts and crevices. *Weaknesses*. It may look invincible and strong, but the cold can exploit those things. Moisture delves into those cracks and fissures, and when it freezes, it ruins. Stone can't withstand it forever. In the end, cold will always win out."

My icy eyes glint with an impenetrable freeze.

A tic in his jaw appears, and for a moment, I wonder if he'll shove the tabletop into me again, if he'll let it crush me to death this time.

I don't care. I'm not going to let another power-hungry king tell me I'm useless.

Turning on my heel, I pass Pruinn and stride out with my head held high, fully expecting the king to kill me.

He doesn't.

Once again, I ignore the sneering fae within the castle, ignore the twins as they lead me back to my room. Ignore the new knob and lock that someone has put on my door. Ignore the pain still pulsing in my body from nearly being crushed to death.

I ignore everything but the cold.

The cold that's filled my veins, the blustery air that collects in my lungs and coalesces into icy shards caught on my lips like cracked skin.

I ignore everything until the room grows dark and my fingernails have gone glacial blue.

Until the assassin returns like I knew he would. With curling shadow and bending light, he appears.

I stand up and face him, though all I can see from beneath his draped hood is the pigment of pale skin circling his lips.

Make me believe you.

"You said my heart might just be a chunk of ice," I say, staring into the depths of his shadowed cowl. "And that might be true."

He says nothing in reply, but I can sense his attention. Can practically *feel* his gaze scraping over every inch of my face.

"But I am the Cold Queen, and my heart beats for my kingdom." I point toward the window, to where the soldiers go on with their endless marching. "I need to get there before the fae do, or Oreans are going to be slaughtered without warning." Dropping my hand, I clasp both in front of me, fingers constricting with conviction. "And I *will* warn them. I will leave this place, with or without your help, assassin."

"They incited a rebellion against you," he says roughly, voice in shreds. "Chased you out of your castle."

"I don't care."

"You ordered your own people to be killed."

Chunks of ice slide down my throat. "I was wrong."

For a long moment, he just stares at me. My chest rises and falls with my fervency, while he keeps completely still. The tension of weighted silence grows so tight I feel I might snap as I await his answer.

When he continues to give none, I can't take it any longer. "Well?" I demand. "Do you believe me?"

Slowly, I see his lips curve through the shadows. "I believe you enough."

An exhale shakes out of me, though I'm not entirely sure what that means.

He turns toward the door and swings it open soundlessly.

"That was locked," I sputter.

He digs into the pocket of his heavy cloak and brandishes a brass key. My eyes go wide with indignation. "You've had that this whole time?"

I can hear his dark snicker beneath his breath, and that's all the reply he gives. Then he holds out his hand, and I hesitate for a moment before walking forward and gripping it. His skin is startlingly warm beneath my icy fingers, marked with the bumps of calluses and lines of old scars.

"If you try to assassinate me…"

He leans in, the flap of his hood brushing against my cheek as he lets out his gravelly voice. "I won't need to. The fae will probably do that for me. Now, hold on tight, Queenie."

I suck in a breath as shadows instantly swarm us, and light begins to bend around us with an unnatural wind. We blow through the open doorway, and the castle becomes something that's no longer tangible.

I only see snippets past the swarm of shadows and prisms of light that engulf us. Bodies are distorted as we caper past the fae like invisible billows of smoke. No one sees us. We exist like the air, like shade and wind. Sound warps, some voices bending like echoes down a ravine, while an ever-present gust blows past my ears.

With the assassin's hand clutched in mine, we make it out of the castle without anyone the wiser. Clinging to every shadowed corner, bending the light as we move like wraiths, we flit past them all. Then, we're outside in the cold, broken land of Seventh Kingdom, where troops of fae march onward. March toward the kingdom that rejected me.

I believe you enough.

I wonder if the rest of Orea will believe me enough too.

CHAPTER 14

OSRIK

There are some really shitty sounds. The kind of sounds that get under your skin and piss you off.

Chewing is one. That shit grates, especially when you've spent years with soldiers and traveling mercenaries. Road jerky makes the sloppiest, longest fucking chews. I've punched soldiers for gnashing on it too obnoxiously.

Another sound that used to bother me?

Wheezing.

When you've spent enough time killing like I have, wheezing is almost as common as swords clashing together. Sputtering and choking on blood usually always follows, too. But sometimes, the wheezing can go on and on for hours and days, until finally it stops, when the soldier kicks off into death. Wheezing is like nails down a porcelain plate. Enough to drive me out of any mender tent.

But now...

I look at the still, sallow form lying on the bed.

Rissa wheezes. With every fucking breath, she wheezes.

I don't know if it's blood in her throat or fluid in her lungs, or some other shit I don't know about because I'm not a fucking mender, but I do know this: So long as she's wheezing, she's alive.

So wheezing has been my favorite fucking sound lately.

I hear the door open behind me, and Hojat shuffles inside. "Here again, Captain?"

"Not again. Still."

I never left. Haven't for the past few weeks.

He makes a tsk and then moves around to the other side of the bed where he starts shuffling around with the bottles on the table. I watch as he readies a clean cloth, pouring tinctures over it methodically.

At this angle, the left side of his face is in full view, the burn scars yanking at the corner of his eye. I've never asked him about his burns. A man's business is his own. But right now, I could use the distraction.

"You ever kill the bastard who did that to you?"

Hojat pauses. "I am a mender, Captain Osrik. Not a killer."

"Want me to kill them for you?" I have lots of pent-up rage I want to get out. Killing someone would hit the mark.

"Just because I said I'm not a killer does not mean that they're not already dead."

"Ah. Rip?" He probably took care of the fucker who did that to Hojat a long time ago, when he first brought Hojat to Deadwell.

"I never asked."

It's better for people like Hojat not to. Some can't handle it. But me? Killing was always the one thing I *could* handle. "Killing isn't for the faint-hearted."

Hojat turns toward Rissa, cloth in hand. "I need to change her dressing again."

I grit my teeth but gesture for him to get to it.

He gives me a look. "Need I remind you that the last time I changed her dressing, you nearly punched your fist into the wall?"

"And?"

When I saw how gruesome the gaping wound was, how much blood still dribbled from it, I was also seeing the blade plunging into her chest. It makes me want to murder the person who did this to her over and over again. Makes me wonder how many times I can stab him until he chokes out into death.

"Captain, healing is not for the faint-hearted."

I cross my arms. "Not leaving."

He lets out a sigh, just as I hear, "What are you doing to our mild-mannered mender?"

I turn around and see Judd walk into the room. "When did you get back?" I ask.

"Just now..." He takes in Rissa with obvious unease. I might leave menders' tents, but Judd? He fucking avoids them like the plague. Can't stand to be around anyone who's badly wounded. "Rip told me what happened," he says, eyes landing on me. "You alright?"

"I fucking look alright?"

His gaze runs over me. "No, actually. You look like shit."

I grunt. Then pause. "Wait, Rip? When the fuck did you see him?"

Judd leans against the wall, trying to seem at ease, but his gaze keeps darting to Rissa. "On my way back from First, after I'd settled a new agreement with the king, I stopped to rest my timberwing in Third Kingdom. At the capital. There was an uproar about King Rot just having left there."

My brows shoot up in surprise. "He was in Third Kingdom? Ryatt said when he left, Slade was still trying to reopen the rip in Drollard."

"He couldn't," Judd says. "Still can't."

"*Fuck.*"

"Yep. Apparently, that set him off, and now he's gone on a revenge rampage."

Hearing that he's gone to Third fills me with sick satisfaction. Queen Kaila is the one who sent her brother and guards here. She and Manu are the reason Rissa is lying unconscious in this mender's room with her wheezing breath and jagged wound. "What did he do in Third?"

Judd smiles. It's a real creepy fucking smile.

"Kaila wasn't there, but he rotted her castle. Some of her guards. Then he went to Derfort. That's where I caught up with him. Had a hunch he'd go there next."

I pause, rolling the name over my mind until it comes to me. "The place where Auren was kept as a kid."

"Yep."

I frown. "But when he first told us about Derfort, we looked into it. That cunt Midas had already killed the man she worked for, plus all his cronies." Midas covered his tracks well.

Judd shrugs. "He wasn't satisfied, I guess. He went and rotted out East and West ends' crime streets. Wiped them out."

"No shit?"

Judd nods.

Guess I shouldn't be surprised. This wouldn't be the first time he's gone on a killing spree. He just usually did it as Commander Rip—not King Ravinger. But now that Ryatt is the new commander, it looks like he's letting his rot come out to play.

Makes me proud. Makes me wish I could fuck shit up right alongside him, but being here is more important.

"Where's he going next?"

"Not sure. He let me have a little fun, then he took off. Didn't want company."

I look back at Rissa. While I was distracted, Hojat started changing her dressing, using silver tools to peel away the old bandage. When I catch a glimpse of her glaring red flesh, I grind my back teeth together.

"Remember how you asked about Third Kingdom?" Judd says, gathering my attention again.

"Yeah…"

He pushes away from the wall. "Come on, I'll show you something."

I shake my head. "I'm not leaving her."

"Captain, if I may…" Hojat cuts in. "My mender novices will be coming in soon to give Lady Rissa her cleaning. For her own modesty, you must step out of the room anyway."

I open my mouth to argue, but he waves a hand at me. "You need to go eat and rest," he tells me sternly. "A cleaning of your own wouldn't hurt either…"

Judd grins. "I do believe our dear mender just told you that you stink like foul ass. Come on. The sooner you leave, the sooner you can return."

I grudgingly get up from my chair. Leaning over Rissa, I gently smooth back the blonde hair from her pale face. "I'll be back, Yellow Bell. You just keep on breathing for me," I murmur. Turning around, I follow Judd out of the room. "This better be good."

Instead of going right to head upstairs out of the mender wing, we go left, down the narrower corridor.

"Trust me. You're going to want to see this."

Intrigued, I follow him all the way down the stairs, to the lowest level of the castle. To where the rooms are cold and the air is wet and the windows are non-existent save for a few inch-wide panels. We pass by the two guards on duty, both of them standing at attention and saluting us as we go through the heavy door.

"What the hell are we doing in the dungeons?" I ask.

Instead of answering, he comes to a stop outside the first cell.

I look inside the dim and dank space, and my eyes go wide when I see the figure inside.

"Told you," Judd says with maniacal glee.

The body on the floor shifts, and instantly, I see who it is.

Manu fucking Ioana.

The man I've envisioned torturing every time Rissa whimpers in her sleep, every time her face contorts with pain. Now I know what Slade was going through when Auren wouldn't wake up after Ranhold. It's a fucking torture of its own.

"Rotting Gallenreef Castle wasn't the only thing Slade did in Third Kingdom," Judd tells me, rocking back on his heels.

I feel my lips pull up into a grin that probably looks more like a sneer—a wolf baring its teeth at its prey. No doubt about it, Manu *is* my prey, and there's going to be a new favorite sound of mine soon.

The sound of Manu's pleas as I wring out my wrath.

I hold out my hand, motioning for the key I know he has. Judd instantly digs in his pocket and passes it to me.

"You want me to stay?" he asks, eyeing me as I shove the key into the lock and open the cell door.

"Nope."

"Good," he says through a yawn. "He was a fucking pain to deal with on my timberwing the whole way here."

I look at his unconscious form. "You knock him out?"

Judd shrugs. "Maybe once or twice."

I snort.

"Had to. After Rip yanked out the rot from him, he was a nightmare. Didn't take too kindly to being kidnapped, I guess."

"He probably won't take too kindly to being imprisoned

and tortured, either," I say as I sit down on the flimsy pallet bed.

"Have fun with that." Judd claps me on the shoulder before he turns and walks away, his footsteps receding until the sound is gone and all that's left is Manu's breathing.

His unstrained, non-wheezing, perfectly fucking normal breathing.

Anger boils under my skin, the wrath I feel molten in my very veins. Fury rises from me like vapor that can only be seen at the sun's peak on the hottest days.

I watch him for several minutes. Take in his wrinkled blue tunic and vest. His long black hair hanging loose. His missing shoes that he probably lost from the flight over here. He doesn't look as put together as the last time I saw him, that's for fucking sure.

But he's going to look a lot less put together by the time I'm through with him.

I continue to sit here while his fingers begin to twitch, his limbs jerking, eyes scrunching up. Then I lean over to the cell door and slam it closed as hard as I can. The loud clang makes him jump awake and flip over onto his ass.

He scrambles up into a sitting position and looks around wildly, and when he realizes he's in a dungeon, when he realizes I'm sitting here staring at him, the blood drains from his face. His ankles and wrists are bound, so when he slithers backwards, he nearly tips over.

"Where am I? What's going on?" he shouts, nervousness cracking up his throat and cutting his words in half. "This is against our laws! I am the queen's advisor and brother. She will start a war over this!"

I say nothing. Continue to watch him as I lean against the cell wall, crossing my arms in front of my chest.

"Where is he? Where's Ravinger?" he demands, his eyes darting left and right.

I stare at him.

"You can't keep me locked in here!" A little spit flies out of his mouth, and his face starts going red.

"Don't just stand there," he yells, still trying to hang on to the idea that he has any control whatsoever. "I deserve a trial. I deserve to have my queen sister present. I can't just be taken and locked up. I want to know where your king is!"

He probably spent days talking and pleading and demanding. But that shit won't work on me.

"You can't do this!" He tries and fails to yank at the ropes binding his wrists, his skin already raw. "I demand an audience with Ravinger!"

His outburst leaves him panting, my continued silence clearly unnerving him. He's probably hungry. Thirsty. Aching all over from the uncomfortable trip. But he knows that those things are only the beginning.

My stare and my refusal to react makes him squirm more. After several minutes, I see him swallow hard.

Now I have his attention.

I uncross my arms slowly, brace them on my knees as I lean forward, and look him right in the fucking eye as my voice drops low.

"Let me tell you how this is going to go."

His hands tremble.

"There's a woman upstairs, lying in a mender bed because she was stabbed in the chest."

Manu's eyes shift.

"She's been lying there for weeks. All because of *you*."

His head shakes back and forth. "I didn't stab her! It was Second's man!"

The dagger that flies from my hand is so quick that he can't track it. Doesn't even notice that I'd yanked it from the sheathe at my hip. He screams as it plunges into his shoulder, his back knocked into the wall behind him. He stares in shock at the weapon sticking out of his body.

"I missed your heart. Just like he missed hers."

A bead of sweat tracks down his forehead, and he sucks a breath in through his teeth as he glances back up at me.

"Your fate is now tied to hers. If she's stabbed, you're stabbed," I say darkly. "If she bleeds, you bleed. If she doesn't drink, you don't drink."

His eyes have gone wide.

"If she has to soil herself in that bed because she's so mortally injured that she can't even fucking get up to take a piss, then you're going to sit here in your own filth."

It's not just his hands anymore. His whole body is shaking.

I drop my voice to barely above a growl. "And if she dies, *you* fucking die, you scheming piece of shit."

He's sweating fucking buckets now.

He lifts his elbow awkwardly to wipe his forehead, but he hisses in pain at the dagger embedded in his shoulder. "What do you want?" he asks shakily. "My sister, she'll pay whatever ransom. She'll make a deal with you. Ravinger wants the import ban lifted; I can make that happen. He wants some information; I can supply that."

I get to my feet and eat up the distance between us before leaning down and yanking out the dagger. Blood spurts, quickly soaking into his shirt and making him cry out in pain. "I didn't mean for that woman to get hurt. Truly, I didn't," he says with a hoarse plea. "I told them to just leave her. They didn't listen!"

"But you fucking brought them here."

I sheathe my dagger and then dig the key out of my pocket and unlock the cell door. I'm out and have it closed again by the time he tries to push up to his feet despite his bound ankles, desperation running rampant across his face while blood soaks through his shirt. "Wait! I said my sister will give you whatever you want! *What do you want?*"

I turn the key with a squeaky click before looking up at him again. "I don't want anything."

My footsteps start echoing down the corridor as I walk away, accompanied only by the sound of him shouting at me to come back.

I lied, though. I do want something. But I already had it. For a fleeting fucking second, I had it, before it was yanked away. And every day Rissa stays in that bed and doesn't wake up, there's less and less chance I'm getting it back.

CHAPTER 15

AUREN

For five days, I return to the field and search the sky. Each soaring bird and split in the clouds makes me hold my breath in anticipation, only to let it out again in a disappointed sigh.

I steal out like a thief in the night, and Nenet escorts me without fail, hiding me away in the back of Keff's cart and moving me under the cover of dawn and dark.

And every day, a few more fae are out there in the field with me, watching.

But while they're looking at me, I'm looking for a rip that doesn't appear.

Nothing else comes of the whispers of my landing, and Wick doesn't return to speak to me. The people do, though. Bringing me offerings, letting their baskets of feathers overflow, all of them careful not to tread on the gilded flowers, as if it will bring them bad luck.

Every night, I return in the back of a bursting cart with

depleting optimism. I wear hope on my sleeve like armor, but it's begun to tear off at the seams, weakening with each passing day.

Meanwhile, my mood has snagged with a single loose thread thought.

What if Slade opened up another rip...but it's just not here?

Annwyn is a huge realm, with more lands than I can remember. If he opened another rip, there's no guarantee that it would be here in Geisel. Which means he could be *anywhere* in this world. We could be separated by miles and oceans, with no way of knowing.

The chance that Slade would end up in this field is probably near to nothing.

It's a depressing thought, one that I've been trying to push against over the last few days. But right now, in the middle of the night and cloistered inside my hidden attic room, with only a short-wicked candle to keep me company, that thought consumes me. I watch the lit flame as it pours a glaze of orange against the walls, and I fester.

I never thought I'd ever come to Annwyn again, and now that I'm here, I realize just how out of touch I am. Everything feels unknown. It's like being five years old again, carted off to Orea for the first time. I'm unsettled, and I feel guilty about feeling unsettled, as if I'm somehow betraying my heritage.

Yet the heaviest guilt comes from the disappointed gazes of the fae. I hear them whispering about how I refused Wick. Refused the Vulmin. Even kids look at me like I've done something wrong. But how can they expect me to help lead a rebellion when I know next to nothing about any of it?

It's strange to return to the place where your roots are, only to realize you're actually a tumbleweed, cut off and drifting.

Sleep continues to evade me, so I give up when it's about

two hours before dawn. On the bedside table is a little pile of rocks I've accumulated—one for each day I've been to the field. I've turned each one solid gold.

I don't know why I keep doing it. Maybe to make little visible markers of the days that pass. Or maybe to remind myself of who I am and what I'm capable of. Despite my uneven footing here, I'm me, and I have my magic.

And while liquid gold still drips easily from my hands during the day and I can still control any gold around me at night, one thing is different.

The black lines that now run through my gold. Black lines of rot.

They're on the rocks. On the gold I fashioned for myself and wear every day. Rot writhes through my magic every time I call my gold-touch forward. It's a constant presence weaving through my molten metal. At the Conflux, I was accused of stealing Slade's power, but I didn't.

And yet...

I stare at the rocks, at each thin vein wrapping around them. His rot twines with my gold like strings floating through water.

How did this happen? Why?

My magic feels different. There's a *pull* that wasn't there before. Not the tempting one inside of me that unfurls, but something that beckons outside of myself.

A beckoning, perhaps, that comes from him.

In some strange way, it makes me feel connected to him, even when we're worlds apart. So, I *like* it—having his rot twisted with my magic. But each time I see it, it makes my chest twinge. My heart ache.

Maybe he'll be there today... a small voice in the back of my mind whispers. *Maybe today, he'll finally come.*

It's warm hope that I don't want to douse.

Forcing myself to get out of bed, I get dressed into

another clean, simple gray dress, wrap my ribbons around my waist, and sling the cloak over my shoulders, buttoning it at my collar. I then slip my feet into borrowed boots that have softened leather and creases at the vamp that curl up like a smile.

Bright side, my feet are completely healed now, courtesy of Estelia. There isn't even an inch of peeling skin left. They look as if they were never burned at all. With my magic back and my body feeling replenished, it's almost like the Conflux never happened. I look like my old self.

Except…my ribbons still don't move. They seem like they're just pieces of fabric that could be draped off a dress.

They just need to heal, I keep telling myself. *They just need more time.*

I don't know if that's true, but that's what I tell myself. They just need more time. Just like *I* need more time. Like Slade needs more time. So we can find each other.

Swiping the gold rocks off the table, I slip them into my pocket, feeling their heavy weight against my leg. I brush through my hair and braid it back, and after blowing out the candle, I make my way down the attic ladder.

As soon as I'm on the main level, I can smell fresh-baked syrup bread coming from the kitchens, so I know Thursil and Estelia are hard at work despite the early hour. My mouth is watering by the time I walk in, soft light coming from the stove's fire and the flickering lanterns set on the countertop.

Thursil glances over his shoulder from where he's stirring a giant pot at the stove, and Estelia pauses mid-kneading.

"You're up earlier than usual," she comments with a smile.

Her hair is pulled back into a bright ribbon this morning, the same exact hue as the orange streaks across her cheeks. But it's the little brass bracelet hanging on her delicate wrist that my gaze lingers on. Because right there at the center, hand-painted on a little white oval, is the broken-winged bird symbol. The same one Wick wore on his ring. The same one Nenet had on her hairpin.

I pull my eyes away. "Couldn't sleep," I answer as I slip into the chair at the middle countertop.

"Nenet won't arrive for an hour still, but you can eat if you're hungry?"

"Of course she's hungry," Thursil cuts in, already moving to pull down a basket. "I'll whip you up some eggs."

"Thank you."

I watch as the two of them work fluidly beside each other, their quiet murmurings bringing a smile to my face.

"Almost done with that bread, love?" Thursil asks. "Don't go knocking out all the air, now."

She shoots him a glare. "The only air I'm going to knock out is yours if you keep it up. I know how to knead bread. Much better than yourself, I might add."

He reaches over and taps her butt. "I know how to knead just fine," he says, squeezing her before she slaps his hand away.

"Mind your manners, or you'll find yourself out of my kitchen."

"We both know you would miss me too much."

She rolls her eyes.

He chuckles good-naturedly, showing off his dimples that make him look boyish before placing a kiss on the swoop of her cheek. "You love me."

"Mm-hmm," she replies, though I catch the smile on her face as he turns away.

Thursil cooks the eggs in no time and then plops them on a plate alongside fruit and slides it over to me. "Eat up, my lady."

"It looks delicious."

I quickly dig in, and between bites, I glance at the clock that swirls above the sink, telling time with the shift of colored liquid that darkens throughout the day. "Aren't you both up earlier than usual, too?"

"Got an extra order today from the inn down the road," Thursil tells me. "All their rooms are let out, so they need more food. Have to prepare their luncheon before we start prepping breakfast here to be on time for the servette to open."

"That luncheon needs to be finished within the hour so I can go deliver it. You know how I feel about not being on time," Estelia warns.

"We'll be on time."

I lick the fruit juice from my lips. "I could help, if you like?" I offer.

Both of them look back at me. "Oh no, you don't need to be doing that, my lady," Estelia says.

"No, really," I say, getting up. "You two have done so much for me. I'd like to help. And stay busy."

They share a look before Thursil shrugs. "Come on over here then, Lady Auren. It's always good to have an extra set of helping hands."

Turns out, it is *not* always good to have an extra set of helping hands.

At least, not when they're *my* hands.

All it takes is for Thursil to watch me stir in some slices of potato for a soup, and he immediately sidles me out of the way. I had no idea there was an incorrect way to stir, but I accidentally burned the wooden spoon, and the shards of ashes flaked into the broth.

I don't think that was the flavor palette they were going for.

Then Estelia had me try to chop up some fresh vegetables, but I ended up cutting my finger and bled all over the place. Not only did she have to use her magic to blow healing essence over the wound, but she nearly burned the bread she'd been making all morning because she was distracted.

While a flustered Estelia ran out to take the delivery to the inn, Thursil had me start making the toast for the servette's morning menu. And you know what? Toast is hard.

After I've burned the fifth slice through the tongs over the fire, Thursil physically moves me aside. "Forgive me for saying so, but…perhaps cooking isn't one of your skill sets?" he says as he gently, although persistently, takes the tool out of my hands.

"No, not really. I never learned how to cook."

I could read by the time I was five, rode a horse when I was even younger, and I have memories of swimming in Annwyn as a child too. But cooking…no.

"But I really enjoy eating," I add, after apologizing for the hundredth time for messing everything up.

He chuckles. "Sit down, my lady. I'll sneak you one of Estelia's puff cakes before she gets back, and you can sort the tea bags. Shouldn't get into too much trouble with that."

I prove him wrong, because I end up accidentally dropping all the tins of tea so they're a mixed-up mess, and I spend the rest of the time sorting them again.

But the puff cake is amazing.

Dawn is nearly here, but Nenet still hasn't come. It's much later than usual, and I'm starting to get antsy, but I keep busy by helping Estelia and Thursil ready the servette by organizing the dishes and silverware while they bring everything into the dining room. The two of them work efficiently together, wiping down the tables, setting out pretty crystal plates and vases of fresh flowers—the blue ones from Saira's field.

"Where'd you learn to do that?" I ask Estelia as she finishes up folding the napkins into pretty birds that will go on top of the plates.

"My mother. This servette has been in my family for generations. We're original Geisels."

"Was your family here when Saira Turley came?"

"They were," she says with a warm smile. "They used to tell me stories about her. About how she met the fae prince right here in our town. About how, after she became a princess and even a queen, she would come back during our holiday in the fields to celebrate with us. Everyone here loved her. She was a good ruler for the fae people."

"She sounds wonderful."

Estelia tips her head. "That's her blood running through your veins."

My eyes flick down to her bracelet again. "So you're a part of the *Vulmin Dyrūnia* too?"

Her gaze follows mine and she spins the bracelet with her fingers. "Nenet told me about your introduction to Wick. He's a good fae, and he's worked hard for our cause, but he's right. We've needed a push to start doing more." She lets go of the bracelet with a sigh. "Something more than simply putting out these blue flowers on the tables and wearing the Turley sigil."

"And you truly believe that this rebellion can make Annwyn better?"

"The Carricks have become tyrants. It started with Oreans, but now it's any fae that they deem lesser. It's a slippery slope, and the thumb of control they've pressed down on us is only going to crush us harder."

"And the Vulmin are strong enough to overthrow them?"

"If we all take a stand, it's possible."

"You think everyone is ready for that?" I ask curiously.

"With or without your return, things are getting worse," she tells me gravely. "We just heard rumors of a town being wiped out simply because someone there spoke against a new law being passed. There's talk of goods being seized from entire farming cities like this one, without any recourse or pay. If any place has been known to be…less than favorable toward our rulers, the people are taxed to death. And that's not even counting the way any Oreans are treated, or any fae who's found out to have Orean blood in their line. They're stripped of their rights."

Unease circles my gut like water around a drain.

"So, yes, Lady Auren. I think the *Vulmin Dyrūnia* are ready to rise up, we just need the push to finally do it."

"And you think *I* should be that push?"

"I think you are, whether you choose to stand with the Vulmin or not," she tells me. "Just by existing, by returning, you've reminded us of how things used to be. We need to act soon, because things will only get worse if we don't."

"I think that *worse* might be catching up to us, love."

Both of us look over at Thursil's grave words. He's standing by the sink window, pinching back the curtain and peering between the slats of the closed shutters.

"What's wrong?" Estelia asks as she leaps up to her feet and starts heading over.

Suddenly, there's a bang at the back door, coming from the storage room that's between the dining room and the kitchen.

Thursil drops the curtain, his expression gone strained. "Stay here."

Estelia comes over to stand beside me, and we watch as he disappears through the swinging doors. We hear the sound of the lock turning followed by murmuring voices, and then he comes back in with a flustered-looking Nenet in tow.

Unlike every other time I've seen her, her hair is down, her silvery strands looking incredibly thin without their usual coif. It hangs in sticky clumps, and her lined face is pale, the edges beside her eyes pulled tight.

"What is it?" Estelia asks.

My heart begins to pump harder as I watch Nenet wring her hands together. "Stone Swords down the street. It took me ages to get here because I was trying not to be questioned." She pauses, glancing at Thursil. "They're checking door to door."

Everyone in the kitchen goes tense.

"What are they checking for?"

Nenet's gray eyes meet mine. "The person who fell through the sky."

Shit.

Estelia makes a strangled noise in the back of her throat. "They know?"

"I'm not sure what they know, exactly, but it seems the whispers have spread enough that they're asking questions. Geisels have not been as careful as they should have been."

"Or someone's greased some hands," Thursil says darkly.

"They wouldn't," Estelia insists.

"Maybe not everyone here is as loyal as they used to be," he says. "After years of this monarchy slowly twisting things, it makes people knotted up. Confuses the lines."

"What should we do?" Nenet asks. "They'll be knocking on the servette's door soon enough."

"Lady Auren can hide in the attic," Estelia says firmly. "We'll show them in, let them snoop around. They won't find her."

"Absolutely not," I say, stepping forward. "You all will stay here, and I'm going to leave out the back door."

"You can't!" Estelia exclaims, her orange cheeks flaring.

"If there are Stone Swords outside, you must stay inside!"

I shake my head. "I'm not going to stay here and get you into trouble."

She snatches hold of my hand, expression desperate. "We want to protect you."

I give her a warm smile. "You have. Don't worry about me. I can take care of myself."

"But—"

"You've done so much for me, and I'm grateful for you—for *all* of you," I say, looking at Nenet and Thursil too. "But it's time I leave."

If trouble is coming to Geisel because of me, then I've overstayed my welcome. None of them deserve to be put at risk.

Estelia's chin wobbles. "I don't like this. I still think you should stay. They won't find you, we'll make sure of it."

I give her hand a squeeze, my heart squeezing too. "I haven't been able to find who I'm looking for. It's time I moved on to stretch my search anyway."

Her shoulders slump, and she finally relents.

I drop hold of her hand. "I'm going to slip out the back."

Nenet pushes forward. "I'll make sure the way is clear, Lyäri."

She disappears out of the room before I can reply, the sound of the back door closing behind her.

"Will you watch the field? Just in case..." My words trail off.

"If anyone else arrives, we'll know about it," Thursil assures me. "We'll keep our eyes and ears open. Send word when you get to your next stop, and we'll reply back with any news."

I let out a sigh of relief. "Thank you."

"And remember, outside of Geisel, I can't promise there will be any loyalists around. That could be a good thing and a bad thing. Good because that means there's less of a chance of people recognizing you. But bad because…"

"I won't have any allies," I say, finishing his sentence.

He nods grimly.

"And you're sure about this?" Estelia asks, worry clear in her face.

"I'm sure."

Her amber eyes fill with tears before she lurches forward and wraps me in a hug. I freeze for a moment, but then I force myself to relax, my arms going around her.

"It's been an honor, Lady Auren," she says into my hair. "I'm so thankful that the goddesses brought you to us." I hug her back, and then she pulls away, darting a hand beneath her eye. "Stay right there while I pack you some food before you go," she says quickly before hurrying to the supply room.

Thursil comes over, face grave. "We can give you more time."

I shake my head. "No. You've done so much for me already."

He looks at me like he's not surprised at my answer, and then he reaches into his pocket and pulls out a pocket watch. It's silver with an embossed broken-winged bird sigil right there on the front case.

"You keep this," he says, handing it over. "And remember that wherever you are, you have people behind you."

Emotion clogs my throat, my thumb running over the embellishment. "I don't know what to say."

"You never had to say a thing," he says with a smile. "Just you being here is going to make all the difference. I can feel it."

Estelia comes back inside, pushing an overflowing bag into my arms, tears clumping up her lashes. "Take this."

I heft it in my arms before securing the strap over my shoulder. "This is way too much."

She narrows her eyes and points at me. "It is barely

enough."

"This sack weighs almost as much as I do."

"Don't argue," Thursil says, landing a kiss on top of Estelia's head. "You won't win against her."

With a shake of my head, I smile as I slip the watch into the pocket of my dress, trading it for my own offering. "Thank you both," I say, and then I discreetly press all five solid gold rocks into Thursil's hand. He raises his brows, but with a pointed look from me, slips them into his pocket without a word.

"Come back here anytime, you hear me?" Estelia says, darting more tears away from her eyes. "You will always have a place with us while you find your footing."

"My footing has never been better, thanks to you," I say, lifting my healed foot.

Another tear darts down her cheek and Thursil slings his arm around her waist, bringing her in close. "Stay safe, my lady."

"Don't you worry about me. I'm tougher than I look."

He nods. "I don't doubt that for a second."

And finally, neither do I.

CHAPTER 16

SLADE

I sit in the dark, watching.

Moonlight flows in through the open-air window. This building is full of them—windows without glass, arches without doors. No impediment to the outside, not when this castle needs every puff of air that the arid breeze manages to eke out.

The night is clear, stars speckling the sky like a face of freckles. But the person in bed has none. Not a single blemish covering any part of her skin. Not that I can see much skin, to be fair. Most of it is covered in a conservative robe that must be stifling to sleep in.

I wonder if that's why she wakes up. If she tosses and turns herself to consciousness because of the suffocating heat. Or perhaps it's that some base, instinctive part of her knows that there's a predator watching her sleep.

Knows that death has come to pay her a visit.

Whatever the reason, Queen Isolte shoots upright in bed,

clutching a hand over her chest. Her head is covered in a plain gray cap, the bottom tied off at the nape of her neck.

She doesn't see me at first. The stream of moonlight doesn't quite reach me. Her eyes aren't yet adjusted. But when her gaze finally lands on my shadowed silhouette sitting on her hard, wooden chair, she lets out a shriek that rivals all the cicadas outside.

I get to my feet at the greeting. She shrinks back and begins to scream again in earnest.

"You can make all the noise you want. No one is coming."

Her shouts cut off abruptly, her body shaking.

When I come closer to her bedside, her back slams against the headboard, and her eyes go wide as she takes me in. The spikes cutting from my arms curve like a dangerous grin, and I imagine the scales on my cheeks may even glint in the dark.

"Y-you're Commander Rip," she says, hands clinging to the sheet as she holds it up to her, like she's worried for her modesty.

"Haven't you heard? I'm not the commander anymore," I say quietly, tipping my head down as I come to a stop at the foot of her bed and lift my hands, showing her the blood covering them. "I've been *set loose*."

Terror fills her face, and then I see her press her forefinger to her thumb and *pinch*. In the next instant, there it is. She unleashes her magic on me, just as she did at the Conflux.

Just as, I imagine, she probably did to Auren.

What she *doesn't* know is that I was the son of The Breaker. What she doesn't know is that since coming here to Orea, I have lived my life torn in two. That when I ripped a gash in the world, I ripped a gash in *myself*. Switching back and forth between forms was a physical consequence of ripping a tear in the world, of my father's magic colliding with mine.

When I first came into Orea, I felt cut in half. Off-kilter. Went through the agonizing shift from one form to the other until I learned to gain more control. I didn't know which part of me to be, and I struggled with that…until I realized that I could use these dual forms for different goals. To show each side of myself and use them both to my advantage. But it always hurt. Just like the rot did when my father forced me to use it for endless hours.

Isolte's pain power was nothing more than a nuisance at the Conflux, and maybe part of that has to do with the rot that runs in my veins. Because what is pain compared to death?

But now? Now, I barely feel her power at all. It doesn't even make me flinch. Because with Auren a world away from me, I'm already in agony. It thumps hard and incessant in my chest.

When I don't collapse into a quivering puddle, Isolte turns frantic. She tries to pinch her fingers together again, again, and again. Trying to squish me like a bug and pulverize my insides.

"Keep trying," I dare her. "It won't work on me."

The blood drains from her face, and her fingers drop uselessly.

"Get up."

She's trembling so hard she gets tangled in her sheets, but she manages to get out of the bed. "Walk."

I can tell she's loath to give me her back, but she follows instructions, walking out of her bedroom and entering the tiled corridor. But when she sees the bloodied heap of two of her guards slumped against the wall—and their decapitated heads lying on the floor—another scream scours her throat.

"Y-you killed them…"

"They were in my way."

She staggers, but I grab the back of her robe and haul her forward. She slumps in my hold, bare toes streaking through the puddle of blood and leaving a thin trail as I drag her.

Again, she tries her pain power. Again, I don't react to it.

"What do you want from me?" she shouts, her thin frame knocking around like she's all skin and bones.

"How many times did you use it on her?" I ask, ignoring her question.

"Who?"

I grit my teeth as we round a corner. "*Auren*. How many times did you use your pain power on her?"

Isolte starts to sob.

"How many times?" I demand, and I drop her back to her feet, though she slips, slicking the floor with more red streaks as she spins around.

"Once!" she cries. "I only did it once!"

"I doubt that."

She's shaking so hard her teeth are chattering. "Wh- where are we going?"

Instead of answering her directly, I keep hold of her collar and push her forward. "I found the Temperance Matrons praying—what a strict schedule you keep for them. Forcing the gray-robes to stay up until midnight in the temple with their foreheads pressed to tile, only to be up to pray again before dawn."

She tries and fails to skid to a stop, the strength in her legs too inferior to put up much of a resistance. "The Guardians of Temperance are highly dedicated," she bites out.

I snort. "And yet *you* were slumbering in your bed."

Her shoulders tense, though that might be because of the third headless guard we pass by.

Hard to tell.

"The thing about the forced devout, or punishments doled out by the pious...is that followers eventually realize what they're enduring isn't for the gods at all. Your *highly dedicated* Matrons are festering with resentment, bitterness, and hate. All they need is an opening, and they'll jump at a chance to get out."

I yank her through one of the doorways and speak right at her ear as I drag her outside. "So I gave them an opening."

The desert air is congested, the night starting to drift away. In the sky, the moon's brightness peels back like a flaking fingernail and scratches out the stars. I take Isolte past the fronds, over the tile embedded into the soft desert sand, and then enter another open-arched doorway.

She grinds her slippery feet against the floor as we go down the corridor, and then she stills as soon as we get inside the circular room. With no windows and the blazing fire burning from an iron pot, the space is thick with hampered heat.

Isolte stiffens when she sees the dozen Matrons who stand against the wall, white wimples covering their heads, their robes lined with the gray stripes of their supposed sins.

"Sisters, help me!"

The Matrons don't move.

I drag Isolte forward. "Your Temperance sisters here have filled me in on exactly the treatment Auren received under your orders."

The queen's worried gaze darts around the dark room until we stop in front of the wooden tub.

"Get in."

Her eyes flare, hands clutching her robe at the neck. "I will not."

"You will."

My dark promise makes a shiver of terror travel over her entire body. She looks at the other Matrons, but they don't help. They don't speak. They simply stand stock-still, faces stiff and hands clasped tightly in front of them, here to witness her humiliation.

Because this is what she did to Auren, so it will also be done to her.

Queen Isolte looks down at her blood-stained feet, and with shaky legs, she steps into the narrow tub and sits down. Her shoulders slant awkwardly, her legs stacking over one another as she tries to fit in the confined space.

The water is tepid, neither warm enough to be relaxing, or cool enough to be refreshing. The fabric of her white robe floats heavily around her, bubbling up as she soaks. With a nod from me, the Matrons step forward and crowd around her. They start scrubbing at her skin over her clothes, using harsh scouring brushes and sharp soap. One of them dumps a bucket of water over her head.

Watching her sputter and cough is surprisingly pleasing.

"Make sure you Cleanse the queen *very* well," I tell them. "Her cruel actions have made her soul fucking foul."

The Matrons nod beneath their wimples and start going at her skin harder. Each of them volunteered information *very* quickly when I walked into their temple tonight. They were all too ready to explain everything she had done to Auren, and even quicker to accept my order for them to Cleanse Isolte themselves.

It seems the queen hasn't gained their lasting loyalty.

Isolte flinches and hisses, baring her teeth at the women, and when one of them lets out a scream and falls back, I go forward and shove the queen's head beneath the water.

She immediately starts to fight, body thrashing, water going all over the place, but her pain power cuts off from the Matron, leaving the woman panting and red-faced, with furious, hate-filled eyes locked on the queen.

I yank Isolte up from the water by her neck. She coughs, looking like a drowned rat, her cap skewed on her head. "Now, that wasn't very nice, was it? Your fellow Matron is simply Cleansing your soul. You have no right to punish her with your power."

"My soul needs no Cleansing!" she shrieks.

I tsk. "Lying is a sin, Queen Isolte."

I shove her head back beneath the water.

Rippled screams pop up from the surface as she thrashes, her pinching pain renewed as she focuses her magic on me once again. It's so harsh I feel it cinch at my lungs, like she's trying to squeeze all the air out of them. But some sick, dark part of me relishes in it. Makes me want to retaliate even more.

I keep her under until her movements go sloppy and slow, until her power cuts off. When I yank her back out, she hacks, her cap now fallen completely off her bald head.

She collapses back against the tub, water drooling past her thin lips and dripping from her eyes. With another nod to the Matrons, the women pick up where they left off, scrubbing their queen from neck to foot, her skin instantly going red and raw.

When they're finished, I keep my grip on the back of her neck and yank her out. Water floods off her robe as she stands there shaking, her eyes so full of hatred that I'm actually impressed.

"Let's take a walk."

Wordlessly, the Matrons lead the way, boxing her in as we head outside. The sun is now cresting over the horizon, blazing bright orange and lighting up the sand dunes in the distance. The women make their way around the outdoor path that winds around the sprawling space of Wallmont Castle. We pass by the desert plants and rotting oranges, while sand sticks to Isolte's wet feet and the hem of her dripping robe.

It's not until we reach the top step of the clay stairs leading down the dune that she jerks to a stop. That she realizes where she's being taken.

Right down to the Conflux. On the same exact path that she led Auren.

"Either you walk or I'll drag you," I threaten behind her.

She hesitates for a moment, but then she forces herself forward, feet slipping a few times as we go. None of the Matrons try to stop her from falling. None of them help steady her. She glares at them all, and when I see her hand twitch, I warn, "If you use your magic against them again, you'll regret it."

Her fingers hang limp.

When we get to the bottom of the stairs, I see the Conflux building lying ruined and cracked before us, still reeking of the rot I infested it with. The dead bodies are all gone, but I can feel the death lingering in the air. I can feel the pull of the rot still embedded in the ground. The poisonous roots twist at my presence, like serpents awakening from the depths, ready to poke back out and bite.

The open-air building is a hectic slop of damage, just as badly scathed as the ground where the spectators stood. The domed roof is damaged, the platform split with decayed roots still visible where they jut out of the crumbling stone.

But my gaze goes to the tiny round cage right there on the stage, to its thin pillars snapped like old bones, torn free from the force of the rip. Spilled out of the cage is a fixed puddle of liquid gold now hardened like cold wax. It's stuck there, shining in the sunlight, with the thinnest bands of black veins running through it.

Gold and rot, intertwined.

This is the last spot I saw Auren. Terrified and trapped, forcibly drained of power while surrounded by enemies.

Being sentenced to death.

When I arrived, when she saw me, she didn't cringe away from my brutal power. She didn't admonish the rot as I spread it out, destroying everyone and everything in my path.

There was *relief* in her eyes. There was love.

But I couldn't get to her then.

Just as I can't get to her now.

The sound of Isolte's mangled gasp wrenches me back into the present. I glance at the waterlogged woman where she's stopped in her tracks. Ahead of her, the Matrons have parted, allowing her to see where I've trussed up her husband.

King Merewen sits there on the ruined stage, on one of the thrones that they'd set up for the Conflux. His head is slumped, gray hair plastered against his forehead, his nightshirt drenched in patches of sweat. Crest stands over him, fangs bared, the timberwing growling under its breath. Along the back wall, more Matrons stand, watching warily. Beside the king, an empty seat is waiting.

She whirls on me. "Where is my son? Where is he?" It's the first time she's shown any care for anyone other than herself.

I meet her eyes steadily. "Safe in his room," I tell her. "Unlike you, I don't punish innocents."

Her pale throat bobs.

I nod toward the stage. "Go ahead, Queen Isolte," I tell her. "Take your throne."

She doesn't want to. Not when she spots the knife sticking from her husband's stomach.

"Neale?" she calls out, voice shrill and shaky. "Neale!"

"Just sit down, woman!" He grits his teeth, trying to clench down on the pain. The timberwing roars at his outburst, causing the king to flinch, which just makes the pain in his stomach worse.

Pity.

Isolte hurries forward and plants her ass on the throne.

Ahead, in the ruined square, several people have started to gather beneath the toppled pillars and torn tarps as they watch this spectacle with open horror. Merchants and laborers, who are already awake to beat the heat of the sun, come to watch an entirely different kind of trial. The kind where only my verdict stands.

I come up to Crest and run a hand down his feathered neck. The beast stops growling and settles beneath my touch.

"Alright, you rabid fucking demon," King Merewen bites out at me. "Give us King Rot's message and be on your way!" Sweat drips down his temple, more of it damming up against his yellowed mustache, blocking the path to his lips.

I tilt my head. "What makes you think I'm here to send a message?"

"That's what you do, isn't it?" he pants out. "Your king sends you off like a dog on a hunt." Every word he's speaking must be agony, considering the way he's grimacing. "You can tell Ravinger that we're even—he ruined my city. You stabbed me in my bed."

Anger flares up in me, rioting and rampant.

"Oh, we're far from fucking *even*."

The spikes along my arms throb. I want to lash out and pierce him through with them. Instead, I shove my Rip form down, sharp canines and scales disappearing, spikes sinking back into my skin in rickety, wavering pulses. I force my form to switch until King Rot stands before them, inky veins writhing up my arms and clinging to my jaw.

King Merewen blanches. "It-it's true. I knew I saw spikes that day," he stutters in fear. "You're him. He's you. *How*?"

His wife cuts in. "You have two forms," she breathes, staring at me as if in awe. "Like one of the gods of old. Two forms merging into one."

"Be glad I'm not your god, for I would give you no mercy."

She swallows hard, bald head leaning against her high-backed throne as she trembles in fear. When I look to King

Merewen, all the blood has drained from his face. Now that he knows it's me, he understands the situation more thoroughly. His watery eyes dart around, as if looking for a way to escape.

There's no hope for that.

Even if he weren't trussed up in that chair. Even if he didn't have a dagger in his gut or a timberwing ready to rip into him. Even if he had a thousand soldiers at his back.

He's at my mercy, and like I said before, I have none.

Not for them.

I let my rage bleed out, a cacophony blaring from the deep pit of hate carved into my soul.

I take a step forward.

"I warned you to leave Auren alone," I say darkly. "But you didn't."

I take another step.

"You kept her here."

Another step.

"Forcibly drained her power."

Another step.

"Put her in a fucking *cage*."

Another.

"And tried to *execute her*." My words are growled, barely audible past the fury in my chest that's constricting every bone and muscle and vein.

I stop right in front of him, hand snapping out to wrap around the hilt of the dagger. His arms strain beneath the bindings, eyes darting down. He thinks I'm going to yank it out. Let him bleed.

Instead, I *twist*.

King Merewen screams.

"You should've run," I tell him, leaning down so we're face-to-face, so I can see every minuscule tic of pain I'm causing him as I continue my slow turn of the dagger. "You should've hidden. But instead, you stayed here, thinking you were safe from me. Thinking that so long as you had fifty guards on watch, that it would be enough."

A gasp spits out of him, a whole body shudder.

My dark tone goes pitch-black.

"You should've known better."

The dagger has gone a full circle now, and the king has started to sob.

I lean in close so that it's just my voice in his ear, so that he can hear just how absolutely fucked he is.

"I'm going to leave this dagger right here, buried in your gut. Do you know why?"

He whimpers.

"Because this blade has cut off the blood flow to your intestines. If this were to happen in a real battle, you'd get gangrene and die a slow, agonizing death. But I want to watch, and I'm not particularly patient. So I'm going to speed up the process."

I twist the blade again, and he howls in agony.

"That's why I've now started to rot your entrails. You feel it, don't you?" I ask quietly, pulling away to see the expression on his face. "Your tissues are dying. Without your blood flow, your organs are too. I bet your skin has already started to turn black and green in some places." I turn to Isolte. "Would you like to see?"

She doesn't say a word, her body shaking so violently that her knees are knocking together beneath her wet robe.

"His blood is clotting up in places, curdling inside his veins as they collapse one by one."

As I speak, the king's face is becoming mottled, bruises swarming as they crawl up from his chest. I press around his gut, the bubbled stomach crackling from the gas caught beneath his blistering skin.

"Stop, stop!" the king wheezes, trying to scream but only

managing whispered wailing.

"You didn't stop for Auren, did you?" I ask him. "So why should I stop for you?"

"Anything—anything," he pleads.

Probably because that's all he's able to say.

"We'll do anything," Isolte says, picking up where her husband left off, and she melts off the throne, knees bent in supplication as she lands on the ground. With hands clasped in front of her face, she curves her spine down into a bow. "Please! It was Queen Kaila! She was the one who convinced us of what we must do. She was the one that told us Lady Ch—Auren needed to be found guilty! Please, spare us!"

I finally let go of the dagger, and I straighten up to look at her. "You're begging me to spare both your lives?"

"Yes!"

She's clenching her clasped hands together so hard that it's possible she might crack a finger.

I tilt my head in thought. "And what if I asked you to use your pain power on your husband, if I told you to use it until he died? Would you do it to spare yourself?"

"*Isolte*—" Merewen clips.

"Yes," she says immediately as she looks up at me, bald head going red beneath the rays of the sun.

I cock a brow. "Is that so?" I ask before nodding toward him. "Then do it. Use your power on him."

Her hands shake as she drops them, but she wastes no time in pressing her finger and thumb together. Pinching, pelting out the pain.

Merewen *screams*.

Isolte keeps pinching.

On and on and on it goes. She doesn't waver. She doesn't stop. No matter how much her husband screams. The people in the square look on in horror. The Matrons have all gone still.

Finally, I tell her to stop. "That's enough."

Merewen slumps, not even fully coherent anymore. With my rot coursing through him, he's already begun to smell. He'll be dead soon. Fever, blotched skin, blisters bursting out with foul discharge, unendurable pain…that's how the rest of his short life will be. That's what he has to look forward to in the next few minutes.

The queen is still kneeling at my feet. With no eyebrows, no lashes, no hair on her head, she looks younger than she is. But the pure and innocent visage she tries to put on can't hide the darkness beneath.

Wicked souls can recognize it in each other.

I glance at the Matrons. "Go."

They scatter off the stage.

When they're gone, I crouch down in front of the queen. Her nostrils flare like she can't take in enough oxygen, body swaying away from me and shaking like a leaf.

"You didn't need much convincing, did you?" I ask. "I tell you to torture your own husband, and you did it without wavering. Without even a plea on his behalf."

"You t-told me to," she stutters. "You are like the god of old…"

"It has nothing to do with me and everything to do with you wanting to save your own skin. If you had any love for your husband, you would've at least hesitated."

All the rot that's poking out from the crumbling stage begins to slowly move, undulating in sinister rivulets. The reaching roots delve through the stone, the ground shaking with its slither.

Isolte's eyes dart around, watching as it begins to surround her, panic flaring in her face. "What are you doing? What is this?"

"You tortured Auren. Made her hurt," I say darkly, and the roots probe closer, inch by inch. "Made her feel trapped.

So that will be your penance."

Her head jerks up. "You said you would spare me! You said if I used my power, you would let me go!"

I shrug a shoulder. "I didn't actually promise that."

"You deceived me!"

"I'm sure you're familiar with that particular sin." Smoothly, I get to my feet and look down at her kneeling form. "Now, pray, Queen Isolte," I say tauntingly. "See if any of those just gods will spare you."

She collapses into sobs just as the stone collapses around her. The rot has spread through the open-air stage, dug through the floor, crawled up the walls. There's a crack beneath her, and then the floor where she's kneeling suddenly gives out.

Isolte wails. Scrabbles. Tries to pull herself out, but the rotting floor has no purchase. Her tears run down her cheeks, snot from her nose runs down to her mouth, and her sweat runs down her brow. She's leaking fear all over.

"Help me!" she cries.

The only help I will give is helping her understand her fate.

"You'll be pinned beneath a rubble of rot," I tell her evenly, while scatters of dust and chunks of stone begin to rain down around us. "You'll be helpless, just like you made her feel. But unlike Auren, no one is coming to save you. You'll die with the weight of the Conflux burying you alive while my rot pinches your every vein. And *that*, in my eyes, is just."

I turn and start to walk away just as the walls of the Conflux fracture. The fissures split up through the domed half-ceiling, and a terrible crack echoes through the square, making the spectators gasp and back away.

I approach the timberwing, his nervousness showing by the flap of his outstretched wings. Above us, the sky has gone yellow, the infection of this kingdom leaking like pus into the clouds.

Gripping the reins, I pull myself up into the saddle, and Crest jumps off the stage, landing in the square. More of the roof begins to fall. One massive slab hits the ground, and that's all it takes for the rest of the Conflux stage to come tumbling down in a terrible onslaught, trapping the royals beneath it.

Within seconds, both queen and king are buried, only the top of Merewen's throne visible, and Isolte's pale arm caught upward like a reaching weed. She's screaming, the sound muffled and choked. Roots still slither through the bricks in obvious threat, but now, she has the roots *in* her too, mashing her veins with poisoned pain.

The air is congested with the grit of the crumble, but when the dust settles, when the people start to clear away the mess, they'll have two dead monarchs and a very clear message of the consequences for going against me.

Crest growls and snaps his teeth, and I look down to see him snarling at the crowd who are staring up at the ruined stage in terror. The Matrons, too, have finally seemed to realize the magnitude of what I just did, of their part in it. Perhaps they'll try to pray for atonement. Or maybe they'll finally strip their robes of the Temperance bullshit and get out of this gods-forsaken kingdom.

One by one, the watchers' knees bend. They bow before me until they're all genuflecting, some with their foreheads pressed down to the corroded ground. Not too long ago, these people were in this very square, falling to the dirt because I'd rotted them through.

Now, they're doing it so that I don't.

The veins running through my skin jut and twist, a hissing sound streaming through my ears with a tempting pull to kill more. I want to wring out retribution until every last drop of blood has been spilled. I want to erupt through the world and leave it to ruin.

But I won't.

Because she wouldn't want me to.

As if on cue, pain in my chest spikes so fiercely that I nearly sway on my feet. It bulges and burrows, the black veins in my skin starting to stutter. My heartbeat slugging in my chest like a drunken punch.

I take a breath, forcing my attention past the pain. The spectators continue to bow. To cower. When I came during the Conflux, they were shouting. *Guilty. Guilty. Guilty.* Roaring with the thirst for Auren's death.

Yanking on the reins, I turn the timberwing around to face them, my voice rising up over the crowd. "That golden female you all were so quick to condemn, the one you were all so ready to watch die…she is the *only* reason I'm not going to kill you all right now. She's the only reason I'm not going to rot the entirety of this kingdom so that nothing—no person, beast, or plant—could survive. So when you kiss that ground your lips are pressing against, you'd better be thanking *her*. Because if it were only up to me, you'd already be fucking dead."

I nudge my heels into Crest's side, and the timberwing launches upward, shooting through the torn tarps and hitting the pus-soaked sky.

I've taken revenge on Kaila, on Derfort Harbor, on Second Kingdom. I've left blood and death in my wake.

But I'm not done.

So I turn my rage toward Fifth Kingdom.

CHAPTER 17

AUREN

When I leave the servette, I sneak out the back door, checking both ways before I head down the narrow alleyway at the side of the building. As soon as I round the corner, Nenet jolts in front of me, stopping just before we collide.

"Nenet!" I whisper, clutching a hand over my chest, pulse clamoring.

"Sorry, my lady. Didn't mean to startle you. Come this way. I couldn't find Keff anywhere, but I wrangled someone else. He'll get you out of the city."

"I don't want to get him in trouble…"

"You won't," she insists, waving me forward. "But the Stone Swords are just down the way, and this is the only road out of Geisel, which means we can't get out of the city yet. We'll have to go to the fields so things don't look suspicious. We can't have an empty farmer's cart heading out of town at this hour."

My heart lurches. I get to go to the field one more time. A final last-ditch look before it's time to cover new ground.

Nenet sees the look of relief on my face. "Thought you'd like that," she says with a smile. "We'll go straight there."

At the end of the alley, I stop just short of the cart, the heavy bag of supplies slamming against my hip. "Wait. *We*? No, you need to stay here with Thursil and Estelia. You can't come with me."

She waves me off. "Bah, nonsense. I won't have our Lyäri Ulvêre out here alone. I'm going with you."

"Nenet, I'm leaving Geisel. This is your home. You can't just pick up and leave everything behind for me."

"I'll do what I like," she retorts, her gray eyes firm. "And I suddenly feel like traveling."

I sigh. "Nenet, it's dangerous."

"Hush, Lady Auren. Let an old fae have her fun."

I pin my lips together, swallowing my argument in the face of her stubbornness. Maybe I can talk her out of it once we leave Geisel, after I have time to figure out where I should go and how to get there.

She peers around the corner and watches for a moment before reaching back and grasping my arm to tug me forward. I slip into the back of the cart and tug off my bag of supplies, setting it in the corner. When I crouch against the side, Nenet follows me in and closes the hatch. All that's in here is a pile of empty sacks and three empty crates. The metal is cool beneath my legs, the sky already lightening through the pale blue fabric overhead.

"Let's hide you quickly."

I lie down, and Nenet starts piling the empty sacks on top of me until I'm completely covered. "Hold still," she whispers before I hear her knuckles rap on the cart. A moment later, it starts to move.

I simmer in the strain of listening, trying to pick up on

anything that might be happening outside. But most of the noises are drowned out by the roll of the wheels and the clomp of the horse's hooves, and minutes stretch out while I breathe beneath the suffocating pile.

Dawn crests, and I get hot and sticky beneath the layers of burlap. After a few more minutes, I can't take it anymore. I shove them off my face, and Nenet glowers at me from where she's tucked behind the narrow crates that aren't doing much to hide her.

Before she can say anything, the cart suddenly jerks to a halt, making my stomach leap. I lift my head up, trying to look through the fabric overhang to see what's going on, but it's too thick to see much more than obscure shadows. From the gap at the back, I see fae clustered together along the side of the road, heads all turned in the same direction.

I see why moments later.

There are soldiers marching through the city, and it's obvious why they're called Stone Swords. Each of them has a sword that looks like it's been carved out of stone, either swinging at their hip or tucked into a sling at their backs. The royal guard aren't dressed in metal armor. They have stone gauntlets on their forearms, and instead of chain mail, a vest of small, interlocking stones in drabby grays and swirled creams cover their chests and backs.

There are dozens of them along the road. Some stop to question fae, others clog around storefronts, their fists raised into harsh knocks as they demand entry. I watch, ears poised to try to hear what they're saying. Mostly, all I can pick up is unintelligible shouts and their booted feet in syncing steps. But it's enough.

It's enough, witnessing the drawn look on people's faces, to see them shouting at the Stone Swords, who shove their way past and kick in doors. It's enough to see Nenet's trembling hands.

I grip the ribbons around my waist and let gold slick against my palms to prepare for the worst, but the cart starts dragging forward again, and Nenet lets out a sigh of relief. After several seconds, the tension drains from me too, the stopper yanked, my gold drying up.

Neither of us talks until we get to the field, and she reaches over and helps clear away the rest of the sacks off of me until I'm free of their cover.

"Will Thursil and Estelia be okay?"

"Don't you worry about them," she tells me firmly. "The royal guard might have a swarm, but they don't have much smarts. They'll search around, rough up some of the citizens for fun, and then crawl back to the pubs for a drink after their day's work. There's nothing to fear."

I give her a sidelong glance. "You're sugarcoating it."

"I always did have a sweet tooth."

I can't help but match the smile she gives me.

"Come. We need to let some time pass before we sneak you out of the city. Give the Stone Swords time to end their search and for things to die down."

She reaches up and sweeps back her frayed hair, twirling the strands together until they're a stuck-together swirl that she loops around her head. "Let's go see if we can find your rip today, shall we?"

Her words make a fist squeeze around my heart, but of course, when I get outside, there's no rip. No tear in the sky, no Slade walking the fields. Just like every other time I've come.

A sigh sears my lips, leaving burning disappointment in its wake. "That's that," I say beneath my breath before I glance at Nenet. "I guess it was silly for me to keep coming out here. I just hoped."

"Hope is never silly. Just look around, Lyäri. Listen."

My head instantly swivels. Two fae are sitting at the back

of one of the other flower carts, their legs swinging down, pants rolled up at their calves. Clutched in their hands are matching pan flutes, the wooden cylinders glossy, the instruments curved and well worn. Both fae perch their lips on the pipes' tubes, moving with complimentary tunes as they blow out a song. Further in the fields, around the gilt blooms, fae are dancing around the flowers, spinning and smiling, as if the troubles of the city and the threat of the Stone Swords can't touch them here.

"Is this safe?" I ask with blooming worry.

"This is *our* field," Nenet tells me, steel solidifying her tone. "This is *her waterless blue*. This is *your* golden circle. The monarchy can strip our traditions and strain our life and search our homes, but they cannot take *this*. Because this is where you both came down to ripple out change, and that will always be true, no matter who sits on the throne. So we will come here and celebrate that, my lady, for as long as a loyalist lives in Geisel."

My heart tips over with some unnamed emotion. "Thank you, Nenet," I say, my throat tight. "I'm glad you were here when I landed."

She grins. "And what a landing it was."

"Lyäri! Lyäri!"

I startle at the shout, and a little girl comes running up to me, smile beaming across her freckled face. She has tiny rivulets of blue skimming across her eyelids and stretching up into her temples until the color on her skin merges with the streaks running through her black hair.

"*Batiellu, Lyäri Ulvêre*," she says, holding out a brown feather to me. "For you, Golden One."

I kneel down in front of her, gently taking the offering. "Thank you very much."

She reaches down to where my cloak has parted, to where one of my ribbons peeks out. She stares at it in fascination. "They say you're the broken-winged bird, but these don't look broken to me." She picks it up, rubs it between her fingers gently and looks up at me. "If you get enough feathers from us, will it fix them?"

There's a twinge in my gut, and I don't know how to answer that, but her innocence makes my heart swell, so I just say, "I don't know."

I don't know how I got them back. I don't know if they're broken. I don't know whether they'll ever move again.

Her face scrunches up in thought. "Well, I hope it does." With a wave, she turns and skips away, back to the dancing fae, and I straighten, clutching the little feather in my hand. Holding it tight.

Her gesture seems to set off a chain reaction, because within seconds, I'm swarmed by more fae. Dozens of them come forward, giving me feathers, murmuring Lyäri Ulvêre over and over again as their fingers gently skim over my ribbons. My hair. My hands, my back. I have to force myself not to flinch. Not to pull myself away or tense up at every graze.

Most of them have the emblem of the *Vulmin Dyrūnia* somewhere on them. A pin, an embroidered handkerchief, a necklace, a patch, a belt, a set of earrings, even a shoe buckle. The broken-winged bird symbol of dawn has woven itself quietly through each one of them like a silent marker.

A quiet stand.

They look me in the eye, their gazes filled with adoration, their touches with reverence.

They look at me like I'm worthy of holding the weight of their trust.

And as each one takes their turn to see me, to smile and touch and speak, something in me loosens. The hard-packed ground of my uncertainty is tilled so that my stunted roots can dig in and spread. So that I don't feel quite as much of an outsider anymore.

When everyone has given me a feather, there are so many that I can't hold them all, and with full hands and a full heart, I'm near bursting.

Because...I've always wanted this—acceptance.

"Do you see?" Nenet asks. "Do you see what's in their eyes as they look at you, Lyäri Ulvêre? You are their hope."

I don't have words adequate enough to reply to that, but I wish I did. I wish I could express how honored I am that they're doing this for me...and how utterly undeserving of their devotion I am.

But maybe I could be.

I watch as they dance around the gilt ring of blooms, their skirts and pants brushing against Saira's blue petals and their smiles floating up to meet the pastel sky.

The same sky that Saira fell from. The same field that bloomed for her, and now blooms for me. Intended or not, coming back has set off ripples throughout Annwyn, starting right here. Right now.

Maybe that rip did open here for a reason.

And maybe Slade isn't going to be able to find me...until I find myself.

CHAPTER 18

AUREN

The only way out of Geisel is through it.

We leave the fields with a full cart of flowers, and now, we can take the sole road that leads out. It's a regular occurrence during harvest, overflowing wagons bumping along the road, carrying their fragrant blooms to sell to neighboring towns. We stayed most of the day, making sure nothing would seem out of place, that we're just another overstuffed farming cart churning out of Geisel.

I have baskets full of feathers and a heart full of hope when I leave the field for the final time. Nenet and I sit side by side, swaying slightly as the wheels roll, not even an inch of space between us with the bushels of Saira's blooms piled all around. Our cloistered cart is flooded with the flower's scent, smelling like the sweetest sea.

Her waterless blue, indeed.

It's early evening, and the sun's face is covered with blunted clouds that bleed blue, marking up the lavender sky with bruises. The moisture of impending rain begins to fill the air, distant thunder rumbling like faraway waves.

By the time we make it to Geisel's main road, fat droplets have started to fall over the roof of the cart, though the thick tarp keeps the moisture at bay. Soon, the sky is pouring down, and the horse's hooves are tracking through splashes of puddles.

It's noisy—maybe that's why I don't hear anything else right away. But the cart suddenly jolts to a stop, and there's a wordless shout from our driver. There are people walking just outside, more voices raised through the storm.

Nenet's wide, gray eyes snap to me. "Your hood!" she hisses as she pulls down her own.

I yank my hood over my head just before the hinge at the back of the cart screeches as the panel drops, and our driver's harried face appears. "Quick! They're checking carts!"

With a vise grip on my arm, Nenet starts to drag me out, flowers scattering in our wake. I barely remember to snatch up the bag of supplies Estelia gave me before I hop out of the cart, my boots landing in a puddle. We're instantly pelted by raindrops in the middle of the packed street, interlocking shops bearing down on us from both sides. I slip the strap of the bag around my shoulder, securing it against me.

Nenet looks around and then pulls me forward, my feet nearly slipping on the slick, uneven cobblestones. As if that weren't hard enough to maneuver, there are carriages and carts all over the road, congested by whatever search is happening ahead. Groups of fae take up the rest of the remaining space, so we're forced to squeeze past people, nearly getting separated several times.

Even with the hooded cloak, rain pours down my face and soaks through my clothes. It's the sort of rain that pummels you from every direction and blinds your eyes with its density.

At the sidewalk, more people are huddled beneath storefront eaves, their distress clear as they look ahead. But the press of the crowd starts to ease when a few fae notice me. Within seconds, everyone starts to give us a berth, whispered *Lyäri*s falling from their lips. Now, instead of fighting against the throng, they're moving us like a tide, smoothly ushering us out of the rain, helping to hide me until we're brought to the door of a shop. Gratitude bubbles through me.

"In here, Lyäri," a female fae whispers.

She brandishes a key, pops the door open, and rushes us inside. As soon as she has the door closed and locked again, she starts yanking the shutters closed.

When she finishes and we're bathed in the darkness of the shop, I shove back my hood, and her eyes go wide. "Goddess grieve. It's really true," she breathes, placing a hand over her heart. "Golden one."

She has a cherry-red braid that hangs all the way down to her knees, twisted over her shoulder in a heavy drape. She's wearing trousers that cinch at her calves, a studded piercing through one cheek, and she continues to stare at me, not even blinking.

"You got searched this morning, Rillo?"

Nenet's question makes the fae jump, gaze cutting away from me as she shakes her head. "Yeah, and they weren't gentle about it, were they?" she says bitterly.

I take a moment to look around, and see destruction the Stone Swords wrought in nearly every corner of her shop. There are freestanding shelves along the floor, but three of them have been knocked over. Shattered glass litters the place with shards of every color, liquids and powders left in puddles.

Everything on the wall shelves has been knocked down too, and it smells like cedar and pine, with a hint of burnt paper. Now that the shutters have been closed, the only source of light comes from a window on the ceiling, but it's warped by bubbled glass and streaming with rain.

Rillo sidesteps the worst of the broken vials and heads for the counter in the corner of the room. When she comes back, she hands us both handkerchiefs. "Here. I'm sorry I don't have anything bigger."

"This is perfect, thank you," I say, and I start to wipe the water from my face. Nenet uses her cloth to squeeze out the raindrops that have stuck to her hair like dew.

"Do you know what's going on?"

The shopkeeper sighs at Nenet's question, tension caught at the corners of her downturned mouth. "They've been at it all day. Barely dawn, and they were here, banging away. Woke me up straight from bed. I came down to open the shop door for them, and they burst inside. Searched all over. Even my upstairs. Under my damn bed. And apparently felt the need to look through my shelves too, breaking open nearly half the tinctures in my shop," she says with a glower.

"Did they say what they were looking for?"

"Not specifically. Asked plenty of questions instead. Wanted to know where I was a week ago. If I heard anything about any insurgents. If I'd ever heard of the name Wick." Rillo pauses and steals a look at me. "If I knew anything about a stranger appearing in Geisel or a mark in the sky."

Nenet curses beneath her breath. "My grandson was right. Someone must've talked."

"Or the Stone Swords are getting better at eavesdropping."

"So now they're stopping everyone riding down the street?" I ask, hating to see such destruction brought onto anyone in Geisel because of me. Hating the fact that my presence is having such consequences. I need to get away from here before anyone else is hurt.

Rillo nods. "And still searching all the buildings. Even doubling back and going back through ones they've already checked."

Nenet's eyes flick to me, understanding bouncing between us. "We need to get out of the city, but I don't think we'll be doing it in a cart." She reaches behind her and pulls up her hood again. "But that's okay, I always liked walking in the rain."

"Use the side door. No one is out that way," Rillo says, and she leads the way through her ruined shop, each of us careful to avoid stepping on the glass.

We walk down a dark hall and past a tucked-away staircase, and then Rillo opens a door, peering out both ways before giving us a nod.

"Thank you," I say, handing the shop owner the handkerchief.

She gives me a small, sad smile. "You keep it, Lady Lyäri. And be careful."

When we step outside, Nenet wastes no time. "Come on."

We slip down a narrow path, the rain appearing to fall down and leap right back up again. But our path leads to a broken carriage, slumped and crooked, taking up the entire side street.

We retrace our steps and then turn left instead of right, but just as Nenet is about to round the corner, I snatch her sleeve and haul her back. I point, and her breath catches when she spots the five soldiers standing with their backs to us. A crowd of people are packed in front of them, expressions tense and disgruntled, voices lobbing back and forth as they argue about not being able to get through.

"You have to go to the main road! Turn back!" A guard shouts.

They're socking everyone in, keeping them herded to the main street.

Nenet and I share an uneasy look before quietly turning

around. Doubling back again, we try to head down the other two alleys that veer away from the main street, but one is blocked with horses, and another is a dead end.

Dammit.

We stop beneath a back door vestibule, only getting some reprieve from the rain as we loiter beneath the low-hanging eave. "We're too close to the square," Nenet says in obvious frustration. "All the shops circle around it this far down. We can't get out. We're going to have to go back to the road."

My mind whirls and my muscles tense. I don't like feeling like we're trapped. "How long until we make it out of the city?"

"Normally? About twenty minutes. But with this crowd, longer." She reaches up to swipe the water dripping from her nose. "We'll be discreet. There's plenty of people out there for us to blend in with, and Geisel will help you." She reaches up and tucks some of my hair beneath my cloak, pulling my hood further down my face. "There. Ready?"

I look up at the sky, gauging the time. It's hard to tell with the storm, but I should have another hour of daylight.

"You need to stay here," I tell Nenet. "I can make my own way out of the city. I don't fear them."

She shakes her head. "No."

"It's *dangerous*," I tell her. "At the very least, we should split up..."

She gives me a fierce look. "Enough of that. Are you broken-winged or broken-eared? I already told you, I'm coming."

"You're stubborn," I grumble.

"And you're hard of hearing—much too young to have that ailment. You should talk less and listen more."

A smile crinkles my cheeks. Her words make me think of Digby. Her matter-of-fact personality makes me think of

Milly. "You know, you remind me of someone."

She arches a brow. "Well, did you listen to them, or did you talk more?"

A little laugh escapes. "Definitely talk."

"Hmm. A bad habit then."

"Probably."

Even though I'm smiling, I kind of want to cry, because I miss everyone—my entire cobbled-together family who's now a world away.

"I'll not be leaving you, Lyäri. That's that."

"But you just met me," I say, trying to get her to see reason, to turn back. "Why put yourself at risk?"

She cackles, like I've just made some great joke. "*Why*s are for eyes, but you don't have to show to know."

I blink. "What?"

Nenet sighs and taps her ear. "Listen. Stop hearing."

"Right. Of course. I'll just...do that."

"Good."

She abruptly spins and walks away, and I have to jerk forward to keep up with her. She maneuvers us through the dizzying paths of the alleys until we find a break between the buildings. Ahead, there's a group blocking the way to the main street, but Nenet manages to shove her way through, tugging me along.

The main road is blocked with carts and carriages and people, even more congested than it was before. Through the pounding rain, I can see Stone Swords searching systematically. They're tearing open carriages, checking carts, shoving their weapons through barrels and stabbing through sacks, more of them pounding on shop windows or kicking in doors.

Just in front of us, one Stone Sword yanks open the back of a cart, letting hundreds of sacks tumble out onto the wet ground. They split open like a festering wound, grain bleeding out all over the road. Another pair of them has a fae male pinned to a shop post, mocking him and punching him in the gut.

This seems like more than just a search for me or some rebels. The royal guard is being destructive. Acting like tyrants. I don't like it.

Nenet pulls me forward, but something up the road catches my eye, and I lean around people in the crowd to get a better look. Squinting through the rain, I strain to see, and when I do, my stomach drops.

Up ahead, Estelia stands in the middle of the street. Her clothes are soaked through, sunset dress plastered against her skin. Her hair has come undone and now hangs in soaking tendrils, and I can see her shouting, though I can't hear her words.

I tug against Nenet's grip, and when she looks back at me, I hiss in her ear. "It's Estelia!" Wrenching free of her hold, I dart forward, surging ahead with a single-minded purpose.

Thunder cracks above as I push myself through the crowd. I make my way forward as fast as I can, slipping through the gaps of people until I reach the front, where everyone has stopped like there's an invisible line drawn across the street that no one wants to pass.

I see why.

The servette is just ahead on the right, the dainty hand-painted sign dripping with rain where it hangs over the door. Flowers line the front of the building, and it would normally look just as cheery and welcoming as its neighboring buildings, except for the windows that have been smashed, the shutters sagging crookedly, the front door kicked in.

My heart pounds in my chest like a warning bell.

Immediately, I see why Estelia was yelling, why a Stone Sword is now holding her back by her arms.

Thursil has been shoved down and forced to kneel in the street, knees buried in a puddle, surrounded by the royal guard. Dripping wet, held down at the shoulders by a pair of them, he's glaring at the fae who's holding Estelia. Barely paying any attention to the male that's circling him.

But I pay attention.

Outrage stirs in my gut as indignation winds and slithers up my torso until it constricts in my chest. I watch like a serpent peeling both eyes open, pupils dilating, tongue flicking out to taste the air.

The male walking around Thursil has his helmet off and tucked beneath his arm, and no rain touches him. Not a single drop.

Water magic. Or perhaps some sort of shielding ability. I squint, and...*there*. Right above his head. The faintest outline of a disc hovering over him, rain pelting off it. So it *is* some sort of shield, but I wonder how thorough it is.

His black hair has a tinge of green that looks like algae running through it, and it's slicked back behind his sharp ears. His chin is wide and square, holding all the angles of arrogance, and the edges of his mouth are bordered by frown lines.

He stops and I see his lips move as he says something to Thursil. My ears strain to listen, but I'm too far away to hear. I do, however, notice the way Thursil's jaw works, the stoic look that crosses his face, and the adamant, stubborn shake of his head.

Algae Hair smirks to himself and then turns toward the crowd, speaking loud enough for us all. "This fae is accused of harboring an enemy to the crown!"

Everyone watches with a grim disquiet, but one of them shouts back at him. "Where's your proof?"

The Stone Sword tries to locate the voice, but whoever it was is lost in the surrounding group.

"The royal guard doesn't need to give proof to the public. We answer only to our king!" he shouts back at the sodden crowd.

"He's not our king!" someone else shouts.

Everyone seems to collectively suck in a breath at whoever dared to say it.

My eyes dart around, but again, I can't find who spoke, and neither can he. The anger on his face is evident by his pinched lips. The rest of the Stone Swords are glowering, eyes scanning, tension mounting. The bystanders glower right back.

There's hate here. It volleys back and forth between the royal guard and the people, soaking through them all even more than the rain does.

Lowering my hand out of the sleeve of my cloak, I let the tiniest drop of gold gather. It slinks to the ground and rolls toward Algae, the barest glint that nobody seems to notice. The small pebble reaches him, leaping up like the splattering rain and landing a hit against his pant leg.

So his shield doesn't cover his whole body. Good to know.

"The treason and conspiracies of the city of Geisel have gone on too long!" Algae shouts. Then he delves into his pocket and thrusts up his hand, showing off what he's holding in his fist.

Gold rocks.

Five of them, all with little black lines coursing through. Bile sloshes in my stomach, and the look on Thursil's face is one of daunting dread.

"This is your price for rebelling against your crown! Gold from the hands of traitors!" He spins around the middle of the street, looking at everyone gathered. "Give us the gilded one, or we will destroy your precious city."

The crowd's fear spikes.

"Turn over the one you are hiding, or we will kill you all."

The rain falls in sharp pellets, but it's the fae's threat that pierces through.

I expect them to give me over. I wouldn't blame them in the least, and like I've been telling Nenet and Estelia, I don't fear the Stone Swords.

But no one shoves me forward. No one starts pointing. And when I look around, I notice something.

Small glimmers through the rain. Flashes amidst the dismal drear.

Dozens, maybe hundreds, of broken-winged bird sigils hidden in plain sight.

It's a tiny painted emblem in a shop window. It's in a carving on an eave. It's branded into a doorknob. A button sewn on somebody's cloak. A tattoo inked into a neck. Chiseled into a lantern post. Hanging from someone's earlobe.

It's everywhere. Surrounding me. Flooded through this city, and I think for the first time, I really understand what broken-winged bird *means*. It's not just the frayed dress that flapped with Saira Turley's fall. It's not just my ribbons that burst from my back in the air as I dropped through the sky.

It's *them*.

It's these fae who feel trodden. Clipped. Their way of life yanked out from under them while they were shoved aside and left to plummet.

I understand that more than most.

They believe if a broken-winged bird can fly despite her fall, then maybe Annwyn can too. Maybe a rebellion can rise up, lifting their realm back to where it should be.

It's not about me. It's not even about Saira Turley.

Like Nenet tried to tell me, it's their hope that they see when they look at me. It's their symbol come to life. And just like when Slade first believed in me, *their* belief helps embolden me, too. Helps remind me of exactly who I am, in that other world and in this one.

The Stone Sword's face darkens with anger. He doesn't like that no one is cowering beneath his threats, that nobody is giving me up. He turns around and marches back over to Thursil with menace.

"Fine," he growls out, hand suddenly fisting Thursil's blond hair. "I'll start with you."

Estelia screams.

The fae yanks out the sword from his scabbard and *swings*, aiming straight for Thursil's throat.

And gold erupts from my fingertips.

CHAPTER 19

AUREN

The clang is so loud that it rivals the thunder.

His blade of stone meets the whip of my gold that's wielded from my clenched fist. My magic wraps around his sword, freezing it in place just a hair away from Thursil's neck.

The royal guard's head snaps to me, his furious gaze locking on my face, algae hair flung into his eyes. "Who dares interfere with the crown's justice?"

"I fucking do."

I step forward and toss my hood back, still gripping the strap of gold like a taut rope. Determination holding its grip on *me*. I'm not going to let him harm Thursil or anyone else on this street.

His eyes rove over me from head to toe, as if he can't believe his luck. As if coming face-to-face with me could actually end well for him.

Idiot.

"Speak your name, golden one, so the justice of the crown can be exacted."

I open my mouth to answer, but another voice beats me to it.

"This is the Lyäri Ulvêre," Nenet spits, suddenly stepping up beside me. "And she is more of the *true crown's* justice than you could ever be."

"Subtle," I murmur as I slip the bag of supplies off my shoulder and let it drop to the ground.

"There's a time for subtle and a time to kick 'em in the balls," she mutters back. "This is the latter."

"Right."

Following her cue and taking advantage of the stunned silence, I yank on the cord of gold, sending the male's sword flying out of his grip. It crashes to the ground, but unlike normal stone, it doesn't crack or crumble. It lands with a heavy thud, unbroken, yet too far away for him to reach.

My gold whip melts onto the ground and starts circling the fae like a bullseye. He looks down at it before that gaze flicks back to me, as if gauging the threat. Assessing. For a second, a wary look crosses his face, and I think maybe he'll make a smart choice.

Silly me. Very few men do when faced with a pissed-off woman.

"Arrest her!"

The Stone Swords gathered around descend on me like flies to a carcass.

I let them—for a few feet anyway. Then I lift my hands and push rivulets of gold out that harden and arc into them, knocking into their pebbled vests and sending them flying. People in the crowd cheer, *Lyäri* coming out of their mouths like a victory chant.

Algae—still without a lick of rain on him—sneers at me. "You will pay for that."

I shrug. "I'm made of gold. I can afford it."

From the corner of my eye, I see Thursil and Estelia reunited, clutching one another. Safe.

"You're done terrorizing Geisel," I tell the royal guard. "It's time for you to leave."

An ugly look crosses Algae's face. "I will burn Geisel to the ground and make you watch unless you submit."

The fiercely fae part of me snarls. "*I don't submit.*"

Upon hearing my answer, he abruptly shoves his hand through the air. The near-invisible disc that hovered over his head moves so fast I barely have time to blink before the shield suddenly backhands me across the cheek. My head snaps to the left, and anger snaps through the rest of me.

He can obviously manipulate his barrier magic for offense, not just defense.

Funny, my magic can be awfully offensive too.

The black-veined gold that's circling his feet shoots up like a fist and knocks him on his ass, upending him in a dirty puddle.

Beside me, Nenet guffaws. "Not so dry anymore, is he?"

My lips twitch. I have to admit, this is sort of...*fun*.

I've come such a long way with learning how to use my magic, with understanding its limitations and mastering control. The fact that I'm here, standing up against so many fae and completely confident in it buoys me. Makes me want to float higher and higher.

The crowd roars with approval, and that fae beast inside of me roars with them.

"Arrest her, you idiots!" Algae shouts, neck flushing with red rage as he points at me.

The royal guard try to scramble to their feet, but every time they do, I use thick paddles of gluey gold to knock them down again.

And again.

And again.

It splatters on their faces, their armor, their feet. Sticking to them in partially solidified streams and smacking into them with a clang.

"This is almost pathetic to watch," Nenet says, sounding absolutely thrilled as she crosses her arms in front of her and grins.

Algae is not so entertained. This time when he shoves his arm through the air like a backhanded slap, his barrier magic slams into my chest, sending me sprawling. If it weren't for the arms of the crowd to catch me, I would've been the one landing in a dirty puddle.

The bystanders dust me off, pushing me upright and shouting encouragements, but as enthusiastic as they are, I don't want anyone to get caught in the crosshairs. So I walk forward, past that invisible line everyone is staying behind, getting away from them. As I go, gold drips from both of my hands, spilling to the ground like a fountain, those little lines of rot pulsing through it.

Spurring me on.

With a flick of my wrists, I make the streams of molten metal roll, like yarn being wound up. With every fast rotation the spheres grow larger and heavier, until dozens of them are ringing out across the cobbles, speeding toward the guards.

In a blink, the globes slam into the soldiers, some big enough to roll right over them, pulverizing their splayed-out bodies in a violent crash, making blood and bone pop out and spill onto the street in a gruesome display.

The smaller spheres knock several Stone Swords off their feet, and as soon as they're laid out, I pounce. The hardened metal melts back down as quick as lightning, a thick coat of it that pins them where they're sprawled in a viscous, tar-like swathe. It binds their limbs, sticking them to the road as they flail.

I walk past them, gold and fierceness oozing out of me. Stepping over dead guards, while metallic rivulets part before me until I stand face-to-face with Algae. Until I can see the fear in his grubby eyes.

"Take your Stone Swords and leave Geisel."

The fae around me shout out in vehemence, cursing the soldiers, spitting at them, their voices raised and their fury heated, my presence bolstering both.

The male sneers. "We will leave. With *you* in shackles."

There's a shout of outrage from the crowd, and suddenly, someone wrenches me back by the hair and slams me to the ground from behind. It's so unexpected that I don't even have time to brace for the impact. My head cracks against the cobblestones, bursting with pain, and I blink, dazed, while rain pelts my upturned face.

I missed one, then.

With a snarl, I turn over and push myself up, whirling round. The Stone Sword who snuck up on me fumbles with his weapon, but he has no time to draw it. I slam my hand into his chest, anger seeping through my skin. Magic bursts out, instantly dousing his clothes and thickening over his armor until it's so heavy he can't stand the weight.

He tumbles to the ground, limbs pinwheeling, head swiveling like an overturned turtle that can't flip over. Panic flashes over his face as he realizes he's unable to get back up. As he realizes how royally he fucked up.

Turning, I swipe the rain from my face, leaving a smudge of gold smeared across my cheek. More sprouts from my palms like vines, and I shoot them toward Algae. He throws up his barrier in front of his head and chest just in time for some of my gold to go bouncing off, but his shield doesn't stretch the entire length of him. Gold vines wrap against his ankles and then slither up, pinning his legs together and planting him in place.

Another burst of his magic hits me, this time going for my hands, managing to momentarily dislodge the gold collecting in my palms. The liquid splashes on the ground, my wrists throbbing from the hit.

I lift the gold back up, hardening it in front of me and making my own shield to block him, but his barrier just passes right through, hitting my wrists again. And again and again.

I grit my teeth as he strikes me in the same spot, making my wrists feel like they're being pummeled with the blunt end of a hammer, my gold shield dropping from the distracting pain. I'm ready to make the vines drag him away straight out of Geisel, but something on his face makes me pause. He's not nearly as afraid as he should be.

"If you don't come with us, there will be consequences."

"*I'm your fucking consequence,*" I snarl.

His eyes cast over my shoulder. "Do it."

I jerk my head to look. And that's when I see someone— *not* a Stone Sword, but just someone in the crowd—move toward Nenet. I don't even notice the dagger they're holding until after they've plunged it into her stomach.

My vision narrows. Tips. Heart stops on a single throb in my ears.

No...

I blink, and it's her, I blink again, and it's Sail. Again, and it's Digby. Again, and it's Rissa. Rotating over and over in agonizing flashes. Blade, pain, punishment, all because of their involvement with *me*.

Not happening...

But it is, because Nenet looks down at the blade like she's both disgusted and annoyed that it's suddenly there. Then she falls to the ground in a heap. People scream. Someone grabs the male who stabbed her, and fighting in the crowd ensues.

I turn to run toward her, but I'm knocked in the back with

Algae's magic, and it sends me sprawling. My slicked palms slap against the cobblestones as I catch my fall, my hurt wrists twinging on impact.

With the breath still shoved out of me, I look up and pitch my hand forward, shooting a stream of gold toward Nenet's attacker. It avoids the people pummeling him, making them stagger back as it hits the male right in the mouth, gorging itself down his throat.

He gurgles, flails, grabs his neck and gags, but the viscous liquid clogs his airway and sinks down into his lungs, gilding his breaths, weighing them down until they're too heavy to pull in. While he struggles, his hood falls away from his face, and I realize it's *Keff*. The quiet, gangly driver who took Nenet and me to the fields every day...except today.

"You fucking *bastard*," I seethe.

I feel no regret whatsoever when he hits the ground.

Pushing myself up, I take in gulping breaths, but the crowd has gone still. Quiet. When I turn around to see why, Algae is right behind Estelia, with a blade to her throat. Thursil is on the ground, unconscious.

My heart leaps into my throat with resounding alarm.

I was distracted. My gold on him must've weakened while I was dealing with Nenet's attacker. Algae must've been able to use his own magic to knock himself loose.

"I can do this all day," he threatens me, an evil smugness marring his face.

Curses fly from my mouth, but they're drowned out by the sound of hooves. My head snaps over just as Wick appears on horseback, bursting past the parting crowd, horse leaping over the gilt bodies in the street.

He rears his mount to a stop, dark eyes scanning the scene. "Stop, Stone Sword! Leave these people alone." He jumps down and holds up a large necklace with the emblem of the broken-winged bird on it. "I'm who you want."

Algae's eyes are hard, and he whips out his hand, sending Wick sprawling off his feet from the force of his magic. "Filthy rebel," he hisses, but he still doesn't let Estelia go. "Traitors, all of you!" he shouts at the crowd before his eyes swing back to me. "Call back your magic and turn yourself in. Do that, and I won't kill her."

Liar.

He knows by my expression that I don't believe him. He also knows that my magic is far superior to his. Which is why when I take a step forward, he sends another pulse of his barrier. It hits me right in the head, smacking me in the skull like being walloped with a real shield. My face whips to the side and my temple throbs, but that only pisses me off more. He's probably trying to knock me out like he must've done to Thursil.

When I see Estelia wince at the press of Algae's blade, I *lose it.*

With a growl, I make the gold around the street gather together and rush him. He wraps his barrier around himself, but it's far too flimsy against the mass of my magic.

A tidal wave of viscid metal slams into him, ripping him off his feet with a surprised cry. Estelia falls back and rolls out of the way, while the wave sloshes over him, sprouting limbs and pinning him down. It undulates on top of him like a furious tide, splashing and striking at him, sticking to his body like thick molasses and crude oil, his magic lost in the flood of mine.

Wicked satisfaction curls from my chest.

More of it floods from my hands and starts to sweep down the road. I pour it out like a glut, let the gold feast on the street until there's so much I can't tell if it's raining water or gold.

And I don't stop.

Not when the last of the remaining Stone Swords are

screaming, pelted with it, *drowning* in it. Not when buildings are splashed with its gleaming spate. Not when Algae's limbs go jerky and rigid, his eyes bugging out of his head as the gold seeps into the sockets and sloshes through his innards.

I'm furious. Feral.

And Annwyn...the air, the very land itself, seems to thrum through me. Like she's saying, *there you are.*

I feel her like a shot of adrenaline surging through my veins and filling me with a staccato thrill, ready to help fuel my fury and push my power to rid her of her tarnished and twisted people.

It *elates* me. Makes me feel everything fae that I'd been cut off from for so many years. And with this vicious elation, I realize something else dark and noxious that's luring my fury out—the black veins that stream through my gold.

It's pushing, seeking to ravage. To *kill.*

"Auren!" someone calls, but I ignore him. Don't pay him any mind. I'm too entranced by the pull of punishment.

Rotted gold floods the street, pouring down the Stone Swords' throats and choking off their screams. It wraps around their limbs, weighing them down, decaying them even as it leaves them gleaming and glossy.

I let more coat the street. Climb up the walls, flood over the cobblestones, splatter across carts. Fling droplets into the crowd. This rot, this land, my magic, my *fae-ness*, it all lures me like a siren song to keep singing, keep destroying.

My heart races, and a part of me knows I should be horrified. But the fae part of me *loves it.* Pushes for *more more more.*

Because they hurt Nenet. They threatened Thursil and Estelia. They tried to intimidate me. Wanted me to *submit.*

The magic is demanding, spilling out of me like a deluge, and people in the crowd start to scream. Not cheering for me anymore, but yelling out warnings instead, shrieking in fear, running away…

Just like that night in Carnith.

Carnith, where I killed the first woman who was ever kind and accepting of me. Where my magic first erupted and I flooded an entire town, killing everyone in my path.

I couldn't control my power then. Couldn't for ten years after, either. But now, I know how to hold the reins. The last thing I want to do is make this town fall prey to my gold the same way Carnith did. I have to stop this.

I slam my eyes shut and focus, forcing an end to the savage call. Reminding myself that I'm trying to *protect* Geisel. Not destroy it.

I clench my fists, hands shaking, trying to shut off the flow, to stop the spread of gilt rot. But I find my magic doesn't want to listen, and Slade's magic is an ensnaring, wicked temptation wanting to consume. It's the overly-sweet scented power seducing me, the bond to Annwyn enticing me. The gleam of my own gold threatening to blind me, and I have to regain control.

"Stop," I whisper beneath my breath.

The rotted gold seems to snarl back.

My jaw clenches. Teeth gnash. My entire body shakes with effort. This is my magic. Mine. I wield it.

"*Stop!*"

The call bursts out of me like a great force of will that I feel all the way down to my bones. Instantly, that feral ferocity that took over shudders and slips.

The savagery snaps off, ending its surge.

It begins to retreat back into me, slinking down with chagrin. Heart pounding, my gaze falls to my hands as the last of the liquid drips to a slow stop, like the turn of a faucet.

Spinning on my heel, I take in the street.

The Stone Swords are all dead, black lines streaked over their metallic corpses. The gleaming liquid has splashed over the entire street, with spatter up on the storefronts and speckles of it staining the bystanders caught in its wave.

They've stopped running, but there's at least half the amount of people that were here before, and all of them are staring at me. Not with awe. Not with hope.

With *fear*.

There's a low whistle beside me, and I see Wick standing next to me, looking at me with an indecipherable expression on his face. He says nothing, but shame crawls up my throat and chokes me.

"Lyäri."

I jerk at the voice, heart leaping into my throat. Turning, I run toward Nenet where she's slumped against the wheel of a cart. I kneel down beside her, the dress at my knees soaking through with rain and blood and gold. Horrible, churning guilt wraps itself through my limbs as I take in the state of her. At how terribly I failed to protect her.

She looks down at the blade still buried in her gut and rolls her eyes. "Typical. Things just start...to get...interesting. And then...*this*."

A half-sob, half-laugh escapes me.

The sound of shuffling draws my eye over my shoulder, and I see Thursil's arm slung around Estelia's shoulders as she helps bring him forward. Together, they sit next to the old fae, both of them looking at her as if in a daze. In shock.

Thursil's hands flit around Nenet like he doesn't know what to do. "Stel..." he pleads.

Estelia's amber eyes go watery. "I don't know, Thursil. I don't know." The orange streaks on her cheeks have gone pale. Like a peel leeched out by the sun.

But Nenet glances over at her. "You know as well as I do that your magic can't heal this."

Estelia's chin wobbles.

"We have to try," I say desperately, looking to Estelia.

"You healed my feet."

"That was different. Just burns on the flesh. This…" Her eyes drop to Nenet's stomach. "But yes, I will try. I need the dagger to be removed first."

Thursil looks stricken.

"I'll do it." Because I know he can't bear to pull the blade from his grandmother, can't bear to cause her more pain.

I reach up and grip the hilt carefully, my eyes skipping up. "Ready?"

Nenet nods.

As quick as I can, I yank the blade out of her. She cries out and jerks back, but Thursil is there to catch her. Estelia instantly leans over and starts to blow out her healing breath over the bleeding wound.

Over and over and over again.

Kneeling there, I grasp her cold, slippery hand, and other fae start to gather around, the mood somber, no one saying a thing. After several minutes, Estelia falls back onto her bottom, exhaustion pulling her down, the orange streaks on her skin nearly non-existent. "That's all I have," she says, heaving. "My magic can only do superficial wounds. Nothing like this. I can't… This—this is—"

"Fatal," Nenet rasps.

Estelia buries her head against Thursil's neck. "You did what you could, love," he murmurs to her, but our eyes go to the stab wound that's still oozing blood.

Still gaping.

My eyes burn.

"Nenet…" Tears track down my cheeks, left to dribble with the rain. "I'm so sorry. This is all my fault."

"Bah." The noise comes out like a strangled croak.

She squeezes my hand, surprisingly strong considering how much blood is soaking through her cloak. "None of that.

Keep fault for the lines in the earth," she tells me, her spiderweb hair plastered against her head like spun sugar left to melt. "You're a *Turley*. Remember that. Remember what...the Turley name means in Annwyn. Remember that the gold blood in your veins...is good."

I want to say that my gold and I almost just destroyed this whole city and everyone in it, but I keep my mouth shut.

She coughs, blood staining her thin lips for a second before the rain rinses it away. Her hand comes down to feel one of my drenched ribbons around my waist. "Broken-winged bird," she murmurs, her gray eyes flicking back up to my face. "Sorry, Lyäri. Looks like I won't...be able...to come with you...after all..."

"Stop talking like that," I tell her, dashing more tears away. "You're going to be fine."

She tries to cackle, but the sound is wet. Labored. The movement makes her grimace. "Terrible liar for such...a talker," she gasps out. "Remember...to *listen*."

My throat tightens. "I will."

I will.

So I listen as the thunder booms overhead. I listen as the rain continues to drop, landing with a metallic clang. I listen as Estelia and Thursil cry and say their goodbyes. I listen as she tells them she loves them. I listen as more fae gather around, their steps mournful.

I listen as Nenet takes her last breath.

I listen to the painful silence that follows.

When I finally get to my shaky feet, when I take in the crowd, they seem to be listening too. Listening and waiting.

For me.

I flex my fingers, let out a steadying breath, and then call to my gold. Because I refuse to be afraid of my magic...or Slade's. *I'm* the one in control, and it's up to me to take it.

This time, I don't let bloodlust fuel me. I don't allow the

temptation of destruction to sing. I tame the beast and force it to move with gentle purpose, to undo the wreckage I wrought.

With reins yanked tight, I make the gold turn liquid once more. Make it retreat from the corpses and drip down the walls, calling it all to pool in front of me. Everyone watches, murmuring, coming closer instead of running away, offering me a second chance at trust as they see me gather it up.

Then, I make it all flow out in a gentle surge.

It floods over the cobblestones, gliding down the length of the slick street. It unfurls beneath everyone's feet, making a few of them jump or cry out in surprise as it moves past. But it doesn't hurt them. Doesn't stick to their shoes or crawl up their legs. It simply continues to spread, until it's all smoothed out and gleaming, the last ripple of the metal settling into place. Until the entire street of Geisel is gilt with marbled swirls of black rot.

I think Nenet would've liked it. And based on the awe in their faces, I think everyone else does too.

With the last minutes of daylight, with the last bit of gold that I can offer, I let drops fall from my fingers, molting out a pile of gold lumps on the ground for the people to take. To use. And with my final drops, I gild their broken-winged bird sigils until they gleam.

The crowd utters *Lyäri,* their hands outstretched to touch me, the veneration on their faces making my heart twist and my spine stiffen. Because Geisel didn't deserve to be terrorized by the Stone Swords, and Nenet didn't deserve to die.

It's clear that I'm going to be hunted, and innocent people are going to be caught in the chase. But I'm not prey, so what I need to do is run with the predators.

Which is why I turn to Wick and say, "I'm going with you."

CHAPTER 20

SLADE

I was easy to infiltrate the underbelly of Fifth Kingdom now that I don't give a fuck.

Without Auren, without worrying about peace or politics, I strode right into Ranhold, threatening palace workers and guards until they told me where I could find the dewdrops supply.

Then I rotted it all.

The new king of Ranhold isn't much to look at, not that I got a very good look. He cowered behind a wall of guards in the entry hall when I stormed through, his round face gone pale with fear, blue eyes watery with the wet terror of tears, blond hair crumpled on one side like he'd been jerked from bed and was on his way to flee when I burst inside.

He was probably terrified I was there to kill him because of his presence at the Conflux. But I have no quarrel with him. He's just a puppet who was placed in a kingdom he has no business ruling. A convenient mouthpiece for Kaila to use.

No, my grievance is with the dew.

I don't know when exactly Auren was drugged, but Digby told me enough, as have my Wrath, filling in the gaps between Auren's words. And that's what it feels like I'm doing—filling in the gaps. Filling in every dark recess that polluted her life.

I promised her I'd be the villain on her behalf.

So that's what I'll fucking be.

Fifth Kingdom supplies all the dewdrops in Orea. The late King Fulke ran quite the operation, farther reaching than I'd realized. But now, those plants will be hard-pressed to grow back since I rotted the entire lot of them, including the seeds.

Thanks to a very talkative worker down in the grow rooms, a stick of a man with more white caps on his face than Highbell's mountains, and a nasally voice. He informed me they'd just sent off a caravan full of the drugging petals to be sold. The last and only shipment currently in transport.

Now, I'm flying over the Barrens, following it. It's heading for Breakwater Port, and I've half a mind to see which kingdom it's going to. But that thought goes out the window when I suddenly see a Red Raids ship hauling ass toward it, appearing out of the frosty fog of the flat landscape like a specter seeping through the veil.

I drop down lower, watching as the snow pirates easily cut off the caravan. Fire claws take up the front of the ship, making the horses panic, the carts tipping over in an icy skid.

Red Raids pour out of the ship, easily overtaking the drivers, and within minutes, the caravan is stripped of its wares. The pirates haul all the goods onto their ship, leaving the drivers with nothing but their empty carts and spooked horses.

So the Red Raids now have a hull full of dew? How convenient for me.

Wicked anticipation fills me.

I keep above them, watching the line of fire claws as they run. The beasts are reined to the ship while their fiery paws easily maneuver through the slick, icy landscape, covering ground with impressive speed.

The ship's polished white boards shine like mirrored glass as it glides down the Barrens like it's cutting through water. And then, through fog and packed snow, the landscape gives way to a cove.

A hidden *pirate's* cove.

What the Raids don't know is that I've been aware of its location for quite some time. Judd told me long ago, when I first approached him about joining my army. Now, I can put the information to good use.

Their secret hideaway is right here, hiding in plain sight. A huge edge of frozen land just past the Barrens, tucked away and easily missed by the casual observer, but obvious if you know where to look.

The bay is small and sheltered, led from a skinny inlet that feeds out into the broad, glacial sea beyond. It hides the bay from view, but the most valuable part of the cove itself is the convex arch that stretches over the beach. The arch is tall and wide enough for the land ship to stop beneath, hidden from both water and sky. There, the Raids unload their stolen goods, either moving the supplies to the other caves further in or hauling them directly onto their sea ships anchored past the shore.

There are three sea ships nestled inside the inlet right now, their sails as white as the snow cliffs shielding them. They bob in the cerulean waters, right alongside chunks of ice. Not a single one carries the sigil of a kingdom, but instead, red strips are sewn into the top of their highest sails. Each sea ship is large and well maintained, in better condition than most of the kingdoms' naval fleets.

Piracy must be thriving.

Too bad they spend their time stealing from others and generally being pieces of shit.

The Red Raids are notorious throughout Orea. While they take advantage of the landscape here in the north by using their unique land ships in the Barrens, their sea fleet terrorizes the oceans and ports throughout every kingdom.

Except mine.

Fourth Kingdom has done dealings with the pirates. Weapons, mostly, since I'm always supplying my army, and they're smart enough not to fuck with me. So I've largely let them be. Until now. They've been on my list since I found Auren, so the fact they stole the dew works out quite well for me.

Breakwater Port is only a few miles up the shore— laughably close to this cove. Breakwater is where all the major trade happens for Fifth and Sixth kingdoms. It feeds into the upper sea, where the rest of the kingdoms' ships come to trade with the colder kingdoms. And despite how many naval ships are sent to try to protect the goods coming in and out, this is the port most often attacked by the Reds.

Convenient. They can stalk the port up the shore and then nip down this inlet with their pilfered goods and tuck into their beachside bolt-hole.

I yank on the reins, ignoring the throb in my chest that pulses with pain. It's been intense for hours, but finally lessening into a dull ache.

Below, I watch the fire claws pull the ship toward the arch, steps strained now that they're off the slick ground of the icy Barrens, while whips crack down from the bow of the ship. When the ship disappears beneath the snowy arch, I have Crest circle overhead. I wait in the clouds, biding my time, landing only after the sun has dipped and taken the temperature with it. Then I let my Rip side take over, let the spikes pierce through.

Time to see if the Raids bleed as red as their masks.

Crest lands past the bend where the salt of the ocean water has ruptured shoreline rocks, denting them with time and force. I see the land ship tucked beneath the arch like a gaping mouth, only two pirates there still, easing out crates and barrels to stow into their hideaway.

All the fire claws have been detached from their reins, and I pass by their separate cavern, its opening barred with a crude iron gate. As I walk past, the white felines growl and snap, glowing yellowish eyes watching me like they're waiting for an opportunity to devour.

They're huge, spanning perhaps ten feet tall, with long fangs hanging from their upper jaws that can easily scrape and shovel past snow and ice to get to prey that burrows beneath the blanket of white. The ones pacing at the gate have flames licking around their paws, burning red and singeing the melted floor, the fire hissing just as much as the cats themselves.

I pass them by, the glow of their paws fading as I make my way around their cavern. Further up is the main beach of the cove. The pirates' sea cave juts out like the curve of a bird's sharp beak pecking at the tide. There's a little strip of land perfect for the skiffs to dock, the empty little boats bobbing up against the slice of snow.

Right now, the water has lost its vibrant blue and instead looks like someone dumped a bottle of ink into it, turning it as black as the night sky. The floating pieces of glaciers practically glow white against it.

It reminds me of another moment—another arctic shore not far from here. Where Auren and I stood on a beach and watched a mourning moon. Where she first started to *see* me but was still too blind to see herself.

Even then, I saw her.

I could feel her strength, her brightness brimming

beneath her surface, just waiting to come out. It didn't matter that the world constantly tried to snuff out her gleam.

She shone anyway.

It's how I found her. Her aura, glowing against the blackest night, lighting up the sky and making the sailless ship glow. It called me like a beacon. As if fate itself was showing me the way. Reminding me for the first time in so long that I wasn't just torn in half and uprooted—but that I was also fae.

Just like her.

Ever since, she has been my light. For someone with a soul as black as mine, who's done the darkest deeds and has the foulest power, her glow is something I will not give up. Without her, I am darkness and death, and that is what I will be until I get her back.

And if I don't, then that is what will consume me. As surely as this pain that's creeping from my chest and threatening to implode. Because the feral fae inside of me is bleeding out.

My feet crunch in the snow as I go down the throat of the beak, making my way to the frostbitten bank inside the sea's hidden cave. The shallow water beneath the hollowed space licks its way up the mouth of the cavern before ending around rocks and a crust of snow peppered around the ground like a scruffy beard.

Iron torches nailed to the rock wall burn erratic flames, battered by the coughing breeze brought in from the sea. I can hear voices echoing past the frost-tipped boulders, see more wavering firelight within.

I walk up into the belly of their hideaway, intruding on their festivities. There are about fifty men tucked in around the bonfire, though probably more within the dark recesses where I can't see.

Most of them have taken off the red face coverings they always wear during their plight of pillage. The cloths hang down by their necks, or are tucked into their front pockets, or shoved up in their hair like bandanas. The red fabric is worn like a warning, meant to incite fear. To alert of blood to be spilled.

I can tell they're all deep into the bottle, passing several around, a crate of henade cracked open. There are spits of skewered fish roasting over the fire, and women and men who appear to be saddles are dangled over the laps of the snow pirates in various states of undress.

When the first Red Raid spots me, shouts echo throughout the cave. Then there's scrambling and swearing, a sudden tension spewing out like vomit. Acrid expressions fill the cave as they take me in, swords threatening to hurl as they rush to their feet, drunken swaying as they try to gain their fighting postures.

One of them takes me in, eyes widening before he pushes forward. "Commander Rip?"

As soon as he says the name, unease heaves through the cave, filling up its hollow gut.

"Were you on the ship that attacked Midas's envoy?" I ask.

He hesitates, caught off guard by my question. "Aye. Afore you came in and bought 'em all off us."

"Hmm." I look around at all the men. "That shipment of dew you just picked up—I want it."

I watch as confusion, surprise, and then wariness filter through the faces. The man who first spoke up itches at the gold hoop caught through his earlobe. The bottoms of his pants are rolled, scuffed boots stuck with snow, and his sword is tucked through the loop of his belt. He looks every bit the loafing pirate, right down to the red face mask hanging at his collar.

"Didn't know your King Rot had any need for the stuff," the man says, ignorant of the fact that he's speaking to the king right now. "It don't usually head that way."

"We already got a buyer," someone else calls behind him. "It's been paid for."

"Where is it going?"

"Don't tell him," someone says at the back.

Hoop Ear shrugs at me and rests his hand on the hilt of his sword. "It's need-to-know," he says with a smirk.

"Well, all *you* need to know is that if you don't tell me where that dew is, I will kill you and every pirate in this cave," I say blandly, as if I didn't just threaten their lives. As if it weren't fifty to one.

Truth be told, I hope all fifty of them rush me. My skin is stretched, my chest gnawing, ribs like fanged teeth ready to devour, to fill the empty pit in my soul.

If the tension was tight before, it's pulled so rigid now that it feels like a taut rope ready to snap.

"Tell me where the dew is."

It's a testament to my reputation that they consider it. I see it in some of their faces—they want to throw the dew at me and run far, far away. They're the smarter ones.

But not all pirates are smart.

"Oh, fuck off, Commander," Hoop Ear says. "You got no authority here. If your king wants the drug because he can't get laid without it, that's his problem. He'll have to put in an order with the Reds like everybody else."

"There won't be any more orders," I say. "You won't be stealing or distributing dew anywhere else throughout Orea ever again."

Several of them laugh and look at each other in camaraderie. "Listenin' to this? What kinda shit he spewin'?"

"Dew's the fastest selling goods we got. We can't get enough of it before it's already gone. You think the Reds would stop that?" Hoop says with a mocking laugh.

"You're going to have to, because it's gone."

More laughter. They don't believe me, but that's fine.

Monsters never need anybody to believe in them. They come out to get you regardless.

One shifty-eyed pirate is wise enough to be wary. "Reds…maybe we should—"

They cut him off.

"Your king send just you?"

"Nah, he probably got his whole army out there."

"I don't think so. I think the commander here is alone."

"I am," I confirm, and I can see they're shocked.

The pirates share a look.

Hoop shrugs. "'Fraid we can't oblige you, Commander. Best go tell your king that."

"Pity you're making that choice," I tell him. "But I have one other question—the quartermaster who used to serve under Captain Fane. Where is he?"

He jerks his chin up. "Goes by Captain Quarter now. Took over Fane's ship. He's up in Breakwater."

"Appreciate it," I say conversationally. Then I palm the dagger from my waist, sending it flying through the air, where it lands between the pirate's eyes with a sickening *snick*.

Shock consumes the cave, everyone watching as he collapses on the ground, dead before his body settles.

"*What the fuck?*"

I shrug. "I did warn you."

Half a dozen of them start running at me. The saddles scream and disappear deeper into the cavern. A sadistic rush of satisfaction fills me as the men attack, feeding the ferocity that's been shoving beneath my skin.

I have no sword, so I'll use my spikes instead.

The first man reaches me with his blade raised, though his feet are clumsy from drink. I punch him in the bicep, making his sword arm go flinging back, giving me the opening to stab him in the chest with the spikes on my forearm. They stretch up to full length and pierce the man between the ribs, his lifeblood dribbling down through my sleeve.

I shove him off, just as three more surround me, but I kick out the knees of one, punch the gut of another, and the third trips over the man I stabbed. I yank his sword from his flailing hand and drive it into his side, letting blood spew out while he releases a scream that echoes through the cave.

The one whose knees took a hit can't get up, but the other man gets bolder as the last two join him in surrounding me. Their trio of swords point at my head as they circle, the firelight glinting off the thick steel.

I grin with feral thrill.

They all launch themselves at me at the same time, but I'm faster. I duck, and the two across from each other swing, blades meeting in a loud clang. With their swords engaged, I hurl my bent body toward the third man, catching him in the stomach and tossing him on his ass, making him let out a grunt.

I feel the other two come up behind me, the back of my neck prickling with the intuition gained from years of fighting battles and my ingrained fae senses. The men are ready to run me through, so I kick out my leg, sending one sprawling.

The last man makes the fatal mistake of raising his sword over his head as he sprints toward me, leaving his chest completely open. I ram my shoulders back, the spikes along my spine stabbing into him from throat to groin.

His scream turns into a gurgle.

I feel his last surprised breath against my ear as his sword drops and the hilt crashes into my chest, right where the pain flares the most. I let out a furious growl and then shove him away, retracting my spikes and letting him fall to the ground in a bloody, groaning heap.

No one else attacks me, and the ones still alive stay down. Everyone else who just witnessed my violence watches me warily. Finally showing the fear they should.

My chest thrums with pain, my adrenaline thumping in my ears as my two forms war with each other. My Rip form wants to fight, slaking more thirst for violence and quenching it with their blood. The other side of me is writhing, rot pulsing, agony knocking against my chest. I shove it away. Shove it down.

"Are we done with that, then?" I ask mockingly. "I'd hoped for more of a fight."

No one says anything, leaving the cave quiet, save for the wind brushing through the torch fire like flapping wings, and the tide sloshing up the snowy bank. That, and the gurgling of the soon to be dead man behind me.

"You." I point at the pirate who tried to speak up before. He blanches at being called out and starts shaking like a leaf, scratching at sores along his hands. He's gangly, with yellowed teeth and a sprout of coarse hair jutting from his pocked chin. "What's your name?"

"Scab, sir."

"Unfortunate."

He shrugs, red staining his cheeks that matches the cloth shoved down around his collar.

"What happened here?"

His eyes go shifty again. "Uhh, happened, Commander?"

"When people ask you, what are you going to say occurred in this cove?" I clarify.

"Oh, yeah. I don't say nothin'." He pauses, gauging my reaction, then quickly amends. "I mean...I tell 'em that you don't fuck with Commander Rip, that's what I say. I tell 'em that we don't sell dew no more...right?"

"That's better."

He pops out a relieved breath.

"Now, those men and women who ran—are they saddles?" I ask.

I watch his throat bob, protruding out like an apple you could pluck from a tree. "Y-yes."

"Did you steal them? Take them by force?"

His eyes drop to the ground, and the other pirates don't answer, which is answer enough in itself.

"You're going to take those saddles on one of those ships and return them to their homes, and you will not touch them. Is that clear?"

"Course, Commander. Whatever you say."

I nod. "How long have you been a Red Raid, Scab?"

"Took the cloth twenty years ago, Commander."

"Congratulations. You just got promoted to captain." I glance at the others. "Anyone have a problem with that?"

They don't say a word.

I look back to Scab. "If I find out you're stealing anymore people, I'll come back and make sure you join these men here," I threaten, gesturing to the dead ones behind me. "Am I clear, *Captain*?"

Scab nods so hard I hear his neck crack. "Sea-clear, Commander."

"Good. Now, where's the dew?"

"Didn't unload it yet," he admits quickly. "Still hitched up in the snow ship."

Good. I'll rot it through on my way out.

"Who were you going to sell to?"

He hesitates.

"*Scab.*"

"It was Second Kingdom," he blurts.

Looks like Judd will get to have a visit there after all.

"And the one who calls himself Captain Quarter. Is he truly in Breakwater?"

Scab looks to the others and shrugs. "I dunno. I

s'pose. That's where he usually is when he's not doin' a run. He's got friends at the Orb who let him stay and don't tell no one he's a Red."

That narrows it down to where I'll need to look.

"Don't make me regret letting you live," I warn him. "Do what I said with the saddles." I pause. "And treat those fire claws with some fucking respect."

"Course, Commander. Thank you, Commander." He presses his scabbed hands together in front of him like he's getting ready to say a prayer. "We're on it. You can count on us, right, Reds?"

They quickly give their muttered agreement, while another pirate says, "The Red Raids are always happy to have a friendship with Fourth Kingdom. Tell your Rot king we's bein' real amenable-like."

I hold back a snort. "Of course."

Turning, I start to head back to Crest. It's time to pay *Captain Quarter* a visit.

CHAPTER 21

SLADE

Breakwater Port is a wakeful hub. The short days and everlasting cold means that nothing stops once the sun sets or a storm comes, because they're used to working through it. Activity continues to churn despite the worst conditions.

On the water itself, I can see skiffs full of boys and girls who are earning a few coins by rowing around in the dark slush, stabbing at the water with their spears to break up any ice that tries to form near the ships.

As I pass in the sky overhead, I see ships moored with precision along the steel dock, sailors emptying out their hulls and rolling crates to the harbor. Their faces are caught in the torchlight that blazes every couple of feet, while the wheels ring along the metal pier. At the shore, boulders sprout up, growing from the icy ground like clumps of weeds and lapped at from the lick of the tide.

I count at least three dozen people walking up and down

the slight incline that leads from water to land, most of them heading for the seaside street and the buildings that line it. The largest ones are the packing houses, where most of the people who live here work. They do the endless job of stuffing goods to send off or opening up the shipments to check them before turning them over.

With one last pass overhead, I eye the inns and pubs and the many fish slop shops. No part of the arctic fish is wasted here. Every catch is chopped up into stews or fried whole, head and all, a constant supply of food for the port, for breakfast, lunch, and dinner.

Now that I have my bearings, I fly back to an empty part of the beach and leave Crest behind some boulders where he starts nosing around in the tide. As I walk toward the harbor city, the busy crowd doesn't notice me. I'm just another body in the dark. Fortunately, I find the *Orb* building that Scab mentioned rather easily. Orb Arch, to be exact. It isn't difficult to find, because its name is literal.

It's a large stone building with no windows, its roof covered in a thick layer of snow, and just in front of its bricked face is an archway made up of polished orbs of all different sizes, the gray and black spheres covered in a layer of frost. Icicles drip down the top where they arc overhead, pointing down accusingly at all those who pass beneath to enter the front door.

As soon as I step inside, I realize it's not a saddle house or a pub like I'd guessed, but a gambling hall. Though I shouldn't be surprised that a pirate spends his nights here.

The low-ceilinged room reeks of alcohol and smoke. Paneled wood walls hold in the cluster of people who are gathered around smoky card tables. There are stacks of coins piled at bent elbows as they hunch over their bets and pints, leaning in, lured by the possibility of winning. At the back, there's a long counter where a barkeep flings out drinks, and in the middle of the room, there are two saddles performing.

They're both on a swing that hangs suspended from the ceiling, the wide, plush sling looking like it's made from bear fur. The man sits on it, swinging them both, while the woman stands. She has one foot on his thigh, the other split up into the air, curved around the rope as she dances to the music coming from the drunk bard propped up in the corner.

I scan the room, but having only seen Quarter briefly, and with the red cloth covering most of his face, I don't know what he looks like.

And I don't have the fucking patience to sniff him out.

So instead, I walk over to the gambling table nearest the door, where a card game appears to be in full swing. I wrench up the dealer by his collar, making him jerk in surprise as I spin him to face me. "I'm looking for a Red Raid."

Everyone at his table jumps to their feet while he flails, trying to kick out at me on instinct. Yet when he gets a look at me, he goes still. I see his eyes flicking over the gray scales on my cheeks, the spikes on my arms, and a nervous tic appears in his jaw. "Commander Rip?"

The rest of the gambling hall goes quiet. The last sound is the squeaking rope of the swing as the saddles slow it to a stop.

"The Red Raid who took over Captain Fane's ship. Where is he?"

The dealer lets me hang him there by his neck and shakes his head. "Don't know anything about any pirates. Don't welcome their lot here. This is a respectable establishment."

I tighten the fabric around his neck until it's biting into his windpipe, lifting him so high that only the toes of his shoes are touching the floor. He starts grappling for purchase, trying to take the weight off. I hold him still as I look around the room.

I might not know who the owner is, but every dealer

always knows the ins and outs of what goes on in these places. If Quarter comes here, they'll know about it.

"I'm not going to ask again. I want to know where the pirate is. Goes by Captain Quarter."

A dealer three tables over gets up, his chin and stare both pointed, wearing a pair of suspenders cocked over his barrel chest. "We want no quarrel with you, Commander. I'll show you to the Red."

"Good choice."

I drop the other man, hearing his shoes slap against the floor as he regains his footing, and I move fluidly through the room. Necks swivel, silence and stares trailing me as I go. The dealer leads the way, past the perched saddles, past the rest of the gambling tables, past the bar.

We go through an arched doorway, miniature orbs glossing the path, and then through a curtained-off corridor. At the very end of the dim hallway, there's a burly-looking man sitting against a door with a heavy pelt of animal fur hanging in front of it.

He looks up at our approach, tearing his eyes away from a thick book. He flicks his gaze from the dealer to me, recognition flaring.

"Commander Rip came to see the pits," the dealer says as we come to a stop.

The guard's expression goes suspicious. "He got a vouch?"

"I'm his vouch," the dealer assures him before digging in his pocket and palming some coins to the guard.

Grudgingly, the man gets up from his seat and clunks his chair off to the side before pushing the pelt over so we can pass through. He watches me closely as I go in, right up until the dealer closes the door behind us.

Inside, the building opens up, far surpassing the size of the front gambling hall. Instead of wood, these walls are made of thick stone, and the floor is packed-in dirt, while the ceiling rises up at least fifteen feet. Yet the sheer size of the space is diminished by just how many people are present.

The pits, as the dealer called them, are exactly that. There's one large pit dug into the center of the room, with several smaller ones scattered around the perimeter.

Fighting pits.

Violence explodes inside the lowered spaces. The crowds gathered around them are corralled off, standing behind wooden fences, steps raised up behind them for more people to watch the fight below. The audience shouts, fisting money into the air in a burst of frenetic energy.

The hall's workers drift around, wearing bright green belts where they shove their paper and quills, while pouches of collected coins are clasped at their hips. Other workers are carrying trays of drinks or bundles of dried leaves for people to stuff inside their smoking pipes, but the rest of the space is packed with gamblers.

As I walk forward, I glance into the nearest dug-out pits. There are two men fighting each other in one, bare chested and bloody fisted. Another has three women fighting against one another using whips. A third has dogs, mouths frothing, hackles raised. But the biggest pit in the center boasts the largest crowd, though it sits empty.

"The one who goes by Captain Quarter is there." The dealer points.

I follow the direction of his finger, homing in on the person standing right at the front, elbows leaning over the wooden fence that separates the audience from the fighters. He's chatting up the people nearest him, gesturing to the sunken, empty arena below.

"Appreciated."

The dealer nods but hesitates. "Always happy to help King Rot's commander."

"Good."

More hesitation. "Always happy for the commander to *also* help in return…"

I let out a sigh, but dig into my pocket and toss him a coin. He nabs it from the air, quick as a blink. "My gratitude," he says with a smile before he turns and disappears back the way we came.

When he's gone, I start making my way through the crowds, sidestepping those gathered. One great thing about my spikes? People learn to move out of my fucking way.

In no time at all, I get right next to Quarter against the fence. He's turned away from me, still speaking, but when the people he's talking to notice me, they quickly disperse, scurrying into the crowd and leaving him with frowns cast over their shoulders at me.

"What…" He turns around, and when he spots me standing so close, he flinches and backs up a step.

His head comes up to my chin, and when his beady eyes reach my face, they go wide. "*Commander Rip?*"

"Captain Quarter."

He looks around, like he's worried someone will hear me. "Go by Quarry here."

"I don't care if you go by Dickhead. You'll answer to me."

He goes rigid, expression filling with anger.

And just because I'm in a fucking mood to rile him, I say, "I can see why you turned pirate. You wanted to keep your ugly fucking face covered with the Reds' mask," I say, gaze flicking over him. "Good choice."

His peeling lips press hard together, scarred cheeks stretching into a snarl. "Fuck you," he hisses.

I smirk. That was entirely too easy. "Struck a nerve, did I?"

"Whadya want?" he asks, impatient now. "Fight's about

to start."

"Funny thing. I was informed recently of a mistake."

He raises a bushy black brow. "Mistake?"

I nod. "I gave the Reds an entire chest of valuables during our last exchange. You were there."

He frowns. "Aye…"

"You took me to inspect the horses I bought after your raid on Midas's caravan, do you remember?"

"Yeah."

"See, we have a problem," I go on, leaning in closer, making it so my spikes nearly pierce into his gut. He tries not to flinch away, but his darting eyes reveal just how nervous he is by my proximity.

I recognize him now, from when I first boarded the Red Raid ship when Auren was taken. Even though I only saw the top half of his face, the way he darts his eyes, his reedy voice, they're the same. I remember how he tried to keep Auren from me, and how fucking terrified she looked as she cowered in front of him. It makes me want to smash my fist in his face, but I hold back.

"It seems you made a mistake on the transfer. I was informed that I didn't get all the horses I paid for."

His feet shift, but he puts on his best confused face. "What do you mean?"

I'm not interested in hearing him play dumb. "You cheated me out of some horses, Quarter."

"No," he says with an adamant shake of his head. He answers quickly. *Too* fucking quickly. If I hadn't already known he was a liar, that alone would've given him away.

"Pirates are usually far better at deceit."

"I ain't lyin'!"

In one swift move, I yank him by the tuft of his greasy dark hair and shove his face into my bent knee. His nose cracks against the bone, but it happens so quickly that he doesn't start howling until I wrench his head back up and blood starts spraying out both nostrils.

He clutches his nose, shaking all over. "I'll make you fuckin' regret that!"

"Don't make threats you're not able to carry out," I tell him calmly as I tighten my grip on his hair.

"Wait!" he says through a wince, hands scrabbling at my hold. "Doesn't gotta be like this. You wanna make a bet?"

"Does it look like I came here to make a fucking bet?"

"I can help," he rushes on. "I always know who's gonna win."

"I don't give a fuck. I want the horses you cheated me out of. One in particular. And you're going to tell me where I can find it."

Cupping his palm to catch his dribbling blood, he says, "I didn't cheat you out of no horses!"

I sigh. Then I punch him in the sternum so hard the breath knocks right out of him and seems to tumble at his feet where he can't catch it. The people gathered around us don't intervene. Why would they? They're here to watch fights. I don't think they care whether it happens inside a pit or not.

"I'm tiring of your lies," I tell him as he clutches the fence, struggling to straighten up. "Tell me where."

He spits at my boots, spraying his blood all over them. I cock an unimpressed brow. "I stepped in shit on the way here, but your blood is still more disgusting." I lift said boot and dig it into his own foot until he winces. "*The horse*, Quarter."

When he doesn't answer right away, I've run out of the last of my patience. Not that I really had any to begin with.

Ready to end it, I lift my arm, prepared to stab him right here and now, but he finally relents. "Okay, okay!" he shouts, holding up both hands in front of him to ward off the blow. "You doin' all this over a fuckin' *horse*?"

Yeah, I am. Because Auren let slip that her horse was

taken by the Raids—Crisp, she said its name was. They were supposed to give me everything they took that night, but Quarter skimmed off the top. By stealing from me, he stole from her. And I won't fucking tolerate that. She's had enough taken from her.

I glare at him and move my spikes closer.

"Alright!" He swipes at the blood still leaking down to his mouth. "I kept a few. Knew the ice pickers needed some new horses, and they were good stock. Got a good price for 'em."

"Where." Not a question. A demand.

"Berg Sheets. Not far from here. They supply the ice blocks to the ships. They needed horse haulers."

I lean in so he's forced to look at my eyes, and fear flashes through his. "You're going to go back to Berg Sheets. You're going to get those horses you stole, and you're going to deliver them to Fourth Kingdom in perfect condition, or I'm going to tell my king and have him rot your asshole and shrivel your dick. Do you understand?"

He swallows hard and gives a shaky nod. "Y-yeah."

I press the spikes along my forearm into his chest. "You sure?"

"Yes, yes!" he cries with a wince. "Lemme make it up to you—this fight's gonna have the biggest payout. I'll tell you who's gonna win."

"I'm not interested in placing bets on a swung fight."

"Not swung," he insists before jabbing a finger at his temple. He lowers his voice to a mumbled whisper. "I just know. Any game, any bet. I can see the competitors and then know which way it'll go."

My attention flicks over him. "Minor magic?"

He nods but looks around to make sure no one else is paying attention. No wonder Captain Fane kept him around. This little trick must've paid out nicely for him.

"What does your magic tell you will happen if you try to cheat me again? Do you want to bet on the outcome of *that*?" I ask darkly.

Quarter swallows hard, his murky gaze filling with trepidation. I offer him a cold smile.

"All your horses will get to Fourth Kingdom. I'll make sure of it," he promises.

"You'd better."

I step away and let go, removing the pressure on his foot while taking away the threat of my spikes.

As soon as he feels better about our proximity, he lets out a breath. "Didn't have to break my nose over a fuckin' horse," he grumbles.

"You're lucky that's all I'm breaking."

He's *not* so lucky that I left some rot in his lung that will slowly spread over time and kill him.

"Get to it," I say with a jerk of my head.

The pirate gives me a dark look, but he turns and walks away. Quickly.

Good riddance.

Suddenly, noise erupts around the pit, wrenching my attention. I look down, noticing that the spectators are riled up because the fighters are finally arriving. Below, there are barred enclosures at opposite ends of the fighting arena, and from within each cage, something comes up from the descending steps. Thick collars are around the necks of two large animals, and attached are stiff metal rods that handlers use to force them into the cages before the doors are slammed shut behind them.

The second I see what's in there, what's going to be fighting, anger flares in my chest, hot and consuming. A fire claw is at one end of the pit, and a timberwing at the other.

Both animals appear to be absolutely savage.

They're also absolutely *scarred*.

The fire claw is a female, and she has long lines of marks through her thick white fur. The scars crisscross all over her body, even on her tail and whiskered face that make her snarling more pronounced.

The timberwing has signs of abuse too. There are dozens of missing feathers that appear as if someone yanked them out—or perhaps done by its own teeth from psychological trauma. Its maw is frothing, and at its ankle is a clamp of metal with an empty hook attached to it, probably to chain it up when it's not in the pit.

When it turns its head to roar at the spectators next to me, I see the telltale streaks of white that curve down both sides of its bark-colored head. This one is female too.

Handlers just on the other side of the caged enclosures remove the leads from the beasts. As soon as the fire claw is free, she turns and tries to attack the handler through the bars, making the man fall back. The crowd erupts into hoots and laughter. The red-faced handler picks up a fire poker in retaliation, its end blunted and red-hot. He slams the end of the pole into the cage, making the animal roar as the brand sears into her side.

My spikes expand and shift, my skin stretching in anger.

Then the cage doors are raised, and the handlers shove the pokers at both animals, forcing them out. The timberwing roars, her mouth wide open, showcasing rows of razor-sharp teeth. The fire claw jumps out of her own enclosure, then immediately spins, going for her handler again. But the man is behind his own protective pen, and he manages to leap back before the beast's teeth clamp around the bars.

When the feline realizes she won't be able to get to the man, she turns to growl at the shouting crowd instead, baring long curved fangs that hang well below her bottom jaw. The timberwing too is pacing, snarling at the spectators above, feathers lifting, while dozens of people shout down at them.

For a moment, I wonder why the timberwing doesn't just simply fly up and attack, but then the answer is obvious—her wings have been cruelly clipped.

My teeth grind.

The handlers jab at both animals with the fire pokers again, trying to urge them forward, to get them mad enough to take it out on the other beast. But surprisingly, even though they're trapped in this enclosure together, they don't go at each other.

This pisses the crowd off, which pisses the hall off, which pisses the handlers off.

A group of men come onto the other side of the fence, and together, they fling in a dead mountain goat, the carcass landing in the middle of the pit.

And the beasts go *berserk*.

Both animals launch at the carcass, and only then do they move toward each other with aggression. Which tells me they're not just held captive and beaten—they're also starved, forced to fight for their food.

They start to descend on the carcass viciously. The fire claw snarls, swiping a fiery paw at the timberwing. The bird beast roars in response, wings outstretched as they both try to fall onto the fresh meat. Saliva drips from their mouths as they clash together with talons and teeth, and the crowd cheers with sickening excitement.

The fire claw swipes furious, flaming claws, making the scent of burnt feathers and flesh fill the air. The timberwing growls in response, snapping wicked teeth, trying to take a bite out of her. Neither of them is willing to give up the food, but they aren't going in for one another's throats, either.

Apparently, the handlers don't take too kindly to this, because one of them comes up and stabs the fire poker right into the timberwing's side—and *laughs*.

I've seen enough.

With one hand on the top railing, I launch myself up and over the fence, landing fluidly inside the pit several feet below. The balls of my feet take the impact, and I look up as I straighten my legs, just as the fire claw whirls on its own handler again, snapping its huge teeth. The coward backs up, too far away for the beast to reach.

So I help her.

I'm at the cage in a second, and I yank the pins out of the hinges and tear the door clean away. The man inside doesn't even have time to try to fight me off. I reach in and grab him by the scruff of his neck and then toss him into the pit, fire poker and all.

There's no hesitation or need for encouragement. The fire claw attacks him. The man screams, the crowd shouts, and I turn my back, striding toward the timberwing next.

She's fallen onto the goat's carcass, tearing into it. When I get closer, she jerks her head up and starts to roar but abruptly cuts off when she sees me. I keep going until I reach the small pen where her own handler is cowering, and my body pulses with fae strength, fueled by pure anger as I tear the gate right off its hinges and toss it behind me. The man inside is now exposed, and he gapes at me, his back stuffed into the corner.

"*What are you doing?*" he screams.

I reach in and yank the fire poker from his grip and then stab the scalding metal into his stomach. He falls, howling in pain, steam rising off him like coal. I toss the poker down to the ground while he clutches his stomach. "Doesn't feel good, does it?"

I turn away and re-enter the main pit, only to find that several men in protective leather vests have jumped in and are heading for me, a couple of them armed with spears. Must be guards that work for the hall. They probably only usually have to deal with crowd control and the occasional violent drunk who gets pissed off at a lost bet. They haven't had to deal with someone like me before.

"You should turn around and leave," I warn as they approach with thick fists and lumped scowls.

"You're coming with us," the one in the front says, and then he moves to tackle me.

But I move faster.

One hit against his temple is all it takes for him to go down. Then the two men with spears rush at me, but I reach out and snatch the weapons clear from their hands with laughable ease. Gripping both, I snap the spears in half over my knee before tossing them away. The men falter for a split second, but fueled by anger, they leap for me once more.

I ignore my stinging knuckles and knock the first one off his feet while ramming my shoulder into the other. He flips in the air like he weighs nothing and lands on his back, gasping for air. A third comes at me with punches already flying, and I grin when one actually manages to graze my cheek. The taste of blood invigorates me even more.

I start pummeling him, jabbing at his face, his ribs, his stomach, while shouts raise up around me, feeding into my furor, but he goes down entirely too fast for my liking.

The last three rush me all at once, jumping over their fallen comrades to get to me, and I meet them with wicked elation. I revel in the fight, in the fucking beauty of fist on fist, flesh against flesh. No swords, no magic, just good old-fashioned violence.

Every hit I give and every strike I take is a release. A *need*. I started it with the Raids, but now I'm truly able to let loose this messy, twisted turmoil I've felt every fucking day since Auren left. So all my pent-up emotion, all this churning guilt explodes out of me in a relief of unleashed violence.

I fight them, but I'm actually fighting *myself*. My failure.

I'm not even here, in this pit. What exists in me is the

uncontrollable fury and fear that's been grating down my ribs, leaving behind coiled shards. The helplessness beats out of me through my fists, pulsating up my spikes, seething down my veins as I throw myself completely into the brawl.

I purposely slow, just so they can land a hit. Again. Again. *Again.*

And I relish in the punishment.

I enjoy that more men jump into the fight. Laugh when a good dozen of them fling themselves at me. My shoulder is rammed, my ribs are pummeled, my jaw is cuffed. Someone kicks out at my kneecap, and I feel it slide sideways, pain ratcheting down my leg, but it's nothing, *nothing* compared to the pain in my chest, so what does it matter? The thrill of this rampage is just a bandage over a gaping wound that can't heal, and I've become nothing but the fight.

Nothing but violence.

Because I can't get to her. My raw power that let me tear into the world is gone. The rip in Drollard is gone. All the villagers are gone. My mother is gone.

Auren is fucking gone.

And I can't get to her.

Can't get to her.

Can't.

So I fight. I bleed and I lash out in insurmountable, savage grief, like I'm trying to fight my way to her, fight my way through this world, fight myself for failing her. All the silent, seething, suffocating panic comes crashing out through a raw clash of brutality.

I'm so caught up in my own head that I don't notice the person with the blade aiming for my chest. But the pile of men fighting me move out of the way for him, and by the time I realize it, he's already thrusting down.

The blade would have sunk in if it weren't for the timberwing that suddenly appears behind him. The beast looms over him, a good five feet taller, her golden eyes flashing angrily, clipped wings spread. Then she opens her mouth, baring those sharp teeth, and clamps down on the man's head, tearing it from his shoulders and tossing his body aside, spouting blood and gore before he can even finish his swing.

The other dozen men whirl around at the new threat, but they can't even cry out before it's too late. The fire claw is there, knocking into them from behind with a swipe of her paws. Blood pours from the scratch marks swiped through their flesh, and flames catch on to their clothes, burning them, melting the hair right off their heads as they run.

I heave, and my senses trickle back in. I realize really fucking quickly just how many hits I actually took, because the pain ripples over me like it's catching up, marking every hurt spot. Awareness trickles back in too, expanding outside of my need to fight and bringing back the rest of the pit.

The spectators are shouting in a crazed frenzy. People are leaning over the fence, placing new bets, watching the slaughter with glee. The volume of the crowd bulges, and it feels like my eardrums might burst.

And all of it infuriates me.

They're cheering for blood, relishing in the slaughter, supporting the exploitation of these animals all to get a rush from the gamble with a chance to line their pockets.

I want to make them pay.

Glaring up at them, I transform, spikes sinking back into my skin. Withered black veins crawl down my arms and ooze across my neck, and I fist my hands at my sides, shoving power out.

Within seconds, my magic slithers up from the ground, crawling up the pit's walls and disintegrating the fence. I don't care if anyone saw me transform from Rip to Rot. The call to kill and punish is too strong.

I hear the people above me shout in fear now instead of

excitement. Three men fall screaming into the pit when the barrier collapses in front of them. They flail on their descent, arms flapping like wind-whipped banners until they hit the dirt with a *thwack.*

I watch in brutal satisfaction as the animals fall upon them with unrestrained viciousness. Yanked off limbs go flying into the air, and blood pours into the ground in brutal slashes. Within seconds, they've torn the men apart. Just like everyone else who entered the pit.

I look around for anyone else I can destroy, but the beasts have well and truly finished the job. There are piles of bodies twitching, gore seeping into the dirt. The ground is scorched with ash, pieces of flung limbs burning from the swipe of the fire claw's feet.

It's impressive.

I enter the now empty safety pen, crouching down into its short enclosure, my fingers wrapping around the iron bars. Rot spreads through it instantly, and I lean away before kicking in the whole door. Inside, there's a dirt path stained with animal piss that leads down beneath the pit. I descend the tunnel to see what's going on underneath this fucking gambling hall.

I find myself in a wide-open underground room clad with iron beams and stone walls. Inside are dozens of cages, with shredded cloths clustered into corners, empty bowls that held either water or food. They each have drains set into the floor to rinse away piss and blood.

The stench in here is fucking *awful.*

Some of the cages are empty, but several are occupied. The dogs that were fighting earlier are inside two of them, licking their wounds. There are small wild mountain cats in another, and hissing snow serpents in the next one over, their scales stark white and their eyes blood red. A wolf. Two foxes. A boar. Clumped together roosters. Some sort of monkey that must have come from First Kingdom. All of them looking feral and coiled, ready to strike with their frenzied need to get out.

Rot spreads through every cage, following my steps as I walk. The metal bars start to disintegrate, and the animals all sit up, snarling, watching, their senses on high alert.

When I get to the very end of the room and reach a set of double doors, I place my hands in the middle and shove them both open with a bang.

The wind of the outside blows in just as the bars to the cages disintegrate into nothing but rusted powder.

When the animals realize they're no longer trapped, they start growling and baying, yelling and hissing. Every single one of them races toward the exit, rushing past me to escape, instantly taking off in all different directions once they're through the doors.

The outside gives way to a copse of skinny pine trees on the blistered hills, their full tips glowing beneath the night sky. The animals race past, disappearing into the snowy landscape as fast as their bodies can take them.

I walk out, but at a noise behind me, I step aside just as the timberwing and the fire claw come prowling outside. The feline sniffs at the ground tentatively and then stalks into the puffy snow. Her feet steam from the contact, her fiery claws sparking and hissing as they sink beneath the plush white. She lets out a sigh like the snow soothes her burning paws, and I wonder just how long it's been since she's been outside. It's clear that this beast, with her icy eyes and white hair, belongs in the snow and the cold. This is her dominion.

The timberwing stands just behind the feline, her broad chest puffed up and wings stretching out as if to test the fresh breeze. I don't know if she'll ever be able to fly again, but the expression on her face looks happy to be out in the free air once more.

I rot the collars off their necks, and the corroded metal falls to the ground. Then I do the same to the heavy anklet at the timberwing's leg. She uses her teeth to yank the cuff the rest of the way off before flinging it away. She looks down at me, blinking iridescent eyes, licking at the gore still stuck in her blood-stained teeth.

At least she's been well fed.

She brushes her head against my arm before turning to leave. With a low rumble, the feline follows, her tail whipping at my leg as she passes.

I cock my head, watching as the two female beasts venture out. Unlike the rest of the animals, they don't bolt. They don't separate. Instead, both timberwing and fire claw begin to steadily and carefully walk away, neither of them leaving the other's side. They prowl across the empty, frigid landscape together, snow cat and flightless bird. Free.

As I turn and leave behind the gambling hall, the last of the violence drains out of me, my injuries pulsing one after the other, wanting to make themselves known.

When I get back to Crest on the empty beach, he's helping himself to a fish he must've plucked from the sea. The feathered beast looks up at my approach, fish bones and innards hanging from his mouth. While he finishes swallowing it, I haul myself onto the saddle and grip the reins.

I glance down, staring at my bloodied knuckles where my fingers are wrapped around the leather strap. With a nudge of my heel, Crest lifts into the air.

My shoulders lower slightly, loosening from the ramrod tension as an exhale purges from my depths. I scoop out the silence of my thoughts, settling in the absolute gravity of my devastation.

I am one of the most powerful fae to ever exist, and yet, I feel utterly *powerless*.

My list of retribution has now dwindled down to nothing.

This list of revenge is what's kept me focused. Kept me going. Kept me *breathing*.

The Merewen monarchs. Kaila and Manu. Derfort. Dew. Red Raids.

Everything has been crossed off, and now I have to come to terms with the fact that Auren is a world away, and I'm stuck here with no way to get to her.

I'll have to return to Fourth Kingdom with a reality to face.

The reality that I don't know how long I have until I go completely mad from the soul-ripping separation from her. How long I have until this pain in my chest consumes me. How long until I'm able to reopen a rip...

Or if I even can.

How long.

Until I can't keep going.

CHAPTER 22

QUEEN MALINA

E ven though the fae had a head start on us, an army travels much slower than two people. Especially when we travel through shadow.

We keep the winding view of the marching regiments in our sights, but stay far enough away that none of the fae detect us. For days, we travel relentlessly across the snow and rocks, passing the cracked, chasmed land of Seventh Kingdom. There used to be cities peppered throughout this kingdom, little villages that existed long ago. There's nothing anymore. Nothing that cold and time hasn't swallowed.

The assassin uses his magic to whisk us through the land. We seem to absorb into shadows in the distance, skipping from point to point. We bend with the light and shuffle around with the wind, always surrounded by the churning dark. It's disorienting and nauseating, and I'm not at all sure how it works, but every day, we get further away from the bridge and the ruin of Cauval Castle, until we're finally out of Seventh

Kingdom.

I feel dizzy and drained when we finally stop each night, but it's nothing compared to the toll it seems to take on the assassin. We travel for hours until he collapses into exhaustion. With heavy limbs and his ever-present hood pulled over his head, he uses his bare hands to dig into the snow, creating a pocket of protection for us to huddle into and sleep.

I watch him now, buried beneath his layers of clothing, shivering in the mound of snow he's dug out like an animal's burrow. He seems to use his bent light and curling shadows to keep himself warm, though I don't know how that works either.

I don't need to.

The cold out here is nothing compared to the cold inside me. I don't shiver. My teeth don't chatter. Goose bumps don't trail up my arms. I lean against the snow inside our little dug den, and it doesn't bother me at all.

What *does* bother me is that the assassin won't speak.

The shadow-jumping is somehow both blaring and mute, sucking the sound from my ears and yet blasting me with raucous wind, so it would be near impossible to speak while we travel. Yet when we stop, before he collapses into sleep, he still doesn't say a word to me.

Just watches me. Day after day. Night after night.

I don't like it.

I don't...dislike it.

It's confusing and infuriating, and yet I stew in the silence he's fashioned, and it's loud. Just like the blaring quiet of his magic.

I've found that, in this loud silence, I'm forced to think. Forced to remember. To feel. To consider. Things that I can usually shove away or ignore. Things I can normally avoid.

I can't avoid them now.

I'm stuck in this contemplative inner study of myself, and I don't like it at all. I don't like what I see. Perhaps the assassin doesn't either, and that's why he stares.

Why does that thought hurt?

His silence is aggravating. I have all these words and irritants and emotions building up, and I feel like I might burst.

I don't want to come undone, stuck in this lonely quiet.

I steal a look at the assassin. We're close. *Very* close. If I was ever caught next to someone this close at court, it would be considered a scandal. Yet out here, in the frigid nothing, social standards don't matter. Especially not when forced to rest in a snow hole every night.

Which is what we're doing now. After a restless sleep, we're sitting together in our snow divot that he dug out in the side of an incline. He's gotten quite good at it. Digging deep enough for us both to crawl in, hollowing it out at an angle so the worst of the wind is kept out.

So our close bodies are huddled in.

Both of us are eating jerky that's only not frozen stiff because he keeps it tucked against his chest in a pocket beneath his cloak. I push the food into my mouth and force myself to chew, but I can feel his stare, and after so many days, I'm frazzled by it. I cough out a bite of the tough meat, nearly gagging as I force myself to swallow it down.

He makes a scoffing noise. It startles me, making my eyes flash up. It's the most I've heard from him in two days. I leap at the opening.

"What?" I snipe. "I can't cough?"

He says nothing. Just stays caught under his hood, a scruffy five o'clock shadow now covering his chin and jaw.

"You know, you could have some manners."

He stays quiet, slouched against the wall of the miniature snow cave, knees bent and arms crossed beneath his cloak.

"The jerky is dry."

Still nothing.

"*Anyone* would cough," I say defensively, still pricking at him.

"No. They wouldn't."

I'm so surprised he actually replied that I just blink at him for several seconds. Until I realize he's arguing. Then I argue right back.

"Of course they would."

He clears his throat, the noise like shifting rocks. "You've never been hungry, or you'd be more thankful for that jerky you're choking on," he says quietly. "You've never had to go days without eating or had to plan ahead weeks in advance, worrying if you'd have enough food for the winter. You've never truly had to go without."

"I've been a *captive* in Seventh Kingdom, and before that I was traveling there in an open cart with a man I didn't know was a fae! Do you think I was served up a five-course dinner every night? No! He gave me jerky too."

"You still got fed, didn't you?" he counters with a snide pull of his lips. "You didn't have to source your own food. You didn't go without. You're a spoiled brat. You don't know how to be grateful for that jerky in your hand, because you were born with your nose in the air."

"You don't know me," I spit. "Don't presume to pretend otherwise."

"Oh, yes. Poor little queen. Born into royalty with every opportunity handed to her."

A humorless laugh rasps out of my throat. "*Opportunity*? That's what you think a magic-less woman gets when she's born from a royal line? Then you are a fool, assassin."

"And you still see yourself as a victim, Queenie."

I glare. He glares back.

Actually, I prefer him not to speak after all.

"How much longer will it take until we reach Highbell?" I demand. I want to be rid of his company—if one can even call it company. I'm sure I've never felt more alone.

"It takes as long as it takes," he answers very unhelpfully.

"What does that mean?"

He hacks off a piece of jerky and chews it with his mouth open, then tips his head back as he downs a gulp of whatever he keeps in his flask. I try not to watch the way his throat bobs, the dark skin at his throat tensing with a hard swallow. I also try not to let it bother me that he's deliberately taking such a long time to answer.

We've been circling around each other for days. Caught entirely too close together and yet thoroughly distanced.

When he finishes, he lets the flask hang down from his hand where it rests over his knee. "It means that I'm expending a lot of fucking energy keeping us hidden as we shadow-leap, and it's not easy doing it at such great distances with you clinging to me the whole way."

Clinging to him? As if I'm some foolish child yanking on a mother's skirts? The nerve of this man.

"*You're* the one who told me to keep hold of you," I snap back.

"Maybe I regret it," he says in a rumble. "Maybe I regret agreeing to take you."

I can't explain the hurt that lands from his words. It shouldn't matter that he's saying these things, and yet, it *does*. Little swoops of frozen clumps suddenly form in my palms, curdling from the unhealed slashes. I fist them tight, stiff fingers curling into the dollop of cold as I let my nails dig in.

"Fine," I bite out. "Leave, then. I'll make my own way back to Highbell."

We both know I'd be lost or dead before I could make it past these mountains, but I stick to my words because this man makes me so *furious*.

He snorts. "And let you get out of warning Orea? I don't think so. You made a choice, and you're going through with it whether you want to or not."

My lip lifts in a sneer. "Is that right?"

Who is he to think he can dictate what I do?

He shoves away his flask and juts up his jaw. "Yes."

"Or what?" I challenge.

Quick as a blink, he's before me. Leaning into my space, body draped over my bent knees. My breath catches and my fists grab his cloak on instinct, like I can try to push him away. But instead, I stay like this, clutching the thick fabric in my cold palms, while his hot breath traces down my face. "You'll make good on your word, Queenie, or I'll finish what I started."

I pause. The moment pauses too. Thickens in the air.

There's a long, drawn out second where the two of us just stare at each other. But the longer we look, something between us seems to pull. To tighten.

From this close, I can see little shards glinting in his dark eyes, the pigment in his irises carrying light patches the same way his skin does. Flecks of colorless light, so tiny they're almost nonexistent, nearly swallowed up by the black. It makes me want to keep looking to see what else I can find in them.

But he's studying me too. Gaze moving back and forth. Sliding over my cheek. Flicking down to my lips.

"Is that what you'd like? For me to *finish* you?" he asks, and my breath catches at the double-sided question.

His voice has dropped, and it suddenly sounds grittier. Hungrier. Maybe he's just hungry to snap my neck or draw a blade against my throat.

Or maybe it's something else he craves.

The thought makes my breath twist. It's a dark thought. A forbidden thought.

Wicked insinuations snake down my spine. Snow slips through my fingers and lands on him in little clots. My stomach tightens, and I wonder what in the realm is wrong with me.

I brace both hands and shove him away.

He falls back against the wall while I scramble out of our tiny hollow, instantly smacked sideways by the force of the wind as soon as I stand upright. I ignore the way my heart is racing. Ignore the shiver that traveled down my neck when he spoke. I take a few long breaths until the heat has drained away and all I feel is the blissful, numbing cold again.

He comes out of the hollow, dusting off the snow from our burrow before crouching down.

"Let's go," I tell him impatiently.

He pauses at my demand, shoving snow into his water hide to look over at me. "Anxious to be in my grip again?" he mocks.

The thought of being in his grip makes a flush dig through my frigid cheeks. It irritates me to no end. "Anxious to get to Highbell and be rid of you."

He laughs and straightens back up, showing off his tall height, and then walks in my direction, passing by entirely too close. The man has issues with personal space.

"Maybe you'll never be rid of me," he says in my ear as he passes. "Maybe I'll haunt you in the shadows for the rest of your life, and one day, when you least expect it, I'll step out and finally slide my blade through your chest."

It's a threat.

Again.

And yet...

I internally shout at my heart to stop pounding. I fight to quell the responses my body gives around him. The last thing I want to do is reveal just how much he affects me.

Because he *does* affect me, though I want to deny it.

I clear my throat and look away. "The fae are already on the move," I say, gesturing toward the winding parade of the army. I can see them marching in the distance, on the other side of this sloped hill. "We've crossed into Sixth territory, so the capital can't be that far off."

His face angles toward the direction the army is headed. "It's not," he confirms.

Worry and trepidation jump up my throat. I need to warn Highbell before they reach the city. "Then let's go. The sooner we get there, the sooner we won't have to deal with each other anymore," I snap, but for some reason, it rings like a lie.

He turns toward me, bright white teeth glinting in a mean smile. "I like *dealing* with you just fine."

My heart skitters. I want to yank it out of my chest and shake it.

"Stop trying to antagonize me," I snap. "I've dealt with kings and politicians and nobles all my life. You think you're intimidating? I've dealt with men far more treacherous and powerful than you."

"Is that right."

His reply is not a question, but a dare. He starts circling me like a shark in the water. I keep perfectly still, refusing to spin, because I don't want him to think I'm too afraid to give him my back.

It's a mistake.

When he's behind me, his hand shoots out and wraps around the back of my neck. Palm to spine, he bends it, until my head is forced back, my eyes looking up at his looming face. "What about now?" he murmurs, tone deadly quiet as he hovers over me. "Have you been more intimidated than this with those more *treacherous and powerful men*?"

I swallow hard, and a wave of warmth fuses itself to my stomach. Shifts lower.

"Yes," I say shakily. But not from fear. Or, at least, not

just from fear. Threat and thrill seem to have joined hands. Gripped hold of me.

His fingers dig into my skin so hard I know they'll leave a mark when he releases me.

If he releases me.

With a jolt, I realize I don't *want* him to let go. I have to stop myself from reaching up and placing my hand over his, urging him to squeeze harder.

What is wrong with me?

"If that were the truth, then you wouldn't be trembling so much, Cold Queen," he says, his voice dragging down my neck and lodging in my chest. "After all, I'm no king or noble or politician."

"Just an assassin," I retort.

He grins, flashing his bright teeth at me, and then gives the barest scrape of his scruffy jaw against the shell of my ear. "Yes. Just an assassin."

An assassin who handles me in a way no other man ever has—true *manhandling*. No one else would've ever dared to touch a queen this way. It makes me feel powerless. Like I'm at his mercy. Takes away my control.

So why do I like it?

Why, when he continues to hold me in his strong grip, do I find myself wondering how many people have died from his hand? It's a rush, to teeter so close to the edge of his danger. I should be flinging myself away, not looking over the brink, wanting to see more.

But I keep leaning. Keep looking.

Abruptly, he releases me, and I almost tip right over onto the ground. I catch myself and cup the back of my neck where he'd gripped me, still feeling a phantom pulse from where his fingers had been. He crouches down again, gathering more snow into his water hide before pushing to his full height and moving a few feet away.

I watch his lithe, powerful legs, watch the strong line of his shoulders beneath the cloak. I don't know why, but I have the strangest urge to peel back his hood and force him to look at me without hiding beneath its cover. I'm so busy envisioning it that I don't even notice he's stopped or the sound of his belt jostling until he takes a wide legged stance and starts pissing in the snow.

"Great Divine!" I flinch away, whirling around until my back is facing him. "Must you do that right here?"

I hear him laugh. "Not gonna go on a trek just to take a piss. Besides, I'm guessing with all those treacherous men you've dealt with, you must've at least seen a few dicks. Or was your dead lover just for looks?"

Furious, I spin back around. "Shut up."

His head turns over his shoulder as if to look back at me. "That's not very polite talk."

I sputter. "You're *relieving* yourself in front of me, and you dare to talk about politeness?"

His arms show a telltale shake before he's stuffing himself back into his pants. "You're easily riled, aren't you?"

"No."

He turns to face me, and I don't miss the flash of daggers at his hip as he finishes buckling his belt. "Sure you're not."

"I want to go," I say, irritated that I sound petulant even to my own ears. At least while we're shadow-leaping, I won't have to see him. His shadows and light keep us mostly concealed from the world, but also from each other.

"We can add impatience to your list of vices," he replies, though he finally saunters over and holds out his hand. The very same one he...*touched* himself with. He isn't even wearing his gloves.

I meet his eye, but the arrogant twist of his mouth makes me snatch up his hand. His smirk grows wider. Before I can tear my grasp away, he spins around, eyes searching the direction of the army before he turns slightly more to the left.

He starts gathering his shadows toward us, but I stop him. "Wait. Why are you turning us that way? The fae are there."

"Yes, but so is the sunlight. There's not as much cloud coverage today. I need the shadows."

"But if I'm not mistaken, one of our outskirt villages is that way."

"I know where the village is."

"Good. Then you know the way. We can stay in a bed instead of a hole in the ground tonight."

"No."

"*No*? What do you mean, no?"

"We're not going to the village."

My spine snaps straight. "I'm telling you we *are*."

His fingers dig painfully around my own. "You're not in charge."

"I'm a queen," I say, chin lifting.

"You're not a queen until someone willingly bows at your feet."

"Then get on your knees, assassin, and *bow*."

The cruelest, most wicked grin spreads up his face. "If I get on my knees, it will be for an entirely different sort of devotion that would have nothing to do with you being a queen."

Embarrassment flares over my cheeks, and my stomach explodes with flutters. The knot in my throat is so thick I can't untangle it enough to swallow. "You...you can't speak to me that way."

"Why not?"

"It's not proper." I don't remember a time I've been so flustered, and considering my recent experiences, that's saying something.

He laughs. "Well, that's your first mistake. Nothing about

me is proper."

"That's more than apparent," I spit back, tearing my hand from his. "You're also just an assassin. I would *never* let you have me in that way."

All the amusement bleeds away from his expression, and his mouth tightens with his bunching shoulders. "There she is. The queen who thinks she's better than everyone."

I bristle.

"I don't think that."

"Really? So you don't think you're above your people?"

"They're my subjects."

"*Subjects*." He sneers at me and shakes his head. "Should've known all that talk about saving your people was all bluster. It's still about you, isn't it? You and your great Colier legacy."

I open my mouth, but no words come out.

He uses the hesitation to point at my face, his stippled skin showing patches of ivory at his knuckles. "Right there. That's the problem. That's why your own people wanted you gone. Because you wanted to be their queen for the wrong reasons, just like I said."

I turn my head away, hating the feeling of shame that tosses into my stomach like stones, leaving me pitted. "Then why did you take me? Why let me out?"

Why not kill me?

"Why should you get to sit in a castle while your people die? You should warn them because *you* did this. It's your fault we're being invaded. It's time you face the consequences of your actions."

Every word he says strikes me like another rock. Like I'm condemned to be stoned to death, each hit landing, because he's right. I made a deal with the fae for my own gain. Led so easily into the temptation of being given a crown and the promise of my rightful rule. Yet…look what happened.

Realization sinks down over my back with a weight that I don't quite know how to carry.

I'm not sure what escapes out of the cracks of my face, but for a split second, I think the assassin almost softens. But it must just be a trick of the light, because when I focus on him, his expression is as hard as ever.

He holds out his hand again. I don't take it.

"Let's go, Queenie."

I don't want to go now, but I don't want to let on that he's gotten under my skin either. So I reach out anyway and let him wrap us in shadows. I take the reprieve he offers, letting myself fall into the blaring, muted wind of light and dark, with only his hold to steady me. It allows me to take a shaky breath and let it out without his eyes watching me. Judging me.

For the rest of the day, that's what I have. A respite from his critical gaze and his biting words, while my stomach topples every time we leap from shadow to shadow. I would never admit it aloud, but I *do* cling to his hand. For some foolish, ridiculous reason, it grounds me, even as his words tip me over and make me squirm in all of these horrible truths I'm left buried with.

It's more crushing than the fae king pinning me with stone.

I dislike it immensely.

I'm used to being angry, but I'm not used to this shame, this guilt. It sits like a cube of ice in my chest, turning uncomfortably in my stomach every time I go over the assassin's words. Every time I go over my actions.

What does it mean to be a true ruler of Sixth Kingdom? What does it mean that my people wanted me dead, that they rejected me enough to run me out? What does it mean that I'm going back there now, after what I've done?

What do *I* mean…if I'm not queen of Highbell?

That's the only thing I've ever been. The only thing I

243

have.

And without it…

Emotion whips around me far more brutally than this magical wind. My own shadows consume me far more thoroughly than the assassins' do.

Because I…failed.

And I think, perhaps, I've been failing for a very long time. Not in the way the men in my life have accused me of, but in who I have become.

Hours later, when my body is ready to pitch sideways from the constant drag of being catapulted along, the shadows thin. I feel a tremor in the assassin's hand right before we jolt to a stop. I imagine it's a bit like being on a ship at sea for weeks and then suddenly disembarking onto steady land. Even when I'm stationary again, I still feel like I'm moving.

I take in our surroundings, finding that we're against a lonely hill with nothing else around, the snow so thick we sink right into it. "Where are we?"

The assassin doesn't reply, and I look over just as the wind picks up and slaps back his hood. I see more of his face for the first time in days and notice the strain at every angle, the heavy circles under his eyes. I hadn't paid much attention when he said he was expending a lot of energy before, but now, I can see the truth of that. My gaze drops to his shaking hands.

He catches me looking and clenches them into fists before burying them beneath his cloak. "What are you looking at?" he growls.

My brows shoot up. "It's a sore subject? For people to look at you?"

"No one *wants* to look at me because I look different," he spits, all fuming bitterness and heated judgment. "Don't pretend you don't feel the same."

I want to lash out at him right back, and I would, if it weren't for the fact that I can feel how tense he is. How…vulnerable. For the first time, I wonder why. Was he made fun of as a child for the patches of light around his dark skin? Have people been cruel to him as an adult? My stomach pricks with thorns, and I realize I don't like to think of people mocking him. Staring at him.

Yet I know the very last thing he'd want from me is pity. So I say, "Looking at you? No, I quite like that. It's *listening* to you that I can't stand."

He bursts out with a noise of surprise, staring at me with a sort of incredulity. Then he shakes his head as if to clear it. "You like looking at me?"

The question is quiet.

Subtle.

Heavy.

My lips part, ready to tell him something cutting. Something to take away the complicated softness of what I said.

The truth comes out instead.

"I do."

He takes in a sharp breath. All full of edges. I can feel it scrape against me, dangerous and honed.

"I like looking at you too, Queenie."

My palms tingle. Gashes blooming with gentle snow.

"*Why?*" I ask him quietly. Ask myself.

The assassin just shrugs. "I don't know."

Neither do I.

I turn away from the moment, from him, because I have to cut away from it before I start to bleed.

"Where are we?" I ask, clearing my throat. Trying to clear away this thickness between us that seems to be expanding every day.

He takes a moment to answer. "The village is on the other side of this hill," he says with a tilt of his head. "But I need to rest. Give me an hour."

I blink in surprise. "You brought us to the village?"

"Nearly."

Looking around, I take stock of the hill. It's not too wide, and aside from the thick snowfall, it doesn't seem like it'll be too difficult to traverse.

I need to put some distance between us.

Which is why I start to tread—slowly—through the thick snow. My dress and leggings are already soaked up to my calves anyway since we've been dumped from snow bank to snow bank all day, so it doesn't matter. Once I'm in the village, I can get warm by a fire, have a hot meal, a comfortable bed...

"What are you doing?" the assassin calls.

"I'll walk the rest of the way there."

"Get back here," he says. "I said I just needed an hour."

I turn to look at him over my shoulder. "Yes, but why wait an hour out in this wind when I could just walk around this hill and be there?"

I keep going, my legs sludging through, thighs burning from the effort. I keep sinking in, sometimes all the way up to my knees, and I'm forced to hike up my skirts and hold them to my thighs.

The assassin curses, and then I hear his lumbering steps coming after me. So I pick up the pace. Holding my skirts up higher, I pant as I trudge, sinking in the snow and shoving through it with each labored step, going as fast as I can.

"Dammit, *wait*."

"Just rest," I tell him.

"*You* fucking rest," I hear him growl, though I can tell he's gaining on me.

I try to go even faster. Perhaps trying to flee from our confessions. From our tense push and pull.

"You said it yourself, it's not that far. I'll rest once I'm inside."

He suddenly grips my arm, stopping me. I almost feel badly about how hard he's breathing. "Stop making me chase you, woman," he grits out.

"I'm not making you do anything, *man*," I retort.

"I need time to recuperate. I don't want to be this drained when we get there just in case the villagers give us trouble."

I pull my arm out of his grip. The spot feels warm, though I try not to notice. "This is Sixth's village. Nobody is going to give us trouble. Highbell might have rejected me, but here in the outskirts, life is quite different. I wouldn't be surprised if they haven't even heard of what happened in the city. I'm their queen."

"I still think—"

"Yes, I'm quite aware of your thoughts, assassin," I say breezily as I start to walk forward again, trying not to show how much I'm struggling in this pathless trudge. "Perhaps keep them to yourself now."

He lets out a gnarled sound like he wants to yank out his hair. "Fine, you stubborn woman. Go. Maybe I don't care if you do run into trouble!"

My lips press together in irritation. "Fine," I snap back. "I don't expect you to care anyway!"

I tromp forward, ignoring the curses that dash from his mouth while I mutter the same ones beneath my breath. I stumble, and he has the audacity to laugh like the bastard he is.

Good. At least disdain is more familiar to navigate than…whatever other emotion we were tipping into.

"*I like looking at you too?*" I grumble to myself with mockery. "Of all the ridiculous, stupid things…"

Why did he say that? He's lying. That's what it must be. He murders people for a living, for Divine's sake. Lying would be nothing to him. He's playing some sort of twisted game with me.

Yet…his eyes looked like they meant it.

When I stumble again, my palms slap down on the snow, the pieces of white sticking to my skin.

I hear the assassin chuckle again at my expense. "Just come back here, Queenie," he calls. "You're going to be too tired to walk all the way there."

He's already counted me out. Fully expecting me to fail.

I am *not* going to fail.

Gritting my teeth, I keep trudging, thankful that I'm cold enough on the inside that the two-feet of snow doesn't paralyze me from the outside. My legs are aching, my body tired, but I keep going.

I'm utterly sick of failing. So I don't care if it seems like this is just one foolish walk—I will get there just to prove him wrong. Knowing he's watching spurs me on.

"It's just snow," I tell myself, calves wedged in, my knees locking with every step as I haul my feet through the heap. "You're a Colier. The snow is in our skin, ice in our veins, cold in our blood. Just keep going," I pant.

I stumble again. This time, I face-plant right into the snow. I'm stuck, clawing at the flurries as I try to heave myself out, when firm hands grip my arms and haul me back until I'm upright again.

Spluttering, I look up at the assassin, the shade of his hood making his eyes look like they're gleaming. He doesn't let go, and despite how angry and embarrassed I am at having him lift me up, I don't jerk away.

I tell myself it's because I don't want to fall down again.

I can't help but let my gaze trace over his features— features he always hides from view. His face is handsome. Dangerous. The patches on his dark skin add to his innate allure, perfectly harboring the dark and light magic he manipulates. It makes him utterly unique, while the gleam in his eyes makes him utterly wicked.

His lips utterly sinful.

The unkempt black hair growing at his jaw is so unlike the perfectly shaven beards and slicked mustaches I always saw at court. In fact, everything about him is different from the men at court. There's a hardness to him. He's not pretty like Jeo was. Not graceful, either. He certainly doesn't possess the silver-tongued smooth speech like Tyndall. The assassin is everything hard and blunt. No fake pleasantries to him whatsoever.

The court would hate him.

I feel a bit of snow stuck to my cheek, and it streaks down my face before plopping onto the ground below. The assassin reaches up, making me flinch back instinctively. He pauses, arching a brow, but then simply uses the end of his cloak to wipe off my face. I stand stunned, my mind blanking.

"Stubborn fucking woman."

I finally snap out of my foolishness and wrench myself from him, shoving his arm away. "There's a reason *assassin* starts with the word *ass*."

"Talking about my ass now, Queenie?"

My temper flares. "I'm talking about you being one."

He smirks. "Sure you are."

I start walking again, but this time, the assassin walks in front of me. With his steps leading the way and bearing the brunt of the snow, the rest of the trek isn't so hard. Still, my legs are shaking from exertion, and sweat is dripping down my forehead by the time we reach the gated entrance of the village. The assassin was right—it was around the hill—though he failed to explain just how big the hill really was.

But, I made it.

When we finally break free of the deep snow and get to the dragged path that leads to the village gate, I nearly totter onto it with wobbly legs. The slick-stepped path is a wonderful respite from the frozen plod.

Ahead, the gate is cocked open, the wooden-beamed fence that surrounds the village like pointed pikes ready to skewer the sky.

"There," I say, dusting off my skirts. "Now we can have a proper rest tonight."

The assassin doesn't reply and instead stops in the middle of the path, nearly making me run right into him.

"Assassin?" I say with annoyance.

"*Quiet.*"

I rear back with offense. "Excuse me?" When he says nothing, I shake my head and go around him. I'm well and truly ready to be rid of him for the night. I don't know what I was thinking, letting him wipe my face before, saying what I said aloud. I should—

Suddenly, he's at my side, his arm flung out and knocking into my belly as I stumble to a stop. "What—"

"Stay," he hisses, barely above a whisper.

My head snaps over to look at him, and I open my mouth to tell him off for barking orders at me, but his tense face stops me.

"What is it?"

"Copper."

I frown. "What nonsense are you spewing?"

"I smell copper."

My frown deepens, but I decide to humor the man, and I lift my own nose to smell. There's nothing. Just cold and snow. "Copper? What a ridiculous thing to claim to smell."

His eyes flick to me. "Blood, Queenie. I smell *blood*."

"What are you talking about? You can't possibly smell that."

"I'm a fucking assassin," he snarls. "You think I don't know what blood smells like? We're turning back. Right now."

Dropping his arm, he turns around to leave, but I move

toward the village's gate. The wood is coated in a permanent layer of frost, and I can see some of the roofs beyond poking over the top.

"Queenie," he growls behind me.

I march forward. "If there's blood in the air, we should find out why."

"*Malina.*"

I ignore him.

I wish I hadn't.

Slipping through the open gate, I stop in my tracks as soon as I'm within the walls of the village. The blood drains from my face, but there's so much of it on the ground that I barely notice its absence.

The sight before me is horrifying. I don't want to look, and yet, I can't even blink.

Behind me, the gate creaks open, and I jump, but it's only the assassin stalking forward until he's standing next to me again. He takes one look around the village and curses beneath his breath. "Let's go," he tells me.

"No."

I walk further into the village, my *no* echoing in my own ears. Because *no*, this can't be real. *No,* this can't be what I'm truly seeing.

Yet, it is.

This village is a small one, maybe only a few hundred people living here at most. A harsh existence, yet one they chose rather than live in the capital or one of the bigger cities. It gave them larger living spaces and seclusion, certainly more spread out than in the slums of Highbell. We had a dozen soldiers stationed here. No more than that, because we didn't need it.

So we thought.

The stone houses are simple, lining up on both sides of the street, windows facing each other like open eyes. Hanging between them, laundry lines are pulled taut, from one house to another, draped above the road. Shirts and trousers clap in the wind with icicles and frost stuck to them. Yet it's not just clothing pinned to those lines. The cords that stretch from window to window sag from the weight of bodies.

Unmoving, lifeless bodies.

Men, women, children. Hanging on the lines right alongside their clothes.

The cords curve down like macabre smiles, blood dripping down from their still-leaking corpses into frozen puddles on the ground. I can smell the blood now. Even half-frozen, the metallic scent slaps at my senses.

The entire village has been slaughtered.

Line after line, people are pinned to the cords, with the smallest incisions cut into their bodies. A coin-sized slash at their jugulars. Another at each wrist and thigh. Slices into their arteries to leak their life right from their veins while they dry out with the laundry.

Most of the blood has frozen, but some still drains slowly onto the street, dripping with icy clinks. Carrion birds are circling overhead, their wings whistling through the air. Some of them have already landed, scaly feet gripping the cords while their white beaks peck and peck and *peck*.

Something in me cracks. A fissure I can physically feel that makes me jolt in place as I slam a hand over my heart. The beat beneath convulses.

My eyes ache.

Hate and horror battle inside my mind.

"The fae came through here after all."

The assassin's voice is low and dead sounding. I suppose he's used to seeing such gruesome death, so he can bring about that numbness to dull him when he faces it.

"*Why?*" I ask, my tongue dry in my mouth. "This is out of their way on the path toward Highbell. There's nothing of value here."

"Isn't it obvious? They didn't come here to march on one kingdom. They came here to kill."

I feel sick.

"My question is, how did they know about this village?" he asks. "As you said, it's not on the way. They purposely sent soldiers here to wipe everyone out."

"Pruinn," I seethe, my hate scraping up through my slit palms, cubes of ice gathering at my molars.

From my peripheral, I see his hood turn in my direction.

"Loth Pruinn—the one who brought me to Seventh Kingdom. He'd been living in Highbell, posing as a merchant. He was gathering information about me, but he must've also been gathering information about settlements all across Sixth. Perhaps even about all of Orea."

I can't look away from the people. The fae didn't just kill them. They made their deaths into a taunt. Treated their bodies with contempt and disrespect, just to show how little they care for us. This death, this *display* is an unfathomable insult.

"We have to get them down."

The assassin pauses. "You want to get them down?"

The anger in me is growing like a glacier, layer by layer. "Of course I want to get them down! We can't leave them like this," I bite out, grinding that ice into little shards that stab into my gums. "I *won't* leave them like this."

I can feel him watching me.

"Why not?"

"Because they don't deserve this," I say thickly. "They're my people. I'm their queen."

Their queen.

I never thought about ruling in the face of something like this. A prosperous Highbell, subjects who respected me, a life of luxury, a dance of politics—that was always expected.

Not this.

Yet, I can't turn my back on Sixth Kingdom. Not the capital with thousands of people, and not this outskirt settlement.

"It's not as if you knew any of these people. Maybe they hated you," he says, and anger quakes inside of me, sloshing frigid water. "Why waste your time and effort doing anything at all?"

"Because you were right!" I shout, whipping toward him with accusation in my eyes and a horrible clawing feeling in my throat.

"Right about what?"

"That I have always wanted to be a queen for the wrong reasons. That I'm spoiled. That I'm a cold-hearted bitch. That my people don't want me. Just like my husband. Just like my father."

To my horror, my voice snaps, pitching higher with an emotion I've held back for so long. I'm not sure I've *ever* allowed myself to feel this way. Not even sure that I *could*.

"I brought the fae over the bridge," I say, tone hollow, heart aching. "It's my fault everyone here is dead. Just like the rest of Highbell and even Orea will be if we can't stop them."

I was born to wear a crown. Yet without magic, I was never enough. No matter what I did, or learned, or gave, or married. I was a failure because I didn't have the power necessary to hold the throne. Because I wasn't able to fulfill my role of birthing an heir to continue the bloodline.

If my anger is solid ice, my sadness is a slush.

"You say I only wanted to be queen for the wrong reasons," I say quietly, cold tears gathering in the thinnest line above my lid. "All my life, I've only been wanted for the wrong reasons. Never for me. Only for what I could give the crown or give the men who wore one. So yes. It's my fault. I was offered my heart's desire. I was offered the right to rule. I was lured with magic, and I took it. I brought the fae over the bridge. It's my fault everyone here is dead. All because I wanted to be worth something. To finally have what I'd lacked. And now, I've doomed the very kingdom I wanted to rule."

The sound of a tinkling crash makes my gaze drop, and I see shards of ice falling from my hands and breaking on the ground.

The assassin watches silently as I turn over my palms. He says nothing as I pick at the layer of ice that's formed over every inch of my skin like glue left to dry. Patches of frost stay stuck to my fingertips, even more gathered at the gashes. Permanent scars slashed into me by my own temptation and weakness. Everlasting proof of my wrongdoing.

A long, tense moment stretches between us, and all that exists in this pregnant pause is a cold, crownless queen, a hooded assassin, and far more confessions than I know what to do with.

Far more deaths than I can atone for.

Finally, after more shards shatter at my feet, the assassin speaks. "Magic responds to mood."

I flinch as he steps toward me, but he reaches down and takes my hand, and I go utterly still. How his palm is so warm I'll never understand, but it sears me. Prickles my skin like my body has forgotten the comfort of heat and his presence is reminding my senses.

With far more gentleness than I ever could've imagined, he turns my palm over in his hands and traces the gash there. Lets miniature icicles drift up with his touch as he digs the cold off my skin and leaves it to scatter in the wind.

"That's why it comes and goes," he says quietly, and that single warm finger of his continues to trace down the bluish slash. Keeps digging through the gathered slurry. My eyes are transfixed on his slow, deliberate touch, and for a moment I forget how to breathe. "Mine used to be the same way, before

I learned to control it. You'll have to get a handle on your emotions."

My eyes snap up to hook beneath his hood. "I'm not emotional."

I learned as a little girl to always keep decorum. To wipe emotion from my face and behave with poise and strength no matter what. To always wear a mask and keep my thoughts and feelings to myself, because my thoughts and feelings didn't matter anyway. If any woman let out even a hint of emotion, she was disparaged. Castigated. Criticized. Mocked.

"You misunderstand me, Cold Queen," he says, finally dropping my hand. I have to fight the sudden and annoying urge to ask him to snatch it back up. "I'm saying you need to get a handle on your emotions as in *use* them. Stop repressing yourself. What are you feeling right now? Right when that ice formed on your hands?"

"Anger," I admit. "Anger and…"

"And what?"

"Sadness." I swallow hard. "Guilt."

The admission falls from my lips like the first sprays of rain. Unexpected. Surprising. Leaving me looking up and wondering where to go from here. Do I dry up or flood it all?

"You know what, Cold Queen?"

"What?"

He gives the slightest curve of his lips. "You might actually have a heart after all."

I let out a shaken breath. "I'm not sure I should count that as a compliment."

"But you will anyway."

He's arrogant.

He's also right.

The assassin slips a dagger out of the sheath at his hip and offers it to me. I hesitate, gaze snatching up. "Time to help your people, Malina."

Yes, it is.

I take the blade tentatively, and though it feels foreign and bulky in my hand, it also feels like a weight I should have to carry.

Together, we walk into the desecrated village, inside the houses, and lean out the windows. Wordlessly, the two of us start cutting down the laundry lines one by one, ridding the insult of the fae, helping to lay the dead to rest.

Though I'm not sure there's any rest to be had.

For the dead, or for us.

CHAPTER 23

QUEEN MALINA

This is the last line.

I've cut dozens and dozens already, yet I hesitate now. I'm gripping the cord in one hand and the dagger in the other, but my eyes are straight ahead. At one of the women on the laundry line, at her slumped head, at the unnatural way the fae pinned her there like a puppet.

At the slight bump on her belly.

Directly across the street, at the window facing my own, the assassin stands. Despite the fact that I can't see his eyes, I know he's looking at me.

I swallow hard and raise the dagger. Start sawing through the cord. Frayed lines come apart, though not as easily as when we first started this task. Death takes a toll on a blade, and it takes a toll on a person, too. I feel blunted, like all my sharpness was dulled in the face of such horror.

Gripping the hilt harder, I saw back and forth, again and again, and when my line finally snaps, the bodies drop. The last of the weight brought down.

Once all the bodies are back on the ground, I stare out the window.

When the first line dropped, something numb threatened to come over me, but for once, I didn't let it. I forced myself to look. To see. To implant each face in my memory.

Line by line, body by body, I've made myself be present and allowed myself to feel. The horror. The disgust. The guilt. The rage. I felt it all, churning through me and leaving me battered like I've been ground to a pulp.

I don't flinch when the assassin suddenly appears beside me in a burst of roiling shadows. Yet I nearly do when he moves with the strange gentleness I'm not used to, as he reaches for my hand and uncurls my fingers from the dagger. I didn't realize how hard I was clutching the hilt until he takes the blade, leaving my hand empty and aching.

"The deed is done, Malina," he says quietly, and my heart aches as much as my hand from the way he says my name.

I look at the bodies outside that cover the streets like rubble. It feels so far from done. More than anyone will ever be able to finish.

"We can't just leave her."

"Her?"

A crack spreads in the hollowed cavity of my chest. Something burns down my face like the fissure is ripping through my cheek. "Them," I correct myself as I tear my gaze away from the woman.

Yet nothing gets by the assassin. "She was pregnant."

There's another crack. It jostles me from the inside out.

"Yes." My voice sounds strange to my own ears. I wonder if it sounds strange to him too.

He says nothing more about it, and I'm glad for that. There's a sort of silent acknowledgment that doesn't need to be voiced. It's already known.

"Your hand is blistered."

I glance down and see that he's right. How soft of a queen have I been that holding a dagger for a couple of hours and cutting down rope should affect my hand so? And yet, it's fitting. I deserve whatever bubbles up. Now I have that to scar my palms too, right alongside the blue-tinged gashes. All marks of my guilt.

"I'm going to gather some food before we leave. You should find some clean clothes to change into." The assassin walks away, his steps treading lightly over the floorboards, and I do as he suggested, though I internally cringe. While I understand the realistic necessity, wearing a dead woman's clothes and pillaging pantries makes guilt roll through me.

I pull on thick woolen leggings and a skirt, and tuck in a button-up sweater before pulling on a coat. All of it is the color of mud. Cloying, covering mud. Perhaps I can think of it as a kind of armor as we approach Highbell. At the very least, it will act as a reminder.

I find the assassin downstairs, new clothes bunched on his body that are slightly ill-fitting. The house feels hollow. The empty sofa, sagging from years of use, the curtains still drawn, a plate on the table with half-eaten food that churns my stomach, a lantern fallen on the floor.

"We can't stay here tonight," I say.

Can't stay in this place where everyone died because of me. Because of what I unleashed upon them.

"And we need to—" I swallow thickly, try to get the bile down. "Burn the village. There are too many bodies, and the ground will be too hard and frozen to dig regardless."

He gives me a nod, and then the two of us walk out, down the street of death, sidestepping the frozen patches of blood. The fae didn't even leave the livestock alive, instead butchering them in their stalls.

They came here to kill.

I avoid the worst of the carnage as the two of us methodically gather all the straw we can find and tuck it around the bodies like a skinny pyre. Then we spread more along the street, trailing it up toward the wooden doorways of the simple homes. I stand at the gate as he sets the small village aflame, sending the people back to the gods through smoke and ash. Burning away the last of the coppery scent and chasing off the pecking birds.

Then, it's done. Nothing left but ash and regret. No one to remember them but us.

And I will always remember.

When night descends, we walk out of the settlement and stay in a hole in the snow far enough away that we can't smell the smolder.

Sleep evades me like I knew it would. I let myself feel far too much today, and the faces of those Oreans flicker behind my lids every time I close my eyes.

When we get up with the morning, the assassin takes one look at my face and passes over his flask. My brow arches as I take it.

"You need it today. Trust me."

I can't argue.

Tipping it back, I let the liquid pour, the burn of the alcohol crawling up my throat. I lick my lips and pass it back.

"We should reach Highbell by nightfall," he says and then digs into the bag of rations and hands me some food. Salted pork. Cold cheese. Stiff bread.

Food from the village.

I slowly take it and start to chew, but my stomach sours, though it has nothing to do with the alcohol. For days, all I wanted was to be rid of the travel jerky, but this feels wrong. Like we took this food when we should have left it.

As if he can sense my thoughts, he says, "The dead have

no use for the things in this world anymore."

"But the world has great use for the dead."

The dead spur us on. To live. To avenge. To honor. To grieve. It's because of the dead that we live.

I swallow down the sticky lump. "I never asked—why does my dear husband want to kill me?"

He pauses before tearing off another bite of his own food. "Will any answer help?"

I consider that. "No."

"Then maybe the question doesn't matter."

Perhaps it doesn't. Perhaps a part of me always expected for Tyndall to do something like this. I've served my purpose after all. I'd be much more valuable to him dead.

"And what about you?" I ask. "He gave you the job. He won't tolerate you not completing it. Or are you still going to stab me through, as you so often like to threaten?"

He continues to chew, and I can't help but notice the way the muscle in his jaw moves. "We have other issues to deal with."

I let out a heavy breath. "Yes. We do."

When we're done, we leave our burrow, leave behind the pyred village as we go on. Though today, the assassin gets tired much sooner than usual. The sun still has a few hours left to shine when we go still. I barely catch myself from falling into the snow when he stops suddenly, yanking the shadows away as he stumbles.

He balances himself against a boulder at the base of the mountain we've stopped at. The bare, snowy mountain I know all too well—the one that houses Highbell Castle just on the other side.

I'm almost home.

He continues to heave, his hand shaking where it grips the frozen rock.

"Assassin?" I ask tentatively, taking a step forward.

"I'm fine," he snaps.

His tone makes me bristle, and in the past, I would've walked away or said something rude in response, but over the last few days, I've learned to gauge his words and determine the root of his moods.

I step closer, hearing the heavy way he's breathing, watching the quake down his spine. I can't see his face—I hardly ever can. Slowly, so slowly, as if I'm reaching a hand out to pet a feral dog, I reach up and start to tug off his hood.

And miraculously, the feral dog doesn't rear back and bite me.

He lets the hood fall.

A sheen of sweat covers his skin, more beading against his beard. His black eyebrows are full of tension, digging a frown between them, and his lips are thinned into a grimace. I can see exhaustion in every inch of his face, can see it draped over his shoulders and hanging off his limbs.

Dark eyes with those slices of light flicker toward me, holding my gaze captive.

"Having a good stare?" he spits at me, like he can't stand my gaze on his face any longer, and it cuts me down. I thought we'd gotten past this, but this ingrained vulnerability in him is still very much there. "That's why I keep the hood on— that's why people call me Hood. They're not very inventive."

My lips press together and I snap back. "Oh, shut up. I already told you I like looking at you. I'm not *staring*, I'm…gazing."

He lets out a snort, though the viciousness seems to have fallen away from his expression. "*Gazing*?"

"Yes," I reply tartly. "That's what one does when they like to look at someone. And I certainly won't be calling you Hood, because I detest when you cover your face. So how about I simply call you by your name? Or should I continue saying assassin?"

He pauses, blinking at me in surprise. Then, his tone drops. "My name is Dommik."

The way he says it makes it feel like he hasn't given it for a very long time.

And yet, he's given it to *me*.

We watch each other for a moment, and my heartbeat rattles beneath my ribs, feels jumpy and bursting.

"Now you've heard my name, you've seen my face, and you know I'm weakened. I'm at the most vulnerable I'll ever be," he says quietly. Pointedly.

"And?"

"And...you know where the dagger is. You could simply grip the blade from my belt and drag it across my throat."

I laugh nervously. "You travel with shadow and light. You can appear anywhere, without anyone being the wiser. I would be a fool to even try."

He turns slightly, shifting his cloak, and my eyes automatically flick down to where the dagger sits. My pulse quickens.

"Go on, Queenie," he rasps. "Do it."

Of its own volition, my hand reaches out, blistered fingers wrapping around the leather-wrapped hilt. Dommik does nothing to stop me. For some reason, a thrill travels down my back.

"You feel that, don't you?" he asks. "Violence is a different kind of power, and you don't need magic to have it."

I grip the hilt tighter. Lift the blade an inch out of its sheath. But my wrist hits his hip, and he straightens up, shifting so his thick thigh comes between both of mine, and I gasp.

But I don't move away.

"There's power in a lot of things that don't require magic," he murmurs.

I swallow hard.

Lift the blade.

The metal shines in the draping sunlight, and flecks of flurry land on its sharpened edges as I press it to his neck. He still makes no move to disarm me, and I wonder.

Does the person who kills for a living want to die?

For some reason, that thought makes my stomach plummet. I quickly lower the dagger, stuffing it back into his sheath with a snap. This taunt isn't nearly as thrilling as it was a few seconds ago.

"I think I held that quite long enough yesterday," I say. "My blisters will need to heal before I can use it properly against you."

He lets out a dry, raspy chuckle, but his hands come to my hips, and I freeze in place, eyes flying up to his face.

"I thought you would've taken me up on my offer," he says, fingers digging in.

My mouth goes dry. For a moment, my mind jumbles, imagining that he's talking about something else. A different sort of offer. All of my focus has homed in on his warming touch, like he's a flame held against ice.

I can feel him melting me.

"Maybe some other time," I reply, though I can't make my tone as glib as I want to. Which is aggravating. I've always been so good at acting aloof. "Now, are you going to sit down, or do you prefer to hunch there until you collapse?"

He scoffs. "I'm not going to collapse. Besides," he adds, moving his face close to mine. "I have a pretty good grip right now."

His hold sears me. I shouldn't like it. But I definitely don't *dislike* it.

"I'm a queen, not a handhold. So if you would..."

Dommik smirks, and my stomach does a ridiculous flip. "Sure, Queenie."

"Malina," I tell him firmly, because I've found I like the way it comes from his lips.

"Malina," he repeats, and great Divine, chills scatter over my arms. His thumbs brush up and down over my waist for a dizzying, drugging moment that I recognize for what it is.

Dangerous.

His thigh is still between both of mine, and he's tall enough that I'm nearly straddling it where I stand. It would be so physically simple, to rock against his leg and build up the fire that he's started to stoke. Realistically though, it would be so very complicated.

Perhaps he can see these inner thoughts spiraling through my head, because he says, "If you really don't want to be my handhold, why haven't you pulled away?"

"You're the one who should pull away, as you were the one to touch first."

He doesn't let go. Instead, he lifts his thigh, just an inch. An inch that makes my entire body jolt. His firm body *right* there...

His dark, dangerous eyes with flints of speckled light delve into me. I itch to reach up and trace the pigmented skin around his lips. To slide my hand under his clothing and rest it against his bare chest, just to soak in more of his warmth.

It's wrong. Entirely, thoroughly wrong. He was supposed to kill me. Maybe he still will, but that danger makes it all the sweeter.

His gaze drops down to my lips, and I forget how to breathe.

Wrong and *Want* blare through me like opposing knocks on either side of a door. Which side will swing open?

Giving me plenty of time to decide, he lowers his head ever so slowly. He's not shaking anymore. His exhaustion seems to have been replaced with a fiery hunger that awakens something inside of me. Makes another icy chip in my chest crack off.

Just before his mouth can press against mine, I turn my head abruptly, panic sluicing down my ribs and soaking into my lungs. "I…I'm still married in the eyes of the gods."

He freezes.

Shame and regret slam into me. I don't know why I said that. I *wanted* him to kiss me. Wanted it *desperately*, and therein lies the problem, because this desperation feels utterly terrifying. Still, I wish I could take the words back, shove them past my molars, and grind them into dust.

"Married?" he hisses. "He hired me to fucking *kill* you."

"Yes, well, it's not a very loving marriage."

He scoffs. "Don't turn cold on me now, Queenie. Just admit it. You like this, don't you?"

"I will *not* admit that," I snip, refusing to look at him, gaze trained on the mountainside instead.

"Interesting choice of words. You didn't answer the question, did you?"

It hasn't escaped my notice that he's still holding on to me, and I do nothing to pull away. My legs part ever so slightly, hips still turned in his direction. If I were to take a single step, our bodies would be completely flush against each other…

"Admit it…" His words are right at my ear, hot breath ruffling my white hair. "I bet if I were to slip my hand beneath your skirt, I'd find the Cold Queen isn't so cold between her thighs."

He yanks me forward, tearing a gasp from my throat, my head tilting up at him as my lips part in shock. Shock…and a surge of desire.

One hand drops down, and he suddenly grips me *right* over my core, my layers of clothing bunching up at his touch. An unbidden moan slips past my lips that makes his mouth curl in a predatory smirk.

"Admit that there's a needy throb beating in your clit, that this cunt is searing hot, aching for me to sink my fingers into it."

I lift my chin in defiance, even though I'm panting. "It's not, *assassin.*"

He laughs darkly, making a thrill pulse through me, my body doing just as he said. "I love when you get haughty and show your claws. It makes me want to bend you over and take you down a notch."

That image immediately springs to my mind and makes a whine crawl up my throat.

"You like that, don't you?"

"No."

"Keep lying," he says, teeth flashing with elation. "I fucking *like* it. It reminds me of being on the chase for one of my marks. And do you know *why* I like the chase?" He scrapes his mouth against my neck, and I know the coarse hair of his beard will leave marks on my delicate skin, but I find I like that too. "It heats my blood. Makes me want to taunt my target. To draw out the hunt even more before my…blade sinks into them." He punctuates the word *blade* with two of his fingers hooking up against me.

I gasp. Want surges, my thighs trembling as my hips drop forward to seek out more of the touch, reaching for something right out of my grasp.

Then he suddenly lets me go, and I'm the one left swaying and panting this time, staring after him in shock. "What are you doing?" I demand breathlessly.

He starts walking off, though over his shoulder he tosses the words, "Still married, right?"

My mouth gapes wordlessly.

"Are you going to sit down, Queenie? Or do you prefer to hunch there till you collapse?"

Insufferable assassin.

But a foreign, strange thing happens.

I smile.

And I don't think I've done that in a very, very long time.

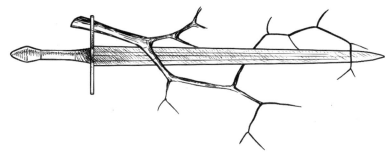

CHAPTER 24

OSRIK

I spend the morning at the barracks in a fight circle to get out some fucking aggression. Punching people took the edge off, and then the training exercises I did alongside my soldiers took off some corners too.

But it all bends back into sharp angles as soon as I get back to the castle to bathe and dress. By the time I'm walking down the corridor toward the mender wing, I'm crushed by it.

Just when I'm about to make it to Rissa's room, I hear raised voices, and when I yank open the door to go inside, I find her thrashing. Head swiveling left and right, back arching up off the bed. Her clothes are soaked through with sweat, and there's three novice menders holding her down while Hojat tries to redo her stitches.

"Stop! You're fucking hurting her!" I growl.

"Captain Osrik, you need to wait outside!" Hojat says.

Fuck that.

I push past the novices, moving them aside so they let

Rissa go. I clasp her face in my hands. "Yellow Bell. Hold still."

Her teeth are gritted so tightly I fear she's gonna break her jaw. "Why's she so fucking hot?"

"She's feverish," Hojat says. "Her wound…"

I straighten up, hands dropping to my sides. Rissa lies back, whimpering in her sleep.

"Let me see."

The mender hesitates. "Captain…"

"Let. Me. See."

Hojat pauses for a second, but then he reaches forward and pulls aside the buttoned part of her nightgown to reveal the wound. A breath hisses out of me. The skin around the stitches is swollen and red. Cloudy pus seeps from it, and the stitches still caught into the jagged skin are crusted with blood.

"It's infected," I say thickly.

"Yes, it is."

My eyes shoot to his. "How could this fucking happen?"

Hojat's face is grim. "I have been diligent, Captain, but her wound is very deep and very severe. We were lucky to stave off infection this long."

"It should be healing!"

His eyes go to his novices, and I hear them skitter out of the room without a word. When we're alone, he says, "Captain, I need you to prepare yourself."

My shoulders bunch with defensiveness. "For what?"

"For Lady Rissa's death."

I look at him with fire in my eyes that burns straight from my gut. "No. I do not accept that."

"Then you are in denial, and that is worse."

I can't stand the look on his face. Some softhearted sympathy that I don't fucking want. My teeth grind, that angry burn in my stomach threatening to tear right through my skin.

"Fix her!"

"I am trying—"

"You are our mender, so *mend her*!"

Rissa whimpers again.

"It's not that simple," Hojat says quietly, like he thinks if he lowers his voice, I'll lower mine. That if he's calm, I'll be calm.

But how can I be fucking calm when her body is spreading with infection and she hasn't been coherent in weeks? "I am doing everything I can. I will continue to do all I can. And right now, that means I need to finish cleaning Lady Rissa's wound and changing out her stitches so I can then try to bring down her fever and get some liquids into her. You need to let me do that."

I start to pace like a wild beast caught in a cage, nearly tearing out my hair as I run my hands through it. "She can't die."

"We mortals don't control that, Captain."

I want to rip apart this room stone by stone and send it crashing into the fucking mountain. Instead, I turn and march out, only to nearly trample over a woman. She isn't one of the novices, that much is clear, since they all wear mender robes, and she's dressed more like a saddle.

She takes a step back and tucks her blonde hair behind her ear. "I'm looking for Rissa, is she here?"

"Who're you?" I bark.

She narrows her blue eyes. "I'm Polly. I heard from one of the soldiers down at the saddle house that she was hurt."

Right. Polly. The saddle who Rissa was tending to while she was coming down off the fucking dew. The Polly who treated Rissa like fucking trash.

She moves to go inside the room, but I block her way. "You're not needed here. Rissa is being taken care of."

Polly crosses her arms in defiance. "I'm her friend, and I

want to see her."

I look her over. "Not high off dew anymore, I take it?"

Anger surges over her face. "Who do you think you are?"

"*I'm* her fucking friend. And you don't see her without my permission."

Her face pinches, eyes glaring at me. "Just ask her! She'll want to see me."

"I can't fucking ask her because she can't fucking wake up!"

Polly's eyes go wide, the anger seeping out of her like I pulled up the stopper on a fucking drain. Then they get all watery, ready to leak out. "How…how bad is it?" she asks tentatively, arms dropping to her sides.

"She might fucking die. That's how it is. That what you want to hear?" I snarl.

She flinches.

"*Please*," she says, her tone now quiet and pleading. "Let me see her. I need to."

When she sees I'm going to say no, she reaches out and grips my hand. "*Please*," she begs again. "I know I wasn't…" She quickly wipes away a tear. "She sat with me when I was sick. Just let me return the favor."

I want to say no. Maybe because I want to punish her for being so fucking awful to Rissa as we traveled here. Or maybe just because I'm an asshole. But it's not about me.

"Fine," I growl, watching as relief spreads over her face. "But not because you deserve it. Because *she* does."

Polly nods. "Thank you."

I step aside, and she wastes no time slipping into the room. I stand there for a second, and then I see the novices coming back down the corridor, holding supplies for Rissa. I stop one of them. "I need a spare needle and thread."

The woman eyes me curiously but hands them over.

Then I turn and head downstairs.

Time to pay a visit to the dungeons.

When I get down to the cell, Manu is lying on the pallet, staring up at the ceiling. I look at the empty bowl and water pitcher on the floor. The menders managed to get some liquids into Rissa yesterday, which means Manu got liquids too.

Lucky him.

As soon as I close the door behind me, he jolts to a sitting position. His vest is gaping, tunic loose. His clothes are filthy, his hair greasy, eyes bloodshot. I haven't come down here since he first arrived. Wanted to let him wallow in fear. Wanted him to feel helpless.

Because that's exactly how I fucking feel.

I can't make Rissa better. No matter how many times I order her to, order Hojat to, she doesn't get better. She doesn't open her eyes.

And now…

I clench my fists and stare at the man responsible for sneaking Second's men in. For one of them stabbing Rissa in the chest. For the fact that she's upstairs with a raging fever and infected blood.

"Lie down."

He looks me over warily. "I'm surprised it took you so long to return, Captain." He pauses. "How is she?"

"You hoping she died so I can fucking snap your neck and put you out of your misery?" I snarl.

"No. I…" Something crosses over his expression. "I didn't mean for her to get hurt. My sister needed me to get Auren to the Conflux. The other lady was just in the wrong place at the wrong time."

"Rissa. That *other fucking lady* is Rissa."

"Rissa." He says it like he's getting a taste for it, and that just pisses me off even more.

"Don't say her fucking name."

"You don't want me to call her lady. You don't want me to call her by name. What do you want, Captain?"

"I want her to *not be dying*!"

The confession comes out of me like a roar. I fucking hate it.

Hate him.

My anger is a corpse dragging behind me. Weighing me down. Plugging my nose with its stench. Death surrounding me.

"Is she? Dying?" Manu asks carefully.

That question makes me want to hurl my fist through the wall. Instead, I kick the leg of his bed, making him almost fall over. "On your back."

I'm a little surprised that he actually does it.

A little disappointed too. I was hoping for a fight because this pent-up rage wants to go somewhere, and I want to take it out on him.

When he's lying down, I yank out the needle and thread from the pouch in my pocket. "It's your lucky day. Rissa's getting new stitches. So you're getting stitches."

He doesn't say a word, but he flinches when I tug back his collar. And then my furious eyes lift up from his wound to his face.

He's down here in his own piss and shit, with wet air and drab light. Eating scraps on the floor like a rat, if he gets any at all. He's here with no one to tend to his wound, and somehow, he's fucking *healing*. With no medicines or salves. He doesn't even have clean rags.

Meanwhile, Rissa is upstairs with the best mender in Fourth Kingdom, being tended to night and day, getting all the best medicines and being kept perfectly clean, and she's *dying*.

How the fuck is that right? How is that *fair*?

I stab the needle through his scabbed-over skin. Hard. I start threading it, making him bleed, tugging the thick string in tight loops and sloppy slashes. His skin goes bloody and tight, stretching at wrong angles, and I should feel some sort of vindication every time he makes a noise of pain, but I feel nothing.

Nothing but this helpless rage.

I don't like feeling helpless. I'm supposed to make others feel that way. I was a damn mercenary for fuck's sake. I made men piss their pants just by being in the same room with them. I'm not supposed to be the helpless one.

I continue to stitch up the wound in a crass, painful crisscross. I just keep lancing deep into his skin and pulling as tight as I can, making blood stream down from all the different spots I've pierced him through.

"This making you feel better?" the asshole asks.

"Sure fucking does," I lie.

I do another stitch. Get another flinch.

"No, it doesn't," Manu says quietly, and I want to punch him in the fucking mouth so he can't say anymore stupid shit.

I feel his eyes on my face as I continue to stab. Thread. Pull.

With his teeth clenched in pain, he says, "I am sorry. For what happened to her. And I deserve it. All of it."

My hand pauses. Gaze stuck on the seeping blood.

"I don't fall for that martyr shit."

He gives off a bitter laugh. "I'm no martyr, Captain. I'm just a man who can admit when he's wrong, and I was wrong."

I stab again. Close enough to the other puncture that it ruins the stitch. "That's not going to save you."

"I know," he says with resolve.

"Then why fucking bother?"

He lifts his other shoulder in a shrug. "My sister was the only family I had who ever cared about me. I was born without magic. That was my first mistake in my family's eyes. My second mistake was marrying another man. My father didn't take too kindly to *that*, because he wanted me to bind myself to a woman who could birth heirs. My third mistake was watching Kaila be married off to a disgusting suitor and not stepping in."

"You think I give a shit?"

"No, but Kaila always gave a shit. When she became queen, she was still taking care of me. Still trusting me, even when I'd let her down. I vowed to never let her down again. To always trust her, to carry out everything she needed."

"Yeah, like kidnapping Auren and sending her to her death."

He cringes. "I swore blind loyalty to my sister. It wasn't personal."

"If you turn a blind eye in the name of loyalty, then you don't deserve to see."

Manu goes quiet.

I know what loyalty is. I'm loyal to the Wrath. I'm loyal to Rip. All of us, every single one, have done fucked-up shit. But I *never* turned my head so I didn't have to look. I always watched head-on. If you're going to commit the crime, you better look it right in the face. Because if you can't, then you know not to fucking do it.

"You would do it again," I say, because we both know it's true. "Don't pretend otherwise."

He actually has the honesty to shrug. "I like Auren. But I love my sister. She needed it to be done, so I did it."

"And an innocent woman is going to die because of it. Auren nearly did too, while you fucking watched."

His face has gone sallow. "I regret that more than you will believe."

I shake my head, holding up the needle to stab him again, but I stop. I suddenly don't want to do it anymore. Don't want to be here. Don't want to listen to him. With a snarl, I yank off the needle and leave the loose thread to dangle, getting stuck in one of the streams of blood. I shove the needle back into the pouch in my pocket and move toward the cell door.

"Auren," Manu suddenly says. "Is she okay?"

"You don't fucking care about her either," I snarl, feeling even more wound up.

"I do, unfortunately," Manu replies with a rueful smile. "That's the problem. It would be so much easier if I didn't care. I think you of all people understand that, Captain."

I glare at him, saying nothing. Then I turn and kick his food tray on my way out the cell door. After locking him back up, I stomp away, feeling no better than when I first walked in here. Feeling fucking *worse*.

Because he's right. It would all be so much easier if I didn't care.

But I found a Yellow Bell growing up out of the ground despite the shitty surroundings, and as soon as I decided I wanted to pick it up and keep it, I was ruined. Ruined with fucking caring for her.

And now I can't stop.

I can't stop, and she can't keep going.

So what's the fucking point.

CHAPTER 25

AUREN

"Stay down."

Wick's mouthed order seems loud, even though he's silent. He's gripping my arm like he's nervous that I'll move, but I know we need to stay absolutely still.

The forest is veiled with thick gray mist that we can barely see through, the ground wet and dense with underbrush. I'm flat on my belly, hands braced against the mud and grass as I stare through the haze.

Ahead of us, a hundred Stone Swords march.

I can feel their every step reverberating up my perched limbs. Their muffled conversations are trapped in the humidity, murmured words I'm unable to decipher. They keep to their winding path, which is barely more than a game trail, and I watch the procession of their blotted silhouettes with wariness.

Around us, pinpricks of phosphorescence shine mutely from the tips of grassy spires, frosting the air with a blue glow that makes the soldiers' shadows look even eerier.

The branchless trees that grow here are shaped like squiggles, as if a child took up a quill and darted it left and right over the paper, bending the line in soft curves all the way to the ground. Most of the sunlight is blocked because each tree has a single giant leaf sprouting from its top, opening like a shell and holding pearly blooms in its pocket that bugs and birds keep flying into.

It's the strangest-looking forest I've ever been in, and peppered all around me, hidden in the brush, are the other Vulmin lying in wait too. We're all watchful and silent, twelve of us hidden in this murky gloom.

I'm glad the mist obscures us, but we'll be spotted if we move or make a sound. So I force my breaths to stay even, force my body to stay frozen in place.

Beside me, Wick almost seems to blend into nature itself. As if he's used to hiding, used to becoming as still as the trees. Droplets of moisture are beading up against his russet skin, and his heavy brow is pulled down in concentration as his muddy eyes stare through the grass.

Things have smoothed out between us since our rocky start.

Over the course of the week that we've been traveling together, I've been able to observe him. The rebel leader seems to be good at what he does. He knows Annwyn like the back of his hand, and he doesn't dive headfirst into fights or kill without thought. Instead, he considers every move with serious calculation and seems to put the other Vulmin before his own safety.

After leaving Geisel, we met up with the rest of his group outside the city. Ever since, we've been on the move, sleeping outside beneath the stars and riding each day as we travel toward one of their safe houses.

But we keep getting deterred with the presence of more

Stone Swords on the road. I think it's safe to guess that word of what happened in Geisel has spread, and the royal guards are searching for me.

This group of soldiers nearly snuck up on us.

Luckily, we'd stopped to rest the horses when our scout spotted them. We only had minutes to take our horses off the path, and then we crouched down here to hide and watch. Watch, but not intervene. Not be seen. Those are Wick's orders.

I look over at him and make the smallest gesture at the soldiers, but he shakes his head sternly and mouths, *no magic.*

He wants to go undetected, wants us to get to our destination without anyone being able to track where we've been, so I understand the need to hide out of sight. Still, it's frustrating to do nothing when a threat is so near. I have to huddle here and watch enemies who might be searching for me as they tromp by, their booted steps sloshing through the muck.

Frustration bubbles through my blood.

Apparently, it's my fate for kings and queens to see me as a threat, no matter what world I'm in.

All I want to do is find Slade.

It should be simple. I should be able to travel across Annwyn, searching the sky for a rip. I should be able to question people and try to figure out how to get back to him. With the magic here in Annwyn, there *has* to be a way. Someone did it before, even if I don't remember how. I still ended up in Orea as a girl, so I'm determined to make it happen again. But the circumstances here have made it more difficult.

Bright side? Even though these Stone Swords and politics are complicating things, I'm still traveling, still able to cover ground. So I'm making progress in my search. I won't let these soldiers or anyone else stop me from my goal.

I know Slade, so I know he's out of his mind trying to get to me. I know that he feels the same restlessness, the same fierce worry and furious determination that I do.

Nothing will be right until we're reunited.

I look down at the gold that's slicked against my palms, at the lines of rot running through it. We'll find each other. He's already a part of me, in more ways than one.

When Wick's hand suddenly tenses on my arm, my thoughts are torn away, and I wrench up my gaze.

Instantly, I notice the source of his unease. One of the Stone Swords has walked away from the trail.

He's coming this way.

I can see the bulky lines of his armor through the mist, the shape of the sword strapped to his back. My breath sucks into my chest as I press harder against the ground. I can feel the tension in the rest of the group grow thicker than the condensed air.

The guard continues to walk toward us, steps sucking into the mud as the grass swishes at his knees. My heartbeat comes up into my throat, my focus sharpened as I track his movements through the haze. More gold smears against my palms, roots of rot ready to dig into the ground.

He's coming closer.

Closer.

My eyes dart to Wick, but he jerks his head again, telling me to wait. Every single Vulmin is probably ready to spring into action, the nerves of the group winding together like a tangible knot.

He's ten steps away now. If he gets much closer, he'll see us.

Seven steps.

Five.

He abruptly stops.

I don't breathe or blink. If he thought he saw something

and has come over to search more thoroughly, I'll have to use my magic on him. I can't avoid it.

Wick's hand digs into my arm even harder, but I shoot him a look. Gold gathers beneath my hands, congealing in a puddle, readying...

A stream of piss abruptly hits the ground in front of us with a splash.

Oh.

All the tension whooshes out of me, and Wick's grip loosens. My nose wrinkles as the stench of urine wafts over us, so strong it makes my eyes water. If the guard took three more steps, he'd probably be peeing right on Wick's head.

Might be kind of funny.

Laughter threatens to bubble up my throat at the thought, but I bite my lip and hold it down. It's probably not the best time for that.

The Stone Sword pees for a *long* time. So long that it's almost impressive. Though if I get so much as a drip of it splashed on me, it's really going to sour my mood.

Finally, the stream cuts off, and luckily, I'm drip-free. I watch his boots as he stuffs himself back into his pants and then turns away. He walks over and rejoins the others, his form once more masked through the brume as he falls back in line.

A breath of relief flows past my lips, and Wick and I exchange a look.

That was close.

The rotted gold on the ground continues to lie in wait as I monitor the rest of the royal guard. The power sings to me in a hushed whisper, like a silent melody only I can hear.

I like the sound. But I don't let it take over like I did in Geisel.

After a few more minutes, the last soldier finally passes by, and everything grows quiet and still once again. Wick, however, doesn't indicate for us to move quite yet. My body is cramping from holding position, and my clothes are soaked, but we wait until he lets out the softest birdcall to signal us to move.

I get up with a stretch, trying to relieve my tense muscles. I dry up my gold, letting it sink back into my skin, and then together, our group starts picking our way through the forest.

The other Vulmin nod to me, letting me and Wick pass them to take the lead. They keep their distance as we walk. Actually, they keep their distance pretty much always.

They watch me with the same awe as the people in the field did. For the most part, they treat me with a sort of reverence that keeps me separated from them. They seem to think of me as another leader alongside Wick.

I don't know how to feel about that. I'm not sure how Wick feels about it either.

I keep watching him out of the corner of my eye, trying to determine if it bothers him that his people are looking to me. I've seen nothing so far, but I don't know him well enough to read his expressions, so I keep my guard up.

Because one thing that usually threatens a man is the thought of being replaced by a woman.

Not that I *want* to lead the rebels, but I don't want to lead a kingdom either, and that doesn't seem to be stopping the fae monarchy from trying to kill me.

It would be really great if monarchs could stop wanting me dead.

At least I have the most powerful king of them all on my side. When Slade and I find each other, he's going to be *so* pissed at this King Carrick.

I'd like to see the Stone King try to go up against my King Rot. Carrick doesn't stand a chance.

Pride flutters in my chest.

GOLD

I will find you, I promise silently.

I don't care how many cities I have to visit, how many fae I need to talk to—I'm going to figure out how to get to him.

I let magic breathe out of me, wrapping around my wrists to keep myself busy. I manipulate the rivulets, making them braid around my arm, the motions keeping me occupied, keeping me centered.

It's been a week since Geisel, a week since Nenet was killed. I've been trying to get my bearings during these endless hours of travel, not only with Annwyn or the Vulmin or Wick, but with myself too.

And I've been doing what Nenet told me to.

I listen.

I listen to the Vulmin day and night, gleaning any information I can from them. It's a bit like feeling my way through a strange house in the dark because everything is unfamiliar. So every conversation I overhear, every new place that we pass, I try to take it all in and learn about Annwyn and the Vulmin as much as I can.

And when I'm not listening to them, I'm listening to *me.*

Whenever I get a chance to go off alone, I use my magic. I listen to the new seductive call that purrs through the rot. I've found that it's not unlike my gold's push for destruction, and I mastered that once, so I can master this too. I practice as often as I can, letting it leak out of me, just to reel it back in. I learned my lesson again in Geisel—that I either control my power or it will control me.

And I won't let anything control me ever again.

I'm not sure how I have Slade's magic embedded with mine, but I suspect it has something to do with that piece of rot that stayed inside of me. It's a deadly, heady power, and I *have* to keep hold of the reins. They've melded together somehow, the rot coming out every time I call to my own power. They're intertwined, as if my gold and his rot are one.

I like knowing that even apart, I have a piece of him with me. It's a comforting presence to have his magic woven with mine, as if it's reminding me that we'll never be truly ripped apart from one another.

Tilting my head up, I peer up at the fragments of sky through the gaps in the trees as I walk. It's my constant habit. I'm always looking up. Always searching for a rip.

Always hoping I'll see one.

Wick looks up with me, probably wondering why I keep doing it, but he doesn't ask, and I don't give up the information.

We're quiet as we make our way through the twisting grove, just in case there are any lingering Stone Swords, but we make it back without issue. Our horses are right where we left them around a shallow gully, their appearance stark against the white tree trunks, their colors cutting through the mist. Seeing them is always a jolting reminder that I'm in Annwyn and not Orea, because they're so much more colorful and unique here.

Blush, the horse I've been riding, has pale gray hair with stripes of opal that run down her sides. The prism streaks are also threaded through her mane and tail, which shine beautifully at night.

Wick's mount is the boldest looking. Instead of swirls or stripes or speckles like the other horses, it has a tri-color of harsh blocks. Brown for its hindquarters, black for its middle, and red at the front. Its muzzle and mane are completely red, the very same color as dripping blood.

It's a bit off-putting.

As we gather around our horses, Ludogar, Wick's right hand, comes walking over. He has shrewd teal eyes and ocean-spray hair the color of the sea, with a foamy white at the scalp. It's in the same style as Wick, with the sides of his head shaved short, and a long strip down the middle that he leaves hanging over his right ear.

I haven't been around him much. He often travels ahead or patrols while we rest. He seems to be as busy and serious as the leader himself, always with some job to do.

I give my horse a pat while Ludogar stops beside Wick. "This is the second group that's been headed in the same direction as us," he says, voice dropped. "Where do you think they're going?"

Wick wipes at his muddied shirt. "Has to be the capital."

I peer around my horse to see Ludogar frown. "But why? There have been way too many reports of him calling for more guards to return there. Why has he drafted so many over the past couple of months? What the hell is Carrick doing with so many soldiers?"

"We're going to find out when we get there," Wick tells him, and I feel his eyes flick over to me. I pretend that I'm not eavesdropping as I swing myself back into the saddle.

"I don't like it," Ludogar says. "Something is happening and we need to find out what it is."

"We will."

Wick's determined answer seems to satisfy Ludogar, because the male nods and walks off to his own horse. Within minutes, we're all mounted, and Wick leads the way, steering us in a slightly different direction than the soldiers without going too far off course.

I ride beside him, maneuvering around the trees and the thickest part of the glowing grass, gaze scanning through the heavy mist. My shirt is covered in mud and starting to dry against my skin in scratchy patches. I wipe at it, but it just smears even more.

Wick looks over and clears his throat. "We'll get to the safe house by nightfall," he assures me, expression looking sympathetic. "I know it's been a hard week of travel as we head toward Werrith."

"I'm not bothered by the travel," I tell him, and I mean it. Because seeing more of Annwyn is…magical. Even when the mist feels like it's trying to choke me, even when I'm covered in mud, I'm still very much taken with how beautiful it is here. The colors are alive, the air is sweeter, the breezes seem softer. The land itself thrums with life and power. It's so very different from Orea.

Wick nods and we fall back into silence, which is what usually ends up happening. While things between us have been smoother, there's an awkwardness that seems to exist, like he doesn't quite know how to talk to me.

It's not like the other Vulmin—they keep me set apart out of reverence. Wick seems to do it because he's guarded. He watches me, and I watch him, and it's like we're dancing around each other, trying to figure each other out.

I don't get a malicious sense from him, but I definitely don't trust him yet either. That's why I'll keep listening. Keep trying to observe everything I can about him. Although, I suppose the leader of a massive rebellion would have reason to be guarded.

But so do I.

He's true to his word though, because we reach the safe house by nightfall just like he said.

By the time the mist finally thins, I feel soaked, even through my cloak. The forest has changed, giving way to branched-out trees. They look more like the ones in Orea, with sharp green leaves and rough bark, and there's a dusting of moss along the ground that has sprigs of purple flowers swirled through.

Our horses clomp over the stubby grass that no longer glows, and my stomach rumbles with hunger. I'm looking forward to eating and cleaning up and then passing out on any surface other than the dirt ground.

Stuffed right in the middle of the wooded area, we come

upon the sprawled-out safe house. It's in the shape of a horseshoe, and it seems like its sole purpose for being built was to wrap around a cluster of giant green boulders that match the moss at our feet.

The house is all one level, the roof low like it doesn't want to compete with the towering trees. It has curved gray siding that's only interrupted by the thin slats of windows as narrow as my arm, which doesn't allow much of a glimpse inside.

Probably good for a rebel house.

We leave the horses in a corral and connected stable, its roof ribbed and speckled with fallen leaves. There are other horses already in the stalls, plus food and water waiting in the troughs.

When we head for the main house, I can see light coming from the skinny windows and hear noises from inside.

This safe house already has Vulmin in it.

I glance to Wick with questions in my gaze, but he gives me an indecipherable look before his eyes fall to the cloak around my shoulders. "Pull your hood up."

My back immediately stiffens. "Why?"

"Just keep it up for now."

He turns and starts walking off before I can ask him more, and my nerves skitter like tiny feet crawling down my back. I subconsciously pull at the ribbons wound around my waist, debating for a moment if I should stay behind, but then I tug my hood over my head and start forward.

I mentally list all the gold I have on me. Arm cuffs. Thick belt. Clasp at the end of my braid. Bracelets around my wrists. All this gold I have at my disposal to use at night, just in case. So that I'm not helpless even when the sun has set and I can't call new gold forward.

It's comforting, because I don't like what's happening right now. Don't like this ominous order to wear my hood and keep concealed. This damn safe house was supposed to feel *safe*. Irritation prickles through me, and I glare at the back of Wick's head as I walk.

As we head for the curved entrance, I keep my eyes peeled. My head swings left and right, and I'm half-expecting someone to jump out from behind a tree and attack me, but no one does.

We tread past the giant boulders, our reflections gleaming in their jade surface. There are spokes of glowing lanterns stabbed into the ground at our feet, their flames flickering in the breeze. At the inside center of the house's bend lies the front door, and there's a broken-winged bird symbol carved into the low-hanging eave just above it.

But my gaze hooks onto the fae standing there waiting for us.

I stay at the back of the group, watching as the male smiles at our approach. His hair looks like the head of a broccoli stalk, tufted in clusters of emerald-green florets, his eyes matching that very same hue.

"It's good to see you again so soon," he says in greeting.

Wick clasps his arm. "It was short notice, so I apologize, Dren."

"No apology needed. The house is always full anyway, so what's a few more?" he asks jovially before turning and opening the door.

I frown. *Why is Wick making me hide if this fae seems so welcoming?*

He leads the way, and our group files into a wide-open room with at least a dozen people inside. Some of them are eating at long benches, others are propped up against the walls, a few are sleeping in various spots along the floor, and there's a group playing cards and drinking.

The bent room feels a bit like standing in the middle of a curving river, but it glows from the flames in the fireplace and a few sconces on the walls, making it feel warm and dim. There's also a medley of furniture inside, with mismatched chairs and sofas, rugs and pillows, benches and tables. All different shapes, sizes, colors, and material. As if they gathered whatever they could and stuffed it in here to accommodate as many people as possible.

As our group clusters in, a few of the fae call out greetings, obviously familiar with one another. I continue to stay behind everyone, keeping my back to the wall, my every sense on alert. I make my gold bracelets melt down, pooling the liquid into my hands, tiny lines of rot swimming through it that flick against my skin.

"Got more of us here than usual. Did that repair up in Breeton Village like you asked. Took a lot of hands. The Stone Swords did a number on it," Dren says with a shake of his head. "But we still have plenty of room. There's food in the kitchen, and you can claim whatever open spot you want for sleep. Stay as long as you like."

Wick nods but tells him, "One night will be plenty, and I'm hoping when we leave, you all will come with us."

Dren looks over, frowning with confusion. "Come with you? Why would we all come with you?"

"Because we have a sign from the goddesses that it's time to do more."

Quiet confusion stuffs itself into every corner of the room. "What sign?"

Wick shifts to the side pointedly and turns around to face me, and the rest of our group steps aside too. "Auren?" he murmurs.

I blink in surprise, uneasiness shifting through my gut. But as he continues to look at me expectantly, I relent and tug back my hood, letting it fall.

The moment I do, all eyes swing to me, and I hear several people gasp.

Dren's eyes have gone as wide as saucers as he stares, the blood draining from his face. "What... She's *gold*. She...she has gold skin like..."

"Like the Lyäri Ulvêre," Wick finishes.

Someone drops something to the floor, and a clatter fills the room. Seems to shatter everyone's shock into a thousand pieces.

Dren shakes his head in disbelief. "But she's dead. The little golden girl was gone. Is this some kind of a trick?"

"No trick, and she's not dead." Wick glances at me, something indiscernible in his eyes as he watches me. "She found her way back."

Every gaze in the room is stuck to me, their unblinking regard clinging to my face. Even the fae who were sleeping have been kicked awake, so I truly have *everyone's* undivided attention.

Irritation swivels up from the scrutiny, tension tightening in my shoulders as I give Wick a look. He didn't have me wear my hood to conceal myself for protection, but so that he could make a dramatic spectacle out of me.

Anger claws down my back, leaving me to fume with the scrapes.

"Auren Turley," Dren breathes. "How can this be?"

"The fates," Wick answers, tone full of authority. "You know what this means, don't you?"

Everyone waits, still and watchful.

Wick's gaze seems to scan over each and every one of them. "It's time for us to mobilize."

Several fae look between each other with concern. A few nod in solidarity. Dren blanches. "*Mobilize*? But we work in the shadows, Wick. You know the Vulmin do everything we can, but what you're asking..."

Wick swings a hand in my direction. "Look at her, Dren. This is the *Lyäri Ulvêre*. She's returned, and she's here for a

294

reason. It's our time," he says with vehemence. "With her, we can finally take a stand. No more shadows. She's brought the dawn with her. Every single Vulmin knows her story. She will help bring us together and forge the way."

I grind my teeth to keep from snarling. I knew what Wick was hoping for when I joined him, but I made my stance clear on being treated like a tool or a prop, and I thought he understood that.

Obviously, he doesn't.

It's one thing to agree to help, it's another to be exploited without consent. The gold in my hand grows hotter, flamed by my ire.

"We're ready," Wick goes on firmly, feet braced, shoulders back. "It's time to fight. Time to take back Annwyn. We need everyone to band together now. Who will join us? Who will step out of the shadows and follow Annwyn's new dawn?"

Silence squeezes between every fae. Their expressions wring out, divulging their inner thoughts, gazes still poring over my face. They're full of surprise, acknowledgment, anticipation, and all of these things douse through the room. Beside me, I can feel Wick's charged expectation like a bolt of lightning ready to surge into the ground.

At the back, someone steps forward, still clutching the cards he'd been playing. "I'll step out of the shadows."

"Me too," someone else says.

"And me."

"I will too."

"I'll stand with the Lyäri."

One by one, they all give their oaths. Like a trickle of promises raining over us, saturating the entire group and buoying them. While for me, it feels like a weight, making it hard to keep my head above water.

Dren nods, one final drop from the downpour to condense

around us. "Alright," he says soberly. "The Werrith Vulmin are with you."

I stand outside the rebel house, arms crossed, leaning against the smooth boulders. I'm tucked between a couple of the smaller ones, perfect to perch on as I watch the narrow window ahead. It shows a glimpse of the kitchen inside, shows the back of Wick's head where he sits at the table with the others, his black hair molded in a tight braid and tied off at his neck.

We've been traveling together for a week. A whole week, and not once did he deign to tell me about this plan of his to incite more Vulmin to join us tonight.

I feel used.

Used and utterly *pissed*.

When I see him stand from the table and walk out of the kitchen, I stay right here, because I know he'll come to me.

Sure enough, a couple minutes later, I hear the door open and shut. Hear booted steps. Then, he appears in front of me. An awkward silence blots the night air, staining us as we stare at one another.

"You haven't eaten yet."

"Too busy chewing on that display you orchestrated," I retort.

A tic in his jaw jumps, but I can see he's not surprised at my anger. He expected it. "I needed them to see you."

"You should have asked me first," I grit out. "What you did in there was *not* okay."

His expression hardens with irritation. "You joined us, Auren. I thought you knew what you were getting into."

I surge up, pushing away from the boulder to square off with him. "I was clear that I had no interest in being a symbol or being used, but that's exactly what you made me feel like tonight," I fume. "You had plenty of opportunities all week to discuss this with me. To speak to me about this plan of yours."

"I don't discuss plans with new Vulmin," he says evenly, as if I'm being the unreasonable one. "I can't divulge information to you. Especially when you turned me down the first time I asked for you to join us."

My eyes narrow. "So because I didn't leap at the chance to join the Vulmin when you first asked, you're acting like an ass?"

Anger flushes over his cheeks. "You have to earn my trust. Just like anyone else who joins."

"Trust goes both ways. And if you *ever* use me like that again without asking me first, you will regret it."

He glares with intensity. "Funny. That sounded like a threat."

"Oh good. Your ears are working, then."

Tension mounts between us, braiding as thick and tight as his hair. I cross my arms in front of me, nails biting into my skin as I stare him down.

Wick blasts out a breath of frustration, his eyes glinting off the spokes of flame from the short lanterns dotted around the path. "You may be the Lyäri, but I lead the Vulmin, and I have to act in their best interest. Right now, I know that *this* is the time we need to strike. You're here for a reason, and everyone will see that. As word spreads of your arrival—and it *is* spreading—I can finally get everyone to band together. To not solely work behind the curtains, but to oppose the monarchy head-on."

I can see the fervency and belief of his words stitched into every line of his face.

"I respect your role as their leader. What I *don't* respect is being used without you consulting me first. I'm not a tool, Wick. I'm not just going to stand still and look golden so that

Vulmin will line up behind you. If you want my help, then you fucking ask me for it."

After the eye-opening events of Geisel, I *want* to help his cause, but not like this. I'm also not foolish—I know it's better to journey with him as I search Annwyn for Slade. I don't want to travel alone, but I will if I have to.

Our gazes stay locked on one another, this battle of wills caught in a silent clash.

"Just give me the respect of talking to me about things that involve me. That's all I'm asking. I'm not your enemy, Wick."

My words seem to disarm him, and he finally drops his weaponized glare. "I know you're not my enemy."

"Then act like it."

A puff of air escapes him, and the tense line of his brow eases. "You're right. I'm sorry, Auren."

His apology takes me off guard, and my arms drop as I shift on my feet.

He lets out a tired sigh and runs a hand down his hair. "You want to know the plan?"

"Yes."

"The plan was to stop at all the major Vulmin houses. To avoid the cities where the Stone Swords have the biggest presence, until there's enough of us that it won't matter. To gather more and more of us together until we get all the way to Lydia—the kingdom's capital. Then, challenge the Stone King," he tells me, his eyes flaring with determination. "Show the Carricks that we won't stand for their regime any longer. That we're going to take back Annwyn."

He's talking about full-out war. Marching on the capital is no minor thing.

His eyes bounce between mine expectantly, but my lips are pressed tight. The only sound is faint chirping coming from somewhere in the forest, though my mind is loud with the reverberations of his expectations.

At my continued silence, his shoulders sag ever so slightly. I watch as he deflates, letting me really see the *person* instead of just the leader. Giving me a glimpse of who he is behind his stoicism and allowing me to see the vulnerability and desperation beneath.

His tone shifts to something softer, his eyes carrying an impassioned honesty within their depths. "They *kill* us. Turley sympathizers, Oreans, any fae who dares go against them. At the first spark of magic revealed, our children are stolen and forced to work for the monarchy. They keep the dissenters starved and tax us down to our teeth. They keep their boots on our necks, cutting off our very air. More fae and Oreans die every year. More of our magic and land dies too. We have to *do* something," he says, his tone distressed, insistent. "We have to stand against this. Who better than a broken-winged bird to show everyone how to rise? Who better than the Lyäri Ulvêre to remind them that the darkness can't stop the dawn?" His eyes flick between mine. "We need your help, Auren. It can only be you."

His words pile on top of me like the bricks of his torn-down wall, each one stacking over my frustration and uncertainty until it crumbles beneath the weight of his plea.

I blow out a long breath, the rest of my anger tumbling out like dropped pebbles left to scatter. "Okay. I'll help you. Because I know what it's like to live under the thumb of a controlling, oppressive king," I begin. "But I'm looking for someone, and he's my priority. I can't promise I'll be here forever. I can't even promise that I'll be by your side when you get to Lydia. But in the meantime, I will help you try to unite the Vulmin. That's what I can do."

He sucks in a breath, surprise and renewed optimism flaring through his gaze. "Okay."

"But from now on, no surprises," I add with a sharp edge to my words. "If you have a plan that involves me, you talk to me about it *first*."

"Deal," he says, holding out his hand.

Our palms meet, and we nod to each other, the weighty significance of our truce settling between us.

"Deal."

CHAPTER 26

SLADE

The many rivers of Fourth Kingdom curve below me, and I fly over the watery lines as they bend through the glittering city. I direct Crest toward the dark, massive shape of Banded Mountain that stands behind Brackhill, its presence looming over the castle like a shadowed guard.

The moat seems to bleed black, its thick trench slashed deep around the castle. Brackhill itself is an inky presence, its tall, smooth walls shining in the night, its pointed turrets as sharp as a quill's tip, writing upon the dark sky with ominous warning.

I fly around to the back of the scrawling spires, to the flat-top roof of my private entrance to the castle. Crest lands, and the watching guards immediately come up to bow. "Your Majesty."

I give them a nod and begin to dismount, but I've barely gotten both feet on the ground before I have a scowling, furious man in front of me. Gray hair and beard disheveled, brown eyes torn through with bloodshot veins.

"Digby."

"Where is she?" he demands. "Where's Auren?"

He looks far better now than he did before. The beating he took at the hand of Midas took a toll on his body, but he's healed since then.

On the outside, at least.

I see a fury and desperation in his expression that's similar to what I feel in my own chest.

"She's gone."

I see the punch coming, but I don't even try to deflect it. I welcome the hit that lands on my jaw. My head snaps to the side, an ache bursting through my face, but I welcome it because I *deserve* it. Because *she* deserves the loyalty and love from someone who would risk punching King Rot in the face on her behalf.

When he raises his fist to hit me again, another hand shoots out and grabs it, stopping Digby before he can swing again.

"That's enough," Ryatt commands. "You got one hit, but you can't beat the shit out of my brother." His dark green gaze moves to me, trailing up and down. "Although, it looks like somebody else already did that. What happened to you?"

"Nothing."

My brother scoffs but lets the matter drop. I'm still bruised and sore from the fight at Breakwater, but the pain has moved to a duller ache, the marks faded.

Digby yanks out of Ryatt's hold and shoves away. The man paces, still limping slightly, though he tries to hide it. "This is your fault." He hurls the accusation right at me like another landed hit.

"It's not," Ryatt defends. "I told you what happened. Slade saved her. It was all he could do."

"But she's *gone*. Without anyone around to make sure that he actually *did* save her. Without me there to protect her. So it *is* his fault. She was taken while staying under his roof, under his protection, and instead of getting her back, he shoved her somewhere none of us can go! Who's going to protect her? Who's going to make sure she's okay?" His voice cracks.

The man cracks with it.

A ragged breath leaks through that he can't seem to stop. And behind those rifts, I see the insurmountable grief and fear that he feels for her. See just how much she means to him.

I wish he would punch me again.

"Enough, Digby," Ryatt tells him.

"No, he's right," I say. "His anger is pointing in the right direction."

My brother shoots me a glower, but Digby looks dubious. "What?" I ask. "You think I don't agree? You think I haven't realized how thoroughly I failed her? I *know*," I tell him, the vehemence of my own self-loathing clear in my voice. "I know I failed her. I'm not going to ever forgive myself for allowing this to happen, and I'm also not going to stop trying to get to her."

His lips press together, his gaze tracking over my face. "Good," he growls before he turns and storms across the open roof and disappears down the spiral staircase.

We both watch him go, and then Ryatt sighs. "He's been torn up since I told him."

"I wouldn't expect anything less."

He gives me a look, and I realize he's shaved his hair so it's right at his scalp. His jaw is clean-shaven too. He looks less like me and more like himself.

He walks over to Crest, but the beast snaps his teeth, making Ryatt stop and roll his eyes. "Mean thing, isn't he? He seems to have done well for you, though."

Crest huffs and then turns his head to look at me. He leans over and nudges my arm until I lift my hand and give him a pet. Ryatt chuckles. "Every single fucking timberwing looks at you like you shit out fresh meat."

I shrug and then pat the beast on the flank. "Go on for a hunt and then rest at the Perch. You did well."

Crest nudges me one more time and then turns and leaps into the air, feathered wings outstretched, probably already lifting his nose and darting his eyes to search for prey.

I can sense my brother's gaze rolling over my face. "You let him get in a good one," he says, motioning toward the mark on my jaw.

I shrug. "It's deserved."

"And it looks like you let someone else get in *a lot* of other good ones."

"It was days ago."

He pauses. "Did it help?"

"A bit, yeah."

I let my eyes drift to the mountain, its silhouette bathed in night's veil.

"It's not your fault," Ryatt finally says. "Auren, Drollard, our mother... It's not your fault."

I say nothing.

Fault is there whether someone wants to claim it or not.

At least Twig wasn't in Drollard when the rip closed. At least the boy's here and safe, because I can't say the same for his family.

"Slade."

I look over.

Ryatt chews on his question before spitting it out. "The rip power?"

My teeth grind and I give a terse shake of my head. "Not yet."

I don't have that power back yet. I can't open a rip yet. It hasn't worked yet.

How long until that *yet* disappears completely?

My hand delves into my pocket. Fingers pressing around the cut piece of ribbon.

"You saved her life. That's what you need to focus on right now. The power will come back, and as soon as it does, we will get Auren and our mother back," he says fervently. "And Digby would rather have Auren alive and somewhere else than dead and here. He'll come around."

"Those shouldn't have been her only two options."

He blows out a breath. "You're just as stubborn as he is."

I take my hand out of my pocket, let it hang defeatedly at my side. "I'm going to bed."

He doesn't try to stop me as I walk past him across the roof, my boots echoing down the steps of the spiral staircase. At the bottom, I pass my gray-haired guard, Marcoul, his pose confident, his expression one of dependable familiarity. "Sire," he greets as I enter the corridor. "I'm glad to see you back."

I don't feel like I'm back. I feel like half of me is so far gone I'm about to snap from the stretch.

I stride down the dark corridors, and even though I pass more guards along the way, the castle feels empty.

Or maybe that's me.

When I'm shut into my bedroom, I fall into bed fully clothed and attempt to sleep. Except her scent is still clinging to the bed, an echo of her warmth leaving me feeling cold. I instantly delve my hand back into my pocket, fingers twisting to that piece of ribbon. If it were just fabric, it would be going threadbare by now.

My chest stabs. Rot gnaws like teeth chomping through my veins and snapping at muscle and sinew. I have her scent, her ribbon, but not *her*. And this is the last place I saw her. Felt her.

I tear myself from the bed, abruptly getting back to my feet. When I walk in my closet, I yank on fresh clothes, pausing when I see the feathered coat hanging up—the coat she wore when we first met. When her golden aura softened from the glaring beacon that shot up into the sky.

Calling me to her.

Auren's golden glow is all I see when I close my eyes. This cloying, agonizing poison stretching through my chest is all I feel. My mother's voice, speaking a single word, is all I hear. Her very *last* word before she went mute forever. It all echoes through me, threatening to drive me mad.

The goddesses are cruel.

All those years, Auren was here. Right *here*, in Orea. That kills me the most. The fact that she was just a couple of kingdoms away all that time, and I never knew.

Now, she's in the fae realm without me.

My shoulders go tense, veins snapping at my jaw, feeling the suffocating emptiness of her absence. Spikes threaten to stab through my spine, punching against my skin in punishment, while the room tilts. It's only once rot seeps through the floorboards, making them creak and sag, that I manage to yank myself back together with the clench of my teeth and pull the rot away.

I can be in constant motion. I can mete out punishment. I can go without sleep. What I *can't* do is sit here a moment longer in this quiet, motionless loathing.

So despite the tiredness dripping down my bones like tar, I stride out of the room with renewed determination. I can't stop. I *won't*. I will keep going. I will keep trying. Because I *will* tear a rip through this fucking world so I can get to her…

Or die trying.

GOLD

I claw into my depths like a beast raking through my innards with ferocious urgency. Every raking swipe is agony, but I keep trying to demand that the raw power unearth. That it spill out from my hidden depths.

But it's empty. Dried up.

Every time I reach for the dregs at my core, I'm only met by a barren void. A hollowness where I was once so full, so capable. An enraged bellow escapes my mouth, the anguished sound bouncing off the mountain and echoing back like a taunt.

This place reeks of shit droppings and blood. That's all I've been smelling for the past three days, every time I come down here.

Here on the dark side of Banded Mountain, where Brackhill Castle can't be seen and the horizon is crammed full with a thick forest, the timberwings have claimed this as their favored hunting ground. Shoved up against the base of the mountain where moss-covered boulders and felled trees litter the ground, it's the perfect spot for the beasts to protect their kill. There's always at least one timberwing here in the shadows, lording over their catch as their maw chomps through flesh and cartilage, picking carcasses clean until all that's left are the bones.

Right now, with dusk fast approaching, there are two of them, one already settled behind a cluster of boulders, sharp teeth crunching through its meal. I can hear the other one every so often too, either stalking prey on the thick forest floor or flying above the trees, the air whistling through its wings. Crest left earlier with a buck bound in his bite.

Every time I hear flapping wings, I half expect Argo to burst through the trees and land in front of me. But he's probably still on a ship somewhere in the fucking ocean, and I don't know what any animal mender will be able to do for him.

Yet another thing out of my control.

I've tried to pour out power here every day since I got back, and still, *nothing*. Rot boils in my veins, fueled by my rage, but the well of raw power stays empty.

It just makes me even more infuriated.

I feel exhaustion tugging at me as incessantly as the wrongness of my separation from her. But I stay fastened to the base of this mountain, failing over and over again. Because failing is better than giving up. Failing means I'm still trying.

At least there's no one around to see it—to see this pathetic attempt to stop failing. No one else comes here. The timberwings won't allow it—not even their preferred handlers or riders. The beasts are far too territorial over this feed site to tolerate anyone else. The only exception, apparently, is me.

Which is why it's *really* fucking stupid when I hear a timberwing land behind me, and then my brother calls out, "You need to rest."

I sigh, dropping my hands down to my sides. "You shouldn't be here."

The female timberwing past the boulders lets off a guttural warning growl that vibrates through the air. My brother's beast lets out a responding one, both equally bristled. At least Ryatt has the good sense not to dismount. He doesn't, however, have the good sense not to irritate me.

"Judging by the amount of sweat staining your shirt and the pissed off look on your face, I'm going to guess that you've been out here for hours. Again."

"You know what I like about this side of the mountain?" I say. "There's usually no one around to say stupid shit."

I hear him sigh behind me, and then the trample of his

timberwing steps forward, talons scraping over the rocks, its shadow casting over me.

"Any improvement?" he asks tentatively.

I snap around on my heel with a snarl on my face. "What the fuck do you think?"

His lips press into a grim line, hands loosely gripping the reins. "I've been trying to give you space since you got back, but your refusal to sleep, to eat, your constant presence here, your revenge crusade… You murdered the Merewens. Rotted half of Third Kingdom. Fucked up Fifth, and none of that made you feel better. You even locked up Queen Kaila's brother."

"He fucking deserves it!" I snarl. "He kidnapped her."

Ryatt raises his hands placatingly. "I get it. I do. But everyone is panicked. All throughout Orea, monarchs are dropping like flies and there's unrest in every corner. You're tipping the entire world off the scale."

"Let it topple." My words are dark, every bit as black as my withering soul.

His eyes flare. "You don't mean that."

I give a humorless laugh. "You don't think so? Nothing, and I mean *nothing*, matters if I can't get back to her."

"Your people, your Wrath?"

He still doesn't get it. So I yank up my shirt, exposing my torso.

Letting him *see*.

I hear him suck in a breath, watch as he takes in the mass of black centering around the organ in my chest. A sickly, poisoned heart, with a snarl of veins staining out of it like dripping ink. It looks even worse in the daylight.

"What is that?"

"My rot," I say roughly, letting my shirt drop back down. "It's like it's rotting me from the inside out. Rotting out my fucking heart."

"Has that ever happened?"

I shake my head.

"So…why?"

"That piece of rot that was left inside Auren…the piece that I couldn't get out? I think somehow, she's using it through her own power. I saw some of it in her gold at the Conflux."

He gapes at me. "She's using your rot?"

"I sensed it inside of her before, but as soon as she went through the rip…it felt like someone dug inside my chest and scooped something out. Like there's a chunk that was ripped out. I'm bleeding out rot. It's infecting me, affecting my magic, and I swear to fuck, sometimes it twinges, like I can almost *feel* her. And all of this, it's just a physical manifestation of what I already knew."

"What?"

"That I can't live without her. I won't stand for it, and neither will my rot. The separation is *killing* me, Ry. In more ways than one."

The blood drains from his face.

When he says nothing, I turn back around, cracking my neck to the side before I stretch out my arms again and try for the thousandth time today to call up the raw power that's abandoned me.

I grit my teeth, my eyes narrowing. Hands shaking with the strain. I feel scales beneath my cheeks scraping beneath the surface of my skin like they want to surge out. But I dig down with intense focus, trying to uncover the magic that's been eluding me for weeks. I pull on the invisible force, but it's like trying to pull up the rope in an empty well. No matter how many times I toss in the bucket and try to drag something out, there's nothing there.

Dizziness suddenly slams into me, and black dots appear in my vision. I feel myself slipping to the right, body ready to fall just like the toppled-down trees around me. But Ryatt somehow gets to me in a flash, catching me beneath my arms before I can collapse. Slugging his shoulders beneath my draped arm, he forces me upright and pulls me toward his beast. The other timberwing that's still protecting her fresh kill gives a roar of warning that rumbles the air.

I brace my hand on his timberwing's chest, panting for breath. "No. I'm staying."

"The fuck you are. Now get on, you stubborn ass, before that timberwing decides to come over here."

"She won't," I tell him, though my words are caught through a strained throat and a warbled tongue.

"Yeah, yeah. All things winged adore you. That doesn't mean she won't take a chunk out of *me*."

He half drags me up onto the saddle, giving my memory whiplash as I recall him doing the very same thing at the Conflux. I feel just as drained now as I did then. More so.

He shoves me upright onto the saddle and then swings up in front of me. Unlike the Conflux, he doesn't strap me in or brace me before he signals his timberwing to launch into the air. The beast rises so quickly that I slide backwards, hands flailing as I almost fly right off. At the last second, I snatch up the saddle strap, gripping it tight and hauling myself back into the saddle while wind thrashes against my face.

"You asshole!" I shout at Ryatt with a growl.

"If you weren't already fucking exhausted and then out here draining yourself—with a *rotting fucking heart*, I might add—you wouldn't have to worry about being too debilitated to stay on a damned saddle," he tosses back.

Any retort I want to make is made useless as the timberwing gains speed, pushing through the trees and making the air rush past us.

But we both know I can't *not* drain myself.

I slump as we fly, though I'm careful to keep my fingers clutched around the saddle strap, even with the headache that's splitting through my skull and the inky dots that keep overtaking my vision. I'm jostled when we land on Brackhill's rooftop, Ryatt once again dragging me forward until my feet hit the ground, keeping his grip on my collar to make sure I'm not tilting.

I shrug him off, hating the feel of being weak. "I'm good."

"Alright, then. Come on," he challenges.

He wastes no time leading me down the spiral staircase, watching me like a hawk over his shoulder, braced to catch me. My sweat-slicked palm grips the railing as my stumbled steps get sloppier by the second, but I stay upright.

The guards nod at us as we pass, not breaking their decorum even though I probably look like shit.

At the corridor, Ryatt stops, waiting for me to catch my breath. "You need to sleep."

"Can't," I gasp out.

His jaw works, green eyes frustrated. "Fine. Then you're going to fucking eat, at least."

I blearily follow him, mostly because I just don't have the energy to argue. He brings me down the corridor and another set of stairs and then opens the door to the sitting room we use as our private dining room.

Instead of Lu being here, plopping fruit in her mouth, or Judd having his feet up on the table, or even Osrik squeezed into one of the chairs and poring over reports from the army, the room is empty.

Lu is hunkering down somewhere in Sixth Kingdom, collecting information for me on the discontent and Queen Kaila. Judd is probably down at the barracks, and Osrik…

Fuck. I need to go see Osrik. Need to check on Lady Rissa.

"Sit," Ryatt orders, though it's unnecessary, since I practically heave myself into the sofa away from the table, body sagging into the pillows.

I tip my head back on the armrest, intending to close my eyes just for a second to get my headache to subside. But it must've been longer, because he's suddenly shoving a plate against my chest, when I didn't even hear him collect food. "Eat."

"I don't want to eat."

Ryatt glares at me. "Lu's not here to tell you off, so I'll do it. You've travelled all over the fucking kingdom, spreading your rot and going on a damned murder spree, and ever since you've been here, you've done nothing but drain yourself. You need to *eat* something. You look like shit and you smell like it too."

I turn and sniff. Shrug. I've smelled worse.

Smelled a lot better too.

He stares down at me, same green eyes as my own, though his are narrowed in frustration. "You're killing yourself trying to create a rip."

I shrug again.

The muscle in his jaw jumps. "Your power probably isn't replenishing because you've been running yourself ragged. Stop rotting shit and killing people for a week. Eat. Sleep. And don't try to open a rip for a few days either."

A few days? Is he fucking out of his mind?

"You expect me to just sit here and do *nothing*?" The very idea of that has the fae side of me going mental, surging through me with fury, snarling at me to get to her.

His attention flicks down to my arms, and when I follow his gaze, I see rotted veins twitching erratically over my wrists. I shove down my sleeves and snatch at the plate of food. He watches as I yank up the sandwich he put together and take a vicious bite.

After that, I realize just how hungry I really am. Ryatt must realize it too, because as soon as I've cleared my plate, he's already there to shove a second in its place, along with a cup of water.

By the time I've eaten my fill and drained three cups, my hands are no longer shaking, the headache has tempered down to a less agonizing throb, and I no longer feel like I'm ready to topple over. I can't remember when I last ate.

"Better?" he asks.

I grunt in response.

"Good." He leans forward in his seat, boots planted on the floor, hands clasped where they hang between his knees as he looks at me. I can see he's trying to go into command mode, because it's an expression I've worn many times when I had to push aside emotions and problem solve. "You need to rest. Give it three days, Slade. Then you can get back at it. You made the rip for Auren once; you can do it again."

"Maybe I *can't* do it again," I lob back, voicing my fear. "That was the only time I did it alone. The first time I made a rip, it wasn't just *my* magic."

Ryatt's jaw tightens, a flash of anger passing over his eyes. We don't speak my father's name. Not ever. If it's at all possible, I think my brother might hate him more than I do.

Frustration bubbles up, frothing at my mouth. "I ripped us into this world, and then I ripped Auren out of it. I don't care what it takes. She's in Annwyn. Alone. Neither of us are saying it, but we both know where our mother and the rest of the village went." My eyes latch on to his. "They're back *there*."

Ryatt's nails dig into the armrest of his chair, as if he's holding himself back, keeping himself seated. "Don't."

He doesn't want to think of our mother being back at my father's estate any more than I do. But if the rip in Drollard closed because I opened another one, then it's fair to reason that everyone got tugged back through it and went right back to where we were before.

Right back to that nightmare.

"It was my doing," I tell him. "So I'll fix it."

He takes in a breath, rubs a hand at the back of his neck as if he's trying to wipe away the tension. I know this is hard for him too. The entire village fucking loves him, and he protected them fiercely. His bond with our mother is unparalleled.

I can't fucking stand his gutted look. It would be better if he was fighting me. Arguing with me. "Where's my brother who's always agreeing when I say I've fucked up and needling me about every damn thing he thinks I'm doing wrong?"

Heavy-laden eyes lift as he watches me tread furious steps into the carpet. "I think we've spent enough of our lives butting heads. Right now, that's not going to help. I want to help fix this. Fix *you*," he says, gesturing toward my chest. "Get our mother back. Help you find Auren."

I stop, dragging my hands down my face.

"The rip at the Conflux?" he asks.

"Closed."

"I could check Drollard again..."

"It's gone, Ryatt," I tell him. "It's all gone."

He lets out a sigh. "Okay. Then you keep trying, but not to the point of exhaustion. It's not helping when you drain yourself. Your magic might need time to accumulate."

If it doesn't...

His eyes flick down. "You're rotting the upholstery."

I yank my hand away from the blackening sofa, the fabric disintegrating and the wood caving in until I pull the rot back.

"You need to rest. I've never seen you this out of it."

I know he's right, but all I've managed to get are a few snatches here and there. Mostly down at the timberwings' kill site, where I've passed out a few times against boulders and bones.

I keep that bit to myself.

If I try right now, I know I still won't be able to sleep. My chest fucking hurts. My mind spins. My two sides feel like they're warring with each other, and I feel far too empty. Too *alone*.

"Can't," I grit out, but then I look at my brother, and an idea comes to mind. "Maybe I can…if I take the edge off."

Ryatt's eyes narrow. "You want to spar *now*? You look like you're one breath away from tipping over."

I shrug. "Fighting helps."

"Fucking hell. *Fine*," he says as he heaves himself up. "You're sleep-deprived and your heart is rotting, so I'll put you on your ass in ten seconds flat."

I snort. "Sure. Go ahead and tell yourself that." I lead him out of the room and down the stairs.

"You'd better sleep after this, or I'll knock you out myself and fucking force you to rest," he grumbles.

Spoken like a true brother.

CHAPTER 27

AUREN

The sky is violet, hovering between day and night. I'm a long way from Geisel now, and we've just arrived at yet another stop on Wick's route. His plan has worked flawlessly.

Every time we reach a new safe house, we pick up another dozen or so rebels. Although today, we've had the biggest addition so far—fifty strong ready to join. All it's taken is Wick's speech and my presence, and they agree to come with us.

It seems most of the Vulmin are like him—ready to take on the monarchy. Others are a bit more hesitant to throw their lives so publicly on the line rather than continue in their quiet rebellion, but one look at me, and they meld in with the rest.

The *Vulmin Dyrūnia* are growing. Every day.

And I'm growing too—in my awareness. In my power. I've been using it more and more, wielding it with increasing confidence and pushing myself into making more difficult things or stretching it out further, pushing my limits.

Speaking of pushing limits…

All the Vulmin traveling with us can't even fit inside the safe houses anymore. Tonight, many of the rebels are sleeping outside, because there's just so many that we're bursting at the seams. Soon, our numbers will be too high to go undetected, just like Wick said.

Luckily, this place has a large gazebo out back and benches along a garden's walking path that people are taking advantage of. Some fae have even taken up residence in the barn. Wick always makes sure I get one of the beds when we stop at a house, but tonight, I insisted on sleeping on the floor and giving the others a turn.

Everyone is winding down now after a particularly hard day of travel in the thick mud from a flooded-out gulch. Wick is sitting at the kitchen bar top, a drink in hand, head cocked as he listens to Ludogar.

"Hello."

My head snaps up and I blink at the fae female standing over me. With my back against the wall of the dusk-colored room, I've been watching the new Vulmin, but I missed her somehow. There haven't been any other females in the group, so her presence is a welcome surprise.

She looks down at me with a smile, and the color of her eyes reminds me of magma. It's a swirl of deep reds and burnt oranges that seems to mix with the blacks of her pupils. At the skin beside her eyes is a trio of red dots in a perfect line that reach her temples. Her hair is auburn, steeped in orange at the ends, and it's short, curling up at the edge of her jaw and neatly tucked behind her ears. Ears which are pierced at each pointed tip with dangling chains that hook to her lobes. On one of them, the broken-winged bird sigil hangs down like a charm.

"Hi," I reply.

"Mind if I sit?"

I gesture to the spot beside me, and she flits down, crossing slim legs beneath her. Several people glance over, including Wick, as if they're wondering why she's approaching me.

She ignores them. "I'm Emonie."

"Auren."

"I know," she says with an impish grin. "I can't believe it. Can't believe you're *real*. My sister's favorite game growing up was to play the gilded Turley girl. Used to pretend that she was off in some hidden island in the sea, biding her time before she returned to defeat the evil king and fall in love with some warrior prince from an ocean realm."

I was actually off in a broken land, not knowing that I was biding my time to meet a spiky-armed fae, but it's not too far off.

"That's quite the imagination," I say with a smile.

"No one quite imagined *this*, though," she says, looking me over, as if she can't believe I'm real. "That you'd be here, with us Vulmin, leading us to the capital like a golden guardian." Her eyes linger on my dirty cloak, on my limp and tangled hair. "Hmm. This won't do. Our golden guardian needs some care. Not surprised, since you've had to travel with this lot of males. Come on," she says, scooping back up to her feet.

"Where are we going?"

"You didn't get a chance to clean up yet."

"The washrooms are full."

"But I happen to know that there's something *better* than a washroom here. Trust me."

I really *do* need to clean up. Traveling every day, staying someplace new every night—sometimes outside—has taken a toll.

Getting to my feet, I follow Emonie through the cramped room. Some eyes watch us as we go, but most of the Vulmin are sprawled out, rolled up on area rugs, propped up on the sofas and chairs, leaning against the walls, slumped over the dining table with their packs shoved under their heads as a pillow. They're resting, sleeping, or eating at every available space.

Emonie takes me through the main living space and out the back door of the gray-toned kitchen. Outside, the night is lit up with a half-moon. It hangs tipped in the sky like it's pouring out thickened buttermilk in a stream of illuminated clouds. The porch has two snoring males lounging in a rocking bench, and at the gazebo ahead, I can see several more prostrate silhouettes.

"Where are we going?"

"The bathhouse," she says as I walk beside her. "I'm trying to make you be my friend."

My brows shoot up. "Wait, there's a *bathhouse* here?"

She grins, showing off her sharp canines. "Yep."

The thought of actually bathing and not having to use a cloth and bucket like I've been doing puts a skip in my step. There have been baths in the houses but too many of us and too little water to go around.

"A bathhouse is a *great* way to make me be your friend."

"I thought so." She slips a hand into her trouser pocket and holds out a glass bottle. "Plus this."

"Please say it's a travel bottle of wine."

She giggles, and the sound is so un-rebellious-like that it makes my lips twitch. "Even better during travel. It's perfumed soap," she says, wagging her auburn brows.

Great Divine. A bathhouse *and* soap?

I crack a smile. "You're good."

"I know," she says breezily. "And by now, everybody else who knew about this place will have already bathed, so we'll have plenty of privacy. Besides, no one would dare come in while you're there. We can soak as long as you like."

She leads us further away from the house, down a dark stone path. After passing a hen house, we enter thinned trees, their leaves the color of lilacs, bark as gray as thunderclouds. After just a couple of minutes, we walk down a slight slope, and I spot the stone bathhouse just ahead.

Inside are four basic walls, but the roof is like an inverted cone, tipping inward and lit up from the moonlight above. It points directly at the center of a large round bath beneath, sending the reflection of the stars to scatter inside its watery depths. It's big enough for at least five people, made of smooth stone with steps leading down into it, and it's *steaming*.

"Hot water?" I think my voice might've actually cracked. "Why didn't you tell me there was *hot* water?"

She beams and starts stripping down. Normally, I'd be a bit more shy, but…hot water.

Within seconds, both of us have yanked off our clothes. I leave all the gold I was wearing in a neat pile beneath them and then climb in. As soon as I sit on the little ledge beneath, I submerge my entire body, head and all. The delicious heat soaks into me, and I release a blissful exhale, bubbles rising from my nose like smoke from a chimney.

When I break through the surface again, I lean back against the wall of the bath, letting my head tip back to rest on the floor behind me. Looking up, I watch drips fall from the point of the coned roof, watch how each drop lands perfectly in the center of the water.

"Nice, huh?"

I hum in agreement, unfurling my ribbons and letting them float around me in delicate wisps.

"Catch."

I barely get my hand up in time to catch the bottle she flings at me. I immediately pop it open, dumping a fair amount of the silky smooth soap onto my palms. I wash myself all over and scrub my hair until it shines. By the time I'm done, I feel buffed and soft and so clean it's heavenly.

Across from me, Emonie lounges back, looking just as relaxed as I feel. "So...I heard some things. About what happened in Geisel."

"Yeah." I'm ready for her to question me about my magic. To ask about what I can do, maybe question the gold.

So I'm completely taken by surprise when she says, "I'm sorry. About your friend who died."

Her voice is gentle, attention steady. So often, people are uncomfortable with grief. It's hard to look it in the eye of others. Because ultimately, we're terrified that one day, grief will reflect in our own gaze, too, and we aren't ready to face it. We're never really ready.

But Emonie, she looks right at me with unabashed boldness, like she isn't afraid of being tainted by my grief, not afraid to look at it too. And I get the sense that it's because she's known grief herself.

I swallow hard. "Thank you."

"Did you know her long?"

Nenet's cackle fills my ears, and a lump of sadness gets caught in my throat. "No. Not nearly long enough."

Others might judge that. They might think grief should be determined by the amount of time you had with someone, but that isn't true at all. Grief isn't based on someone's length of presence. It's based on the impact of their absence.

Emonie looks across the water at me, and I feel like she's seeing *me* and not the Lyäri Ulvêre. "Some people are in your life for only a moment, like a shooting star. Quick and short, but they light up a part of you for a second, and their brightness lingers even after they're gone."

I nod, though I have to blink back the emotion that threatens to drag me under. "You speak like you have some experience with that."

She gives me an enigmatic smile. "Oh, I think you'll find that lots of Vulmi have stories like that. Stone Swords are notorious for their cruelty, and the monarchy is notorious for public executions to teach us *conspirators* a lesson."

I get the feeling that she doesn't want to talk more about that, so I latch on to another part. "Did you say Vulmi?"

"*Vulmin Dyrūnia* is a mouthful, and I always thought Vulmin sounded a little mean. So I call it Vulmi for short. Sounds much nicer, yes?"

I huff out a small laugh. "Are rebels supposed to want to sound nicer?"

She shrugs and blows at a bubble from the soapy water.

"You know, you don't seem like the rebel type," I tell her.

Emonie grins. "It's my friendly, sparkling personality, huh?"

"Yes. Everyone else here is a little…"

"Boring."

I laugh, palms skimming over one of my floating ribbons. The silky strip is smooth under my fingertips. "I was going to say reserved."

"My parents were both Vulmi."

I don't miss that she said *were*, and I wonder if the public executions she mentioned have anything to do with them, but I don't want to pry.

"I grew up in it. Grew up with everyone here, so I'm used to them and they're used to me. I'm just a lot more fun, because life's too short to not have a good time when you can," she tells me, her expression straightforward while the steam around her twists and curls. "You're lucky I'm here to be your friend. You look like you could use one."

"I do?"

She nods. "You look sad. Even when you smile."

Ouch.

Right on cue, the spot at the center of my chest twists with a brutal pang. "I…miss someone," I admit, trying not to let the raw emotion scrape down my throat. "I'm looking for him and he's looking for me."

"I'm sorry."

"It's okay. We'll find each other."

She starts cupping water in her palm, letting it dribble back out. Every single one of my muscles is relaxed in the warm soak, and the quiet night air has made me sleepy and contemplative. Melancholic. Has given me time to breathe away from all the people, to be still after all the travel. And in my stillness, I always think of him.

"What's he like?" she asks.

"Wonderful. Intense. A bit…rotten," I say with a smirk.

"*Oh*. A dangerous male. I like those too."

"When I first saw him, his black aura terrified me."

Her eyes widen, magma depths churning. "You can see his aura?"

"I can, and he can see mine."

She lets out a longing sigh, letting more water drip from her hand. "Not many fae get to. No wonder you're dying to get back to each other. Even if he is a little rotten, as you said."

I smile, but my cheeks are hollowed out with yearning, with missing him. "I love his rotten side, but he has a heart of gold just for me."

"I think you're giving *everyone* a heart of gold when it comes to you. They're all smitten. You really took the whole gilded Turley thing literally, huh?" she adds, gesturing toward me. "Instead of having one gilded thing, you're a *whole* gilded thing. It's flashy. I like it."

I chuckle, and then she stands up, clearly not worried about her nudity as she climbs out of the bath and starts drying herself off with one of the stacked drying cloths against the wall. "Come on. We have to be up early, so we'd better get some sleep."

I pet the surface of the water, loath to leave the heated bath. "Can't we just sleep here?"

She smirks, toweling off her wet auburn hair, the orange ends looking darker from the soak. "And then I have to explain to Wick why I let our famed Lyäri drown in the middle of the night, all because she really liked hot water? No thanks."

"I won't drown." My protest is a little weak, because, well, soaking in here *has* made me sleepy.

She starts tugging her clothes on, her lips twisting into a smirk. "You're made of gold. Can you even float? Won't you just sink right down to the bottom?"

"Ha ha."

As soon as I drag myself out of the water, she tosses a drying cloth at me, along with a pile of clothes. "Those are extras of mine, and they're clean. I'm a bit shorter than you, and sadly, not as curvy, but I think they'll be alright."

"Thank you." I only had one other dress packed from Estelia, plus the clothes I've been wearing, so Emonie's trousers and shirt are a much appreciated addition. I quickly dry off and squeeze out the water from my hair and ribbons.

"So…what's with the fabric glued to your back? Taking that broken-winged bird thing literally too? It's very theatrical."

I chuckle, looking at her over my shoulder as I slip on my gold arm cuffs before pulling the brown shirt over my head. "They're not glued."

"Weird," she says as she looks at them. Then she seems to catch herself, and quickly adds, "I mean *pretty*. Very pretty. And unique."

Snorting, I step into the pants and stuff my feet into clean, thick socks and then put on my boots. My ribbons trail down past the hem at the back of my shirt. They'll take more time to completely dry, but I loosely wrap them around my waist like a belt so they won't drag in the dirt. "Ready."

She gathers up all our old clothes. "I'll get these washed in the morning."

"You don't have to do that. I can—"

"We'll take turns," she assures me.

Together, we walk back to the house, and I melt down my belt, holding the malleable metal in my palm. It takes a few tries, but I manage to manipulate it into a comb. It's simple but effective, and I can't help but smile at how much better I've gotten at using my gold-touch. Humming a bit beneath my breath, I start to brush through my hair.

Emonie trills in excitement. "Now *that's* impressive."

I pass the comb over, and she sighs as she rakes it through her short hair, the ends soon flipping up with a slight curl. When she hands it back to me, I melt it down again, letting it gather around my waist beneath my ribbons once more.

As we walk, Emonie starts flitting around the path and collecting things. I watch her picking certain leaves, grabbing up mushrooms, and snapping off berries along the forest floor. She stuffs everything into a pouch that hangs off the loop at her pant waist, excitement bouncing off her with every new item she finds.

"You like foraging?"

"Mm-hmm."

She cinches the pouch closed before offering me a few of the berries. I take them, and both of us pop one into our mouths. My tongue floods, the sweet sourness making my jaw tingle in the best way.

"My parents taught me to always be looking for things to use for food or medicine—or anything useful, really. Being a Vulmi means you travel a lot, and we're not always lucky enough to sleep in a house or have food readily available, and we hardly ever have access to any kind of healer. I like to collect useful things."

I read between the lines. Emonie knows what it's like to go hungry. To be hurt without help. To sleep in the cold. It's almost impossible not to like her, and honestly, it's a relief to finally have someone to talk to.

Friendships never came easy to me in Orea, but with Emonie, I just feel an instant, effortless connection. A warmth that I recognize between her soul and mine. It revives something in me, making me feel more like myself again. Making me feel not so alone.

"*Oooh*, look!" She's already bent down, yanking up something from the ground. She holds up a piece of twine proudly. "This is a good find."

I frown as she puts that in her pouch too. "How'd you even see that?"

"I always know where to look," she says with a wink.

When we get back to the dark house, the rest of the Vulmin seem to be asleep, aside from a few who are standing watch and walking around the outside. Inside, we pick our way past all the sleeping bodies, and then the two of us claim an empty spot at the top of the stairwell, next to the blue balusters.

"Of course I'd become friends with the Lyäri on the night she insists on sleeping on the floor," Emonie grumbles.

I huff out a quiet laugh and then watch as she disappears into one of the rooms. When she comes back out, she has two blankets and two pillows in her arms.

"How'd you get those? I would've thought everything would've been claimed already."

"I just told them the Lyäri needed them," she says with a shrug as she hands me the pillow. "You really should use your position to your advantage, you know. Good thing you have me around."

Shaking my head at her, I toe off my boots and slump down to the floor, my tiredness catching up with me. I keep the banister at my back and stuff the pillow beneath my head, while Emonie sweeps the blanket over me, covering me chin to feet.

She lies down beside me, propping her head on her own pillow and wrapping herself up in the second blanket while letting out a jaw-cracking yawn. Even with the rug beneath us, it's definitely not the softest place I've ever slept. It's also not the worst.

For a few minutes, I lie here, looking up at the paneled ceiling, hearing dozens of others as they snore and breathe and shift in their sleep.

"Thanks. For the bath, and the pillow, and…for talking to me," I whisper awkwardly. "Not as the Lyäri, but as just me."

She flashes a grin in the dark. "Look at us. Friends already because my plan worked. It was the soap that really made you like me, huh?"

I smile and shift my head deeper into the pillow. "No, you had me at the hot water."

CHAPTER 28

AUREN

The woods are all brambles and low-hanging branches, and sweet-smelling yellow leaves dotted with pockets of pink pollen. The morning sun is bright, and I have my back braced against a tree and fingers dug into the dirt.

The gilded, rotted dirt.

It's getting easy to handle now, this combination of seductive power. Easier to control. To hear, but not let it deafen me. I feel the presence of the rot as if it's added a new facet to my gold-touch, like a glass crystal held up to the light.

My power has this new connection with the land too. It seems like Annwyn is thirsty for the gold I let drip. Like she soaks it all up and sighs with relief.

But my magic isn't the only thing I try to work with.

All twenty-four ribbons lie on the ground around me like rays stretching out from the sun. I feel the earth's beat beneath them, feel the warmth from the dirt and grass. Yet no matter how many times I try to move them, they don't budge an inch. They stay lifeless. Separate. No movement curling playfully through their lengths.

I miss them.

Tears prick my eyes, but I loop them around my waist with gentle movements, tucking them in safely against me, and tell myself they just need more time.

With that thought, I glance up at the position of the morning sun.

Time to go.

So I gather up the gold, calling it back. I meld it into a ball, rolling the metal between my palms until it hardens, and then I slip it into my pocket.

Slade was right about always keeping some on me. I should've been more equipped. If I'd had more at my disposal during that night at Brackhill Castle, maybe I wouldn't have gotten kidnapped. Maybe I would've been able to stop those men from killing Rissa.

Regret clangs against the walls of my heart.

For a moment, I recall her stubborn face. Her clipped words. The tentative, sharp way she went about becoming an actual friend, as if she was still too apprehensive to be a flower without the thorns.

I liked her prickly personality. I liked those glimpses of softness beneath the barbed exterior. Even though she wasn't very nice to me in Highbell, there was always something about her that I admired. Plus, Rissa was the one person who understood what it was like living in Highbell all those years as a saddle. We had that connection of the past, no matter what.

Now, she's gone. Because I wasn't prepared enough. Because I let my guard down.

I can't do that again.

After wiping my hands on my pants, I start making my

way back to camp, yawning as I go. There was no cozy house for us to stay in last night. Instead, we crowded inside a dilapidated barn with rotted boards and a charred roof, over a hundred of us packed in together on grass and straw.

Just when I'm about to break through the tree line, I hear a branch snap before Emonie suddenly appears next to me, her auburn hair a bit messy, a leaf dangling from an orange-tipped curl at her ear.

"Great Divine," I say, hand slammed against my thumping heart. "Where did you come from?"

"Look," she chirps, shoving a leafy branch in my face. "I found Lick Loot! Want to try it?"

My nose wrinkles at the bough, its leaves the color of mud. "No, thanks."

Yesterday, she got very excited about an old shoe with its sole ripped off and laces missing. I have no idea what she's going to do with it, but she stuffed it in her pouch with a smile on her face.

"Suit yourself," she says as we continue to walk. She snaps off one of the leaves and shoves it into her mouth, twirling the stem with her fingers as she sucks on it. "Mmm. Sugary."

"Good foraging morning, I take it?"

"Yep." She carefully plucks off the rest of the leaves and puts them in her pouch. "How about you? Have a good magic morning?" Surprised, I turn to look at her. "What? You didn't actually think I believed you were always going off because you had to *go*, did you?"

"So you followed me?"

"A few times," she admits with an easygoing shrug. "It's nothing personal, I spy on everyone."

"*Now* you seem more like a rebel."

"Vulmi," she corrects. "And thank you."

I start to laugh, but then I notice something about her.

"Wait. Your eyes. They're…a different color."

She turns to me, batting them. "Yeah, you like them? I got them from the fae whose house we stayed at the other day. Pretty pink color. What do you think? Romantic, yes?"

My own eyes twitch. My stomach does too. "Please…tell me you didn't forage someone's eyeballs."

Her delighted giggle scares a bird in a tree above us. "No, silly. I have glamour magic."

Surprise shoots through me. "Oh."

She reaches over and twirls her finger in my hair. "If I touch someone, then I can take something of theirs and use it for glamour." I watch as her short auburn hair turns as golden as my own.

I have to fight not to let my jaw drop. Seeing someone else with my hair is eerie. "Whoa."

She shakes her head, and just like that, her own color returns, the strawberry-orange ends bleeding back into view. "I can glamour other people too, not just myself, but it takes a lot more magic and concentration."

"Wow. That's impressive."

"Thank you," she says cheerfully.

Up ahead, I see movement in the overgrown field as we approach the barn. People are filtering in and out, packing up, shoving food into their mouths, and saddling their horses as they ready to leave.

I head straight for Blush, my sweet opal-swirled mare, only to find Ludogar, Wick's right hand, buckling her straps. His sea-stranded hair is combed straight back today, dripping slightly at the ends like he dumped a bucket over himself to wash. He's never been around me much, even after all this time we've spent traveling together. I get the feeling he likes to keep to himself.

"You didn't have to do that. I could've saddled her," I tell him as I approach.

He smooths a hand over her rounded cheek, and I notice the bloom of a pale pink right there, which does make it look like she's blushing. "Ahh, but you see, Blush here is my first love."

I blink in surprise. "I didn't know she was your horse."

"Yep," he says as she noses his arm. "This old girl and I go way back."

"I didn't mean to take your horse."

"Don't worry, I have another. Blush isn't keen on the riskier rides I go on sometimes. She also likes attention, so I think she quite enjoys being your mount. It's good for her ego."

I smile. "Well, I'll take good care of her and show her off as often as I can."

"Good," he says with a small tilt of his lips, but I have a feeling he's assessing me, his teal eyes trying to dig down deep. "I'm Ludo, by the way. I never officially introduced myself."

"Don't take it personally. Ludo isn't friendly," Emonie declares.

"Em," I admonish.

"What? He isn't." Her glamoured pink eyes swing back to him. "Isn't that right?"

The male shrugs.

"I've noticed you're usually out scouting or doing some other job," I say.

He tips his head. "I keep busy."

His eyes flicker behind me, and when I turn, I see Wick walking over, his long hair drooping on the left side of his head, leaving the shaved side exposed on the right. He stops in front of me, black brows pulled low. "Can we speak?"

I nod and he takes us around the side of the barn, away from the large group. We walk alongside the wall, its crumbling, split boards and dangling nails as our backdrop. When we're nearly at the middle of the building, Wick stops and turns toward me, and I study the drawn planes of his face. "I wanted to talk to you about where we're going next."

I pause. "Okay."

He's kept up his side of the deal, making sure to always talk to me about what to expect with every safe house we travel to. But his tone and his hesitant expression are making my own anxiety spike.

My hand slips down to my waist, thumb hooking over one of my ribbons.

"We're picking up another group of Vulmin, but they won't need much convincing. They'll have one look at you and be ready to take on their new mission without a single word from me."

"That's good, isn't it?"

"It is. For the Vulmin. But I fear it will be difficult for you."

I frown. "Why?"

He pauses, his shoulders rounding slightly, face strained with something close to...worry.

My fingers curl tightly around my ribbons as if they can brace me. And I'm glad I have hold of them, because his answer staggers me.

"Because the next place we're going is Bryol."

I rear back in shock.

Bryol.

My foundation shakes at hearing that word, the whole ground beneath me left to waver and tip. Bryol—my childhood home.

We're actually going to my *home*.

I don't know whether I'm filled with more excitement...or dread.

Returning to the place I lived with my parents brings up so many emotions that I don't know how to stand still. I can't—not with how hard the earth seems to quake, how loudly my skull clangs.

My hand comes up, bracing against the dilapidated wall, gold trickling down my fingers and coating the wood in slow drips.

"I wanted to prepare you," he says quietly, and my eyes lift, even as my vision wants to tunnel.

"Thanks." My voice sounds far away.

Wick vacillates, boot toeing at some buried farm tool long-since rusted and covered with dirt. "If you don't want to go…"

My head snaps up. "I want to go," I say firmly. "I just…"

I just need to make the ground settle again, need to steady myself.

"I never thought I'd ever go back."

He nods as if he understands, still watching me closely. "Alright. Then we should head out. We'll be there by dusk."

Dusk.

So soon. Just a handful of hours.

For nearly my whole life, Bryol has been a far-off, unreachable place, and now, I'm going to be there by *dusk*.

"If you change your mind…"

"I won't," I tell him.

After he walks away, I stay beside the barn, giving myself a moment alone. I drop my hand, leaving a streak of gold against the wood. I know my parents are dead, I know this, and yet, hearing that I'm going to Bryol makes me feel as if I'm going to *them*.

After a couple of minutes forcing myself to breathe, to process, I turn back and head for the group. When I round the corner, I see all the Vulmin have already mounted their horses.

I feel everyone's gaze as I walk to Blush and get myself onto the saddle. I look straight ahead, gripping the reins, trying to appear strong and sure. Wick and Ludogar take up the lead, while I take up the spot right behind them, with Emonie at my side.

As we begin our travel, I focus on the scenery to calm my rattled heart. There's a haze of fog trying to stick to the flatlands like steam over a teacup, and between the endless grass is this dusty path we're traveling on and no buildings in sight.

Emonie stays quiet beside me, but I can't stand the silence.

"So," I begin, trying to latch on to whatever topic I can. "You mentioned a sister before. Is she a Vulmin too?"

She seems startled by my question, her eyes turned back to her own color, swirling with orange and red. "No. Definitely not." She laughs, but it's not her giddy giggle. It's more of a force of breath. "She's not the Vulmi type."

I get the feeling I shouldn't have brought it up. "What part of Annwyn are you from?"

"All over. My parents always traveled. We never really had just one place we stuck to, so I stuck with other things instead," she says, leaning down to pet her horse, stroking against his dappled white coat. He has a soft bluish mane, and she's used the twine she collected to braid little plaits into it. "Thistle has been with me since I was a girl. He's just about the only thing I still have."

My heart aches for her. I might've been stuck in one place for over ten years when I was little, never able to leave Derfort Harbor, but I know what it's like to feel like nothing is yours. Nothing constant or familiar.

"What were you doing for the Vulmin before you came with us?" I ask, hoping I've chosen a better topic.

She gives an impish grin, her auburn hair looking particularly orange today at its short, curled-up tips. "Stealing from the Stone Swords."

My eyes go wide. "Stealing what?"

"Messages mostly. It was a lot of hanging out at taverns and flirting."

"*Mostly?*"

She lifts a shoulder. "I may have foraged a few things from them here and there."

"Like what?"

"Coin. A *very* risqué portrait carried in one of the captains' pockets—of *himself*," she giggles. "Plus, a nicely carved pipe. Some yummy chewing sap that tasted like jam. And…one of their swords."

I sputter out a surprised laugh. "You took one of their *swords*? Those things are huge. Aren't they heavy?"

"Not at all. The Stone King makes them with his magic. They're strong but surprisingly light. Very long though. I prefer a short blade, myself."

"How'd you manage to steal it?"

"Told the soldier I wanted to *touch it*," she says with a wag of her brows. "He was mightily disappointed when he realized I was talking about his sword and not the other rock-hard piece he had on him. Although, I must admit, that *was* impressively lengthy too. But I never get involved with Stone Swords." She wrinkles her nose in disgust at the thought.

"What about other rebels? Do you *get involved* with them?"

She teeters her head. "Here and there. But males are so exhausting, you know? Always demanding commitment when it's convenient for them."

"Run into that problem a lot?"

"Of course," she replies with a wistful sigh. "Plenty of them fall madly in love with me. But I live a treacherous life of a Vulmi. I can't be tamed, Lyäri."

A laugh tapers out of me. "And you shouldn't be."

Emonie glances over. "And what about this…dangerous lover of yours? Did he tame you?"

The smile on my face goes sad, a fresh pang of longing pinching the center of my chest.

"The opposite. He set me free."

I can feel her mottled gaze on my face, but I stare straight ahead. Eyes skipping up to the sky.

The sky makes me think of him, the land makes me think of my parents, and I'm hovering on the horizon between them both.

"I heard we're going to Bryol," Emonie says quietly.

I manage to speak despite the hard lump in my throat. "Yeah."

"If you decide you don't want to go, I'll hole up with you."

Appreciation swims in the depths of my whirlpool stomach. "I'll let you know if I change my mind. Thanks for the offer."

"Of course. Friends stick together."

I don't know how I've gotten so lucky since being in Annwyn. First by meeting Nenet, then Estelia and Thursil, and now her. It reminds me that I'm not alone.

"Besides," she goes on. "You can turn things shiny. Imagine the things I could forage from you."

I snort. "That's called stealing."

"*Collecting*," she amends breezily. "Besides, I think a bit of sharing between friends is normal. Healthy even."

"Of course."

"I shared my soap. And my clothes."

"I turned your sigil earring gold," I reply, head tilting toward her pierced ear and the pretty chains dangling down from the pointed tip. "It really sets off your gleaming charisma."

Her slender finger brushes over it. "I know. You just understand me so well."

For the rest of the day, Emonie helps distract me from melancholic thoughts as we banter back and forth, talking about nothing and everything.

And all the while, apprehension eats at me. Our group chews up the distance of our destination, time biting through the day one nipped hour at a time.

Then, just before dusk, we reach Bryol, and I find it's quite hard to swallow.

CHAPTER 29

AUREN

The city is a clutter of ruin. A patchwork of crooked destruction.

Bryol sits on the horizon like a scar. Bubbled up with pocked buildings, smears of burnt stone still stained an inky black. The entire place is blistered with rubble and wreckage.

It looks like a great fire spread throughout the city, and then a giant came along and stomped it all out, crumbling every building beneath its bulky feet.

One lone street weaves through the havoc. A seam in the middle of the frayed fabric of what must've once been a thriving metropolis.

"Great Divine." I sit atop my horse, looking out at it all, eyes skimming as if I can try to find one spot that hasn't been destroyed.

I can't.

This isn't a city anymore. It's a wasteland.

Wick sits atop his horse next to me, the others gone

ahead.

"What exactly happened here that night?" I ask. My voice is thick, but the moisture in my eyes is thicker.

"There was a short war. It was quick—only lasted a few months that time. Just another swift boot of the monarchy kicking against the rumbling rabble, squashing the fae who dared to resist or speak up. Every time our discord becomes too loud, the king makes sure to deal with us quickly." Bitterness churns in his tone, making it foam up with bubbling anger. "But a battle didn't need to happen here. The unrest was near the capital. There weren't even many Vulmin soldiers stationed in Bryol."

"They attacked it because of my family."

His gaze lashes out with a rope that tethers to mine, looping in place. "Yes. They didn't like that the resistance whispered their support for the Turleys and wanted your family to retake the throne. So the Carricks sent soldiers here to send a message...and to remove their biggest threat. Though they never admitted it."

My stomach churns, gnarled and bunching.

"Why hasn't it been rebuilt?"

"Monarchy won't allow it," he says bitterly. "And truthfully, no one wanted to. It's a gravesite now. Without a Turley in Bryol, it's going to stay dead anyway."

It looks like a gravesite. Wedges of buildings jutting up like gravestones in a row down the street. Shots of bloomed greenery grown up over the bowed land like flowers left by loved ones.

"But it's your home. You needed to see this."

My nod is heavy. Wick's is angry.

"This is what the Carrick monarchy did. They killed *thousands* of people. Razed an entire city. All because after hundreds of years, the Turley name is *still* a threat to them, and they can't stand it. When a Turley wore a crown, there were no undue executions for fae daring to speak up. There were no exorbitant taxes, no one arrested for being Orean, no half fae seen as *lesser*." He bites out that last word with gnashed teeth and curled lip, the little nicks of scars on his forehead standing out more with the reddish hue of his anger. "It's not a monarchy anymore, it's tyranny. And so long as we sit around and don't rise up to finally go against them, things like *this* will keep happening," he says, jutting a finger toward the city. "With your help, the Vulmin can overthrow King Carrick…and then you can take his place."

My head snaps over to him. "I have no desire to wear a crown. I'm supporting the Vulmin so fae can stop being terrorized by the monarchy. That's it."

His black brows pull together, eyes studying me intently. "But you're *Auren Turley*. You're alive, and you landed in Saira's field. Don't be blind to the fact that the Vulmin will want *you* to take the throne now that you're here."

Blind?

I yank my gaze back to the city, gnawing on his words. Remembering how Thursil said something similar. First, Nenet accused me of not listening. Now, Wick's accusing me of not seeing. But I am. I just have no desire to look in the mirror and see myself as something I don't want to be.

Silence churns around us for a couple of minutes, and Wick watches me like he doesn't quite believe me. Then, he lets out a breath. "You might feel differently. As you spend more time here. As you take more in," he says quietly. "Are you ready to go into the city?"

I nod, though I'm not sure if I'm ready at all. If I ever could be.

With a click of his tongue, he leads his horse down toward Bryol, leaving me on this hill alone.

Leaving me to listen.

And see.

The streets of Bryol are an uneven seascape of frothed dust from crumbled buildings and waves of debris that sluice through the city. It's a backlash of violence, anger still cracking through the stonework in severed silence.

My footsteps though…my footsteps simmer with the undertow of regret. Melancholy hangs off my arms and slumps down my shoulders, and I wouldn't be surprised if I dripped it down the street. This place has wrapped its arm around me and plunged a dagger of pain through my chest.

"Where are you going?"

I don't turn around at Wick's voice. My attention is too choked, heart too flooded.

I've left my horse with the others, in the rifted building just behind us, where stringy trees and fringed bushes clutter all around the outside. There's a gash torn down its stone face in a diagonal scrape, big enough that our horses were able to walk right in. It's big enough that all of us, horses and all, can fit inside. We're supposed to wait here until one of the Vulmin checks things over with the group we're meeting in a small village just past the city's crumbling walls.

I've only taken three more steps out onto the street before Wick's beside me, hand on my arm. "Auren, you shouldn't wander alone."

He's saying my name here, in the same place where my parents spoke it. A fresh wave of despondency trickles through me.

"I'll be fine."

There's a beat of silence. He's probably remembering what he saw me do in Geisel. "Still, this place is unfamiliar to you."

That's where he's wrong.

GOLD

Because despite the rain of ruin that's flooded Bryol...I know this place. Even though it's been over twenty years since I was here last, I know it. It feels familiar to me, right down to my bones. There's a little thrum through the ground, as if it's recognizing me too.

"I'll come with you."

"So will I," Emonie says, coming up to stand at my other side.

"And me," Ludogar adds.

More Vulmin have trickled out of the building, gathering around me in a silent presence that radiates quiet support.

Gratitude bloats, floating up like bubbles to help lift my weighted-down heart.

With all the Vulmin keeping pace behind me, we start walking through Bryol.

Our boots crackle along a dusty spume of ash and ground dirt, ankles threatening to twist over the crumbs of buildings piled up beneath our feet. Most of the debris is scattered at the edges, the worst of the buildings' carnage laid to rest. But all over, plants have retaken the ashen shambles, sprouting up through the tiniest crevices, bursting through broken ceilings, dangling down tipping walls.

Despite the destruction and the overgrowth, my feet somehow know where to go as we wind down the streets. Something tugs me forward. Maybe some long-ingrained memory. Or maybe something else pulls me toward the city's unbeating heart.

The Vulmin don't say anything. Not as we climb over a particularly bad spot, not as wooden spires have to be hauled away to unblock our path. Not as we pick our way through the various buildings and help each other over the wild wreckage. They all just follow me without hesitation. Letting me lead myself to my past.

Until finally, my feet bring me here.

Here, on what used to be a picturesque street. I face a two-story house that's now a hovel of dumped-down slabs. Knuckles of rock clenched between rust and ash, a punched-out roof smothered with char. My childhood home, just a topple of skeleton walls, all bones and teeth and nothing in between.

Nothing but a fist of memories that suddenly thumps against my skull, as if I had to get here to open up the lock that bound them.

Up and down this bricked street, there used to be staggered houses, one after the other, in neat little lines. I'd run in and out of them, playing with the other kids, laughter and shouts pealing like bells.

There were humming trees that sang in the summer, with puffstring vines that trailed down in feathery fluffs and brushed against their exposed roots. We'd hide beneath their canopies, all while their song danced through our hair. I'd race my father on the way to the morning market, where he'd buy me warm, sugared berries pinned to a wooden skewer.

I'd swim in the crystal lagoon and ride my mother's horse with no saddle. I'd watch the lightbreathers when they traveled through, putting on great performances in the night sky big enough for the whole city to see.

And this house.

This was where I would come home to each day. It had a bright yellow door with a running trim of a decorative eave hanging over it. Inside, there were stairs with beaded rails. I had little suns and stars painted on my bedroom ceiling to help me fall asleep at night. Bundles of willow branches hung beside the fireplace for luck. Jade leaves floated in dandelion water to bring harmony under our roof.

I learned how to walk here, to talk, to play, to laugh, to love.

Inside this skeleton house lies a piece of my heart.

GOLD

The building now is nothing but a lump of coal. Cracks run jagged through its sagging face like wrinkles strained from a sob. The whole street is ruined, but my house…this one took the brunt of the fire. As if this is where it started. As if this is where it all began.

You're the last-birthed Turley.
It never should've happened.
Then Darkness fell onto Bryol.
To remove a threat.

My house. My family. My city. Thousands of people, and this all happened because Turleys lived here. Because *I* lived here.

Tears burn my eyes, as hot as the flames that once burned these walls.

Behind me, the gathered Vulmin watch.

I wonder if any of them remember what Bryol used to be. I wonder what they think as they see a Turley standing in front of her black-charred home, crying tears of gold.

Maybe my tears thin the veil between past and present, because I suddenly hear my mother's faint voice at my ear.

"My little sun, where is your shine?"

"It's here, mama," I said to her, even as I cried. Because no matter the reason for my sadness, she could fix it. She could *always* fix it.

"Good, my girl. Because all I want is for you to be happy. You have your own light, little sun. So you must carry it with you when it grows dark. But you can do that. Because we are strong, aren't we?"

I feel more than hear Wick come up to my side, his gaze locked on the same sight as me. "This is why we fight," he tells me quietly. "Because this is *wrong*. What happened here should never be allowed to happen again."

When his head turns, I look over to meet his stare. I don't even try to wipe away the tearstains trailing my cheeks.

"You should *never* have been taken, Auren. Your parents should *never* have been killed."

A crumpled-up sob tosses down my throat.

"But I want you to remember something, Lyäri."

"What?"

His brown eyes dig down, burrowing into my trampled spirit. "The Carricks didn't win that night. Not completely. Because they didn't get *you*."

He surprises me when he grabs my hands and holds them gently. Surprises me when I see the depth of sadness in his usually stoic face.

"You *lived*, Auren."

Then why does my heart feel like it's died?

"Although they tried, they couldn't extinguish all the light of the Turleys that night. You've been a beacon in the dark, even while you were gone. And now that you've returned, you're Annwyn's dawning sun."

My heart throbs like an open wound, fresh tears scratching down my cheeks. Grief digs in her nails, making sure I'm left to bleed.

Left to scar.

How long was it after my parents pulled me out of bed that night? How long did it take after they ushered me outside with the other children to be taken to safety? Was it minutes after we walked down the street with our guards? Did violence come to my house before my bed was even cold?

Did my parents try to fight, to flee, to get to me? Did they die on the street, or did they burn right here in our home? Were they already dead when I was taken?

I don't have the courage to ask.

But I hope that they died thinking I was safe. Thinking that their death wasn't in vain. I hope they took their last breath believing I was okay.

I fold my legs beneath me. Knees bent, head up, tears dripping.

I wasn't killed that night, but a part of me died, anyway.

Emonie comes up. With light steps, she leans down, placing the broken-winged bird charm from her earring onto the ash.

As soon as she steps away and sits beside me, more Vulmin take her place, each one of them setting down their own sigils. Until there's over a hundred of them lying at the foot of my home, glinting among ash and rubble. Until all of them are kneeling with me, here on the hallowed street.

A silent tribute.

A wordless bond.

One that means more to me than I can ever possibly say.

With a kiss pressed to my fingertips, I then rest my hand to the ground. Let my gold stream.

I hear several of the Vulmin gasp aloud, many of them getting to their feet to back away, all of them watching as the tree sprouts up, reaches, growing taller and wider, its branches spreading, leaves springing, flowers blooming high overhead.

Until the tree stands taller than any broken wall on this whole street. Until the bark gleams and its black-veined leaves let the last of the sunlight stream through.

A solid gold tree, roots dug down where mine were severed. Turley gold. Grown up where they tried to snuff us out.

When I get to my feet, the Vulmin rise with me.

My mother's voice is an echo through the breeze.

We are strong, aren't we?

Aren't we.

CHAPTER 30

AUREN

The group of Vulmin we meet up with actually turns out to be the entire village. Erected behind Bryol, past the fields where crackle grains shift with sparks of static, and lavender moss fattens the hillside rocks.

They call this village *Naonos Erith*. The Clamor of the Blaze.

Because while Bryol may lie quiet since death came during the Hundredflame Battle, the people here carry its lasting din. With devastated rattles in their chest. With a cacophony of quieted grumbles. With a racket of dissenting tears. Their reverberating discord blares through every single scarred building that now stands.

They used pieces of Bryol's ruin to build it. A circle of homes cloistered in close against one another. One shop. One stable. One communal garden. One water well with a rusted pump. And one hundred fae.

That's all that remains from the thousands that used to

thrive in the city's walls.

As we approach on horseback, I see that the entire village is already outside.

Waiting.

As soon as they see me riding beside Wick, as soon as realization sinks in, I see the change overtake them. Eyes widening and mouths gaping, fingers lifting and whispers hissing. The moment my presence sinks in, their collective clamor *roars*.

The Golden One Gone.

Lyäri Ulvêre. The gilded girl returned.

Lyäri Lyäri Lyäri

I'm filled with their blaring sound, and then I'm surrounded with their presence.

Hands are outstretched, faces smiling, others wailing, all of them trying to get closer to me as I sit on my horse. It's overwhelming. Makes my hands tighten on the reins. Even Blush doesn't know what to do with this level of attention, her nervousness apparent by the way she paws at the ground and pricks her ears.

"Auren Turley has returned to Bryol!" Wick calls out. "We come to gather all Vulmin, between here and Lydia. To march against the monarchy and bring our new dawn. It's time to step out of the dark." The villagers are listening to him intently, their eyes alight. "Who will join us?"

Combined bellows lift in the air so loud I flinch, and then I'm practically pulled down off my saddle. All the Vulmin dismount, and it's like being caught in a swell, a surge of people moving around me, and I have to move with it. We're ushered into the heart of the village, and within minutes, a bonfire is lit that casts sparks up into the darkening sky, and a large animal is roasting over it in preparation of a feast.

"Here, Lady Auren," a male fae says, ushering me to sit on a heap of fur at the fire.

The moment I plop down, people flock to me. They smile, welcome, give me their names. I do my best to greet them all, but the attention is staggering.

They watch me as I'm not just their symbol, but their savior.

"Lady Auren has returned home!" someone shouts on the other side of the flames. He's tall and brawny, with two large hoops hanging from either ear. Everyone turns and listens to him, the noise dulling down, making me think maybe he's some sort of village leader. "The Lyäri Ulvêre is back to Bryol. The *Vulmin Dyrūnia* is ready to march. The Clamor is ready to march with them!"

Voices of approval crush against my ears, the energy of the village frenetic.

"Let us feast and celebrate the return of our Lyäri! And tomorrow, we rise with our Dawn!"

Another raucous cheer fills the air to near-bursting.

Then, it's a blur of villagers dancing, music and singing, or a lightbreather who makes a show in the night sky. Where tendrils of light float up, telling the story of Saira Turley's bridge. Of a girl who didn't give up. Of a girl who kept on her path.

I'm plied with food and drink and more drink and more *drink*.

It tastes like smoked vanilla and goes down with decadent warmth, the crackling foam top sending bubbles right to my head.

Delicious.

Just like the roasted meat. And the bread husks peeled open that are doused with creamy butter. The sugared berries pinned on a skewer.

I dance with Wick. With Emonie. With Ludogar. With all the Vulmin in the entire village. I melt down the gold from my arm cuffs and make them into strings that sway around us like tall grass, glinting against the firelight beneath a sky that sings of home.

I let my ribbons dance with me, and even though I can't move them, they move with *me*. They spin through the air and drag across the ground, and for a moment, I can pretend that they're back to the way they were. I wish for Slade, the Wrath, Digby and Rissa, Nenet and Estelia and Thursil, Sail and my parents…wish that they were all here. With me.

But maybe there's a reason I'm alone.

And maybe…I'm not really alone after all.

I wake up with a splitting headache.

Those smoked vanilla drinks were entirely too delicious going down. I'm not exactly sure how many cups I consumed, either. Feels like a lot.

Bright side?

It's better than all the times I'd wake up with these headaches in Highbell after drinking too much wine and fermenting in despondency.

As soon as I open my eyes, the headache chisels into my eye socket and has me groaning. My roiling stomach makes me want to yank up the covers and hide beneath them. I can't though, because Emonie is on top of the blankets and grunts at me with a hiss of threat when I try to snatch them.

"If you move me, I will forage someone's shoe and throw it right at your beautiful face," she grumbles, eyes still shut.

"I'll turn your hair solid gold so you can't lift your head from that pillow," I mutter back.

She hums croakily. "That actually sounds nice. Then I wouldn't have to get up."

She's got a point.

"Come on." I shove an elbow into her side. "If I'm up, you're up."

A huff escapes her smooshed lips. "You're a bit mean after a celebratory village feast."

"You snored in your sleep all night."

She sits up, her hair stuck around her head at all angles, the orange tips curling every which way as she tries to finger-comb through it. "I'll collect something you can stuff into your ears."

I snort as I get up, swinging my legs over the bed with one eye shut. "I don't know what we were drinking last night, but that stuff was…"

"Amazing?"

"Yeah, honestly." As soon as I'm on my feet, I sway and slap a hand to my mouth. "Great Divine, I think I might vomit," I say through my fingers.

"Really?" She looks around. "Better gold yourself a bowl."

I shudder and take a deep breath, forcing myself to exhale through it. "I can't be vomiting in someone's home."

She hums. "It would be a bit off-putting, since they just sang songs to celebrate you all night," she says as she comes over and picks a twig out of my hair. "Come on. Maybe there's a pond we can dunk our heads in."

Maybe that'll numb away the skull chisel.

But as soon as I get to the door, I think I really might have to go collapse back onto the bed and hide under the covers. Luckily, I'm saved.

Elisabeth, the lovely fae who let me borrow her bed last night, is also apparently a divine being and the most beautiful soul in the world, because she has a cure in hand the moment we stumble out of the room.

She takes one look at me, her blonde ringlets bouncing at her shoulders, and presses a cup into my hands and then another into Emonie's.

"What is this?" I ask warily, looking down at the bit of clumpiness that's floating on the top.

"Best you not ask, Lady Auren," she says ominously.

Emonie clinks her wooden cup against mine in a toast and then tosses it back. I tip my own cup and gulp the liquid down, trying not to think about the floaty bits. It tastes like pickled chocolate with a bit of soil, but the moment it hits my stomach, I get instant relief.

"Wow," I say, letting out a breath.

"Better?" Elisabeth asks.

"Much, thank you."

She smiles and takes the cups, dress swishing as she strides away. I look around and see Wick, Ludogar, and a handful of other Vulmin who also stayed here last night, picking up their bedrolls and tidying up their presence.

Everyone, except Wick and Ludo of course, looks like they need Elisabeth's helpful concoction too.

"Enjoy yourself last night?" Wick asks as he approaches.

"Yes, although, I probably shouldn't have…"

To my surprise, he shakes his head. "You should celebrate your return to Bryol. Don't feel guilty about that. These are where your roots are. It's a happy occasion."

"But you didn't celebrate much?"

He gives me a rare smile, and I can't help but match it. "I've just got a stronger stomach than you."

"My stomach is plenty strong."

"Really? *I* didn't need Elisabeth's fog juice, unlike you."

I shrug. "Then you're really missing out on the full experience."

He chuckles. "Go eat some breakfast. Fill that weak stomach of yours."

I roll my eyes, but…I *am* hungry.

Elisabeth, bless her soul, has the table laid out with a big bowl of thick cream with berries swirled through it, slices of salted meat, and dipping bread that's soaking in some kind of syrup.

"I made sure I saved a fresh loaf just for you," she says with a wink.

"You're the fairest fae in all the land," Emonie tells her dreamily before she quickly grabs up a piece. I do the same, the two of us dunking the bread into the cream until we polish off our plates.

Afterward, I wash up using a bucket of water someone brought in from the well. When I come out dressed in the brown tunic and pants Elisabeth gave me, I find Wick and the other Vulmin with serious faces. They're gathered around someone I haven't met yet, though as she stands beside Ludogar, it's easy to see the family resemblance.

She has the same sea-blue hair as him, the same froth of frizzy white along her scalp that makes it look like the way a tide bubbles up along the shore. Her eyes are sharp teal, and she seems like the older sister to Ludo and has a couple of inches on his height. While he's wearing a tunic and vest, she's in a simple gray smock with a cloak and a white apron that frills at the edges.

"How many?" Wick asks her.

She shrugs. "That I don't know."

His gaze flicks to Ludo, and the fae tilts his head in thought. "Fancy a rescue mission?"

Wick smirks and looks around at the others. "What say you, Vulmin?"

Everyone grunts their approval, and I use the noise to move without notice, sidling up next to Emonie where she's standing against the wall. "What's going on?" I ask quietly.

"Lerana is Ludo's sister. She works as a spy in one of the nobleman's houses in Riffalt City. She has some news of some Oreans we might be able to pick up along the way."

My brows lift up in surprise.

"It's one of our most common missions," she tells me. "We try to track down Oreans who need our help. Sometimes, they're being forced to work for terrible fae, and we sneak them out and give them a new life in a Vulmin village where they can live in peace. Other times, Oreans reach out and we help get their ears molded for pointed tips and new birth papers that list them as full fae. We do whatever we can to help."

"So it's true." The fae's voice draws my attention away from Emonie as I look across the room at Lerana, whose teal eyes are now locked on me. "My brother told me about you, but to see you in person…"

"Nice to meet you."

"The honor is mine, Lady Lyäri," she says, pressing a hand to her chest with a smile. "Word has spread of your return. The whispers are catching on. I believe you've come at the perfect time."

Let's hope so.

She turns back to Wick. "I should return. I'll await your arrival."

He nods as they get to their feet, the other Vulmin doing the same. "I'll get a plan together. Tell Brennur to expect us within the hour."

She nods and then leaves the house, her brother following behind.

"I'll go pack," Emonie says, slipping away just as Wick comes walking over.

As soon as he's beside me, he tilts his head toward the door, and I follow him outside. The morning air still smells faintly of smoke from last night's bonfire, and the villagers who are cleaning up look over, giving me greetings and smiles.

"You heard the tail-end of that, but Lerana is one of our most valuable spies in Riffalt. She holds a position as a servant, feeding us important information from a nobleman's house. He's a big supporter of the Carrick monarchy."

"And there are Oreans in his household?"

"Not his—but a neighboring one. From what it sounds like, they're not there by choice. Normally, I wouldn't hesitate at sending a group in to retrieve them, but this particular household is incredibly risky. I need to go there myself."

"And you're wondering what to do with me," I guess.

He nods. "The whole city is crawling with Stone Swords. I don't want to leave you with the other Vulmin as they continue on toward the kingdom, but the estate where I'm going will be dangerous."

"I'm dangerous myself."

His lips quirk. "Yes, you are. Which is why I think you *should* come with me, but I'll leave the decision to you. I have a plan to keep you safe, and it requires a disguise, if you're okay with that. I think it's important for the Vulmin to know you're helping to rescue these Oreans rather than staying behind. It will show them how strong you are—that you're willing to fight. Now that we have larger numbers, we should do more missions like this together on our way to the kingdom. Let word of you spread among all of Annwyn, not just the Vulmin."

"I want to help," I say honestly. "And if these Oreans are in a bad situation, I want to get them out. A disguise doesn't bother me."

"Good. We'll leave within the hour, so get ready."

I'm filled with a soul-renewing purpose. This mission with the Oreans is exactly what I need—exactly what I want to do. It makes me feel like I'm not just a golden symbol, but that I can actually *help* the people who need it. To start actively making strides to aid their cause.

There's no need for me to *get ready*, as Wick said.

Because I already am.

CHAPTER 31

QUEEN MALINA

I think Dommik might have been less dangerous when he was simply trying to kill me. Something has changed between the assassin and me. Now that he's touched me, nearly kissed me, I'm not sure how to behave.

We were supposed to have reached Highbell last night, but since he became too exhausted to continue, we ended up staying in a little cave he found at the side of the mountain.

We could've gone to the safe house where I went when I fled the castle, but I didn't suggest it, and neither did he. He killed my guards there. Killed Jeo there. Tried to kill *me* there.

It wouldn't feel right if we were to return now. It seems like ages ago, and I feel like a different person since I fled that place.

Perhaps I am.

Perhaps the assassin is too.

I can't help but think how things would be different if he'd been successful that day. If he'd been able to plunge his blade through my chest. None of this would've happened if he'd killed me. The fae wouldn't be invading. The two of us wouldn't be…in this strange push and pull.

Part of me still wants to hate Dommik for killing Jeo and the others, yet that hate has shifted to myself. Ultimately, it *was* my fault. I took Jeo on as a sort of rebellion. After so many years of watching my husband flaunt his harem of saddles, I wanted one for myself to shove in his face. Jeo was pleasant. Uncomplicated. I enjoyed his company, and I enjoyed the freedom I felt with him. He was killed for no other reason than staying loyal to me, and I left him there in the snow.

Dommik was right. I did have a heart of ice.

But I'm trying to make it thaw.

"Your thoughts are so loud I can hear them from here."

I glance up at Dommik as he treks back inside the cave. At least he walked away to relieve himself this time. He stops in front of me and passes over the water skin along with some bread wrapped around a slice of hard cheese.

"Care to share what it is you're thinking about so hard?"

I pick at the crust. "Jeo."

He hesitates. "The lover."

He doesn't pose it as a question, but I nod anyway. "Lover might be too generous a term. Can you call someone a lover if you pay them to be with you?"

"I wouldn't think the Cold Queen would have a saddle."

"Yes, well, when you're in a loveless marriage and can't birth an heir, which is your sole purpose for living and only duty to the kingdom…then one's husband leaves your bed quite quickly," I say bitterly.

Dommik watches me as I nibble on the bread. "Can't say I know much about duties to kingdoms, but I do know people, and your husband seems like a smarmy ass."

We share a look. "I think that would be an adequate

description."

After we both eat in silence for a while, he says, "Are you ready? To return to Highbell?"

I'm not sure it matters whether I'm ready or not. I have to go, regardless.

"You have to make them believe you," Dommik warns.

"I know."

"It won't be easy."

I know that too.

When we're both finished eating, Dommik shadow-leaps us away. Once we reach Highbell, I won't be traveling this way anymore, and I find myself wanting to savor it. The bent light and billowing shadows have become like a comforting embrace. I can't see his body, or mine, can't hear his voice or see much of the world, but I can feel his hand. A hot, steady, callused palm gripped in mine that never falters.

What must it say about me, that the most dependable hand I've ever held is in the grasp of my assassin?

We stop at midday, right at the road that leads to the city. I can see the Pitching Pines in the distance, those incomprehensibly tall trees that barricade us from the worst of the blizzarding wind.

Up the mountainside sits Highbell Castle. Right now, it's gleaming in the dappled gray daylight that filters in through the clouds. Snow covers its turrets and ice hangs from its belltower walls, but the gilded monstrosity is never dulled enough for my liking.

"I gotta ask..." Dommik begins as the two of us stare at the castle. "Was he trying to compensate for something?"

My lips curve. "A great many things, I think."

"Bold move to gild an entire castle."

"That's all Tyndall is," I reply. "Bold moves and smarmy charm."

"But you're still married to him in the eyes of the gods?"

he taunts.

"For now." My gaze casts sideways. "Perhaps I should simply hire your services. You can assassinate him instead of me."

He turns, hooded face revealing a hint of a smirk beneath. "Can you afford me? I'm expensive."

I gesture to the castle. "Take whatever gold you can hack off as payment."

Amusement ripples through his face, and he opens his mouth to reply, but suddenly, his eyes dart over my shoulder, and his entire face hardens. He shoves me a fraction of a second before an arrow flies right toward his chest. Before it pierces him, he explodes into billowing shadow.

I fall hard, landing in the stiff snow with the breath knocked out of me. I turn and try to push myself up, but someone suddenly grips my hair in their fist and wrenches my head up, neck stretched as they stand over me. I scream as a blade starts swinging toward my throat.

But shadow erupts, and a spray of blood bursts in my face.

I blink as a fae soldier falls to his knees, and it takes a moment to realize that Dommik just sliced his sword through his neck. The fae's head falls, pointed ears stabbing into the snow.

A bile-soaked scream lodges in my throat and makes me choke as I blink down at the severed head. I scramble back, slipping in the bloody snow, before I manage to get far enough away from the splatter that I can get to my feet.

The assassin stands over the fae's body, hood pulled low, arms flexed at his sides, and sword hanging from the tense grip of his hand. Blood is soaking into the snow, steam rising from the rivulets. The fae's marbled blade lays uselessly at his torso, his long blond hair now stained red.

I almost died.

One more second, and he would've sliced that sword through my neck.

Subconsciously, my hand lifts to my throat like a protective barrier as I continue to stare. My vision mottles with black spots.

"Hey."

He was going to kill me. My scalp still hurts where he gripped me. It was so close. I almost—

"*Queenie.*"

My view is abruptly cut off from the fae as Dommik stands before me. Searing hot hands grip my ice cold cheeks. "Look at me."

It's like my body has to listen to him. Has to comply. My gaze flies to his, and we lock eyes.

"You're in shock. Breathe in and out."

I do as he says, realizing that the black dots I keep seeing were from lack of air, and they slowly creep out of my vision the longer I keep breathing.

"Good," he rasps. He drags his thumbs across my frost-touched cheeks, rubbing flakes away. "Good," he says again. Then his hands drop, and I watch in fascination as he dips the corner of his cloak into the snow and then gently starts wiping the blood off my face.

"You saved my life."

He says nothing, just gives a few last swipes over my cheek.

"You were supposed to kill me, but you saved me just now instead." Ice crusts against my palms and pinches into my skin.

"Can't have the fae collecting my bounty, now can I?"

I want to scoff but all I manage to do is grimace.

"Come on. The Cold Queen doesn't get shaken from a mere assassination attempt, does she?" he teases.

I want to laugh. I want to cry.

Instead, I sniff and lift my chin. "Of course not."

I see him grin. "There she is. The unshakable cold."

He dusts me off, but when my eyes start to drop down to the fae again, he turns me away to face the city once more. "Don't look behind you. Look ahead."

Looking ahead frightens me even more. But as he said, I have to be the unshakable cold.

I hear him scraping around in the snow for the next couple of minutes. When he comes up beside me again, I see he's done his best to pile snow up over the body, head, and all the blood. The ground is lumpy, but no one will know what's hiding beneath unless someone walks over it.

Dommik dusts off his hands. "With the presence of that fae scout, I don't think we have time to walk into the city and take stock. Last time I checked, the scouts were only a couple of days ahead of the rest of the army. We should shadow-leap straight up to the castle."

I nod, but trepidation fills me. I'd hoped for time to sneak into the city and find out what's been happening since I left. I have no idea if Tyndall is back or if everyone still thinks I'm dead.

"Ready?"

I use the ice in my chest to fortify me, to freeze layer upon layer until I feel like I can stand taller. Pushing my shoulders back, I then grasp his hand. "Yes."

We lurch away with his magic, but it feels like only seconds before the comfort of his shadows pull away from me again. Too soon, we're whisked in front of Highbell Castle, inside the shadowy cover of the stable overhang.

Before us lies the front drive, the path open and leading right to the main door. A main door that looks as if it's been hacked at. As do the front walls that once shone with polished perfection.

I gape at it wordlessly.

GOLD

Gilded bricks have been chiseled into, pieces of gold snapped off the window panes, ax marks cutting up the walls. Besides the visible damage to the castle itself, there's another startling difference.

The drive should be open and clear, save for a horse or even a carriage if Tyndall has need of it. Instead, the front of the castle is utterly full of people. So many that we're crammed at the very back of the thick crowd. I creep back even more, nearly pressing into Dommik, but no one is paying us any attention. Everyone is facing the castle ahead.

"What in the realm..." My voice trails off as the crowd makes a collective noise, and then someone speaks. My gaze snaps upward to the high balcony.

A woman stands there, addressing the people below, and she looks so startlingly different from me. Her skin is bronze, her hair lush and black, hanging down to her waist in sleek waves. She has curves so unlike my slim figure, and a turquoise gown that plunges between her breasts, revealing far more cleavage than is proper. She oozes so much feminine sexuality that more than half the crowd seems to be riveted with desire, and the other half are looking at her like they'd do anything to please her.

Yet the thing that makes my stomach plummet is the glittering crown that sits atop her head. All at once, I realize who she is. The seashells and azure gemstones in the crown confirm it. Queen Kaila Ioana, ruler of Third Kingdom.

Why is she in Sixth Kingdom, in *my* castle, standing on *my* balcony?

"It appears that there's a queen in your castle," Dommik murmurs behind me.

"What is Queen Kaila doing here?" I hiss.

"Third Kingdom?" Dommik asks, a hint of surprise in his tone. "She sure is a long way from her beach."

Her voice lifts into the air as she addresses everyone. "I

completely understand the concerns of the kingdom, and I am here to rectify them."

She's here to rectify them?

Her words carry so perfectly that she doesn't even need to shout. Her husky voice drifts over the crowd, sounding like she's right beside me as she speaks. A trick of her tone, perhaps? Or is she using her voice magic?

"With his last words, King Midas beseeched me to step in and care for his people. That's why I came, and I am so thankful to the gods that I arrived when I did. I can only apologize for not getting here sooner." She presses a hand over her heart. "As his grieving betrothed, I will fulfill his last plea. It's what he would have wanted."

I can feel Dommik's eyes on the side of my face.

Kaila's words are screaming in my ears.

Last words.

Grieving betrothed.

What he would have wanted.

"He can't be," I whisper, shaking my head. "He can't possibly be…" My vision is tipping, my thoughts confused. "How can he be dead? She must be lying."

Dommik says nothing, but I can feel the confusion in his tension. He strikes me as a person who doesn't enjoy being caught off guard. I suppose with his line of work, that wouldn't be the best thing.

"He can't be dead," I say again, feeling like I'm my own version of an echo.

"I will personally be in the throne room every single day, opening the doors of Highbell so I may hear your concerns," Queen Kaila goes on. My gaze drops from the balcony, her words drowned out by the pounding in my ears. My eyes search through the crowd as if I expect to find Tyndall amongst them.

I don't.

I do, however, see a woman, brown eyes locking on me as her eyebrows shoot up in surprise. I freeze, and the sight of her pricks my senses. She's slight, but the way she holds her body screams strength. She doesn't look like a peasant or a noble. She's something else. She has dark brown skin and wears black leathers like a fighter, and her hair is shaved short. It looks like she has shapes shorn into her scalp. The shapes almost look like—

She turns her head, and I get distracted, my gaze pulling toward the soldiers up by the castle door. I frown at the sight of them, forgetting all about the woman.

Third Kingdom soldiers are standing shoulder-to-shoulder with Highbell's guards at the castle entrance, integrated with one another. Silver and gold, standing united under the beautiful presence of this other queen. We're allied with Third Kingdom, sure, but this is different. This is a show of unity that is just that—a *show*.

"She's trying to take my kingdom," I grit out.

Obviously, that's what she's doing. She's spelled it out. Not just with her words, but this ostentatious display, where she's acting as this beautiful benefactor come to graciously save Sixth Kingdom out of the kindness of her heaving heart.

My cold hands go colder, and my fingers dig into my palms, scraping against my frosted skin.

Tyndall sent an assassin to kill me, so that he could marry *her*? So that he could have not just Sixth and Fifth Kingdom under his control, but Third as well? He was going to have power over nearly half of all Orea, and then somehow…he suspiciously ends up dead?

My head is spinning.

My anger spins louder.

Like someone swinging a rope round and round, making it whistle through the air, so high pitched it makes me want to cringe.

How dare this woman think she can come here and lay claim to my kingdom.

I start walking forward.

"Queenie," Dommik hisses at my back. "What the fuck are you doing?"

I ignore him and start pushing my way through. Having to squeeze past everyone makes me more determined to get through the crowd, so that they'll know who I am. So that they'll see I'm not dead and that this other queen can't simply stand on my balcony and try to stake claim to what isn't hers.

Grieving betrothed. The absolute *nerve.*

Her continued words clash around in my whistling ears. "I am so incredibly proud to stand here before you and act as Sixth Kingdom's steward and help get Highbell back on steady feet." She smiles beautifully, lovely eyes casting across the crowd like they're her horde of adoring children. "And being from Third Kingdom means I have stepped on many a ship and crossed many a sea. I can safely say my feet are the steadiest you'll find."

The crowd laughs collectively.

I shove through.

I'm at the halfway point where the crowd is thickest, where I have to push more aggressively, when the people start to look over at me. When they start to *see.*

Then they're pointing and shouting, moving away, everyone's attention turning toward me.

"It's the Cold Queen!"

"It's Queen Malina!"

"The Cold Queen is alive!"

They have no idea how accurate that nickname now is.

I stop when all the people have moved aside, creating a path between their bodies, one that parts all the way to the front steps of the castle.

I stare up at the supplanter queen. "I am Queen Malina

Colier Midas and ruler of Sixth Kingdom. My throne has no need for a steward."

The grounds go quiet. Shock covers Queen Kaila's face before she quickly covers it up. She whispers something to her guards before looking down at me with a frown. "Queen Malina perished. She was killed by the very people you stand beside."

Internally, I flinch, but my face shows nothing as the crowd stares at me, and I lift my voice high, force it to stay even and strong. "I was not killed. And you cannot be betrothed in the eyes of the gods or the people, because King Midas was my husband."

Everyone just watches me—and not in the same way they watch her. They watch me with distrust. As if *I'm* the supplanter.

Kaila's thick lips press together.

She doesn't like that I'm ruining her carefully orchestrated show. I can see the frustration in her hard, umber eyes as she looks down her nose at me. I know what I must look like. Unbathed, unbound, clothes ill-fitting and humble, full of a slushed hem and wrinkled creases. Tendrils of my white hair ripped from the braid that hangs down my back, and I wonder if Dommik truly removed all the blood off my face from earlier or if there are still traces of it on my pale skin.

I don't care about any of it. She can't supplant me when I'm standing right here in the courtyard.

"If you are truly Queen Malina, where have you been?"

I hesitate.

Then, I feel his presence behind me. I don't know how I know it's him. Perhaps it's the scent of smoke that clings to his cloak. Or the slight tick in temperature that I feel radiating at my back. But I know Dommik stands there, a silent, hooded presence to help steel my spine.

There's no time to dither. Not with the fae so close behind. So the fact that there's a good portion of the city here within Highbell's walls to hear the truth directly from my lips is a blessing from the Divine.

So I square my shoulders and say, "I was in Seventh Kingdom."

Surprise spreads through the crowd like a gap. It stretches between me and them, widening like their gaping mouths.

"Seventh Kingdom," Queen Kaila repeats in monotone. "That *kingdom* doesn't exist anymore. There's nothing there. The edges of the world crumbled away hundreds of years ago."

"I thought that too. Until I went there."

She stares at me. I can feel everyone waiting, the gap stalling its spread. "Alright…and why did you go to Seventh Kingdom?" she asks carefully.

"I was…led there. By someone. But it was a mistake. A trick. They used my position, my confusion, and my blood. Now, war is coming to Orea."

This time, the beautiful queen can't hide her surprise as she rears back. "*War*? With Seventh Kingdom? Seventh Kingdom doesn't *exist*. Why are you speaking such ridiculous lies?"

"Not Seventh Kingdom," I tell her, voice raised over the people in the crowd who start to shout at me. I pause, but I know I have to tell it all. Tell my part in it. "I gave my blood to the fae, and they used it with their magic to repair the bridge of Lemuria. Now, they're coming to take over Orea."

The courtyard goes violently still. There's no mere gap anymore between the people and me; there's an entire canyon that divides us. One that I fall into alone with my echoing words.

The weight of their gazes makes my shoulders stiffen and curve. There's hatred and surprise and disbelief and…the look someone gives you when you're utterly unwanted.

I stand beneath their stares and bear their incredulous

hate. There's so much space between us now that I'm not sure I could ever close the distance.

As if that weren't horrible enough, Queen Kaila then tips her head back and *laughs*. The sound is just as husky and decadent as I would expect, and it spreads through the air, instantly changing the tension of the crowd, making them erupt into laughter too.

My ears burn. Everyone surrounds me, laughing at me. *Laughing.*

Humiliation gouges into my face, pitting my soul. I want to hide from their mockery, but I stand tall instead.

"It's true!" I shout, forcing my voice to carry over their ridicule. "The bridge has been remade! The fae have sent an army, and they're marching on Highbell!"

The laughter turns more raucous.

I have never been so mortified, so angry, so frustrated in my entire life.

Queen Kaila stops laughing long enough to look down at me with delighted pity. "Fae have not been in Orea for hundreds of years."

"That's not true. There have been some—at least three that I know of—who were here. There could have been more. And they've found a way to fix the bridge, and now they're marching on us, set to slaughter us all."

The crowd mocks me.

Kaila smirks at me.

Even Highbell's guards standing sentry just a few steps away look at me with derision.

It goes on and on, and I feel more than hear Dommik's fury shaking through his body. "Say the word, and I'll get you out of here," he growls at my back.

It's tempting.

But I hold my tongue.

"Enough," Queen Kaila announces, as if she's the power

here and I'm nothing but a nuisance she accidentally stepped on with her shoe. "One does not laugh at a queen, however mad she may seem."

My hands go so cold I worry my bones might snap if I bend my fingers even an inch.

"Queen Malina has obviously suffered a great ordeal," she goes on speaking to the people. "Come, help her inside."

Guards march forward, one of hers and one of Highbell's. I snatch my arms out of their grips and turn, looking at the crowd instead. "I know it's hard to believe! I know the fae shouldn't have a way back to Orea—that they've been gone for so long their existence seems like a myth. But it's true! I saw them with my own eyes, and they'll reach Highbell soon."

A few of the people frown, but for the most part, everyone looks as if they wish they had rotten fruit they could throw at me. This time, the guards snatch at my arms and start hauling me toward the castle, and I can't wrench out of their grips.

"You must listen!" I shout desperately, head whipping around, snow falling from my hands and dusting uselessly at my dragging feet. "You must prepare!"

I know how I must look. Crazed and filthy, nothing like the poised queen they're used to seeing. But this is so far beyond concern for my own image. I need them to believe me. Need them to prepare.

All I can see is that slaughtered village behind my eyes. Yet even as I'm hauled away like a prisoner into my own castle, with mockery and curses lobbed at my back, I go knowing that I have a shadow following behind me.

So I hold my head high, steeling myself as we enter Highbell Castle.

Into the belly of the gilded beast.

CHAPTER 32

QUEEN MALINA

Queen Kaila is enjoying this.

The slight smirk she wears looks like a perfected accessory as much as the glittering earrings that drip down her lobes.

We're sitting at the formal dining table together, but the chair at the head is blatantly empty. We both looked at it, both bristled at the other, and then we settled for the seats across from one another instead.

Still, even if she's not sitting at the head, her silent statement is clear—she's in charge.

She enjoys that it's her guards that line the room. That it's her kingdom's colors of silver and blue that adorn the napkins and silverware and place settings. There's even a centerpiece filled with blue-tinged water with floating candles on top of it. She's put her little touches inside this castle already, when all my own Colier touches were stripped away years ago.

She's enjoying the fact that she sits here perfectly put together, while I look haggard and harried. Instead of taking me upstairs so I could bathe and change, she ushered me straight here. As if she's hosting me in *her* castle.

The nerve.

I would normally fight against this sort of silent subterfuge, but there are much more important factors at play than my pride taking a hit. Besides, she can try to intimidate me with her colors and her guards and her presence all she likes.

I'm not alone.

Of their own volition, my eyes flick to the back of the dining room where the corner is bathed in shadow. It looks empty, save for the gilt wallpaper that's been peeled away.

It's not empty.

Dommik is there. I can *feel* it. The space probably looks like an ordinary shadow to everyone else, but I can tell the difference. Perhaps it's because I've been traveling in his shadows for days on end, so I have some sort of connection to them.

Or perhaps, I just have a connection to *him*.

Either way, it's a silent comfort knowing he's there.

Not wanting to give anything away, my attention trails around, and I note how thoroughly this room has been ransacked. Even her kingdom's colors can't hide that.

There used to be gold-threaded drapes hanging from the tall windows, but those have been ripped away, save a few clumps of the fabric still stuck at the top. The gilt rug is gone, and someone even yanked off the floor trim. Little scuffs and chunks are scored into the walls, and the light sconces are noticeably absent. The chairs we sit in aren't the ones that used to be here. They're all simple, made of plain wood. I'm sure that the only reason the table still sits here is because it was far too heavy for people to steal.

I wonder how many came through and plundered the castle. I wonder if it helped cool their anger.

"That announcement outside was unwise," Queen Kaila says, the first to break the silence. I've rankled her enough to do that, so it's some concession.

Unlike outside, her face is now devoid of the charm that she wore in front of the crowd. Sitting in front of me is a very different queen.

"I'm not interested in wisdom in the face of impending threat."

She taps a nail against the crystal glass in front of her. "You want your kingdom back. I understand that. I also understand the need to play the game. What better way to get your people to back you than an *impending threat*, as you called it." Her hand smooths over the table. "Though this lie about the fae is extreme."

"It's not a lie," I say through gnashing teeth. "There's a fae scout dead in the snow just outside the city. There's an entire village razed, every single person slaughtered. Send some of your soldiers to go confirm."

Kaila waves a hand dismissively, cuticles perfectly manicured. I drop my own hands into my lap, hiding my jagged, crusted nails.

"Malina—may I call you Malina?"

My spine goes stiff as steel. "You may call me queen, for that is what I am."

Her eyes dance, as if this response is a glittering challenge she enjoys. "Your Majesty, I believe we can come to some sort of agreement."

I nearly roll my eyes. I can imagine what *agreement* she'd put forth, and I'm not interested.

"When did he tell you I was dead?"

She blinks, obviously taken aback by my change of subject. "Excuse me?"

"Tyndall. When exactly did he tell you I was dead, and how far after that did the two of you decide to marry?"

"Such details aren't important now," she replies breezily. "Obviously, his information was incorrect."

She's treating this—all of this—as if it doesn't matter, when she doesn't understand how very wrong she is. "It wasn't *information*. He reported I was dead because he thought he'd ensured it."

She arches a brow and looks around at her guards with a wry shake of her head. "I'm sure you're not speaking treason against the late king."

I bare my teeth in a wicked smile.

"I'm sure you shouldn't throw out that word *treason* when you're trying to sit on someone else's throne."

She gives me a biting grin right back.

For several seconds, that's all we are. Sharp teeth and cool contempt.

"Your death was announced, Queen Malina," she says to me, as if that should be the end of it. "The lines of your Colier heritage were crossed out in the books, and with no heirs…" She lets the sentence hang.

It slips around my neck, tightening like a noose. The shadows in the corner flicker, ever so slightly. Reminding me to breathe.

"Highbell was in an uproar when I arrived. There were riots in the streets, purgers in the castle. I put an end to all of that. You should be thanking me."

I look at her incredulously. "*Thanking you?*"

"Yes," she says firmly, hand smoothing over her lustrous black hair. "Your people hate you. They were glad you were dead. I made them stop looting, stop running wild through the city and committing crimes unchecked. Since I've arrived, I've instilled peace again. They trust me. Adore me. Unlike you, I'm very good at being liked."

I'm sure she is.

Everything about her looks as if she's used to having people like her. She's young, beautiful, alluring, charismatic...warm. From head to toe, she's exactly what a queen should be.

Everything I'm not.

My smile slips. My mind falters. There's a little bit of snow that weeps from the center of my palm and drips onto my lap.

Perhaps...perhaps she's right. Maybe Highbell is better off with her.

Something hard and jagged and bitter gets stuck in my throat. It coincides with this ugly, piercing pain that seems to twist in my heart.

Is Highbell better off without me?

I don't like the answer that whispers in my head. I don't like the way that answer staggers me, like there's no even ground for me to stand upon.

What am I, if not a queen?

But my eyes drift to that corner again. Catch on a flicker of bent light. That twisting pain lessens, just a bit. Enough for me to breathe, though the breath that exhales out of me is tired. Worn. A weariness that isn't physical, but something soul-deep.

I no longer have the stomach to sit here and play political games with the woman across from me. Because in the grander scheme of things...none of this matters. There might not even *be* a Highbell anymore if we can't stop the fae.

I rub at the building headache that's starting to form at my brow. "This isn't about politics, Queen Kaila. This isn't even about me retaking Sixth Kingdom."

"Really?" she asks dubiously. "So you'd be content letting me ascend the throne and take control of Highbell?"

"Yes," I answer, letting her see the truth in my face.

She rears back in surprise, and I think I've even surprised

myself.

Her brown eyes flick between mine. "*Why?*"

"Because if that's what we need to do in order to save Highbell—to save Sixth Kingdom and the rest of Orea—then so be it," I answer honestly. "The fae are here, and we need to prepare Highbell and protect the people. If we don't, everyone is going to be killed and this city will be overrun."

Silence rains down between us. Like a storm cloud breaking loose, tendrils of its fog untying to let a torrent of hush descend and douse us with it. I wait in the breadth of the downpour, soaking in Kaila's expressions, letting her soak in mine.

"All personal issues aside, Highbell needs a queen," I say, all the haughty fight drained out of me. "They don't believe in me right now, because I have let them down, but they will believe *you*. Help me," I implore. "Prepare Highbell for attack and defend this city with me."

She watches me intently, as I imagine a cat might watch a mouse. Yet I'm not trying to put myself at odds with a predator. I'm trying to make sure that Highbell isn't defenseless prey.

I wait with bated breath, trying to show her exactly how serious I am—hoping she can see the severity of the situation through the cracks in my usual cold facade.

Finally, she sweeps away the flood of silence and nods. "Alright, Queen Malina. I believe you."

Relief soaks through me, body wrung through. "You do?"

"Yes."

She gets to her feet gracefully, and I shove back the chair to stand as well. There's so much to do. So much to discuss and plan for.

"You go upstairs and get yourself cleaned up," Kaila says. "In the meantime, I'll gather the rest of Highbell's guards. There weren't many when I arrived, as most had abandoned their post, but I have rectified that."

The two of us stride toward the doorway. "We'll need all soldiers capable of fighting," I say. "The bell must also be tolled to signal for the city to retreat to the castle. The people need to get behind these walls as soon as possible. That includes provisions and whatever animals we can fit."

Kaila looks contemplative. "Alright. After you've had time to clean up, we'll speak with the advisors."

My gaze shifts as a shadow stretches across the floor.

"I'll be quick. We must act fast."

"We will," she says with a nod.

Separating from her, I leave the dining room and make my way across the main hall. My steps slow, however, when I see castle workers chipping away the last of the white paint still on the wall.

The paint I ordered to try to cover the gold beneath.

With scrapers in hand, the men work to peel away the layers bit by bit and then use a rag to wipe away the curdled white, leaving them to scatter on the ground like piles of dust.

Or snow.

My hand pauses where I grip the banister railing before I force myself to face forward once more and start my ascent up the steps. The palace has been looted, the paint's been stripped away, and Highbell is gold and empty, with no king and a different queen.

And I don't mean Kaila.

As I go up to the higher floors, I note all signs of damage where people ripped things away. I notice every missing item. Anything the people could feasibly take, they did. The gold-threaded carpets on the stairs, the curtains, the gilt frames, the sconces, all gone. There used to be a gaudy luster to this castle. Now, it just looks scorned.

When I get to my floor, I head down the corridor to my

room, but there's a woman between two of Kaila's guards walking toward me. She has long black hair that hangs limply over her shoulder. There are circles beneath her eyes, and her lips are dry and peeling in places. Yet the most noticeable thing about her is her rounded belly. It protrudes out from a simple white dress, a ribbon tied just beneath her breasts that accentuates her pregnancy even more.

When she sees me, her brown eyes go wide. "Queen Malina!" she exclaims, lurching toward me. "You have to help me! It's—"

One of the guards grabs her arm, and she jolts, looking up at him. "Come along, miss. Don't bother Her Majesty."

He and the other guard lead her away, the man giving me a small nod as they go. Frowning, I look over my shoulder at them, watching as they head for the stairs. She's familiar, but how do I—

"Malina."

I freeze at the whispered voice, every muscle in my body pulling tight. My heart pounds so fiercely that my ears are drowned out in its beat.

I'm hearing things. I have to be. Just a trick of the—

"*Malina.*"

I whip my head around the other direction where the voice is coming from.

Tyndall?

Squinting, I barely see someone disappear around the corner at the end of the corridor with hurried steps.

It *is* him.

Emotions flood through my body too fast to grasp on to; I can't tell which one I'm even feeling. My palms go frigid— my whole body frozen in place.

Great Divine, *how* is it him? Kaila said he was dead— talked about it publicly. Unless…she lied. Unless she's done something, or perhaps they did something together, some grand scheme, and he's not dead at all.

I turn and stride in the direction where he went, hurrying to catch up. Yet when I round the corner, I can't see him. All the light sconces down this corridor have been ripped off, leaving one lone window to light the way.

"Tyndall," I call quietly.

I hear footsteps retreating, heading up the set of stairs.

Picking up my grimy skirt, I hurry forward and rush up them, nearly slipping on the bare steps as I climb up. The top of the balconied landing is just as dim, and I'm out of breath when I reach it, leaning against the gilt railing as I try to catch my breath and strain my ears.

"Tyndall, what is going on?" I demand, looking left and right, trying to figure out where he went. Does he need to hide from Kaila and her people?

"This way," he calls.

Turning around, I cross a threshold and enter a dark room. There's no light save for a single candle set on a table.

"Malina, come here."

The odd tone of his voice makes my steps falter for a moment, but when I hear something behind me, I quickly bolt forward. I bang my elbow on something as I pass by. "Ouch," I hiss between my teeth and rub the spot as I turn around, squinting. "Tyndall, what's wrong? What's happening?"

He says nothing, and when I walk forward, I nearly stumble over something on the floor. I catch myself before I go toppling down, but then a loud clang bursts behind me. I flinch and spin around, my heart in my throat. "Tyndall?"

All of a sudden, light flares in the room, and I squint at the invasion. As soon as my eyes adjust, my stomach plummets. Kaila stands there before me, with several of her guards holding glaring lanterns.

She, however, is holding a key.

That's when I see—when I truly realize where I am.

The gilded cage.

The cage at the top of Highbell Castle, where no one was allowed to go except Tyndall himself and a few trusted guards, because this is where he kept *her*. His favored pet. His golden Precious.

"What's going on?" I say, rushing forward, gripping the barred door and realizing that was the sound—someone slamming it shut behind me and locking me inside. I shake it anyway, eyes flying up to Kaila, who looks warm and soft in the lantern light, though the casting shadows make her face take on a more sinister air. "What do you think you're doing? Where's Tyndall?"

She cocks her head. "Dead. As I told you."

I glance around. "No, I heard—"

She blows out a breath, and a stream of mist seems to slip out like pipe-smoke from between her plush lips. Except, instead of the scent of tobacco, the sound of my husband's voice permeates the air.

"Malina, come! This way. *Malina*!"

My eyes widen in realization. In panic. "Your magic," I breathe. "You tricked me."

She has the gall to smile, the vapor and voice fading away into nothing. "You arrived at a very inopportune time for me," she tells me with chastisement in her husky tone. "I finally gained a true foothold here, and your arrival will confuse some of the people. But no matter," she says with a shake of her head. "As I said, you're not very well liked. I'll figure something out to clean up this complication you've caused."

My breath fumbles, blowing out in a cold cloud of white. "You…the *fae* are coming, Kaila! We don't have time for this."

She rolls her eyes. "Spouting lies won't help you. You think Tyndall didn't warn me about you? He told me all about

your little underhanded attempt at taking control of Highbell."
A cruel smirk plays on her lips. "That didn't work very well,
did it?"

My teeth grind in anger.

"You left this city in an uproar, but I fixed all of that. You
can't walk in here now and try to take it back. Highbell is
mine now. But you're safe. Until I figure out your use."

She turns and motions toward the guards, and they start
filing out, taking the light with them.

"No!" I rattle the bars, my hands clenching them so hard
it hurts. "You're making a mistake! We have to prepare!"

Kaila turns, only two guards waiting with her. "All I *do*
is prepare, Queen Malina. That's what a queen must do in this
world. We plan. We play. We plot. That's the only way we get
to keep our crowns. The men are lazy. They get to keep
whatever is handed to them, but not us." She shakes her head,
shiny black hair glistening in the firelight. "We queens must
always plan ahead and manipulate circumstances in our favor.
Take Mist for example."

Mist...

"She'll give birth soon, I think. A bit early, but the
menders say the babe should live. It'll be small, which will
work very well in my favor."

Her hand drifts to her own stomach, her dress banded
below her breasts and hanging down loosely all the way to the
hem. The sort of dress someone might wear if they were
pregnant.

Or pretending to be.

In an instant, my mind finally catches up to her words. To
the familiar pregnant woman in the corridor.

Kaila shakes her head. "You really should have taken
him up on his offer, you know. If you'd simply agreed to claim
the saddle's babe as your own heir, Midas might not have
hired that assassin to kill you. He might not have agreed to

marry me. Now, I will not only have his vow of betrothal that he announced before his death, but I'll have his only heir too. Which means Sixth Kingdom is well and truly mine."

Ice runs through my veins that has nothing to do with magic. My breath comes in quicker, thickening in my mouth like fog.

Kaila's eyes glitter. "When a king falls, a queen can rise. But only the ones who know where to step."

"Did you kill him?" I blurt out.

She smiles, showing off her bright, perfect teeth. "I didn't have to. But it was quite convenient of him."

The proud look on her face is so familiar, because it's the same look I always carried. "I don't understand. You have Third Kingdom."

Her shoulder tips up. "I don't just want a kingdom. I want an *empire*."

Anger and panic war in my chest, battling through every heartbeat.

"You'll have *nothing* if you refuse to listen to me, because we will all be killed. Orea as we know it will be no more."

She doesn't acknowledge what I've said at all and looks around the room instead, as if she's appreciating the cage she's trapped me in. Her blatant disinterest at my words makes me shake with anger.

"Ironic, isn't it?"

"What?" I snap.

"You, here. Being locked up in this very cage."

My back goes ramrod straight.

Her brown eyes find mine, her face illuminated softly from the candle still burning on the table just in front of her. "You let your husband lock up his gilded pet here."

"*Let him*? Tyndall was going to do as he pleased. It had nothing to do with me."

She hums in fake contemplation and taps a finger against her bottom lip. "I don't think that's true. It's quite cruel to have kept her here, and yet, you did. Now, you've taken her place."

"I didn't keep her here," I argue. "She was perfectly content being his little golden whore. She was doted on every day, given every luxury and—"

Kaila cuts me off, head tilting. "Did you ask her?"

"I… What?"

"Did you ever ask her? Or were you simply so jealous that you didn't care?"

A reply fails me, and she steps forward until we're nearly face to face. "Admit it. You liked that she was kept locked in here. It helped you feel like she was being adequately punished for capturing the attention of your husband."

Shards of ice feel like they're bracketing against my ribs. Closing in around my lungs and making it hard to breathe.

"Personally, I would've played with her a bit—driven her mad with voices until she snapped." She stops as if she's considering it. "Or I would've just killed her. But to each her own. You played your own game, but you lost."

My lips press in a hard line, little chips of cold nearly piercing through the skin. "I was playing no game."

She smiles condescendingly and slips the key to the cage into her pocket. Then she reaches down to pick up the candlestick on the table behind her. "To answer your question more fully…I didn't kill Midas," she tells me. "His gilded pet did."

My eyes go wide.

Everything in me stumbles in shock.

She beams. "So very scandalous, isn't it? What was it you said? Oh, yes." Pursing her mouth, she blows out my voice through a stream of magic.

She was perfectly content being his little golden whore.

As my voice fades out, Kaila smirks at me. "It seems you were wrong, because that little golden whore killed him."

I shake my head. "You're lying."

"Am I?" she taunts. "I suppose I could be, but in this case, the truth is much more interesting. Tell me, did you know he was a fraud?"

I go still. "What?"

Her smile grows wider, eyes dancing over my face in utter joy. "No, I didn't think so."

She turns and starts walking away. "Kaila!" I shout. "Listen to me! The fae are coming! Unlock this door this instant! You can't keep me in here!"

At the door, she looks over her shoulder at me. "Queen to queen, I'll let you in on a little secret. That gilded whore is *much* more than she seems. And so am I. What are *you*, Malina?"

With that haunting, echoing question, she sweeps out of the room, taking the last of the light with her.

What are you?

I was a daughter. A princess. A Colier heir.

I was the wife of King Midas, ruler of Highbell and the Sixth Kingdom of Orea. People flocked to see his gleaming castle that was worth more than all the riches in the entire realm.

What are you?

I look down at my hands brimming with snow.

I'm the Cold Queen, caught in someone else's cage.

And what an ugly prison it is.

CHAPTER 33

QUEEN MALINA

I've walked the length of the cage over and over again. Bedroom, washroom, through the library, through the atrium, glancing out at the iced-over windows and seething the entire time. Everything behind the bars seems to have not been ransacked by looters, probably because it was locked.

Even though it's still daylight, the bedroom is incredibly dark, the sole window blocked by a thick layer of snow. I never realized how dark it is up here. Save for the atrium, every caged-in room is dim at best, weighing it down with a lonely gloom.

I'm glad there's no light to see better.

All of *her* things are still here, completely untouched. Bed unmade, clothes hanging, gloves laid out, combs set on her vanity, though the mirror has been shattered. I wonder if she did that. Just like I wonder at the multiple vats of wine stacked at the corner of the room.

Did you ever ask her? Or were you simply so jealous that you didn't care?

Kaila's words keep repeating in my ears as if she's still using her voice magic against me, but it has nothing to do with magic and everything to do with a grudging guilt that's sitting in the pit of my stomach.

I went my whole life without feeling that emotion, and now, it keeps piling on.

I don't want to feel it. I don't want to pity the pet that so often warmed my husband's bed. I don't want to see things from her perspective, though when *I'm* the one behind her bars, it's difficult not to.

I used to catch him watching her. Seeing the obsession in his eyes. I *hated* it.

If what Kaila said was true, if Auren truly did kill Tyndall… I just can't seem to make that train of thought line up with all those I had in the past.

And yet…

My eyes fix on the gilded bars. I always thought it was another flashy show for my husband to have this built for her. That she was important—precious enough—that he needed her under lock and key. I thought she liked the attention, liked being his favored pet. But maybe I was wrong. Maybe she didn't want to be kept.

Did she hate him as I did? Did she hate him even more?

Those questions jar me, but before I can try to answer them with new eyes, shadows coalesce in the room. Familiar shadows.

I rush forward, hands wrapping around the bars with relief. "What took you so long?" I demand, though my voice betrays my shaken anxiety.

"Couldn't fucking find you," Dommik says, and I can hear his frustration and worry as it grates down his throat. Tossing back his hood, he stalks forward and takes in the room, the bars, me. "They locked you in here?" His question is a growl, and the protective anger he feels on my behalf takes away the sting of my captivity.

"Where have you been?"

"I followed a few of the guards when you and Kaila walked away, because I wanted to see what I could hear from them. I didn't have a good feeling. But I swear, it was only for a moment. I had eyes on you. Until I didn't." He scrubs at his bearded jaw with frustration. "I've been searching everywhere for you, Queenie. Didn't expect to find you here."

"Can you get me out?"

He slips his hand into his pocket and pulls out a couple of metal picks. Kneeling down, he starts working on the lock with determined focus.

"You can't just shadow-leap me out?"

"I can't go through solid objects."

"Back in Seventh Kingdom, you went into my room…"

"I had the key, remember?"

"But I never heard the door open."

His eyes flick up to mine. "I'm good at being quiet."

I swallow hard.

"And…how many times did you sneak into my room without me knowing?"

"*Often.*"

He says that word suggestively. Voice even rougher than his usual rasp.

My stomach fills with flurries. "And…when I bathed…"

His lips curve, fingers paused on his task, his handsome face completely focused on me instead. "Do you think I watched you?" he asks in a low tone—a *wicked* one. "Do you think I stayed hidden in the shadows while you peeled off your dress and sunk into the cold water? That I watched the nipples on your tits pucker?"

A flush creeps up my cheeks, but I clear my throat. "It would've been very improper if you had."

The thought of him watching me, desiring me when I didn't know he was there, when we hated each other, fills me with that twisted thrill that only he can bring me.

"Well…I didn't," he finishes, tone back to normal.

I deflate.

"But I was tempted," he adds as he gets back to picking the lock.

I waver slightly on my feet, gripping the bars for stability. "Well, I am glad you didn't follow through with your debauched and immoral impulses, assassin."

He lets out a chuckle, shaking his head. "You're very good."

"At what?"

"Lying."

The lock pops and he stands up, swinging open the cage door. He holds out an arm for me with a flourish. "Your Majesty."

I sweep out of the cage like I'm shucking off a weight. I can't imagine being trapped in there for hours or days. For weeks, months, years…

How did she stand it?

"So, I take it Queen Kaila won't be helping after all?"

I shake my head. "No."

He looks around the room before his steady eyes land back on me. Waiting.

I take a breath and wipe my hands on my skirt. "Come, assassin. If my usurper won't see reason and start preparing for the fae to attack, then it's up to us."

"Really?" he asks. "You still want to help Highbell even though they laughed at you? Even when they're supporting Kaila?"

Determination narrows through my eyes. "Highbell is my home. I won't just stand by and let it be destroyed. It's my duty to protect it, whether they want me to or not."

Something like quiet pride flows through his face, and then he reaches down and takes my hand, his warmth pressing into each finger. "You're sounding like a queen for the right reasons now." He pauses for a second. "No more *enough*."

No more enough?

My brows pull together in a frown of confusion. "What? You're speaking nonsense."

"Before, back at Seventh, I told you, *I believe you enough*," he explains. "The *enough* is gone now. I just plain believe you, Queenie. Believe *in* you."

Flecks of snow seem to collect right at the corners of my eyes.

"You do?" I ask shakily, like I'm offering something fragile in my hands, hoping he'll take it. Hoping he'll take *care* of it.

He dips his head, and then so tenderly I feel like my skin might shatter, he presses his lips against my forehead, shocking me all over again. It's there and gone in a flash, and I might even think I imagined it, if it weren't for the bloom of warmth that seems to travel from that spot, tingling all the way over my scalp.

"I do."

A shudder lets out through my lips.

How is it that the person meant to kill me ended up being the one who saved me?

"Ready?" he asks.

I have to be.

It isn't difficult sneaking through Highbell with Dommik's magic. We slip down to the floor below, passing by more wrung-out, pillaged rooms, the shadows showing glimpses of broken furniture, stolen tapestries, chunks missing from the walls and gilt banisters knocked loose.

Once we make it outside, Dommik shadow-leaps us to the barracks. It's a drafty, bulky building that reeks of sweat and metal, erected behind the castle and not far from the stables. One large building takes up the most space, dedicated to their training area. The rest of the buildings are an offshoot, spreading out to their living spaces and dining hall. These barracks are the one spot that's not gilded, but lie unchanged from the original stonework that my family had built long ago.

Dommik takes us right inside the training area, cushioning us into a cloistered corner. The last time I came here, I was just a girl who'd become interested in boys. I used to sneak in and crouch beneath the equipment bench where the sword targets were stacked so I could watch without anyone knowing I was here.

I watched the men who bared their chests, sweating despite the cold. Watched as they spit and swore, making my ears blush at the things they talked about. Then, I'd slink away, not daring to ever tell my father where I'd been, not even if I got lashed for it. I'd simply come to hide and watch again the next day.

Yet this time, instead of hiding from the soldiers, I have to step out to face them.

Dommik pulls away most of his shadows, allowing me to see. To hear.

"Are you sure about this?"

I nod. "Yes."

He yanks away his magic completely, and as soon as he does, I walk out of the dark corner of the fighting hall and stride over the sandy pit. The room's high ceiling makes it feel bigger, the stench of sweat and metal clinging to my tongue.

As I stride forward, men stumble to a stop, some getting hit from their sudden loss of attention. Surprise ripples through the entire room, until every soldier is staring right at me.

When I'm standing directly in the middle, I look around at them all. Outside, the wind whistles past the high windows that line the entirety of the four walls.

"What are you doing here?" a man with a slick of sweat-soaked mousy brown hair asks. There's a threaded notch at the collar of his jerkin, signifying him as one of the generals, and if that didn't alert me to his superiority, the arrogant look on his face would.

"This is my home, General, and there is a threat coming to Highbell. I would think my presence would be expected."

He levels me with a look and rests his hand on his belt. "We thought you were dead."

The rest of the men stare at me, as if they want me to apologize for being alive instead.

"You were misled," I say simply.

"Still doesn't explain what you're doing *here,* in my barracks."

I bristle. Technically, it's *my* barracks, but it's pointless to argue.

"As I said. There's a threat coming. I'm sure you've heard what I said in the courtyard earlier."

He smiles, showing cracked teeth, as if he got punched one too many times in the mouth. "Aye, we heard it. Had a good laugh over it too," he chuckles, and the sound sets off at least a dozen others to laugh as well.

I don't react to the sound. I've already been laughed at today, so I have my walls up to defend against it.

"The fae are coming, General. I'm giving you orders to gather the men and prepare for attack."

He kinks his neck as he regards me. Everyone else is quiet, waiting to see what he'll say, their gazes bouncing between us.

"We're taking orders from Queen Kaila now."

"You didn't swear your oaths to Queen Kaila."

He chews at his cheek like he's chewing up his thoughts. I've no doubt he was one of the soldiers who abandoned his post during the riots.

"Highbell is better off with Queen Kaila than for us to listen to a madwoman who ordered us to kill our own citizens."

Shame slams down over my head like a bucket of water, and the men's accusing stares take on a more honed edge. One I understand. I *did* order them to do that during the riots, and I thought it justified to do so. Instead of truly listening as a queen should, I lashed out and made things worse.

Dommik's eyes on my back feel as piercing as ever. I don't like for him to see or hear about the way I behaved before.

The general must smell blood in the water with my continued silence.

"Now, you're here, ordering us to fight for you again?" He shakes his head as he looks around the room, making the others join in his dismissal. "No, we won't be doing that. We've had enough of your *orders*."

"I was wrong." The words are gummy, hard to unstick from my tongue and let them fall out. I've never admitted such a thing in my entire life, but I admit it now.

I expect them to all be shocked. To listen to me now that I've admitted fault.

They do not.

"Yeah, and Queen Kaila seems *right*. We want her as our queen. Not you."

His declaration is a blow to my face, but I don't turn my cheek. Not even when I feel every single man in the room exude that same scathing sentiment.

I press my hands together in front of me, dig my fingers against my torn palms. "She can be your queen all you like, and she may well and truly be a better one than me. But Highbell is, and always has been, my *home*." I look him steadily in the eye, let him see the truth of it in my white hair and icy blue eyes. "My family has lived and reigned here for generations, and we Coliers have *always* been loyal to Highbell. If nothing else, you know that about me," I say firmly. "The fae are coming, General, and their numbers are vast. We must ready for attack."

They're staring at me, my words sinking in, and for a moment, the general himself seems to consider me, making hope surge in my chest.

It plummets a second later when he shakes his head.

"We've heard enough. It's best you go back to being dead, Cold Queen."

With the utmost sign of disrespect, he gives me his back and walks away, and I'm left standing here as every single one of the soldiers walks away with him.

Devastated desperation has my eyes glossing over. Has a single tear getting caught in the corner, freezing before it can even drop down my cheek.

Feeling shaken all over, I turn and make the long walk across the room toward the door. Only once I'm outside with my back pressed to the wall do I close my eyes and let out the quavering breath.

"Malina."

My eyes peel open to see Dommik standing in front of me.

His eyes run over me, and I wait for him to ask if I'm okay. Instead, he says, "Do you want me to kill that man?"

He's perfectly serious.

A dry laugh cobbles up my throat, the tension leaving me.

I shake my head. "No, assassin. Keep your dagger to yourself."

"What about Queen Kaila?"

"No," I tell him, as tempting as it is. "Despite what happened, the people listen to her—trust her. When the fae come, I think the city will need her presence to band together."

He looks disappointed. I, however, feel slightly better knowing he'd kill her if I asked him to. At least I have one person on my side.

These men don't understand. They didn't *see*. If they had, they'd know death is coming to Highbell. I can't let this place face the same fate as that outskirts village, but I don't know how to stop it. I only know that I don't want to see it slaughtered.

I walk forward, gaze falling down the mountain to the city below. To *my* city. Not because of my royal lineage, but because this is where I've lived my whole life. Where my family lived.

"You tried, Malina," Dommik says as he comes up to stand beside me on the flattened snow trodden down by hundreds of soldiers' footsteps. With the barracks at our backs and the empty mountainside just behind, we're cast in shadow. The wind whips around us, my loose hair spitting at my face. "Just say the word, and I'll get us out of here. Find us someplace safe."

I reach back and re-braid my hair, pulling the white strands as tight as I can before tying it off at the ends. Then I square my shoulders, my view still on the city. "I'm not leaving Highbell."

Dommik pauses for a moment at the ferocity of my statement. "So what are we going to do?"

No one ever asks me that.

That's the question I've had to ask other people all my life. My father, my husband, my advisors.

Men.

Whenever something needed to be decided, I had to ask. I had to wait around for the men to decide. Nobody asked or even cared much for my opinion. Nobody ever waited, like Dommik is waiting now, for me to come up with a plan. Nobody trusted me to do so. I had to resort to offering unwarranted opinions or pointed questions, driving them to reach the conclusion I'd already thought of, to make it seem like it was *their* idea in the first place.

For once, the question is for me, and I have an answer.

"We're going into the city," I say as I turn on my heel, steps sloshing through the thick snow as I head for the stables. "I'm going to need a horse."

CHAPTER 34

QUEEN MALINA

Despite the fact that I am an excellent rider, Dommik insists on sharing the damn horse. We're in the stables, the animals firmly locked up in their pens in preparation for the snowstorm that seems to be blowing in. The stablemaster jumped in fright when we appeared in the corner, but one look at me made him skitter away without a word.

Or perhaps it was the hooded assassin in my company.

"I started having formal riding lessons when I was two," I point out as I watch him ready the saddle. The horse's body is thick with long white hair, mane trimmed and braided intricately.

"And I've been riding wild stallions barebacked since my cock got hard for the first time. You're still riding with me, Queenie."

He finishes tightening the straps and then walks over to me. Without warning, he grips me by the waist, making me gasp, and sets me atop the horse as if I weigh nothing at all. Then he mounts himself behind me, leg swinging over as he sits in one fluid motion.

I shift in the saddle, my skirt not made for riding like this, but he simply reaches down and tugs it up until the fabric is bunched at my thighs. If it weren't for the thick leggings I'm wearing, my legs would be indecently on display. "I don't think—"

"Good. Don't," he interrupts.

He reaches forward with both arms on either side of me, and I expect him to take the reins, but he picks them up and hands them to me instead. I grip them, and he moves his hands to grip *me*. One staying at my bunched skirt, and the other splayed against my stomach.

"I can ride alone," I say, though my voice sounds breathy now. His touch is bleeding warmth into me despite my clothing. Though it's *nothing* to the heat that erupts when he suddenly yanks me back into him until my ass is flush with his groin.

I suck in a breath.

His head comes down, mouth at my ear and voice deliciously rough. "You're riding with me."

All my previous arguments have died away. I can't think of them with his body so close to mine, and I find I don't want to.

"Admit it," he says huskily. "You like it."

"I don't…dislike it."

He chuckles, and the sound sends a shiver down my spine.

Clearing my throat, I try to ignore his hard body behind me and snap the reins to direct the horse forward. We trot out of the stable, across the flat, snowy yard, passing soldiers as we go. They all gape at me, but none of them try to stop me.

Once we reach the road and begin our descent down the

mountain, half of my mind is trying to come up with some sort of a plan, but the other half is completely preoccupied with the feel of Dommik.

I seem to think about him a lot lately. It's difficult not to, especially when his splayed fingers start to rub circles over my stomach, making it dip.

Yet even that hasn't distracted me fully from the terror I feel every time I have to travel on this road. The way down the mountain is perilous, but I can't allow myself to fall into distress. So I use Dommik's touch as the distraction I need, focusing on him instead of the winding slope.

Every time we hit a slick patch, he tightens his hold on me, brings my bottom closer to his groin. Normally, I'd be in a carriage with the curtains shut tight, not willing to look at the height. But here we are on horseback, completely exposed, yet I'm preoccupied by the hard length pressing against me.

His hand skims lower, distracting me as those fingers of his continue to slowly rotate. Heat gathers between my legs, and my eyes flutter closed of their own volition, my mind imagining what it would be like if he were to go even lower.

I desperately want to shift in the saddle, and I nearly lift up so I can get closer—

The horse jolts, screeching out a neigh as it slips on a patch of ice, my eyes flying open with terror. The animal stumbles, trying to find its footing, and I let out a scream, certain we're going to go careening off the edge of the mountain, my fear of heights rushing up so fast my head spins.

But Dommik snatches up the reins and, with expert maneuvering, gets the horse to calm, somehow helping it regain its footing. I breathe hard as we lurch to a stop, eyes blinking down at the edge we're just two feet away from, hands white-knuckling the saddle as I shake all over.

"Great Divine. That was…"

"Scary?" he volunteers.

"Your fault!" I snap.

He has the audacity to laugh. As if we didn't both just nearly perish over the side of the mountain.

"Got a bit distracted, Queenie?"

I grit my teeth, though I'm still breathing hard. "This is why we shouldn't have ridden together!"

"Oh, I disagree. We should do *a lot* of riding," he says wickedly.

My stomach flutters with a burst of icicle butterflies. So I jab my elbow into *his* stomach to ensure he feels something irritating too.

He lets out an *oomph*, which is reward enough.

"Keep it up, Malina," he says, his tone darkly playful.

I look at him over my shoulder, our eyes meeting. "I intend to."

His lips curve. "Good."

With a click of his tongue, Dommik leads the horse the rest of the way down the mountain with slow, sure steps, keeping his hands to himself this time. My body is able to cool, until I once again can pretend that neither desire nor fear has its grip on me.

Once we reach the bottom and make it to the bridge that goes over the chasm and into the city, I let out a sigh of relief, glad to be back on even ground. Yet that relief is short-lived, because now, I have to face the people.

The people who detest me.

After crossing the bridge, we're swept up in the city's entrance. A low wall drags across the length of the chasm behind, but in front of us, there's a wide stretch of cobbled stone that glitters with a light layer of snow. There are several streets that lead in different directions into the city, their tidy lanes packed tight with shops and people.

I retake the reins from Dommik and direct the horse where I know it'll be busiest—the square.

No one pays us much mind as we go, probably in part to do with Dommik at my back, his cloaked height blocking me somewhat. When we reach the square, the market is still going. There are carts with awnings laid out, people filling baskets with the goods they purchased as they exchange coin beneath the pavilion. Yet it's clear they've been watching the sky too, as some of them are starting to put away their wares and shut up the shutters on their carts.

The last time I was here, I was trying to win my people's favor, and they rejected me, threw things at me, hated me— and that was with a retinue of guards and a fully enclosed carriage for protection. Now, I come with only Dommik and a horse.

Vulnerable.

Yet, I remind myself that they're far more vulnerable than I am. They just don't believe me yet. It's my responsibility to make sure they do.

I urge the horse right into the middle of the square, where merchants and shoppers move out of the way as I yank to a stop. I stand in the stirrups and then swing my leg over and hop down, skirt settling back at my feet.

Surprise spreads over the market when people turn to look at me, when they realize who I am.

Dommik lands behind me, staying there with the reins in hand as I walk forward through the crowd, making sure I have everyone's attention. Making sure they see me—my Colier white hair, my face, my eyes.

As they take in my presence, I can feel their shock and confusion. Their anger and disgust. It's clear that like the guards, everyone here would've preferred I'd stayed dead.

It doesn't matter.

I'm not here for me. I'm not here to win them to my side

or to gain their favor this time. So as I stop and turn in a circle, I let them see my bedraggled state, let them see the desperation in my face as I lift my voice high enough for them to hear me.

"People of Highbell, I can see that you know me, that you realize you were told lies about my death. I've come to warn you. There's an enemy marching on us!"

There's a palpable reaction of distrust in the air as they gather around me with wary distaste, like my words have offended them.

"I traveled to the edge of our world. I saw the ruins of Seventh Kingdom with my own eyes. The bridge of Lemuria was remade, and the fae have returned to Orea to attack us."

My voice catches on the blustery wind, and I continue to turn, to try to make sure they can all see me, all hear me. They've given me a wide berth, from nobles to beggars and every status between.

"I was your queen once. All I want is to protect Highbell."

"Lies!" a man calls from the crowd, his clothes ragged and heavily layered, a spun cloth wrapped around his head to keep the cold away. "Queen Kaila is here to protect Highbell now. We don't want you and your lies!"

His words set off even more angry shouts, even more dismissal.

"I'm telling the truth!" I cry out desperately, eyes searching through the crowd, trying to find even one person who seems to be heeding my words.

There are none.

"The fae are here! You need to get to the castle, or flee, or prepare to fight. Because they *are* coming whether you believe me or not."

People turn and start walking away. Turning from me as if who I am means nothing to them. As if my words hold no consequence. My breaths scrape up and down my throat as the cold wind blasts my face, and I feel completely ineffective.

Useless.

Desperation catches in my throat as I shout through the storm, feeling like I'm trying to snatch at air, my grip empty, unable to catch their attention or care. "Wait! I know I have failed you. I know you rejected me. But this has *nothing* to do with me. You must prepare!" I shout, urgency clawing at my voice.

Everyone disperses, leaving me in the middle of the square alone, left with the shuddering wind. Merchants tie up their carts, vendors close up their stalls. Shopkeepers have gone inside and locked their doors, and the shoppers and beggars have all turned away.

Turned their backs.

Panicked frustration gorges on me, a beast tearing out my insides and chomping on my guts.

No one will listen to me.

I have been a royal all my life. Servants, guards, nobles, advisors, they've all *had* to listen to me. But now, when it actually matters, when a queen is trying to entreat her people, to save their lives, their neighbors, their children, their homes…my words fall on deaf ears.

It's different that Queen Kaila dismissed me—she has no true connection to this place. It's even different that the guards didn't put stock in my words, for they've seen me give atrocious orders. But for the people to turn away, to not even *consider* what I'm saying might be true…

It means I have utterly failed them.

I stand in the middle of the emptying square, watching them all leave. Watching my people reject me again. My hands burn with cold. I can't keep failing like this. Not with everything on the line.

Perhaps Kaila is right. Perhaps I'm not wanted.

But I am *needed*.

That thought fuels me. Bolsters me. Fills me with determination like nothing ever has in my whole life. Highbell needs me. They don't know it, but I do, and I won't fail them again.

Turning, I march back the way I came. I don't wait for Dommik to lift me up. I brace my foot in the stirrup and swing my leg over, setting myself atop the horse as I yank my skirts up and grip the reins. Dommik settles himself behind me, gripping me around the waist once again, not saying a word as I urge the horse forward.

The wind of the impending snowstorm picks up as we race back down the street, my white hair whipping free of its braid, strands scratching over my eyes. At my back, Dommik wraps his cloak around us both, though he needn't bother. I relish the cold. It feeds something in me with every frigid breath.

The first of the snowfall starts spitting out when I yank the horse to a stop at the bridge. I jump down and walk over and then pace in front of it, eyeing the length, eyeing the other side that leads to the mountain. To the castle caught snugly at its side like a mother holding a babe on her hip. Between us, the frozen chasm yawns, sucking in the wind of the coming storm like a wheezing snore.

There's one road.

One snowy, open road that leads from Seventh Kingdom. This is where the fae army will enter. They'll crest from the hill and start marching down, and they can either go left up the mountain to the castle or cross the bridge and come into the city.

I can't get Kaila or the guards to listen to me. I can't fortify the road itself since it's too open. And I can't get the people to flee and hide behind the castle's walls. So instead, I'll have to protect the city with a wall of my own.

At the entrance of the bridge, right where it meets the short wall blocking the chasm, I drop down. With my legs tucked beneath me and knees braced on the stone bricks, I hold my palms out.

"What are you doing?"

I don't answer Dommik. All my focus is right here, on my hands. On the gashes cut through each palm and the sharp shards of ice stuck to them. And I beg.

On my knees in desperate prayer, I beg.

I don't beg the gods, because what have powerful men ever done for me? No, I beg the magic instead. The magic I shouldn't have. I beg desperately for it to do something, *anything*, to help me save the city I endangered.

Please...

The wind howls.

Snowfall starts to drizzle down from the sky.

And I beg and beseech and *pray*.

Dommik watches me. A kneeling queen and a silent assassin, the two of us a seemingly unlikely pair. Except, we have more in common than most. We've both brought on death. He's just honest about it. He wields a blade and spills others' blood. I let someone spill *my* blood, and now the enemy will wield their blades against my people.

What I've done is far, far worse.

Please...

My eyes are shut tight, my hands shaking, everything in me coiled with a desperation that seems larger than life itself.

Because I regret.

I regret allowing my powerless life to mold me. I regret not standing up to my father. I regret marrying Midas. I regret allowing him to keep a woman in a cage. I regret looking down on the very people I was meant to serve. I regret taking everything for granted.

I regret becoming this bitter, cold woman, and I want to

let that cold *out*. To make it do something *good*.

Please…

I keep praying to this power, keep begging this mercurial magic, and then, my teeth begin to gnash on frost. Ice forms on my hard-pressed lips and cracks against my tongue.

And somehow, as if it listened to my plea, the magic starts to *surge*. To rumble up beneath my flesh and through my blood and finally, *finally* answer my call.

I suck in a breath as I watch ice begin to coalesce in my hands. The scabbed shards that are always stuck to the gashes begin to puff up like clouds. They stretch, reaching for the other, and the two pieces merge into one. As soon as they do, they begin to grow. Like frost forming over a window, it builds up layer by layer, thickening until it's a block of ice so big and heavy that I drop it on the ground with a grunt, unable to hold its weight.

I stare at it. At this perfectly formed brick made from solid ice, slightly cloudy with frost that's as white as my hair, a blue tinge the same color as my eyes. And finally, I have an answer to Dommik's question that he asked me outside of the barracks.

So what are we going to do?

Since no one is going to listen to me, then I'll just have to defend Highbell myself.

Brick by brick.

CHAPTER 35

AUREN

Instead of a babbling brook, we follow one that sighs. The stream's croon seems to pause between breaths and then lets out an exhale of relief, like someone finally falling into bed after a long day. Rocks steep lazily beneath the surface, making the water tint with rivulets of green.

It's the exact shade of Slade's eyes in the sunlight.

As I sit on top of Blush, leading the horse alongside the brook, I fiddle with the collar of my tunic, swiping a thumb across the loneliness that swells from my chest. I want to look Slade in the eyes again. I want to tell him all the things that I should've said right from the start. When I was too scared and too broken to know what was in front of me. When I was too full of doubts and scars to trust myself and my heart.

I was so sure that I was going to make the same mistakes I'd made with Midas. I thought I couldn't possibly have real love with Slade. Thought he couldn't possibly love someone like me.

Love happens in all kinds of ways.

He was right when he said that. Love *does* happen in all kinds of ways. But our kind happened like the dawn.

The dawn doesn't question when to appear. It simply does.

He walked into my life with the surety of his presence, and from that point on, the night began to wane.

I was trapped in lonely darkness for so long that I couldn't recognize the way the world began to illuminate— not right away. I was blind for so many years that, when my horizon began to brighten, I tried to turn away. To squint and blink and shut my eyes against it because I thought, of course, I couldn't have that. Of course I'd stay in the dark.

But I didn't.

He showed me what it was to face the sun and not shy away. He let me approach it with my hesitations, let me ease into it without being blinded.

Let me choose.

I'm in this light with him, basking in its warmth, and even our distance can't take that away. Because no matter where we are, the sun always dawns. No matter where he is, I love him.

"We're almost there."

My thoughts scatter and I look away from the brook to Wick. He and Ludogar are riding in front of us, Emonie is beside me, and two other Vulmin named Marox and Ogith are behind us. We're the six that Wick chose to take on this mission to rescue the Oreans. All the other Vulmin stayed behind in the village. We've been riding for a few hours now, going to meet up with the fae who will be bringing us to Riffalt City where the Oreans are being held.

I straighten in the saddle, trying to stretch my back, and Emonie digs around in her pouch before extending her hand to me. "Here."

Taking the offering, I find a bit of syrup-drizzled bread. I instantly pop it into my mouth, the burst of sweetness coating my tongue and leaving a hint of citrusy sour that makes my lips perk. "Mmm, thanks."

One thing about Emonie, I never go hungry during the long days of travel when I'm riding beside her. She's always plying me with food to snack on. Right now, it's a good distraction since I'm a bit nervous about going on my first real rebel mission. But I'm also invigorated. Ready to do something meaningful.

"Lady Lyäri," Marox calls forward. "I also have some food you can have if you're hungry."

"As do I," Ogith adds.

I look over my shoulder at the pair. Marox is scowling from beneath his bushy red beard at Ogith like he doesn't appreciate the tag-on. Ogith gazes straight at me, his black hair wind-swept, his freckled face open and sincere. They've both been incredibly attentive since we left. I've already had offers to drink their water and to take their cloaks when it rained earlier this morning.

"I'm alright, but thank you."

Ogith's pale blue eyes go a bit dejected, but Marox sits up straighter in his saddle. "Anything you need, Lyäri, we will get it for you."

"That's very kind of you, but you don't need to go to any trouble for me," I say as I face forward again.

"That's right. She has me," Emonie chirps.

I snort as Wick begins to veer us away from the gentle brook and head deeper into the thick brush around us. The trees we pass have trunks adorned with black moss, like a broad body tucked into a cloak. Bright green leaves the shape of tears weep down overhead, shading us from the sun, and the ground is thick with overgrown bushes. The six of us ride single file down a narrow game trail with Ludogar at the front, cutting through some of the thorny branches that block the path.

We break through a particularly dense spot of brush, and then, it seems like the world opens up. Our group dismounts, leaving our horses behind to graze and nose around near the small pond as we approach the meeting place that seems to be a realm of its own.

A row of huge pillars stands as tall as trees. The stone is semi-translucent in a deep violet color and is incredibly old, with parts crumbled away and the rest cracked with age. Vines wind around them, sprouting through the fissures and clotting with little white reeds as puffy as the clouds.

Whatever this building used to be before, it's clear it was grand. Now, nature seems to have taken it over, and time has worn it away. There are a few shallow steps leading up to it, nothing but open sky in place of a roof.

Wick leads us between the crumbled walls that stand on either side, but I watch my feet. The floor has the same see-through stone as the pillars, but beneath it and right down the center, there's an underground river, making it seem like we're walking on purple water. Every once in a while, a small fish darts by, pale scales looking like the streak of a star shooting past.

"What was this place?" I ask in a hush. I'm not sure why, but something about being here makes it seem like I should whisper.

"An old temple," Wick says, thin streaks of sunlight dappling his face. He takes us to a spot where the wall has split, parts of the purple stone fallen in a pile with a thick layer of spongy vines grown over them. "The fae we're meeting should be here soon. In the meantime, we can relax."

I nod as we all cluster together, and I sit on one of the cushioned rock pieces. Emonie walks to the wall and clicks her nail against the purple stone, letting out a low whistle while fiddling with her pouch.

Ludogar shoots her a look. "Don't even think about it."

She glances over her shoulder at him as she continues to walk the length of the wall. "What?" she asks innocently, though her molten eyes dart left and right.

His teal eyes, however, are unwavering. "You cannot, under any circumstances, steal something from this place."

She stops and holds up a finger. "Firstly, it's called *foraging*. And secondly—" Another finger juts up, but she pauses. "Umm...why not?"

He lets out a huff and looks at the rest of us, but Wick sits down and busies himself with taking a drink from his water skin, while Marox and Ogith avoid eye contact.

"This place is *sacred*," Ludo says, like it should be obvious. "It was built for the goddesses."

She hums thoughtfully. "Which one?"

His brows draw together. "Does it matter?"

"*Does it matter*," she scoffs. "Of course it matters. Say this was the temple of Dronidylis. She was the goddess of favor and filch. She would *love* for someone to steal from her temple. It would delight her."

My lips curve up in amusement. I see Wick fighting a smirk behind his drink. Even Ogith and Marox share a look of mirth between them.

"This wasn't the temple of Dronidylis," Ludogar says irritably.

She taps another part of the wall. "How can you be so sure?"

His words falter, but not his scowl. "Just...don't steal anything! It would bring us bad luck."

"Did you not hear me? *Favor and filch*," Emonie retorts. "I'd argue that we would get good luck." Then she looks to me. "Droni is my favorite goddess."

Not surprising.

Ludogar sighs and shakes his head, looking up at the trees growing high overhead like he's trying to see the sky and find a goddess up there who will help explain things to her.

Unbothered, Emonie plops on the floor, legs folded and back up against the wall before she starts picking at the little vines dangling next to her.

Just when I lean back to get comfortable with the wait, I hear a sound behind me. I turn quickly as Wick gets to his feet, and see a hobbling old fae making his way toward us.

"Good, you're here," he says in greeting.

He has shoulder-length brown hair streaked gray from age, and a short beard that looks like a perfectly shaped square hedge. His skin is pale with hues of gray like a clouded moon. He's wearing a black leather vest over his tunic and creased pants with a red belt looped around his waist. As he walks, he taps a wooden cane against the floor, sending an echo through the ruins of the temple.

"Brennur," Wick says as he walks over to meet him while the rest of us hang back. "Thank you for agreeing to come back for us."

The slightly hunched fae gives a quick nod. "It was a task, I won't say it wasn't." He looks over at Ludo. "Lerana insisted it was urgent when I brought her back."

"Yes," Wick answers. "We're grateful you were able to bring her and return for us."

Brennur stops and lets out a tired sigh as he leans on his cane. "Of course, of course. You know I do all I can for the Vulmin. But why do you want to go to Riffalt?"

"There may be some Oreans there who need our help."

Brennur's wiry eyebrows lift.

"We'll need your help with that as well," Wick finishes.

There's slight hesitation in the old fae's face. "That is *very* dangerous…"

"You'll be well compensated."

"You know I don't care about that," Brennur says with a wave of his knobby hand. "But to sneak Oreans out of Riffalt is a great risk."

Wick gives him an enigmatic smile. "Everything worthy of risk is worthy of doing."

"Yes, yes. Fine. Of course, if that is what the Vulmin mission requires, you know I am at your service," Brennur says as his eyes begin to skim around the rest of us in the group. "Now, let's see, how many am I—"

The moment his eyes land on me, they go wide. There's a shock of silence that seems to stab through him, making him stagger back from the plunge. Then, he yanks it out with a gush. "Y-you. You're Auren Turley."

I give him a polite smile. "Yes."

His face seems to drain of all color before he whips toward Wick. "How is she here? How is this possible? She's *dead.*"

"That's just what the monarchy declared," Ludo says.

"And we all know how often they lie," Wick adds. "The Lyäri Ulvêre is alive and well, and she has returned."

Brennur's hand shakes on his cane. "How is this possible?" His gaze keeps tracking back to me, his eyes the color of clay.

"The goddesses brought her home," Wick tells him.

"Maybe even Dronidylis," Emonie says under her breath, making me crack a smile.

"What's she doing *here*?" Brennur asks.

I step forward and answer, because I'm tired of being talked *about* instead of talked *to*. "I'm going to Riffalt to help the Oreans."

His expression is dumbfounded, with traces of fear filtering through as he looks from me to Wick. "You expect me to bring her to Riffalt City? Are you *mad*?"

"Auren can take care of herself," Wick replies, and a

surge of pride goes through me before I nod at the old fae.

But he shakes his head, making his squared beard bobble. "Absolutely not. I cannot take her *anywhere*, least of all there. I can't be seen with her! None of us can! Do you know what will happen to us if someone realizes who she is? Tales of the Turleys might not be talked about in cities like Riffalt, but they will figure out who she is quick enough. And if Lord Cull or the other nobles hear word of it…"

"He won't. No one will see her. We just need you to take us to Riffalt. I will handle the rest, Brennur. Trust that I know what I'm doing is in the best interest of the Vulmin."

His lips press down hard, thinning them out. "I don't like this…"

"You took a vow to the Vulmin," Wick tells him. "And so did I. I won't put you at undue risk, but these missions always pose a danger. It must be done."

Everyone watches and waits as he chews on Wick's words. He's clearly torn, a frown split between his brows in a jagged line.

Finally, he relents through gritted teeth. "Alright."

"Thank you, Brennur." Wick claps him on his shoulder, making him teeter slightly. "Lead the way."

Brennur casts a look at me again before turning and walking away, cane clicking against the floor. I follow behind him, trailing his slower steps, and Emonie walks beside me. This close, I can smell his leather vest, the scent earthy and with an underlying tone that makes my nose twist, reminding me of wet bark.

Our group doesn't have to follow him for long. We get outside of the temple ruins just on the other side of the pillars, and Wick motions for the rest of us to stop and wait. Too bad I have no idea *what* we're waiting for. I watch as Brennur begins walking around, gaze trained on the ground at his feet as if he's looking for something.

"What's he doing?" I ask quietly.

"Riffalt City would take too long to get to by horse," Wick tells me. "We're traveling using much faster means."

I wait for him to divulge further, but his gaze is back on Brennur.

Everyone watches as he continues to walk around, and then he seems to find what he's looking for when he taps his cane against the ground and mutters something under his breath. He toes off his sandals and then flips his cane around, hooking them by their straps. Without a word, he extends his cane out, and Ludogar comes over and takes the hanging shoes. As soon as he does, Brennur flips his cane around again and starts walking forward in a determined line.

What in the world?

He halts just past the old steps in front of a purple pillar. Still looking down, he then begins to walk in a circle with deep concentration, his bare feet treading over the cracked ground.

My confusion deepens. "What…"

He goes around and around and around again. After his tenth rotation, the path beneath his feet begins to sprout with blades of grass in a perfect ring. They're short at first. Stubby things cutting up through the broken stone, bright green like the first shoots of spring. My brows lift in surprise.

Magic.

As he continues to walk, the loop grows fuller, bolder. Dainty flowers bloom up in whites and purples with little petals that unfold like a butterfly's wings. The grass becomes thicker and greener, and pebbles appear that glisten pale blue like dew drops left behind from a rain. There's a gentle hum beneath our feet, and my skin tingles with the trace of whatever power Brennur is using.

Finally, when the grass is up past his ankles and the flowers are in full bloom, he stops walking and looks around at the three-foot circle with a considering expression before he steps off and glances at Wick. "It's ready."

Marox steps forward. "I will go first and ensure all is safe for the Lyäri."

Go first…?

"You and Ogith both go," Wick tells them.

"Perhaps it would be best to travel one at a time," Brennur says, motioning to the circle. "The trace here isn't very big."

But Wick shakes his head. "We'll fit two. It's safer, even if it is a tight fit. It will be quicker for you as well, so we don't strain your magic."

Brennur nods, and then Marox and Ogith stride forward. I watch as they both step past the grassy ring to stand in the center. It's just barely big enough for them both to stand in, but as soon as they're back to back, the ground hums again. The grassy ring that surrounds them blows with a breeze, bending the flowers and splaying the leaves.

Then, the two of them disappear. Just like that.

My mouth drops open. "Wait. Is this…"

"A fairy ring," Emonie says, practically bouncing on her toes. "I *love* passing through fairy rings." When Ludogar snorts, she shoots him a look. "Don't pretend you don't like it too."

"Why?" I ask.

"You'll see," she says with a grin.

"Emonie, you go with Ludo," Wick tells her. "I'll travel with Auren next."

The two of them stride forward and step into the ring. Emonie shoots me a wink. "See you on the other side."

Within seconds, they're gone too.

"Ready?" Wick asks, looking over at me.

Ready?

"A little '*Hey, we're going to be traveling through a fairy ring today'* would have been good information to have," I hiss beneath my breath.

He blinks in surprise. "I apologize. I assumed..." He shakes his head. "I forget how little you know of Annwyn. I should have explained it earlier."

Well. Now that he apologized, I can't keep hissing at him about it. "Okay. Thank you. And...what is this going to do exactly?" I know of fairy rings, but only that they once used to be throughout Orea when fae lived there. I never used one, so I have no idea what to expect.

"We'll step in the ring together. Rings have a twin. This one is here, and its sister will be in Riffalt City, where Brennur traveled from. When we pass through, his magic will pull us there. Then Brennur will follow us, closing both rings so no one can follow."

I hesitate.

"You'll be perfectly safe in the ring, I promise."

With a tight nod, I walk forward with him. Together, we step into the ring, our backs to each other, while I face Brennur. The old fae stares back at me, nodding in encouragement, and the strangest sensation crawls down my spine. Then, a shot of heat surges up my heels, enveloping my entire body in an instant. My gold surges to my palms in response, flaring to life, just as the world around me warps.

It's quicker than a blink, the air itself feeling like it creases around me like a ball of paper scrunched in my fist. My vision wrinkles and my surroundings go gray, as all the colors of the world get smashed and mixed up together into one drab hue.

My ears crackle like they're opening up from a big yawn, and something invigorating surges through my blood, like the ring's power is fueling me. Then, the heat shooting through my body becomes a refreshing cool breeze. And it *should* feel refreshing, just as the ring's energy should revive me.

Except my stomach coils into knots. Anxiety shoots down my limbs. A cold sweat breaks out all over me, and I don't like it at all. None of it. I want out.

I open my mouth to yell, but there's no voice in this strange vortex, which makes me panic even more.

I want to get *out out out out out*—

The scrunched-up world suddenly starts flattening again, like a steady palm smoothing out the creases.

And then, it's over.

With a gasp, everything is as it should be, and I'm standing in an identical fairy ring, though I'm somewhere else entirely. The temple ruins are gone, and in its place is a simple bedroom. Everything is completely ordinary in it, except for the circle of grass and flowers growing right up through the polished wood floor.

Emonie comes forward, tugging me out of the ring. "What did you think?" she asks with a bright smile. Her excitement is jarring to the panic that was just coursing through me.

Glancing back at the ring, I have to suppress a shudder, "It was…strange."

My fall through the rip has obviously affected me more than I realized.

"But *good* strange, right?" She has a wide grin on her pretty face, her eyes carrying a faraway look. "I always feel so…*alive* after going through a fairy ring."

"It is quite revitalizing," Ogith offers. "It's the connection to Annwyn that you're feeling. A fairy ring is made by making a connection to the land's core. Kind of like tapping into the world's vein. When you pass through, you're feeling a piece of Annwyn's beating heart."

Emonie grins at him. "You know a lot about fairy rings."

He blushes, freckled cheeks turning crimson. "My great grandmother was a ringer."

"Rare magic. Especially these days," Marox says over his shoulder where he's standing at the bedroom door, looking out through a small peep hole.

"*All* magic is rare these days," Ludogar mutters.

"Which is why the Vulmin are incredibly lucky to have Brennur," Wick says as he walks across the wooden floor. With all six of us in here, the bedroom seems quite small. "He's helped us complete a lot of missions."

"All in service of the cause," the old fae himself answers as he appears inside the ring.

"All's clear here," Marox announces, though he keeps his gaze on the door's bubbled glass.

Ludogar glances to Wick, and the two of them exchange some silent communication. Then Ludo passes Brennur's sandals to Ogith to hold, before slipping out the door.

At the sound of shuffled feet, I look over and see Brennur begin his slow track, bare feet passing over the ring of grass, flowers bending beneath his heels. With every pass, the green liveliness of the grass begins to eke out, the flowers wilting, petals drifting off as the grass turns brown and dry.

He keeps circling, the ring dying with each step, until finally, everything has come loose and lifeless, nothing but sparse blades and dead stems pulled up from the floor and scattering around like dust.

He steps out of it, nearly stumbling over to the bed to sit down with a tired sigh, his shoulders sagging more than before. Emonie and the others may feel energized from traveling through the fairy ring, but he looks worn out.

Ogith goes over and slips on his sandals for him, looking up at him with concern. "Alright, Sir Brennur?"

"Fine," he replies, waving a dismissive hand.

Just then, the door opens and Ludogar comes back in. "We're clear."

My stomach twists with nervous anticipation.

Brennur gets back to his feet, toes curling in his sandals. "I should go. Can't be missed or brows will be raised."

"Yes, go," Wick nods. "We'll see you at the meet point in a few hours. Marox, Ogith, you stay with him. You know what to do. Keep your eyes and ears open, and protect him at all costs. Remember, we have no friends in Riffalt."

Tension mounts in my muscles. For the first time since arriving in Annwyn, I'm going to be in an anti-Vulmin city, surrounded by non-Turley loyalists.

The two Vulmin nod, their faces resolute. Then they follow the old ringer out, and Ludogar shuts the door behind them.

When it's just the four of us, Wick looks around, his expression set in grim determination. "Alright. Getting to Riffalt was the easy part. Now, things are about to get a lot more difficult."

CHAPTER 36

AUREN

Wick's declaration doesn't deter me. I knew this was going to be a difficult mission, and despite my nerves, I'm looking forward to the challenge. I don't like to think of Oreans being hated here, any more than I like the way fae are hated in Orea.

"You have a plan?" I ask him.

"I do—Ludo and I finalized it on our way here, but we have to hurry and meet Lerana, so I'm going to make this quick," he says, looking at both Emonie and me. "Ludo's sister got word about some Oreans being kept in Lord Cull's estate—a very powerful and notorious nobleman here in Riffalt. She works as an undercover servant at a neighboring estate, so she's going to help us get in. You two are to be eyes and ears *only*. That means all I want you to do is see what you can find out while you're there. But under no circumstance are you to put yourselves at risk. This is a fact-finding mission only, not a rescue mission. I will handle that part once we confirm the Oreans are there and if they actually need our help."

"Okay," I say with a nod.

"Remember that Riffalt City, and especially where we're going, is dangerous. So it's important we all stay in our roles. Which is why I mentioned a disguise for you, Auren."

Realization dawns on me and I look over at Emonie. "Your glamour magic."

She grins. "Yep. As long as you're okay with it, of course."

"This mission requires discretion," Wick tells me. "We know you're powerful, but you're not the only one with magic. There are a lot of Stone Swords here, and the captains are all hand-picked because of their magical abilities. Even some of the grunts have power—it's why the crown drafted them. The nobleman, Lord Cull, is a powerful bastard and close with the king. Luckily for us, Lerana said he's not here at the moment. So our focus is to get in, assess their situation, and get out. Discretion and your safety are of the utmost importance."

I nod in understanding before my eyes flick back to Emonie. "What do you need me to do?"

"Nothing at all. I already collected some things from the others."

"And by *things* you mean…"

"Eyes, hair, that sort of thing."

She makes it sound like she's hacked them off and stuffed them in her foraging pouch. "Right."

"Ready?"

As soon as I dip my head, she reaches out and presses a palm to my chest, fingers resting over my collarbone. "Hold your breath for a second."

I suck the air into my lungs and keep it there, and in the next instant, I feel a pulse directly under her hand. She drags her touch down, and the pulse reverberates along my limbs and up my neck. The slight vibration morphs to something like water pouring down my skin, and I watch as the gold of my complexion changes, fading into a dreary gray that I recognize from one of the Vulmin back at the village.

The wet sensation follows her touch as she moves to graze down my arm and then cup my cheek, making my lips feel wet and my ears go cold. She gives me a wink before tapping a fingertip over my eyelids. Instantly, my eyes feel as if they're being flooded, like someone is pouring a cup of water right into them.

I blink through the tears, but the feeling goes away as quickly as it started, my eyes drying up. Then her hand moves to my hair. I watch as she twirls strands of my golden locks around her fingers, and the color slowly leaches out and turns an inky black, though the length stays the same.

"There." Her hand drops away, and the three of them look at me in assessment. "Oh, wait. Almost forgot." She reaches up and taps me on both ears, and I gasp at the pinching sensation that radiates at the tops, feeling the distinct points now at the tips.

I swipe a finger beneath my eyes and lick my lips, looking down at myself. It's eerie to see my hands a different color. "Well?" I ask.

Emonie nods. "You still kind of look like you, I didn't change your face shape or anything. You're just not...shiny."

I snort.

"What about those?"

At Ludogar's question, we all look down at the golden ribbons around my waist.

"Can't do anything about those," Emonie says.

I reach down and pull my shirt over them a bit. The ones peeking through could pass for a belt. "How's that?"

Wick looks me up and down. "You'll do."

"Dazzling compliment."

"*Dazzling* is exactly what we don't want you to be in this city."

Emonie pats me on the arm reassuringly. "You're still dazzling on the inside."

A laugh escapes me. "I thought you said using your magic on other people was difficult?"

"It takes a lot of power," she admits, wiping a bit of sweat from her brow.

"We should only need a few hours," Wick says. "In and out."

Emonie's fiery eyes churn with determination. "I can do it."

If she says she can do it, I believe her.

"Okay," I say, looking around at everyone. "Then let's go rescue some Oreans."

When the four of us leave the room, we walk down a set of stairs and then hit the main level of a busy inn. It's about five times the size of Estelia's servette, with none of the dainty decor or pretty flowers. The dining room here is filled with benches and long tables, with stains on the wood and smoke in the air.

It's loud. Fae are going in and out, more of them slopping up food or slamming down drinks. Wick leads the way past them without hesitation, keeping his head up as we go by the busy tables and head for the door.

As soon as we're outside, Ludogar takes the lead, making a sharp right. Emonie walks beside me, while Wick takes up the rear watching our backs. We're spread out enough that people can weave between us, but close enough not to lose sight of one another on the busy street.

And the street *is* busy, though unlike Geisel, with flower carts and people traveling up and down the street-side shops, here, it's busy with soldiers. Stone Swords litter the place, cluttering up every corner with their intimidating presence. Most are marching in formation, postures straight and faces stiff.

I glance over at Emonie to gauge whether or not we need to be worried, but she looks completely carefree…and is swinging a basket in her hand.

"Where did you get that?" I ask from the corner of my mouth.

She just winks over at me.

Great Divine.

"This is just a suggestion, Em…but maybe *don't* steal in the dangerous city swarming with Stone Swords," I mumble.

Her lips quirk, but I can practically hear the giggle that wants to bubble up her throat. At least Ludo is walking ahead of us. He probably would've thrown a fit if he'd seen her.

As we continue to walk, I keep my eyes peeled for trouble. The street is paved flat and black, and the buildings are just as plain and austere. No embellishments, no mash and mix of woods and colors. Everything is gray stone, each front face smooth and flat, boasting the same sized doors and black-framed windows.

When we pass by another formation of marching guards, I lean closer to Emonie. "Why so many?"

"Riffalt is an outpost. They have a training camp here."

No wonder this place isn't safe for Vulmin.

"But…" she goes on, eyes scanning the street. "It does seem like there are more than usual."

"You there!"

Emonie and I jolt, eyes whipping around to the Stone Sword just ahead. He has yellow hair plaited back against his scalp, and a close-cropped beard embellished around his scowling face. The fae he was talking to scuttle away, as if glad he's moved his attention on to someone else.

My stomach plummets when he starts marching over, arms swinging, the skin at his knuckles red as if he's fresh out of a fist fight.

Shit. What does he want with us?

He stops in front of us and looks us over. "Where are you two going?"

He keeps himself planted in front of us, sharp eyes assessing. Up ahead, I can see Ludo has stopped walking and appears to be glancing in some windows of one of the buildings, like he's debating whether or not to go in, but I know better.

"We're just out shopping, sir," Emonie tells him brightly. "We need all sorts of things for tonight. You see, it's our cousin's birthday, and he is *quite* picky on what he likes for his meal. So we need to get down to the butcher and get his favorite cut, and then the florist so we can decorate the table, and then we need to track down some fresh spices, since he likes his meat quite flavorful, and then we—"

"Quiet." He cuts off her chatter, his yoke-colored eyes sliding over my face and slipping down my body in a way that makes me want to knee him in the groin. "What's your name?"

"Nenet," I say without hesitation.

"Nenet. What's your cousin's name?"

"Ludo."

The real Ludo glances our way for a moment and then starts meandering over, back to looking through windows. Out of the corner of my eye, I see Wick pass us, though he stops near a couple of fae to our right, charming them with a smile as he strikes up conversation in order to stay close.

Nervous sweat is starting to gather at the back of my neck, but I keep my face expressionless. Emonie shifts on her feet, a slight give away at her own anxiousness. We're on a crowded street swarming with Stone Swords, and if I have to use my magic, Wick's whole plan of discretion will be gone.

The guard continues to eye us, and my heart pounds in my chest as my palms heat, gold-touch pressing just beneath my skin, ready to surge out.

He leans in close to our faces, making a big show of lording over us as if he wants us to feel like we're so much smaller than he is. "You know, *Nenet*, I don't think I believe you."

I see Emonie glance at me, and my heartbeat thrums loudly in my ears.

"You two are going to come with me."

His hand shoots out to grip my arm, and I go stiff for a half-second before I grip *his* wrist with my free hand. He looks up at me with surprise, but I smile at him sweetly.

"Sir, I think there's some mistake," I tell him. "We're just doing our errands."

"Release me at once," he growls. "You have no right to touch a Stone Sword, and if you don't come with me now, I'll *drag* you."

The threat has me tightening my grip.

He's too incensed about the fact that I've challenged him to notice the rotten gold that's now slipping in through the cracks of his split knuckles.

Who knows what he'll do to us once we're off the streets. I saw the Stone Swords in Geisel. The way they terrorized that town, the way they were ready to kill Thursil without hesitation. I won't let him terrorize us.

"I don't think you heard my *cousin*," I tell him. "We have things to do. So we won't be able to go anywhere with you."

He opens his mouth to argue, but there's a terrible choking sound that comes out instead.

"Are you alright?" I ask, my brows pulling down into a

frown.

He jerks away from me and looks down at his hand, but there's nothing there to see. All the gold has already made its way through blood and muscle and bone, tiny rivulets that have now swarmed to his lungs.

I can feel it—almost see it in my mind's eye where it's infected his body. My gold has latched on to his lungs, filling them, weighing them down. The rotted lines slither like snakes, sinking their fangs in to decay the very breath he tries to take.

The rotten seed in my chest warms. My fae beast grins.

The guard gasps, wide eyed, his breath going putrid as he struggles to make a noise.

"Oh dear." Emonie frowns as she takes his arm and starts pulling him behind one of the parked carriages. "You don't look too good, sir."

"No," I say with a shake of my head as I help her prop him up against the wood. "He doesn't look too good at all. We'd better leave him to rest."

He shakes his head at us in a panic, though he's bent over, clutching his ribs, his focus on trying to breathe. He won't be able to for very long.

Wick comes strolling over and smiles at us. "There you are."

"Cousin!" Emonie gushes before she threads her arm through his. "Let's go. This poor Stone Sword appears to be a bit sick."

Wick's eyes flick away from the gasping guard, and then he quickly escorts us away. Together, the three of us bustle around the carriage and back into the crowded street. There's a shout behind us, but none of us dares to turn around or stop walking.

My heart pounds, faster and faster. Wick's bent elbow is rigid beneath my hand.

We keep going, and Emonie chatters happily like she doesn't have a care in the world. Up ahead, I see Ludo loping through the crowd. Wick's body stays tense beside me, but he keeps up conversation with Emonie as if nothing is amiss, their steps unhurried, their faces relaxed.

When there are more shouts, my stomach leaps, and I turn to glance over my shoulder, but Wick stops me. "Don't," he hisses beneath his breath. "Just keep going."

Stone Swords run past, and anxiety spikes so high between us that even Emonie's words peter out. Every second that goes by, I'm convinced that we're about to be swarmed by Stone Swords. My ears strain to listen for anyone rushing up from behind us, the corners of my eyes pulled with tension.

But then, we veer off at a fork that takes us away from the busy street and onto a gravel road of small white pebbles. It winds up and away from the main city, toward a slightly sloping hill, and I finally let out a relieved breath as the noisy crowd fades. Emonie and I share a look.

Wick loses the tension in his body. "What happened?" he asks.

"He was questioning people on the street, I think. Something about us set him off. He wanted to bring us somewhere to question us."

"What did you do to him?"

"Gilded his lungs."

Emonie whistles. "Impressive."

Wick sighs. "Well...at least I know you won't hesitate to protect yourself."

"She was brilliant." Emonie beams at me.

"I just killed someone," I point out.

Wick picks up on my unease. "He would've killed *you*. Stone Swords don't question people for answers. They question to bully and torture and kill. Don't feel bad about defending yourself and your identity."

I nod, because while I don't just go around killing people without thought, I will do it to protect myself and those I care about.

"I'm going to hang back again, just in case. I'll keep an eye out," Wick says before he falls behind until it's just Emonie and me again, while Ludo is even further ahead.

Now that we've ventured away from the main city street, we've left behind the uniformed buildings for spread-out greenery. The grass around us is kept short and shorn, looking like no one, not even animals, is allowed to walk on it. The road is lined with orderly trees all the same distance apart, the leaves tinged with blue and perfectly trimmed on either side to create an arch overhead.

We walk for some time beneath the spotted shade, only occasionally moving aside for a fancy carriage to pass us by. Emonie swings her basket in her hand and hums beneath her breath, the wind blowing her amber hair so the curled-up orange ends keep fluttering along the edge of her jaw.

"So your hair and eyes, are those yours or is it glamoured?" I ask her.

"Oh, they're mine. Like I said, glamour magic takes a lot of power. The longest I've been able to hold a different eye color for myself was two days."

"It's a handy power."

"When I was younger and I first got my magic, I would swap hair and eyes with my sister all the time after I'd done something I shouldn't have. She got *a lot* of lectures about things she didn't do," she says with a lilting laugh. "It came in quite handy."

"Where is your sister now?"

The smile falls from her face. "She went off and became a noblewoman. Doesn't have much time for me anymore."

I can hear the sadness in her voice despite the way she tries to cover it up. "I'm sorry."

"We all have different paths, right? Take this one for instance. It's really...neat," she says, looking around at the uniform road with her nose wrinkled. "Kind of makes me want to mess it up a bit. Kick some rocks off the side, bend some of these branches down..."

"Let's not draw any more attention to ourselves today."

She blows out a disappointed breath. "Alright." Still swinging her basket, she looks over at me. "So, what's Orea like?"

"Well...there's six different kingdoms. I lived in the coldest one for a long time. But I've been to nearly all of them. There's snow and deserts and marshes and jungles... There's ugly parts and beautiful parts. There's good people and bad people."

"Sounds a lot like here."

"The sky is different. So are the trees and the sun. Annwyn smells sweeter."

Emonie makes a noise under her breath. "Wait until we get to Lydia. I bet you the air there smells worse than Orea. That's where our land is dying. It stinks something awful."

"Because of the bridge?"

"That's what we think," she says with a shrug. "It's been happening since it was broken. It's like Annwyn is punishing us for breaking the bond with Orea."

Emonie and I grow quiet as a small group of Stone Swords marches past us, and I wonder at this broken bond between realms. Wonder what will happen to Annwyn and everyone here if the land keeps dying.

When we make our way around a slight bend in the road, we see Ludogar ahead, stopped beside a fae with a horse. They exchange a few words, and then the male passes the reins over to Ludo before quickly turning and walking away.

I watch as Ludo smoothly starts leading the horse forward. Emonie snorts beside me. "Okay, see, I only took a little old basket, but he just took a *horse*. That's much more noticeable."

She's got a point.

Now, the road starts opening up to private paths that lead to large, elaborate estates. Most of them have thick hedges that line the drives, each one meticulously trimmed with edges so sharp it looks like you could cut your finger on the corners.

Just when I thought the estates couldn't get more extravagant looking, we reach one that's far larger than the others we've passed. It has immaculate trees lining the long drive, and in the distance, there's a lake cut into a perfect square at the front.

The manor sits just beyond it, with green hills covering its back. There's an intimidating solid iron gate sitting propped open like a gaping mouth, and this is where Ludo swoops in with the horse in tow, disappearing behind it.

Nervousness passes over me, but I shove it away, sharing a look with Emonie before the two of us follow him.

The surrounding fence hides the road from view, the walled-in iron gate and stone pillars a good head taller than me. Just to the left of the drive, we spot what looks like a tiny guardhouse. It's only big enough for one person to fit inside, though it's empty right now, apparent from the square cut into the wall like a glassless window.

Just behind the small building, we find Ludo talking to his sister, Lerana, while the horse snuffs at the grass beyond them. As we approach, Lerana reaches into the open doorway and then hands Emonie and me wadded-up clothes.

"Here, put those on," she instructs, and I shake out the bundle, realizing it's a long gray skirt and an apron.

Emonie stows her basket in the guardhouse, and the two of us then step into the skirts. Mine is long enough to hide my pants beneath, the hem skimming the toes of my boots. I loosely braid my ribbons and then feed them through the belt loops before I tie the apron on over them, and then make sure all the discreet gold I have on me is covered.

Meanwhile, Wick and Ludogar each get a flat cap from Lerana that they've stuffed over their partially shaved heads. Ludogar's short bill barely contains the riot of hair that hangs down his left side like a waterfall. They've also stuffed red cloths into the front pocket of their jackets that are now buttoned all the way to their necks.

Now, we all apparently look as if we can stroll onto a nobleman's estate like we belong there. I hope we can pull this off, but my silent worries are stacking up. My neck and shoulders feel tight, my breaths tense. I don't want to let the Vulmin or the Oreans down. And despite the fact that I will defend myself and the others, I don't want to leave a litter of bodies in my wake either.

"Alright, listen carefully, because I'm running out of time before I need to get back," Lerana says with a no-nonsense tone, her own sea-blue hair braided tight and wound around her head. She levels her teal eyes on Emonie and me. "The story is, you two work with me as servants in my lord's estate that neighbors this one. I'm bringing you over here to help serve *this* estate today, because they need the extra hands. Apparently, the arrival of the Oreans has put a dent into Cull's housekeeping."

Emonie and I nod.

She looks to her brother and Wick. "You two will be reporting to the stables. The horse master has ordered a new horse, so you'll be delivering it," she says, gesturing to the horse standing beside Ludo. "If you give a good showing, they'll purchase him from you. But the horse master is very particular, so expect it to take a couple of hours. He'll make you do a thorough showing, so I hope you two got acquainted with one another on the walk over."

Ludogar pats the animal. "We'll be fine."

"You'll have eyes on the outside, while Lady Auren and Emonie will have eyes on the inside. I wish I had more information to point you in the right direction, but I don't, and this is the best way I know how to get you onto the estate."

"This works perfectly, Lerana," Wick assures her. "Thank you."

She smiles at him, her teal eyes warming, and then lets out a sigh. "Alright. Ready?" she asks, looking critically back at Emonie and me. "Can you pull off being handmaidens?"

"I've played many parts in my life. Handmaiden should be a walk in the park," I say, trying to play off my nerves with a little laugh. Inside, my gut is tightening.

I can't let them down.

Wick steps forward, burying me beneath his grave expression. "If *anything* goes wrong, if there's even a *hint* that someone might suspect you aren't who you say you are, I want you both to leave immediately and find us at the stables, with or without information on the Oreans. The nobleman who owns this estate is a mean bastard, and even though he isn't here, he'll have guards. Remember that you can't trust anyone—not even the other servants. What we're about to walk into is incredibly dangerous, so be on high alert. And if anything feels off, you get out. By *any* means necessary."

I don't have to ask him to elaborate on what he means by that.

"Got it," Emonie says.

Apparently, neither does she.

He stares at me a moment longer, looking like he's going to add something for a second, but then he just nods and says, "Good luck."

Emonie and I turn and follow behind Lerana toward Lord Cull's estate, and the gold bands around my arms tingle with anticipation. As I walk down the grassy drive, eyeing the ominous -ooking estate in front of us, I take in a deep breath. Readying myself—*reminding* myself who I am and what I'm capable of.

I can do this.

I glance back at Wick, and when he gives me a nod, I give him one right back. The simple exchange boosts my confidence, and when I face forward again, I crumple up the last of my nerves and toss them away.

For the first time since joining them, I finally *feel* like a Vulmin.

So it's time I act like one, too, and save some Oreans.

CHAPTER 37

SLADE

I'm sweat-slicked beneath my heavy armor, my breath stuck in the humid confines of my helmet as I clutch a sword in each hand. Inside the fight circle, I face three soldiers. Beside me, Ryatt is facing off against three of his own.

This is what we've been doing. It's the only way I can manage to get a couple hours of sleep. The first time we came down here, we pummeled each other pretty good before word caught on. Soon, news spread that we were sparring—Rip and Ryatt. Their former commander and their new one. It's been a good boost to morale with the change in command, and a good way to set Ryatt apart. But for me, it's been more about the fights.

Every time we come down here now, the circle soon bursts with crowds of soldiers, the energy sizzling. It's been the perfect distraction for me. One that Osrik also partakes in, since he's been in need of distraction too.

My muscles ache with satisfying strain as I move against the soldiers, countering their attacks and pushing them to be quicker, more aggressive. Above us, the sun is searing through cluttered clouds that are pouring down a slosh of messy rain. Puddles litter the dirt, making everyone's armor blotchy with mud spatter.

The three soldiers I'm up against are good—well trained, solid footing, clever maneuvers—and the fight is exactly what I need. They work together, trying to contain and overpower me. They don't take their eyes off my spikes, but they also don't cower away from them either. Since they're used to seeing me, they've learned to not let my spikes intimidate them, but to be smart about how to avoid their sharp ends. Which means they get in some solid hits.

I still put them on their asses, but the metallic taste of blood in my mouth fills me with pride.

Hoots and hollers raise from the soldiers spectating, and I get ready to call for more challengers when Ryatt's voice rings out, bringing the fights to an end.

I scowl at him as he comes to stand beside me. "We can keep going," I tell him.

His face is wet from the rain, though now that he's shaved his head, he doesn't have soaking wet hair to contend with. He also doesn't have the humid helmet like I do.

"No. We're done."

He leans down and helps up one of the soldiers I flattened. The man gives me a bloody grin before walking out of the circle with the others.

"You heard Commander Ryatt!" Judd calls from the sidelines. "Go back to your training!"

The crowd starts to dissipate, and I turn to follow my brother to the overhang just at the edge of the fight circle. He tosses in his training sword, and I follow suit, but irritation is pulsing down my veins. "I wanted to keep fighting."

Ryatt's tunic is stuck to him with sweat and rain, and unlike me, he's not wearing armor. Further widening the gap between Rip and Ryatt. He hasn't even been wearing black anymore. His tunic is white, his pants brown.

"Look at you," he says as he eyes me like he can see my glare in the slits through my helmet. "You're fucking swaying on your feet."

I glance down. The ground does seem to be tilting a bit.

He jerks his chin. "Come on."

I bite my tongue on a retort and follow beside him. At the fence, Judd is standing with Keg. The army's cook has pieces of wood braided into his hair and a grin on his face. "Ho there, ex-Commander," he says to me jovially. "You hungry? I can whip something up."

I shake my head. "No thanks, Keg."

He looks at me dubiously. "You sure? I think even *I* could knock you out right now. One swift kick to the arse and you'd be down."

I suppress a snort and arch a brow. "You want to test that theory?"

Keg seems to consider this and then quickly shakes his head. "Nope. No, I'm good, actually. And I got soldiers to feed, so…lots to do. Better get to it." He claps Judd on the shoulder, gives us a perfunctory nod, and lopes away with the other soldiers.

"Actually, I think he *could* knock you out," Judd says as the three of us start walking away. "You do look unsteady."

"Don't start."

"How many hours of sleep did you get yesterday after the fight circle?" Ryatt asks.

One. But he doesn't need to know that.

"Plenty."

He shakes his head. "Yeah. Right."

We walk through the grounds, and I'm pleased to see the

soldiers deferring to Ryatt as he passes. Moving out of the way, tipping their heads, standing at attention, saluting. He greets some of them by name, striding past with a confidence I've never seen him have—not as himself, anyway.

I hear him and Judd talking, but they're right. I'm fucked. Now that the fight is draining out of me, my head feels heavy, my muscles shaking. I spent all morning trying to open a rip, then came down here to fight. Now, my rotting chest fucking aches, and I barely have the strength to walk up past the stables and into the line of trees where I left Crest.

With Ryatt's help, I yank off my armor and stash my helmet, pulling my spikes and scales back in before I tug on my shirt from where I kept it in the saddle bag.

"Try to sleep more than a fucking hour this time, or I swear to fuck, I really will knock you unconscious," he hisses at me as I drag myself into the saddle.

Guess he's more aware of my sleep schedule than I thought.

I grunt at him and then nudge my heel into Crest. The beast leaps into the air, flying back toward Brackhill. By the time we reach the roof, the strength of the fight has drained out of me completely.

The poisoned chasm in my chest, however, hasn't.

I stagger off the roof and down the spiral stairs, unable to walk straight as I bounce off the walls of the corridor before making it to my rooms. When I reach my bed, I stumble onto it, rolling onto my back with a grimace. I don't even toe off my boots. I do, however, manage to dig into my pocket and drag out the strip of Auren's ribbon.

The gold is the same exact color as her eyes at night.

I grip it tight in my fist as the days—*weeks*—of exhaustion seem to suddenly wash over me. Catch up to me. Knock into my skull and cinch around my limbs in a way that I know I won't be awake after a mere hour this time. My body is shutting down.

My black heart chugs with painful pulses, spreading poison throughout, and I close my eyes, feeling darkness start to drag me under.

With Auren's scent clinging to the sheets and with *me* clinging to these remnants of her. With the rot in my chest reaching up and out, like it's reaching for her...

I finally, *finally* sleep.

And I dream of her.

She's bathed in sunlight.

There's nothing but shine and warmth, as if her very essence surrounds me. She's always been radiant. Always burned hot.

Like the sun itself.

I reach out my hand in the golden ether, and she reaches right back with a look that squeezes my heart.

The moment we touch, she pulls close, tucking herself against my chest. She turns her head and presses her lips against that aching, rotting, poisoned spot of me, and I shudder.

One touch, and she takes away the pain that's been stalking me. The drain that's been eating away at my lifeforce.

A shaky breath slips out past my lips.

When she hears it, her fingertips come up to smooth against my furrowed brow. Dancing down my jaw, making the rot beneath my beard writhe, like it's trying to reach up to her. I feel the seed of rot in her own chest thump in answer.

I take her hand in mine, look down at her with an ache. "Where are you?"

My voice echoes.

She smiles—a smile that reaches up to her gleaming

eyes. Then she moves her other hand down to rest over my heart, and I go heavy all over. Eyes drooping, mind falling. Going down, down into the dark.

But I hear her beautiful voice in a whisper just before all the light fades away.

"I'm here."

"Is it working?"

"Yes, he's stirring, Commander."

Their voices and a sharp scent start pulling me out of sleep. But what really jolts me is when something jabs at my chest. I hiss at the intense and sudden pain, my fist flying up before I even open my eyes.

But my hit is caught in a fist, and someone really fucking strong shoves my arm back down. Eyes snapping open, I look up and see Osrik pinning my hand. He gives me a shitty grin. "Is that any way to greet me?"

"Os," I say through gritted teeth. "Could you kindly fuck off?"

With a chuckle, he releases me. "There's those kingly manners."

As soon as he removes his weight and lets go, I take stock. I'm in my room, and Ryatt, Judd, Os, and Hojat are all hovering around me—the latter putting away his smelling salts. "Why are you all crowding around my fucking bed like I'm a corpse in a coffin?"

"Not far off," Judd says, head tilting to motion at my chest.

I look down and immediately grimace. I'm shirtless, so everything is exposed, and my chest is a fucking *wreck*. My black, rotted heart is showing through stretched skin, as if the organ has begun to swell, trying to burst right through. All around it, the sickly black roots have lengthened and grown thicker, pushing against the surface, and my skin...it's peeling. As if I were out in the sun too long. Except instead of being burnt, the skin is dead, chuffing off in ashen flakes.

"Your permission to apply this salve, Sire?" Hojat says.

I eye the sludge already cupped onto his fingertips in a tacky mound. "One of your concoctions?"

"Of course."

That's what I was afraid of. Hojat is always coming up with different experimental mixtures, but the ingredients are usually enough to turn even the hardiest person's stomach. Though, they usually *are* effective.

"Just don't tell me what's in it," I grit out.

Hojat's scarred face twists as one cheek lifts in a smile. "As you wish, Sire."

With quick, efficient movements, he starts slathering the gunk on my chest, which fucking hurts, but the scent...

"Goddess, Hojat. That's fucking foul."

Judd cackles at my bedside.

The scent must hit Ryatt's nose too, because he takes a step back.

"I'm not sure anything topical will actually help," I tell the mender.

"Perhaps not," he concedes. "But at the very least, it will soothe the aggravated skin."

"*Aggravated*?" Osrik says with incredulity. "It's not aggravated, it's fucking *decaying*. It looks like shit."

"Thanks, Os," I mutter.

He ignores me.

"You could've mentioned you were rotting from the inside out when we were in Derfort," Judd says from where he sits in *my* chair, legs crossed at the ankles. "Just might be something worth bringing up to your closest friends."

"I was busy."

"I should kick your ass."

I roll my eyes but hiss again when Hojat goes right over the center at a particularly painful spot. "You can't kick my ass, Judd."

"Fine. Os, punch him for me."

Osrik clocks me in the head so hard my entire body jolts. "*Fuck!*"

Hojat doesn't miss a beat. Just keeps slathering.

I glare at Os. "You fucking asshole, I'm *rotting*."

He crosses his huge arms in front of him and shrugs. "Tell us next time."

"I told Ryatt!"

"Yeah, and you haven't talked about it since or told me it was getting worse. And you've been asleep for *three fucking days*," my brother snaps.

"I—Wait. Three days?" I glance around my bedroom, seeing daylight stream through the windows, and realize that I actually don't feel weighed down with exhaustion like I was before. "I've been asleep for three days?"

"Yep. We were starting to get worried," Judd says. "We've been trying to wake you for an hour."

"I'm fine."

"Do you see the state of your chest?" Ryatt hisses. "We needed to make sure you weren't actually dead already."

"I said, *I'm fine.*"

Hojat hums over me. "I don't think so, Sire."

When the army mender is concerned, then it's probably not good. But…three days. Maybe my magic has replenished enough. Maybe I can finally fucking open a rip.

I look down as Hojat finishes slathering. There's a part of skin just over the center of my heart that isn't as black as the surrounding area. A bit of a sickly brown instead.

I start to sit up, but Ryatt pins my shoulder. "What are you doing?"

"I need to get down to the feeding grounds."

His eyes widen. "What? No. Absolutely fucking *not*."

"I know I look like shit, but I actually feel better," I tell him. "And three days...maybe my power was replenished in that time. You know I have to check. Have to try. For Auren. For our mother."

He glares at me while the others watch.

"Fine," he grits out. "But you have to eat first, and then I'll be going with you. You can try for an hour today. That's fucking it."

I start to argue, but Hojat cuts in. "He's right. You must eat. It is important to keep up your strength, lest you find that you have none."

My molars grind together, but I give a terse nod. Hojat then places a gauzy cloth over me, and when he's finished, he lifts my wrist, frowning at the way the rot looks as it writhes like thick streams of sludge beneath my skin. He presses his fingers against a vein, and his frown deepens. "Your pulse is very erratic."

"Well, his heart is rotting, mender, so I think that's to be expected," Judd says dryly.

"Looks like someone shat out coals on his chest," Osrik adds with a smirk.

Judd howls in laughter. "It fucking does!"

I sigh and let my head fall back onto my pillow. "I need a new Wrath."

"You wouldn't say that if you saw me in action in Derfort," Judd tells me. "I was so damned Wrathful it was downright poetic."

Os rolls his eyes. "I'm more Wrathful than you."

"Yeah, but you're an ugly, scowling giant. Everyone expects it from you. They get surprised with me."

"So?"

"*So*...I'm friendlier, and I look nice, so my wrath comes

as a surprise to people. Which makes me scarier."

"Fuck off. I'm still way fucking scarier than you," Osrik says, crossing his arms.

Judd looks affronted. "What the fuck? Ryatt, tell him."

"I'm not fucking telling him."

"Hojat!" Judd springs on him. "What do you think?"

"Don't involve our poor mender in this insanity. He deals with enough of our shit," I tell Judd.

Hojat gives me a grateful look and puts away his things. "If that's all, Sire, I should return to the Lady Rissa."

I cast a glance between him and Os. "How is she?"

The mender hesitates. "She has not improved."

Fuck.

My eyes flick up. "Os..."

His face goes hard. "No."

Alright then. It's clearly not open for discussion.

A knock suddenly sounds from the other room, making all of us turn. Ryatt strides out of my bedroom, into my entry room, and I hear him talking to someone. I swing my legs over the side of the bed and force myself to my feet. I don't even sway this time.

Waving off Hojat, I crack my neck and then stagger for the closet. I grimace slightly as I pull on a new shirt, but the pain has definitely been slightly numbed from whatever the mender slathered on me.

Just when I come out freshly dressed, Ryatt is returning. "What is it?" I ask.

My brother's expression holds a hint of surprise. "It's King Euden Thold from First Kingdom."

Judd and I exchange a look.

"What about him?"

"He's here."

I do my best to look like my heart *isn't* rotting through my chest, and then I slam my crown of twisted wood on my head. Ryatt, Os, and Judd accompany me as I go downstairs, but when we reach the dining hall, it's empty. One of my guards walks up, informing me that the monarch of First Kingdom is out in the gardens with my Premiers.

The four of us change direction and go outdoors. But as soon as we cross the threshold, Osrik stops with a strange look on his face. "Os?"

His eyes slowly shift to me, and he clears his throat. "Catch me up later," he says. Then he turns and walks back inside, shoulders stiff.

"This was where Rissa…" Ryatt trails off, motioning toward the garden.

Fuck.

This was where Rissa was stabbed. This was where Auren was fucking kidnapped. A fresh wave of rage rolls over me, and my shoulders bunch.

"Slade…" Ryatt prompts.

"Yeah." I force my footsteps forward, following the sound of voices.

When we reach the onyx fountain, I see my Premiers, Warken and Isalee, standing with the king. Warken has his hands clasped behind him, dressed head to toe in black, the silver strands in his shorn hair glinting slightly in the sunlight. Isalee stands with her husband and nods to whatever the king is saying, with a polite smile on her face. Her black gown is in perfect order and her hair is swept up, the spirals pinned in place.

"Ah, here he is," Warken says when he notices me. As I approach, I see he has a strained look on his face, which immediately makes my hackles rise. If Thold is fucking with my Premiers, we're going to have a problem.

"King Thold," I say as I walk over.

I immediately see the reason for Warken's grimace. The serpent king has a bright green viper draped around his neck, its long body curled around his bicep, tail flicking against him every few seconds.

At the Conflux, my focus wasn't on King Thold. Before that, I hadn't seen him personally in years. But now that I'm in an audience with him, it's clear that time has passed since we last saw each other.

There are some gray strands through his black hair that weren't there before, and his brow is creased, though no other lines wrinkle the dark brown skin of his face. He's dressed in gray, his sleeveless tunic trimmed in deep green and embroidered from collar to cuff. He carries himself with all the grace of a royal. Back straight, serpent crown perched on his head, formidable air. There are three guards behind him, twisted black and green ropes latched on to the shoulders of their armor like a row of serpents in his kingdom's colors.

"We weren't expecting you," I say as I come to a stop before him.

"No, I imagine not." His snake turns its head to look at me, tongue slipping out to test the air. "As I was just telling your Premiers, I apologize for the sudden appearance, but after what happened at the Conflux, I deemed it necessary to come in person."

"You mean when you took part in an attempted execution that should never have taken place." My tone is laced with my anger, biting just as sharp as his viper.

He holds my gaze, but I can see the way his heartbeat quickens from the vein in his neck. "I came here in good faith, King Ravinger."

"You can come in bad faith for all I care. This feigned

sincerity does nothing."

As if it understands my brush-off, the viper hisses in my direction, fangs bared and red eyes locked on me. Warken shifts and Isalee backs up slightly, but I don't move. King Thold cocks his head at my unflinching expression. "You don't fear snakes, King Ravinger?"

"Why would I, when I could rot the fangs from its mouth?"

He hums thoughtfully, finger lifting to the chin of his snake to soothe it. "And is that your intention, King Ravinger? To rot those who have wronged you?"

"So you heard about my...trips around Orea."

I get a sick sort of pride that he obviously got reports of what I did in the other kingdoms and immediately flew out here to try to patch things up so he doesn't meet a similar fate.

"I heard you rotted the front of Gallenreef Castle and every guard in the vicinity, including one of Third's advisors."

I shrug a shoulder. "Just his throat."

King Thold's lips press together. "I heard...that you may have taken something from Queen Kaila."

"She took from me first," I practically snarl. "And you would do well to also pay attention to what Queen Kaila has been doing these past months."

"Her reach of power has not gone unnoticed," he tells me. "I have eyes watching her progression in Fifth and now her attempts in Sixth."

"King Ravinger was completely in his rights to retaliate against her," Warken puts in. "Just as he was in Second Kingdom."

Thold dips his head, though he continues to watch me carefully. "I'm not surprised to hear that King and Queen Merewen are dead. And I'm not here to argue your rights of retaliation against them."

"Then why are you here?" I ask, though we both already

know why.

"I've come here in person to ensure that retaliation does not come to First Kingdom." He pauses. "Or to me."

"Maybe you should've thought about that before going against me."

A tic of frustration appears in his cheek. "I'll remind you that, before I went to the Conflux, you sent your envoy to renegotiate with me and I accepted that renewed alliance. My imports are on their way to your shores as we speak, as I promised to Sir Judd," he says, motioning toward my Wrath.

"Imports that should have been heading to my shores anyway, but you initially cut them off because of Queen Kaila and her discordant spewing. You were in breach of your treaties with me. So this *renewed alliance,* as you called it, doesn't endear you to me."

His snake tightens around his arm while Thold's gaze skims over the others before settling back on me. "I should not have broken our agreements."

Surprise shuffles through me at his admission, though I don't let it show on my face.

"No, you shouldn't have. And now, here you are, trying to ensure I won't mete out retribution for your part in the Conflux."

His expression tightens. "I had no true part in the Conflux. The only people who did were Second and Third, whom you've already dealt with."

"You *were* a part of it," I counter. "You were behind that barrier with all the rest of them."

Irritation has his shoulders stiffening, brown eyes flashing. His snake responds, hissing in my direction. "I was called to a royal Conflux, and so I went. It was a request I couldn't deny as an Orean monarch, as you well know. We are bound to the Conflux law."

I feel my rot scrape against the skin at my neck. "Yes,

and you, along with every other ruler there, condemned an innocent to death, even when the laws clearly state that *all* monarchs must be in attendance for such a verdict."

King Thold's eyes flicker from my blackened veins. "That is true...*unless* the monarch in question is unable to make sound decisions or cannot physically make the journey. The way that Queen Isolte was telling it, you were under some sort of spell by the golden woman."

My gaze is steady. Icy. "Queen Isolte was mistaken."

The two of us stare at each other, the tension mounting.

Fortunately, Isalee interjects, her voice smooth and sure as always. "We all know that Queen Isolte is—*was*—ruled largely by her religious beliefs. A religion, I will point out, which often condemns women. It is a doctrine we in Fourth do not condone."

Thold hesitates for a moment. "I know not of their doctrines, but I do know what I saw with my own eyes, and that is the fact that the Lady Auren was indeed using gold-touch...and what appeared to be rot was also flowing out of her. What say you about that?"

When I don't reply, Thold asks what he truly wants to know. "Is it true or not, Ravinger? Did that woman steal your magic? Did she steal Midas's magic? Are we all at risk?"

I can feel my Premiers glance at me. Can feel my brother tense.

"No." My reply is steady, unwavering. "She did not steal anything. Why do you think Midas kept her in a cage for so many years?"

Thold's expression folds with distress. "What are you saying?"

"Midas never had gold-touch. It was always her."

He starts to pace, making his viper shake its head in agitation at the sudden movement. "Are you saying that a magic-less man wore a crown for all those years?"

"I am."

He stops in front of me. "If that's true—"

"It is true. There is no *if*."

"You must understand the implications of that," he says, glancing from me to the others. "If that information were to get out...it would shake all of Orea. People would riot, the magic-less trying to lay stake to thrones."

"Which is why I didn't announce it publicly," I reply. "Not until I was forced to do so at the Conflux. Yet I was not believed because of the narrative that Queen Kaila and Queen Isolte had both circulated."

"But that doesn't explain the rot. Why did it appear that rot was in her gold?"

I wave him away. "It was mine," I lie easily. "I can use my power at great distance. I was trying to rot through the floor so I could get her out."

His dark brows pull together in a frown. "But—"

"I've answered your questions, King Thold, and that's more than I owe you. Lady Auren is not a threat in that way. She does not have the ability to steal magic. You and your serpents are safe, I assure you."

He considers me, hand coming up to stroke the viper's tail. "Curious magic happened that day. For a moment, I thought I saw spikes come up from your arms. Just as I thought Lady Auren was using rot through her gold." He pauses for a moment, as if debating whether or not to continue. "The magic you used wasn't rot, either. Whatever you did tore the air like parchment, and then Lady Auren disappeared through it."

I say nothing.

"What did you do, Ravinger?" he demands. "Where did she go?"

My pissed-off patience has had enough. "You're not entitled to answers, Thold. *You* cut off trading with Fourth

Kingdom. *You* broke our agreement. And *you* stood with the others during the Conflux. Those are reasons enough for retaliation if I see fit, as you are *very* aware."

His expression tightens, and his guards shift forward ever so slightly at my threat. "That is why I am here in person. I think you can understand, Ravinger, that above all, we strive to protect our kingdoms. I see now that I was misled at the Conflux. I would much rather have you as an ally."

I'm sure.

"Forgive me, King Thold," Warken cuts in. "But as my king pointed out, you broke treaties. Severed trust. Played a part in the punishment of someone under his protection. So why should Fourth Kingdom realign with you?"

"You need the imports," he answers immediately. "Your land isn't even a fraction as viable as mine. As you know, since Sir Judd was sent to dissuade me from the trade block."

I push my hands into my pockets and stare him down. "But who's to say I can't simply rot your kingdom and take the exports by force?"

For the first time, Thold loses his temper, and his anxious heartbeat pulses loudly. "I don't want war, but I won't abide threats," he says through his teeth. "Our kingdoms are better off in a symbiotic relationship rather than at odds. We both know that First Kingdom has the largest quantity of food exports in the world. My lands are rich in agriculture, and since the rest of Orea has still cut off trade with you, especially now, your kingdom is in need of what mine can provide."

We *do* need his exports, but neither my Premiers nor I give away anything in our expressions.

"If you try to take it by force, we both know it will be at the cost of many lives, and many acres. It's in both our best interests that we avoid all of that and reinstate our alliance. I won't have First Kingdom suffer because of misinformation and misunderstanding," he says, voice stern, eyes determined.

I let him sweat for a moment. Let him stew. It works well for me that he's here, trying to broker a deal. It also works well for me that he's nervous.

Because he fucking should be.

Thold lets out a short sigh. "You stay in your kingdom, and I'll stay in mine, and our relationship can flourish once more. You may be able to ruin my land, but your people can't eat rot. Can't live on decay. Like it or not, you *need* my kingdom thriving, and I don't think you want the hassle of killing another monarch. Not when it's far easier for you to accept this realliance."

I stare at him for several seconds before my eyes shift to Warken and Isalee, and one look from them tells me we're on the same page.

"I will have to discuss this proposition with my Premiers."

He bristles in frustration but gives a stiff nod. "Fine."

I pull my hands out of my pockets and turn around. "Judd, could you escort King Thold inside and ensure he's taken care of?"

He gives a nod. "This way, Your Majesty."

With one last look, Thold follows Judd inside, his guards sticking to his heels. When Ryatt and I are alone with my Premiers, I let out a breath, shoulders loosening.

Warken gives me a sidelong look. "How long do you want to make him wait?"

I hum in consideration before turning to Isalee. "What do you think?"

"Three days," she answers without hesitation. "Any longer, and he'll start to come up with nefarious alternatives. Any shorter, and he won't sweat enough."

I smirk. "Ruthless."

"We're Fourth Kingdom," she says with a shrug.

"Besides, he'll demand an answer by then. I can tell."

Her husband nods. "Thold is right, though. We need his imports, and it does show good faith that he agreed to disregard the trade block *before* the Conflux."

"I still want to rot him in his sleep."

"About that…" Isalee's dark brown eyes bore into me. "Next time you decide to execute monarchs, warn us ahead of time. Do you know the amount of hawks that have arrived? My hands are going to be covered in calluses by the time we finish answering all the messages."

I wince slightly. "I apologize."

"You should," she says, not giving me an inch. "Warken and I have been dealing with the fallout from every kingdom."

Her hand digs into the pocket of her dress, and she pulls out scroll after scroll of hawk messages, like she stuffed them in there just so she could toss them at me at her first opportunity. It's effective. "Fifth Kingdom, Third Kingdom, Second Kingdom," she lists them out as my eyes skate over the various broken seals.

"It was all necessary."

She waves a hand at me. "That is debatable. A debate we should have had together, *before* you acted," she says. "But you are the king."

"We all know you two run this kingdom more than I do."

"We have no power, and you have no patience for politics. We are a good partnership, so long as it's that—but a partnership requires communication."

"You're right. Consider me perfectly chastised."

"Good," she says with a firm nod before her eyes flick up to my hair beneath the crown. "You need a trim."

I snort.

"How is the fallout?"

"We're managing it. But we knew when we took the position as the Premiers for *King Rot* that there would be the occasional public issues we would need to handle regarding your particular temperament and power," she says diplomatically. "We're staying on top of it."

I give her a smile. "That's why you two are the best."

"For the most part, there's a renewed sense of fear of our king, especially from the people in Third Kingdom," Warken tells me. "Second Kingdom is a mess, and they hastily crowned the Merewen heir—though the boy is quite young."

The prince whose barrier kept me from the monarchs—kept me from Auren. Let's hope he will be a better ruler than his parents.

"His first order of rule was to declare Fourth Kingdom an enemy."

"To be expected. I have plenty of enemies."

"Indeed." Warken cocks his head. "Why Breakwater Port?"

"Red Raids," I tell him. "Found a gambling hall that was responsible for animal fights. I didn't care for that."

Isalee makes a noise of disgust. "Neither did the animals, I'm sure."

"Is there anything else we should know about?" Warken asks.

I can feel Ryatt staring at the side of my face. When I hesitate, he clears his throat, making my Premiers glance between the two of us.

"Oh, Divine," Isalee says. "What is it now?"

It's clear Ryatt isn't going to let me ignore it, so I'm forced to tell them the truth. And he's right—my Premiers need to know.

So I say it as matter-of-factly as I can to get it out of the way. "Well...it seems my heart may be rotting out of my chest."

The two of them gape at me, mouths gone wide.

"*What?*" Isalee demands.

"It's not ideal…"

"*Not ideal*? How long has this been going on?"

"Since the Conflux," I tell her. "We should come up with a contingency plan. Just in case."

She pinches the bridge of her nose. "You are giving me far more gray hairs than I should have at this age."

"You look beautiful."

My compliment doesn't deter her.

"You have landed a heap of issues on Fourth's lap. You are absolutely *not* allowed to die, is that clear?" she says sternly, brown eyes narrowed on me like a mother disciplining her child.

My lip twitches. "Understood, Premier."

"At least not until we get a handle on how we're going to manage the public reactions regarding what you've done, resecure our kingdom, and ensure Fourth gets what it needs in the fallout of the trade block." She lets out a sigh. "Then you can die. And we can retire."

"You would be far too bored without a kingdom to run."

She sniffs. "Perhaps I'll go to Second and help the new young Merewen."

"You don't like the desert heat."

"Fine," she relents. "But if I have to answer missives, so do you. Come, you can help deal with the consequences of your actions, King Rot."

"I actually need to go…" My words trail off at her vicious glare. "Never mind. I can spare a few hours."

"Good," she says with a saccharine smile, while Ryatt gives me a shit-eating grin. But then her eyes flick to him next. "You too, Commander."

All of that amusement he had on his face at my expense has now been erased. "Me?"

"Yes. You. As the army's commander, I have need of your counsel, and you will need to know our plans."

"Oh. Right. Of course."

Now, it's my turn to give him the shit-eating grin.

When Isalee turns and starts to walk away with Warken, Ryatt glares at me. "Fuck off," he grumbles.

At least he has to endure the next few hours of politics and paperwork with me. As soon as I'm done, I'll get back down to the timberwing feeding grounds to see if my raw magic is back. But a part of me is dreading it.

Because if it still won't work after three days of rest...

Then I'm not sure it ever will.

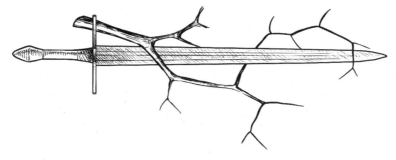

CHAPTER 38

OSRIK

With the sun at high noon, the street is busy with people. It's like everyone and their fucking mother is out in the city, buying shit or fishing at the river. I finish tying up my horse at one of the hitching posts at the side of the road, under a grouping of trees and grass, and then cross the street.

When people see me coming, they move out of the way. I'm not like Judd. They don't smile and wave at me, hoping for my attention. That's usually the *last* thing people want from me, and that suits me just fucking fine. I don't want attention from anyone either.

Except one person, and she still hasn't opened her eyes.

The shop I'm headed for is right here on the street, facing the water. A wooden sign hanging from its eave swings in the wind, and it has a picture of a leaf painted on it that's gone faded.

I yank open the door, and a little bell above rings as I step inside. The space is crowded with plants growing out of different sized pots on the floor or up on the shelves, or even hanging from hooks on the ceiling. Three steps into the place, and I accidentally walk into one, smacking my head on the clay pot and making soil dump out on my shoulder.

"Oh, careful there, sir!" A wiry woman pops out from behind the counter and comes around to greet me, her brown hair ruffled up around her head and tied off with a green ribbon. "Captain Osrik! What a pleasant surprise to find you in my shop."

Surprise, sure. Pleasant? Fucking doubtful.

"Do you need to put in an order to resupply the plants for the army's medicinal uses?"

"No," I say as I look around the shop, noting a couple of women over in the corner, hovering around some leaves.

"Oh, okay," the shopkeeper replies as she starts walking over to the wall and reaching up to a shelf with a sign that says *HERBS*. "Perhaps some dried spices that are good for traveling when you need to flavor up your rations? I'm running low, but I've got some excellent—"

"Don't need that either," I say with a grunt.

She stops and glances at me, wiping her hands on her apron. Then she walks closer again, lowering her voice. "Did you need some of those mushrooms? I know some of the other soldiers like them to take the edge off..."

For fuck.

"*No*. I just need some fucking flowers."

"You want...flowers?" she asks, like she must've heard me wrong.

The other two women turn and look at me.

I shift on my feet. "Yeah. Flowers. You got any?"

She nods slowly. "Of course, I have all sorts. In the garden out back."

When I gesture for her to lead the way, she takes me

behind the counter to the open doorway beyond. We step into a garden that's about three times the size of the shop. There are flowering plants everywhere, growing up in rows.

"We have the favorites, of course," she says as she walks down the dirt path. "Roses, daisies, jasmines, peonies, lilies... Are you looking for anything specific?"

I clear my throat as I accidentally trample over a plant with stubby blue flowers.

"Yellow bells," I grunt.

She stops and turns with a frown. "Hmm. Apologies, Captain Osrik, but I don't have any of those."

My shoulders go stiff, and my gaze shoots around the outdoor space. "You got plenty of yellow flowers; I'm sure you have them."

"I know every plant I'm growing," she replies, tapping her temple. "I don't carry yellow bells. No one tends to buy those. They're also quite poisonous."

Frustration cricks in my neck. "You're a damn flower shop. I need a flower."

Why is this so fucking hard?

She hesitates. "That particular flower just isn't very popular here. Not many like them, I suppose."

"*I* fucking like them," I snap.

The woman rears back in surprise at my sharp tone, and I grind my teeth in irritation, trying to tamp down my anger. It's not her fault.

"Just check. Please."

With a wary nod, she turns and heads down the path to the various yellow flowers and walks through them, checking the blooms.

I just wanted some fucking yellow bells to put on Rissa's bedside. Not that I've ever gotten flowers for a woman before, but it seemed like something she might like. Now, I'm twitchy and frustrated and remembering how bad she looked this morning. Sallow. Worn out.

I hate it.

When the woman comes back empty-handed, she shakes her head with a regretful look on her face. "Apologies. As I said, I don't have them. But I do have some other quite beautiful blooms that are yellow. There's—"

"Forget it," I mumble before whipping around.

I march back through the shop, my booted steps sounding way too loud, the browsing women eyeing me and whispering as I pass by. I wrench open the door so hard that the bell above rips off, knocks into my head, and then clatters to the ground.

I stare down at it and try real fucking hard not to see it as a bad omen.

When I get back, I nearly run into Polly just as she comes out of Rissa's room. Her face is all blotchy red, eyes swollen with a handkerchief stuffed against them like it'll help stop the leak spewing out of her eyes.

"I can't keep seeing her like this. I can't keep coming here to watch." She shakes her head and looks up at me all glassy-eyed. "Thank you. For letting me visit her, but I can't anymore." Before I can say anything, she turns and rushes away down the corridor, leaving me to scowl after her.

I have half a mind to drag her back into Rissa's room and make her sit at the bedside and help care for her. Just like Rissa fucking did for her day after day.

But I don't. Rissa doesn't need her. She has me. And unlike *Polly*, I won't abandon her.

When I enter, I find Hojat in the room. He gets up from his chair beside her bed, and his grim face makes my muscles bunch. My bones lock up.

"It's soon, Captain," he says quietly.

A cold, sickly dread gushes into my gut.

I give a sharp shake of my head. "No."

He stops me before I can storm past him with a gentle hold on my arm. I don't like the look in his fucking eyes. "Yes," he says, like he's trying to let me down easy. "I'm sorry."

My gaze shoots past him to Rissa's sleeping form. One of the novices steps away from her, her hands clasped, head bowed. She's brushed out Rissa's hair. It looks pretty. Soft and light. She's been changed into a clean nightdress too. Pink, like the color her cheeks used to get every time she blushed at something crass I said. But there's no embarrassed flush now, no gaze sparkling with fire.

She's sleeping. Not thrashing or crying out with delirious fits. Just lying there.

Wheezing.

Wheezing so slowly it makes me grimace.

"I'll leave you alone with her to say your goodbyes," Hojat says softly, while I swallow hard.

Denial wants to rush up, but it just…drains out of me instead. I don't take my eyes away from her as he and the novice leave the room, shutting the door behind them.

When it's just us, I step forward, almost tiptoeing, like I shouldn't disturb the quiet. I don't want to break it, don't want to startle her. I slump into the chair next to her and place the little brass bell from the plant shop on her bedside table. Probably shouldn't have taken it, but I didn't want to return empty-handed.

Reaching forward, I grab hold of her hand. It's hot with her fever, but the worst part is how limp it is. How fucking lifeless.

"Brought you this, Yellow Bell," I tell her, but my voice sounds too rough. My hand looks huge compared to hers. She feels delicate. Fragile. I'm afraid to squeeze too hard in case I break her fingers. "They didn't have your flowers. At a *flower shop*. Can you believe that shit?"

She doesn't reply. Her eyelids don't even twitch.

The pauses between her labored breaths are fucking terrifying.

"Brought you a bell instead. It sounds kind of annoying to be honest. Not like your voice. Your voice is…nice."

I cringe. I suck at this shit. I'm almost glad she can't hear me. I've never been good at words. Not good at giving compliments. But right now, I wish I was. Because if I were, I'd give them to her.

I'd give her whatever fucking words she wants.

"Wish you'd wake up and mouth off to me, Yellow Bell," I murmur as I scrape my callused thumb over the back of her soft hand. It's softer than feathers. Like silk or something. Too soft for the likes of me. My hands are scarred and rough, with ripped cuticles and thick skin from all the years I've gripped a sword.

She takes another slow, wheezing breath before silence draws out between us.

What happens when she just…stops? When that drawn-out silence turns into *just* silence?

Emotion quick and hot rushes up my throat and stuffs inside my head. I've tried raging. Tried torturing. Tried arguing. Tried denying. But now, in this wheezing silence, the truth glares at me like a judgmental bastard.

She's dying.

She has been. Since that dagger went into her chest. Since I carried her into this mender room. She wasn't ever going to come back out. I wasn't ever going to hold her again.

Every time I've sat here at her bedside, death has been spreading over more of her, like a sheet coming to cover her up, going higher and higher.

I didn't want to see it, but there's no denying the infection spreading from that wound. If she were one of my soldiers, I would have broken the news to her family already, sent a message to prepare them for the worst.

But she's not a soldier. She didn't enlist for violence or sign her name accepting the threat of dying on a blade. She should die of old age a long time from now, after she got what she wanted. The thing she wished for most.

Her independence.

She wanted to go away. To go far enough to escape her past and live without being beholden to anyone. Without having to cater or coddle or please any fuckheads to earn a coin like she had to do for years. I was the selfish bastard that asked her to stay. Look where that got her.

With a blade nearly stabbed through her heart and an infection burning her alive.

"Can't even get you fucking yellow bells..."

She called me her mistake. Said we were wrong. Maybe that's true, because I can't seem to get anything right. But when she kissed me, that *did* feel fucking right.

In a world full of wrong, I wanted one right thing.

I press my finger against the pulse on her wrist, feel the weak flutter, and it makes me so fucking *angry*. I shove my gaze at the clear window, like I can glare at the gods.

"Not her," I snarl at them. "Not yet."

It's a pissed-off prayer, and I don't even fucking pray. Don't even know if I believe in the gods. But if they're up there smug as shit in their simple sky, then the least they can do is come down here and help this complicated woman who doesn't deserve this.

"She needs more time," I tell them. "*We* need more fucking time."

I thought we had all the time in the world.

"Just give us that," I snap. "Never asked you for shit all

my life. Just give us this."

I wait, listening. Glaring out the window. But nothing happens. Not a strike of lightning or a growl of thunder. She doesn't suddenly open her eyes.

Hojat wants me to prepare myself. To say my goodbyes.

But how am I supposed to see her through to her end when we barely got to start?

My gaze trails up to her lips, now chapped and pale, a frown dug deep between her blonde eyebrows like every breath hurts.

I feel that hurt right in my chest.

It burrows deep. Jabbing in with her next labored wheeze. Hearing the way her inhale scrapes and whines as if it's ready to give up makes that cottony emotion in my head rupture, like stuffing that bursts out of a seam.

I never get teary-eyed. Never let emotion seep out. Not even on the battlefield when my own soldiers died at my side. But right now, right here, I find a furious, grief-ridden sob rasping from my throat and tears searing my eyes.

I lean in and place a kiss on her burning brow, and then I tip my head against hers, eyes shut with anguish. "You were supposed to wake up," I tell her as torment slides down my tongue. As the evidence of my misery lands in dots against her pink nightgown. "We were supposed to have time to make this mistake over and over again, until you finally realized how right it really is."

But time doesn't fucking listen to me any more than the gods do.

So *I* listen instead, because that's all I can do. I listen to her every breath that gets harder and harder for her to take. I listen to all the things I never got to say.

And I listen to my own goodbye that she'll never get to fucking hear.

CHAPTER 39

QUEEN MALINA

"*Sit up straight, Malina. Honestly, is it so hard?*"

My father hisses this at me from the corner of his mouth. It's impressive how he can speak like this, barely moving his lips.

Impressive how he can convey such anger in his tone while keeping his expression completely flat.

I lengthen my spine and slam my shoulders back. I've been sitting here for hours, holding court, listening to the people as they come forward and give us their condolences.

Because my mother is dead.

It still sounds strange, like it isn't real. Except it is.

My mother is dead, and her corpse is in the atrium right now, where her death rites are being carried out. That's where I should be. Up there with her, where the gods can look through the atrium windows and accept her soul's ascent. I want to be with her when her soul slips away. Maybe her incorporeal spirit will remember me as she passes into the heavens.

Yet father won't let me, so here I sit in the throne room. Normally, the white walls and blue carpet that runs up the stairs to the dais make it feel icy and open, but with the black drapes of mourning and the packed crowd, it feels claustrophobic.

More and more people come forward, leaving boughs from the Pitching Pines at the bottom step of our platform, while we sit at the trio of thrones, my mother's seat startlingly empty.

I'm dressed all in black with the mourning veil hanging from the tiara on my head and draping down my face. At least the sheer fabric is dark enough that no one can see the silent tears that drip down my cheeks.

It's not until hours later, when the people have finally gone, that my father allows me to peel myself up from my throne. His advisor informs us that mother's body is wrapped up and moved away already. I can't help the sob that escapes me, my grief echoing through the empty room. When the advisor bows and leaves, my father's eyes skate over my veiled face.

I so desperately want to ask him if he misses her as much as I do. If it doesn't quite feel real. But he wouldn't appreciate questions like that.

So I say nothing.

Yet as he looks down at me, I see something in his eyes soften—just for a moment. His hands come up and grip my shoulders, and I almost flinch. Father doesn't give loving pats or hugs, or anything like that, so his touch is foreign, making me go stiff.

"Why are you crying?" he asks.

I blink at him, wondering if I misheard. "Because...Mother."

Why wouldn't I be crying? She's dead! *I want to scream at him.*

Of course, I stay silent.

"It is important that you do not show weakness in front of our people, Malina."

My head bows under the condemnation of his words. "Yes, Father, but I—" I catch myself, horrified by the argument I almost let slip.

"But what?" he demands.

I hesitate, but I know it's no use. I have to answer him. "I wanted to be with her during her rites," I say in a small voice. A despairing one.

Her body is already wrapped up. Already moved away.

I'll never see her again.

That thought hits me in the chest and steals the breath right out of my ribs and makes me want to fall to my knees and sob. But I can't.

My father squeezes my shoulder in what I think might be a rare show of affection, and my eyes snap up to his face. "This is what it means to be royal, Malina," he says. "Yes, your mother, my wife, died. But their queen died too, and it was our responsibility to sit here and allow them to pay their respects. To grieve."

But what about my respects? What about my grief?

"When you're a ruler, you make sacrifices for your kingdom," he says as he shakes me, as if he wants to rattle the sadness right out of me, like knocking pebbles from a jar. "Your feelings come second. You listen to them, you act for them, even to your own detriment. Kingdom comes first."

He drops his hands and gives me one last look. "Wipe your face and go up to bed now. We have her funeral in the morning, and the bell will start tolling at dawn."

I dip my head and walk away, reeling with sadness. Reeling with his words too.

But I don't cry again.

In Highbell, the sky is constantly cluttered with clouds, making the sun limp and futile. If it gives off warmth, it can't be felt, nor can it be used in marking the hour since it's always covered. Instead, snow is how I tell the passing of time.

The storm that falls around me has been steady and unyielding, sloughing off the crust of the icy clouds as wind whips around me. Already, there are thick heaps of snow caught alongside the short wall that braces against the chasm, more of it drifting toward the mouth of the bridge and trying to pile up around me.

This mouth is where I still sit, stone cutting into my bent knees. I'm long past the point of feeling the bite. I'm not sure where our horse trotted off to, and there's no one to watch, since it seems all of Highbell retreated inside their homes to escape the storm. Dommik and I are the only ones out here.

It feels eerie.

With gritted teeth, I smooth my palms over the ice brick I'm making, arms burning as I hold its weight. Dommik plucks it up from me as soon as I've finished forming it, and then whooshes away in shadows, appearing several feet up. I squint up past the snow and wind, watching him place the heavy brick on the top of the wall we've built. The bricks are stacked along the entire entrance of the bridge, and since each slab is about a foot thick, it's already quite high.

Dommik stacks them diligently, one after the other, all across the row. Then, once we get a good ten feet high, we start doubling up the wall. Then tripling. Making it as thick as we can.

We work all through the night.

Past the pealing of the midnight bells. Past the worst of the storm, where the clouds dump mounds of snowfall onto the ground. It doesn't deter me in the slightest. Instead, it's as if the storm is helping—pillowing where I kneel on the ground and slipping onto my lips to moisten my parched mouth.

I work almost in a trance, focusing only on the cold power that slushes through my veins. Ice pours from the gashes in my hands and continues to bleed out frozen magic—magic that allows me to make brick after brick.

My people might hate me, someone else might sit on my throne, the fae might be marching on us, and I might not know what else I can do with this new magic…but I can do this.

I can do this.

Dommik doesn't try to talk to me, he simply works alongside me in silent support. Somehow, we don't need words. He knows exactly how to help, and does so without complaint. Even as the wind whips at his hood and his bare hands go chapped. Even as snow gathers on his shoulders and leeches the warmth from his heated body. I make them, he stacks them, and he doesn't try to direct me or argue with me or say he knows better.

When morning crests, the storm finally abates, letting out a few last sprinkles of snow shavings. Yet as the pale gray light of morning arrives, so do the people.

The first of them mutter and keep walking, but soon, they begin to gather. Just a few at the beginning, but then the gathering steadily grows, and with more numbers, the bolder they become.

The realization that I'm using magic ripples through them, surging along the steps of disbelief, surprise, confusion, and anger, each emotion rising with fervor. They begin to voice their complaints about the bridge being blocked, the way to the castle cut off.

"What are you doing?"

"She's trapping us in!"

"Cold crone bitch! You're no queen of ours!"

"She's using magic against us!"

"Take this down!"

"Queen Kaila won't stand for this!"

They ridicule me. Curse me. Hate me. But I keep going.

Dommik appears at my back, growling fiercely when a group of them gets too close. He grips a dagger in each hand with a threatening warning, a sneer on his lips as light bends around him.

It's enough to keep everyone from growing too aggressive in their hatred and trying to harm me or drag me away. Their verbal lashes don't stop, though, and I hear it all. My body may be numb to the cold, but my mind is open to the onslaught of their heated words that continue to pour, gushing out like steam, making me flinch one after another as they scald me.

—the cold queen lied about having magic—the frigid bitch—get out of the fucking road—she blocked the bridge— she's gone mad—go back to the grave—you should've stayed dead—

I keep working. I won't stop until the last brick is stacked along the twenty-foot wall. I don't care that my hands are shaking. I don't care that sweat beads at my brow, freezing there before it can even think to drip.

The hate, the doubt, the insults, I let them hit my back and strengthen my spine, and I just keep going.

—she's trapped us—she's trying to keep us from our new queen—we don't want you here—not our queen—stop her— smash the wall down—

Those threats make me pause.

I can't afford for them to tear down what I've so painstakingly built. This is the only protection they have from the fae marching down this bridge and into the city.

I've been forming these ice bricks for countless hours, but this time, instead of bringing my palms together to form the block, I turn around and press my hands flat on the ground.

Fueled by the need to keep the wall safe from my own people so that I can keep *them* safe, I silently direct the magic, hoping that it will listen to me, pushing it to the ground, spreading it, thickening it.

Until it makes a perfectly flat, slick layer of ice to separate us.

The crowd gasps and backs away, but a few at the front of the horde don't move quickly enough, and they slip and fall. Now, they can't get within twenty feet of the wall—or me.

Perfect.

I move to get up, yet as soon as I'm standing, I sway slightly on my feet. Dommik is there in an instant, catching me by the elbow.

"Queenie?" he murmurs.

"I'm fine," I assure him, brushing off the snow from my back, shaking it from the mussed plait of my hair.

"You're using too much magic. Used too much all night," he says quietly. "You need a break."

I glance at him sharply. "There's no time for a break."

He doesn't argue, because he knows I'm right.

I walk forward, assessing the barrier we've created. Since I was able to slick the ground, maybe my magic can do more. Placing my palms on the wall, I focus on the ice, spooling it out like a fishing line, spinning it from my hands and sending it to the top of the bricks.

I take a few steps back, watching as a swoop of half-formed ice spreads along the entire top of the wall, and then it solidifies like tines on a fork, making a perfectly spiked stockade.

Pride surges through me. My magic is *listening* to me.

Turning, I address the angry crowd. "This wall will slow the fae down, but it won't stop them."

"There are no fae!" someone shouts.

"There *are*," I reply, voice cutting through the wind. "And I'd much rather you were all behind the castle's walls, but since I knew you wouldn't go, I'll defend you here as best I can."

"Give us lies so you can trap us, you mean!"

Others cry out in agreement, others hurl curses.

Frustration gnaws on me, like blunt teeth digging in. Yet my stomach churns as doubt thrums down my spine. Is this a terrible plan? I don't know. I was never trained for military strategies. The only lessons I had on wars and battles were from a purely historic point of view. And yesterday, I couldn't even get my magic to do anything at all.

A wall seemed like something achievable, something I could do piece by piece. All I can do now is hope it buys us some time.

"She's not lying!" Dommik growls at them, and it's the loudest I've ever heard him speak. "This is your queen! Listen to her!" he shouts desperately.

People curse him too.

"Get inside!" I tell them. "Fortify your houses, gather your weapons if you have them, or flee into the pinewood if you can, but I can't promise anywhere will be safe."

For the first time, a few scattered faces finally turn worried, glancing around as if maybe they're starting to doubt. To think that I might be telling the truth. All I can hope is that this trickle of worry grows into a downpour. If I can't have their trust, perhaps I can prompt them to act from pure paranoia.

"Flee. Hide. Fight. Prepare yourselves for war, because war is coming whether you believe me or not!"

The crowd is quiet. The wind whistles through us.

I turn toward Dommik and hold my hand out to him, and he arches a brow in question. "I need to be on the other side of this wall," I tell him.

I have more work to do.

The moment his hand encloses over mine, shadows collect us, and my stomach dips as we leap on top of the wall. I barely feel my feet slipping on its surface before he's already leaping again, this time, landing us on the other side of the bridge while shouts of surprise sound from the crowd.

I turn around and face the wall from this angle, taking a moment to acknowledge just how impressive it actually looks. It sits thick and tall and the spikes along the top are forbidding. Yet it won't hold forever. At best, it will only delay the fae.

So I need to do more.

Mimicking my earlier move, I kneel down, pressing my hands to the ground. With concentration, I start feeding sloshes of freeze over the arc of the bridge. It's slow, ice creeping over the cobbled stones inch by inch, but once I spread the slippery layer over the entire length, I let out a ragged breath. This time when I stand, my swaying is so prevalent that I nearly tip right over, and I would've if it weren't for Dommik catching me.

"Queenie..." he warns, this time saying it with a sharp tone. To anyone else, they might think him angry, but I can tell that he's concerned.

For me.

"Stop worrying about me," I tell him. "I need you to go scout. Find out where they are. Let me know how much time we have."

"You expect me to leave you?" he grits out incredulously. "When you can barely stand and the people in this city want to toss you over the bridge?"

"Well, they can't get to me, can they?" I ask, gesturing to the wall.

Honestly, I shouldn't have to point it out.

He makes a disgruntled grumble under his breath.

"Go," I tell him. "We need to know how close they are."

"Fine," he snaps. "But if I come back and you've passed out, I'm going to fucking kill you."

I arch a brow coolly. "If that threat was supposed to instill some level of fear in me, then perhaps do it with your knife next time?"

He eats up the space between us, making me lose my blasé attitude as I suck in a breath. When he stands in front of me, he leans in close, his chest pressed against mine. Somehow, his dagger *has* come out to play without me even noticing until the sharp edge is pressed to my neck.

Then he starts dragging it *down*.

Over my collarbone, between my breasts, almost scratching through the fabric of my dress—but not quite. I gasp when it glides down my belly button and circles there, and I stop breathing completely when it starts slipping down my thigh.

His mouth is at my ear. "If the thought of me playing with you with my blade gets you hot, just say that," he purrs.

My eyes flare, my cheeks are flushed, and when he pulls back and puts the blade away, I have to fight not to let out a noise of disappointment. At least the crowd can't see us.

I brush my hands down the front of my dress as if I can brush away the tingling trail he left behind. "It does *not* make me hot."

His lips curve at the lie.

"Should I scoop up your skirt and see for myself?"

"*No*," I snap, shoving him away as he chuckles deeply.

I've lost my mind…and my body, apparently, because he's right. I *am* hot—all over—but *especially* there.

"We have a battle to prepare for."

He shrugs a shoulder. "Don't you know? A pre-battle fuck is what all the soldiers do. Gets their blood pumping.

Reminds them what they'd miss out on if they lose."

"Another reason why women are superior," I mutter.

His chuckle comes back tenfold. "You'll find no argument from me."

"That's a first."

"Careful, Queenie," he says, teeth flashing. "I might think you're flirting back with me."

Is that what I'm doing? Flirting?

I clear my throat and force my mind to go back to the task at hand. "Go, assassin."

"Okay, but remember what I said."

"Yes, yes, threats and demands. Now go away."

I hear his chuckle even after he disappears in his cluster of shadows. Then, I'm alone in front of a slippery bridge, with the wind whipping at my hair and a gleaming castle lording high above me at the mountain at my back. Maybe the gold of Highbell will tempt the fae enough that they'll go there first.

One can hope.

Without Dommik's watchful eye, I let myself slump. I didn't dare let myself do it in front of him or the people, because I have to be strong, but using my magic all night has taken a toll. Though it doesn't matter, because I still have more I need to do.

I kneel down on the bridge and open my palms, urging more ice to form. Even though my hands are shaking and my eyes are burning from exhaustion, the magic answers my call.

Slowly, I figure out exactly what I want to form and how. I envision a long spike like a spear, and the shape coalesces between my palms in dripping, frigid water that ices over. I stretch and mold it, while frost builds up on my lashes and more shakes from the ends of my hair. Then I make the spike solidify into the ground, angling toward me in piercing threat.

Perfect.

I do it over and over again. Elongating the poles of ice,

hardening them, making the tips end in sharp lances that could puncture someone through. Until I've formed enough of them to stretch across this side of the bridge's entrance. One more deterrent before the army reaches the wall so they won't be able to simply storm the city.

When I'm done, I fall forward, hands braced in front of me and barely managing to hold me up so I don't face-plant. I'm shaking all over with snow caked to my hands—hands that are raw and peeling back with flakes of white skin. My cheeks are chapped too, and I can feel a swipe of frost spread on each side where my hair keeps getting caught.

I give myself a few moments to breathe, to shake, to stare at the icy ground in front of the barricade. My breathing is ragged. My eyes tunnelling. But I shove myself to my feet again, because I have to do more.

I have to, when all I really want to do is crawl into a bed and sleep. When everything screams at me to flee instead. When I remember I'm draining myself to protect a city who hates me.

Because kingdom comes first.

CHAPTER 40

QUEEN MALINA

"Queenie."

I'm in a carriage being jostled left and right. The movement is jarring, making my stomach leap into my throat and a groan grate out past my lips. I *hate* riding down this road. That's probably why I can't remember—I can't stand to look out the window, so I close my eyes and keep the curtains closed. I must've dozed off this time, but it seems it only made my motion sickness worse.

"Queenie!"

I snap open my eyes to see the assassin. I'm not in a carriage, I'm in his arms, and he's shaking me so much I can feel my skull rattle. I open my mouth to shout at him to stop, but I cough instead, little pieces of ice grazing past my tongue and slicing my throat.

Dommik's hand slams against my back until I elbow him in the gut hard enough to make him stop. "I'm not choking!"

He huffs at me but at least settles for gripping my arms

instead of trying to knock out my esophagus. Then he's spinning me around on his lap, and I swear I will ice him through if he keeps handling me like this.

He stops me so we're face-to-face, all so he can snarl at me. "What was the *one* thing I told you not to do?"

I take in his wild-eyed expression and the snow caught in his wind-blown hair. His hood is tossed back, which is an immediate giveaway of his frantic mood.

I sniff haughtily. "I can't recall."

"I told you to not fucking *collapse!*"

"Oh. That." I force myself off of him, scooping up some snow for my mouth to soothe my parched tongue and raw throat.

"Yes, *that.*"

With shaky legs and a dizzy head, I get to my feet, swallowing down the slush with relish. "Well, I don't remember collapsing, so how can you be sure I did?"

I think, perhaps, the assassin might start having a fit. His eye is twitching, and the growl that gurgles in his chest can't be healthy.

"*Malina.*"

"Did you find the fae?" I ask, cutting him off.

He's not to be deterred. "I leave like you tell me to, and then when I return, I find that you've used your magic so much you drained yourself into *collapsing.*"

"You keep saying that word, and it's getting on my nerves."

"*You're* getting on my nerves!"

"Then leave me be, assassin!"

He surges forward and grips my arms again. "I can't leave you be, you insufferable, cold woman, because for some *fucking reason*, you've gotten under my skin so much that I now crave the ice of your touch."

My breath catches and I stare into his dark eyes, at the

little flecks of light that float through them. "You...you crave me?"

"Yes," he snarls, his voice rubbed raw in grit. "I can't sleep, because I'm too busy watching you breathe. I can't think, because my mind wanders to you. And when I should've just slit your throat a hundred times over in Seventh Kingdom, I didn't, because I wanted to watch you instead and see how far down your cold really went."

My breath feels shallow, his grip on my arms exuding a heat that seeps in all the way through my skin. His presence, his voice, his touch—everything about him, from the dangerous air he carries to the handsome lines of his face— they all pull me toward him. Make my nerves light up and my senses magnify.

The man meant to bring me my death makes me feel more alive than ever.

"And?" the question drags out of me in a whisper. "How far does my cold go?"

Right now, I can't feel my cold at all. All I feel is his heat. Against my breasts as his chest presses into me, through my sleeves where he's gripping me, the searing breath on my cheek as he exhales hard.

"It goes all the way through," he says roughly, though his touch has gentled. "But you know what I figured out, Queenie?"

My mouth feels dry despite the lump of snow I just swallowed. "What?"

"Your cold burns far better than fire."

He pulls me forward and kisses me.

His hot lips land on my icy ones, our temperatures at war. I go weak in the knees again, but this time, it has nothing to do with exhaustion and everything to do with a rapturous need.

He kisses me with adamance, like he's demanding entry,

and I *want* to let him in, but something stops me. Not to be deterred, he grips me by my jaw, warring with me to open. When I still don't, he slides his teeth over my bottom lip and *bites*.

"Ouch!" I snap, though it's muffled from the press of him.

"Let me in."

I shake my head frantically, wanting to pull away but wanting him to hold me even closer.

He pulls back to look me in the eye, and I'm not sure how he sees so much, but his face softens and his hold on my jaw gentles, his thumbs brushing over my cheeks. "Let me in, Queenie."

We both know we're not just talking about the kiss.

I tremble, because I'm so pent up, so filled with want...

So incredibly terrified.

Every man I've ever opened for has always trodden on me. Burned my heart to ash and left me to scrape up the remnants. So perhaps my heart *is* made of ice, but if it is, it's because I had to freeze it just to get all the flaked parts to stay together. I became the cold that everyone saw me as, and the cold protected me.

Because what is a burn if you're already numb?

"Let me in," he murmurs for a third time. He's asking. Waiting. Not a demand, but a true request. To let him in and give him a chance.

To give *us* a chance.

His eyes bore into me as he waits for me to decide.

Maybe I'm a glutton for punishment. Maybe being on the brink of battle has my desires surging up because I know there's a chance I might die. Or maybe, it's just him—and somehow, he figured out a way to thaw me.

Whatever the reason, I lean forward, pressing my lips to his, and...I let him in.

The kiss is a clash of heat and cold, of lust and fear, of desperate want and shattering uncertainty.

The kiss is life changing.

Which is incredibly ill timed, considering our deaths might be on the horizon.

We shouldn't go together at all, but we do. I've never felt such a connection with someone, and as we meld together, I never want our kiss to stop. Never want *us* to stop. Because Dommik has challenged me to be a better person. A better queen. But he also fills me with a fiery desire that I don't want to subdue.

I want to urge it on.

The most beautiful part of this kiss is that neither of us is in charge of the other. There's no war, no fight. It's a mutual caress between our lips and tongues, an equal give and take, a dance in which we take turns to lead and follow.

When he pulls away, I'm still caught in his draw, just like the shadows that always curl around his body, as if always wanting to wrap around him. I blink up at him and he gazes down at me, and this push and pull between us seems to settle.

"There," he says, something like a promise lingering in his tone. "Something to look forward to after this battle."

I give a humorless laugh, his scorching hands still clasped on my cheeks. "There might not be an after, assassin."

His eyes darken—even those specks of light that are caught in the recesses of his irises. "Make sure there is, Queenie."

The way he seems to have faith in me to ensure such a thing is shocking. No one has ever had faith in me about anything before, and that fact brings me back down to reality. Back to the hard truth of what's coming.

I take a step away to clear my head from his nearness. "Did you find them?"

His expression sobers. "We have hours. Nightfall, at the

very most."

My stomach dips, but I nod. There's still so much to do.

"Nice addition," he says, nodding toward the fortified bridge. "No wonder you collapsed."

I busy myself trying to dust off the snow from my dress, but I'm soaked through. "I need you to take me into the city."

"Why?"

"We have more work to do."

His eyes flare in angry disbelief. "Malina, you just collapsed—"

That word again.

I pin him with a sharp look. "Yes, and you know, that was quite a refreshing rest. I'm ready to do more magic now."

"You're a pain in my ass," he rumbles.

"You kissed me, but now I'm a pain in your ass?"

"Going to keep thinking about that kiss, aren't you?" he mocks. "Maybe you'll dream of it the next time you collapse?"

"That would ensure I vomit as soon as I wake."

Dommik laughs, and I can't help but crack a small smile. Then he digs a hand into his pocket and shoves something at me.

I take it and look down with a scowl. "Why are you giving me this awful jerky?"

"You want to do more?" His head nods to my hands. "Then you eat that first."

I wrinkle my nose. "This really will make me vomit."

"Don't be such a spoiled royal. Eat so I can at least pretend you have some energy before you go off like the stubborn woman you are."

I can tell he's not going to be amenable until I do this, so I eat the jerky as quickly as I can, though it's incredibly tough, and the taste is no better than it was before. When I swallow the last piece, he double checks that I'm not hiding any in my hands before he passes me his water to drink.

I gulp it down. "There. Now, let's go."

The sky is starting to darken, the cold growing bolder and thicker with every breath. Dommik has taken me to several spots throughout Highbell, and strategic streets now have ice barriers and walls blocking them too. Nothing like the scale of what I made at the bridge, but something to help protect the more vulnerable parts of the city. No bricks, just solid sheets of thickened ice frozen across roads.

I've had to be quick, because the people either scurry away when they see me using magic...or start to curse and attack me when they think I'm just walling them in.

I glance through the solid ice barrier I've made while I catch my breath, my hands shaking against its cold length. Beyond, the shanties lie in their crooked rows, the filthy street and roughshod buildings now blocked.

They don't have gates or locks or even strong walls. If the fae come through this way, they'll all be crushed. Unlike the noble houses with their guards and fences, and probably even some safe bunkers, the people who live in the shanties have nothing except teetering houses.

At least my walls are another obstacle the fae will have in their way. My hope is they'll decide not to bother with these streets at all, but at the very least, it will slow them down.

I was lying to Dommik earlier when I said I felt refreshed. Now, I feel like death. My limbs are heavy, and the slices on my palms ache constantly, the layers of my skin peeled and raw and bloodied.

"Enough," he says when I continue to slump against the wall.

I can see children on the other side as they come over and

press their faces against the ice like it's a window in a sweet shop. The sight of them makes my ribs tighten. There are so many lives at stake.

"I'm alright."

"No, you're not," he snaps before yanking my arm over his shoulder as he wraps his own around my back, gripping my waist to keep me upright.

"It might not work at all. These walls are weaker, and who knows what kind of magic the fae have. They could simply burst through and—"

"You're trying. That's what matters."

I'm not sure he's right about that.

My father used to tell me that what mattered most was what would end up written in the history books, and everyone knows that the ones who write history are the victors.

"Take me to the bridge again—inside the city this time," I tell him.

"Malina…"

"I know," I say harshly. "But I have to try again before the fae arrive. If I can get even a small percentage to believe me…"

He blows out a breath. "We need to hurry."

Dommik leaps us back through the city, and I prepare myself to be ignored again. But I go over the words I can say to implore them, steeling myself for the inevitable rejection. A few minutes later, we settle on steady ground, and the shadows fade away from us.

I blink, eyes adjusting to take in the city's entrance, only to widen in horror.

The road in front of the bridge is teeming with people, and at the entrance where I painstakingly built the ice wall, is Queen Kaila, with four timberwings lounging behind her in the snow. Her blue-and-silver-clad soldiers are with her, along with dozens of Highbell guards, and they're ripping the wall down.

Destroying it.

From here, I can't see how they broke past the spiked barricade on the other side or crossed the slippery arc of the bridge, but I can see the soldiers starting to tear my wall down brick by brick.

"No!"

I rush forward, but Dommik grabs my hand before I can, and instead, shadows me past the crowd. He brings us right to the front of the spectacle Kaila is holding, her bright teal dress gleaming, her smile dazzling. I realize that she's sitting on a stack of the ice bricks they dismantled from the wall. Someone's cloak is draped over them, and she sits there like she's on a throne, while surrounding her on the ground are piles of items and boughs that people have left to her in offering.

She is sitting on *my* bricks. Bricks that took me all night to create. All night to build into a wall that they're now tearing down. All so she could…sit here in the city, while people bring forward gifts of adoration to lay at her feet like it's some sort of damn holiday celebration?

I want to cry.

I want to *scream.* Somewhere in the deepest recesses of my head, I do, the sound reverberating through my skull, though only I can hear it.

Frustration swells through me to a level I've never felt before. "Why?" I shout as I rush forward. "Why are you doing this?"

Kaila turns and looks at me as if she's surprised to see me. Did she still think me locked up in that cage in the castle? So unconcerned with my presence that she forgot to look?

"You," she says, narrowing her eyes on me.

"Put them back!" I shout to the guards as I storm forward. "Put them back *now*!"

"This has truly been you?" she asks, gesturing toward the ice. "I thought you didn't have magic?"

"She's been walling us in!" someone calls from the crowd.

"*How* do you have magic?" Kaila asks. Wasting time on suspicions of me, when she should be fixing the damn wall she's *ruined*.

"The fae are coming, and you're taking down the *one* defense we have!"

"Enough," she snaps. "Guards! Take the mad queen away."

The guards stop tearing down the bricks and start coming for *me* instead. Dommik is beside me in an instant, dagger in hand and shadows already gathering, but my hand snatches out and I grip his arm as all the blood drains from my face. "Wait."

"Wait? For what?" he snarls. "I'm not going to let them take you!"

"*Look.*"

My tone is filled with terror, and Dommik follows the direction of my gaze, his lips instantly pressing tight. "*Fuck.*"

The guards are on us both, grabbing hold of our arms, but I don't even feel it. I'm too busy staring at the movement just past the base of the mountain.

At the fae army marching toward us.

They're a grayish mottle of stone-armored soldiers walking in unison down the winding road around the mountain's base, the sound of their synchronized steps starting to echo over the chasm that separates us.

When Kaila notices that we aren't reacting to the guards, she turns, and her eyes widen as she looks past the bridge and toward the mountain, where she sees the fae.

The crowd starts to see them too.

There's a gasp that seems to spread through everyone, a deafening silence as the shock and horror sinks in.

Kaila's guards gather around her, but she leaps to her feet and sucks in a long, drawn-out breath. It's more than just a simple inhale. A wisp of magic comes with the pull, and suddenly, the amplified sound of a fae shouting orders echoes through the air.

"Fae, let's greet these Orean scum. Charge the city! Leave none alive! Lead Magicks, attack!"

The magicked voice that Kaila brought forth is the only warning we get.

Far to my left, a massive stroke of lightning suddenly cracks down in the middle of the crowd. The flash momentarily blinds me with an unnatural purplish hue that burns my eyes. Screams rend the air, and charred, smoking bodies are left in a gaping pit where the thunderbolt hit, leaving dead bodies in its wake.

The air stings with fae magic that pinches my skin.

There's another crack of lightning that hits further away, this time striking one of the city's buildings and splitting it in two. Before the walls even finish falling in crumbling destruction, a shockwave ripples through the ground itself, knocking everyone off their feet.

I go sprawling, smacking into Dommik's body, but he cushions my fall, while the guards who were holding us are knocked away.

Since the crowd is so packed in, everyone falls into one another, until the gathering is a tangle of frenzied, unsteady panic.

The people behind us are screaming and scrambling up, with no care of who they trample over as they start to flee like animals in a stampede.

"The fae! The fae are here to attack!"

"The army is here!"

Dommik wrenches me up to my feet, and together, we rush toward Kaila, past the cracked ice on the ground. She's still staring at the road, at the fae marching toward us, while her guards and timberwings gather around her with obvious distress.

She looks like she's in a shocked trance. She's not blinking, not even moving, save for the inhales she keeps sucking in. I'm not even sure if she's aware of the random voices she's pulling, though I can hear dozens of the fae. Goading each other on, giving orders, talking about their attacks, one after another in a jumble that's difficult to discern.

"Kaila!" I shout as I climb up the icy blocks to reach her arm and shake her.

She snaps her head around to look at me in a daze. Her beautiful face has drained of its usual color, her hands shaking.

"I'll try to fix the wall, and you get your guards to form a line! Use your magic to call down Highbell's royal guard!"

The queen of voices just looks at me, her gaze tracking back to the army. "It's impossible," she whispers. "Fae don't *exist* anymore."

Frustration trounces through me, because we don't have time for her to have a crisis of denial. "*They do*. But this city won't unless you help me defend it!"

She glances back at the bold rows of soldiers marching closer, and then determination crosses her face as she nods. I let out a sigh of relief. With her voice magic, we can listen to what the fae are ordering their soldiers to do, we can anticipate their attacks, which can buy us precious seconds, and plan countermoves somehow.

"Use your voice magic to tell the people to stop panicking before they kill hundreds of their own neighbors!" I shout, gesturing back to the fleeing crowd. "Then you can announce through the streets and direct them! I'll tell you where to lead them!"

Another lightning bolt surges, making Kaila scream,

hands clapping over her ears. A second later, the ground shakes again, but this time, Dommik braces me for it. Kaila nearly falls over, but her timberwing slants out its wing to catch her.

She grips hold of its feathers and scrambles up its back until she's mounted, eyes skating over the screaming crowd. Some of them are yelling at Kaila for direction, some of them are sprinting away, others are hurt or dead, and more are crying, shouting for loved ones or trying to drag lightning-struck bodies away.

It's bedlam.

"Tell everyone to head for Pillar Row!" I shout up at her. "You need to get them to listen!"

She fists her hands in her timberwing's reins and then glances at the guards. They're a mess, unsure what to do, some of them starting to frantically shove the ice bricks back in place, but it's too late.

At the center of the wall, blocks are missing from the top all the way down, leaving a large gap, while several more bricks on the right have been knocked loose from the quaking ground. More topple, nearly crushing one of them just as we're hit with another shockwave.

I lock my knees and lean into Dommik as the ground sways, while another bolt of lightning comes dangerously close to hitting us, so much so that all the hair on the back of my neck lifts.

"We need to move!" Dommik shouts in my ear, still not letting go of my arm, as if he's waiting to whisk us away at a moment's notice.

"Kaila! Hurry!" I call to her.

She looks at me, a moment between queens where we understand what's at stake. Understand the implications of what's come for Highbell. For Orea.

Then, she turns and snaps the reins on her timberwing,

taking off into the sky. I wait as she gets higher, knowing she's going to try to head off the chaotic crowd and use her magic to help direct the hysteria.

Except…she doesn't.

She keeps flying. Past the crowd, higher and higher in the sky.

People below all around me, scream her name in anguish as they watch her abandon them.

"Queen Kaila!"

"Don't leave us!"

I stare in horrified shock as she does exactly that.

She leaves.

I knew she wasn't going to believe me until she saw them with her own eyes. Knew all she was preoccupied with was her own power play and politics. But I never imagined that once faced with the reality, she'd desert us.

She disappears above the clouds, out of view, without so much as a backwards glance.

Upon seeing her flee, some of her guards rush over and snatch at the reins of the other three timberwings in a mad rush. Two of them go on one, then four guards try to scramble on the other. One of the men goes sliding off, unable to hold on when the beast takes flight, his voice hoarse as he begs them not to leave him behind.

The last timberwing has five guards all battling each other, trying to get on its back first. Three of them do, while a fourth tries to cling to its leg as the animal leaps into the air. The man grips fiercely, but it's obvious the timberwing doesn't take kindly to the guard hanging off its foot. The animal reaches back and roars at him before knocking the guard loose. The man goes free-falling with a scream, before landing in a bloody, broken heap in the crowd, the impact crashing in my ears and making me flinch.

Another beam of lightning strikes. Singes. Kills.

The fae army is getting closer, swarming down the snowy path, ignoring the winding road at their left that goes up the mountain to the castle and heading straight for the city instead.

They're going to be at the bridge within minutes.

Around me, blackened pits are peppered across the street where the lightning has hit, the scent of scorched bodies making bile rise up in my throat. And the sound...

The sound of so many Oreans fleeing, screaming, *dying*...it cracks something wide open in my chest and fills me with a resolute certainty.

"We need to get out of here!" Dommik shouts.

But I shake my head. "No."

I break away from him and run for the bridge, and though the ground is icy, I don't slip. Behind me, people are still calling for Kaila to come back. A tumult of pleas against the pandemonium, while I come to a stop at the wall and slam my hands against the bricks.

Because I will not leave.

Even with fear so heavy I nearly buckle from the weight of it. Even with a horde of fae before me ready to kill. Even with a city of people behind me who hate me.

I might not be the queen they want, but I'm the one they have.

And I will not leave.

CHAPTER 41

QUEEN MALINA

Above us, snow has started to leak from a punctured cloud.

The ground lifts and ripples, like a blanket being shaken out, knocking people off their feet. Forked lightning cracks open the sky, targeting the largest groups of people as they try to flee. Somewhere in the city behind me, I hear a building tumble down, its crash reverberating through the streets.

I may be queen, but chaos reigns.

With unsteady feet, I finally make it to the torn apart wall, and I slam my palms up against the frost-covered ice. Skin sinking into the freeze, I call to the magic, forcing ice to stretch across the gap, filling in the space as thick as I can manage. Layer upon layer it grows, bubbling up and distorting my view to the other side.

When my arms drop, the filled-in sheet of ice is much thinner than the bricks, but at least it's not gaping open anymore. Though, the same can't be said for me. I feel as if there's something torn open within me—cut through my body and draining me of life.

But I have no other recourse. All I have is this taboo magic. Magic that I shouldn't have, but magic that I will use every drop of in order to help right my wrongs.

Dommik appears at my side, lips downturned when he sees the state of me, though he says nothing. My gaze whips around, thoughts spinning, gathering, trying to think through the awful noises of screaming and running and the hits blasting down from the sky.

To my right, the rest of Kaila's guards are fighting amongst themselves, panicked at being left behind and clearly at a loss as to what to do. "Get yourselves together!" I yell at them.

Their heads swing in my direction.

"Start heading off the stampeding crowd. Order everyone to get to Pillar Row."

"You're not our queen," one of them snarls. "We don't have to take orders from *you*."

"You're right—but *your* queen just abandoned us all here to die. And that's exactly what will happen to us if you don't listen to me!" I yell back.

To my surprise, one of the Highbell guards walks forward. "I'll do it," he tells me as he tightens the straps on his gilt chest plate. He probably thought when he woke up this morning that he only needed to wear it for show—to glint in the snowy daylight as he stood beside Kaila. "I'll do whatever you need," he declares.

The other Highbell guards nod with him, taking steps forward.

"Good," I say, though what I really want to do is fall down in relief. "Tell as many people as you can to go down the row. Get them to the Pitching Pines—do you understand?"

"Yes, my queen," he says before the group of them rush away in different directions. Beacons of gold getting caught up in the swarm, all of them shouting, trying to cut through the noise and hoping some people will hear their instructions.

Suddenly, a lightning strike hits just to the left of us, sending Dommik and me sprawling. My hair is raised from the charge, eyes blinded momentarily from the lavender shock of light. When I get back to my feet, I see the hem of my skirt is singed black.

Too close.

I press against the wall and peer through a crack between the icy bricks to see the other side of the bridge. There, at the front of the army, is a fae whose hands are wrapped in tiny threads of lightning that spark and twist around his fingers.

Not a single fae forked off to take the winding road up to the castle. Instead, they've all marched here, toward the bridge.

The entire army gathers behind the lightning fae, their stomping feet coming to a stop, just short of the bridge's entrance. The spiked barriers I made have been partially dismantled from Kaila's people, but the fae make quick work of the rest of it. A horde of them come forward and start hacking away at the sharp spikes with loud clangs, breaking them into pieces.

Within minutes, they've dismantled the barriers enough to pull them away, leaving the path of the bridge open, their regiments gathering up in perfect lines.

I swallow hard, queasiness pinching my stomach with a level of fear that makes it hard to think.

I'm out of my depth. I was trained to be a princess, to be married off to a king. Tutored in politics and dancing, taught how to sit and eat and dress and speak and sew. I was *not* trained to lead a battle, and magic or not, I feel staggeringly inept to face the army that stands before me.

But if I don't, who will?

My father's voice rings in my ear, just as the castle's bell begins to toll out its blaring warning. My fear doesn't matter. My *life* doesn't matter.

Kingdom comes first.

The lightning-wielder moves away, and my eyes widen when I see the archers march forward and span out on either side of the bridge. They line up on the snowy bank and go down on one knee, one after the other, then point their bows into the air.

I suck in a breath, but my inhale stutters short just as the bowstrings snap their release.

"*Arrows!*" Dommik shouts, but the surrounding cacophony is too loud for anyone to hear him.

The arrows arc over the chasm toward us.

Living in Sixth Kingdom all my life means I've experienced every kind of snowstorm. When the arrows rain down, it sounds just like the sharpened hail that would sometimes crack the atrium windows and dent the roof, except the aftermath is so much worse.

Dommik launches himself at me, and the second he has my hand gripped in his, he engulfs us in shadows.

The seconds inch by, feeling like an eternity, feeling like a blink.

When he yanks them away and we no longer have their wraithlike protection around us, I look down to see three arrows have punctured the ground right at our feet. They would have pierced us through.

I lift my gaze, ears pounding with the barrage of new screams. Behind me, countless Oreans have been struck, some fatally, arrows distending from their bodies like quills that bleed out red ink.

They're attacking helpless citizens who are fleeing, people who aren't even capable of fighting back. Just like the village they slaughtered, they're here to kill without qualms.

The fae don't give us a single moment to recuperate from the first wave. There's a shout for the archers to loose another bout of arrows, and with it, fury looses from *me*.

I react on pure instinct, tossing up my hands over my head, and an arc of ice *explode*s out of me. In an instant, it stretches from the top of the wall and curves back, curling like a tidal wave in a frozen sea. It spans at least a hundred feet above us, shielding the last of the crowd below.

Gasps of shock flare to life, sounding muffled beneath this blue-tinged ceiling, just as clinks of hundreds of arrows crash against my barrier. Some of them nearly pierce through, making fissures spread like spiderwebs.

But…it holds. No one else is hit.

"Queen! Queen!"

My attention is wrenched down, where a little girl is clutching my skirts. Her brown hair is a tangled mess, and she's crying so hard that she's shaking all over. Tears stream down her agonized face, and there's an arrow pierced into her tiny leg at the thigh. The only consolation is it doesn't seem like it's gone through, but blood has soaked into the rags she wears.

I kneel down in front of her just as she falls forward into my arms. "I can't find my mama! I can't find her!" she wails hysterically.

Great Divine.

She can't be more than five years old. I look around wildly at the last of the people retreating down the streets deeper into the city, none of them seeming to be a mother searching for this little girl.

"I need to go home! Help me go home to find my mama, please! It hurts!" she sobs while she clutches me.

"It's alright," I say, trying to soothe her, though I've never soothed a child in my life. I rub her back while I look down at the arrow in her leg.

It has to come out.

"We're going to help you find your mother," I tell her before one of my hands slips down to the arrow. When she sees where I'm reaching, she starts to panic, but I grip the arrow and yank it out as fast and firmly as I can.

She screams and tries to shove me away. "It's alright," I tell her again, but she's crying so hard she's gulping and choking on air.

"Dommik. Take her. Take her home and try to find her mother."

He hesitates, his expression conflicted.

"We *have* to help her."

He leans down and picks up the little girl, and she buries her head against his neck and cries. "Do you know where you live?" he asks, and she nods her head.

"Go," I urge as I get to my feet. "Hurry."

His face goes tight and he takes a step closer to me. "You get away from here as *soon* as those fae start to cross the bridge. Understand? Fucking promise right now, or I won't go."

The sound of the girl's cries are peeling away a layer of my heart, yanking off the muscle in bloody, painful strips. "I will. Just get her out of here and find her mother!"

With one last look at me, he vanishes.

Without Dommik by my side, I feel more vulnerable than ever. Fortunately, the people have fled the city's entrance, the last of them disappearing into the dense streets.

I barely get a chance to feel that relief when I suddenly hear a horn blaring for the fae to charge. Then, the sound of hundreds of footsteps begin to rush the bridge. I scramble forward, looking through the cracks of the bricks.

The first of them race forward, but the stones are slippery with ice. They go crashing down, making the fae behind fall on top of them, until there's a huge dogpile caught up at the front.

Behind me, the streets are emptying, most of my people now out of view. The further away they can get and the more time to flee, the better chance they have.

Down the bridge, the fae are scrambling, trying to get their feet beneath them again. Pride swells in my chest when I see them retreat back and off the bridge. Something I've done is actually working. When they're back in formation on the snow, I see the army move aside, letting one soldier march through the fray.

It's one lone fae with jet-black hair and pale skin, a mark of red across his stone armor. He walks right up to the entrance of the bridge until he reaches the cobbled bricks. Stopping, he glances down at his feet, then lifts his gaze and looks at the icy wall.

What is he doing?

I get my answer a moment later when he opens his mouth and breathes *fire*.

It roars out of him in a stream of red, sparking angrily like struck flint as it hits the bridge. It crackles over the stones while he walks forward with determination, the ice burning up and puffing out of existence as soon as he passes. With every step, he melts the freeze, his fire eating up the snow and leaving only burnt stone behind.

When he's halfway over the bridge, the army behind him begins to follow in perfectly lined rows. The thump of their synchronized steps seems louder than the lightning when it struck.

A promise of death marching forward.

As he gets closer, the fae's fire gets bigger and brighter. A red threat against my icy blue defense.

I tremble, looking back at the streets. Save for the spitting smoke of charred bodies or those riddled with arrows who were left behind, I'm alone. The people have all fled further into Highbell, and hopefully, toward the pines.

They need more time to get away. As much as I can give them.

Turning back around, I press my hands against the wall. Ice pours from my palms and I thicken the wall at its weakest point—though, I'm at my weakest point, too.

Through the cracks, I watch the fae's slightly distorted silhouette as he stalks forward like a demon, his sparking fire so bright I have to squint. He gets closer and closer, and my heart pounds in terror.

I clench my teeth and divert my power. I envision it flowing past the wall and then shooting into the fire fae in sharp shards that pierce him through. But what actually forms is nothing except splinters of ice that he simply bats away.

Useless.

He laughs, and the sound seems to echo down through the chasm and come back around to mock me.

The army behind him is my living dread. I can feel their synchronized steps reverberate up through my legs, and I know with deadly certainty that the wall isn't enough. Not nearly enough.

I'm stricken, shaking, *losing*.

I glance down at my feet. *Maybe I can try to ruin the bridge.*

My eyes lift up to the mountain—to where Highbell sits snug against it. We'd be cut off from the castle completely, but it's a last-ditch effort I need to try.

I fist my palms and close my eyes, fighting past the intense feeling of unnatural exhaustion that's draining me. I form and mold and *push*, and then shoot out as much magic as I can, aiming it up as high as I can toss it.

A massive mallet of ice shoots up and over the wall, and then goes plunging down when gravity grips it. The fire fae stops and looks up at it in daring, but he backs up before it can flatten him. Just before it crashes against the bricks, hope leaps in my chest because maybe it's big enough, solid enough to—

It shatters.

Breaks into a million tiny pieces against the bridge.

All those livid words I tossed at their king, and I've lost.

My ice is no use against stone.

I can't stop them. Can't stop *him*.

I stand with my shoulders drooped, panting, while snow is scraped across my cheeks and salted over my lips and flaked down my lashes. I brace a raw, bleeding palm against the wall just to keep from collapsing, and I look up at the fire fae, who smiles menacingly at me before he starts to close the last of the gap between us.

Every instinct in me is screaming to run away. Every sense is pricked as his deadly magic advances. But I lock my knees. Steel my back. Pour my panic into my power and stay right here.

Sparks flare as he reaches the other side of the wall. As soon as he comes to a stop, he cuts his flames off. I can feel more than see him looking at me. A mile between us wouldn't be enough—a realm between. But all I have is this wall, three-bricks deep.

He makes sure to stand right in front of me, and I see his warped smile spread over his face. Then he starts blowing fire right at me, billowing it toward me like a fiery fog. I flinch on instinct, though I can't feel its heat.

Yet.

I grit my teeth, feeding more ice into the wall, refusing to drop my hands. Refusing to back down. Because if I can hold them off for even another minute, then it gives my people more time.

And time is all I have to give them.

My power continues to bleed from my hands, thickening the wall, but his fire is setting off sparks, hissing and spitting out steam into the air. I will the ice to hold, to pour out of me, to fortify, but his flames are relentless. It's eating away at it, melting it, weakening it.

Water pours down, flooding from the melt.

But I don't drop my hands.

Not when the wall above me starts to curl inward and dissolve. Not when water slushes down at my feet. Not when frosted blood oozes from my palms. And not when my hands start to burn from the flames just on the other side.

I can see the fire fae now as clearly as if I were looking through a window. Can see the army behind him, waiting, swords in hand.

My last defense, one that took me all night to build, and I've only been able to slow them down by minutes. All this effort, exhaustion, energy, and it barely matters. I've barely made any difference at all.

Frozen tears trickle down my face and shatter onto the ground.

The thinning wall rains down, unable to resist his flame as it drips. When the barrier between the two of us is so thin that it's ready to snap beneath my fingertips, the fae stops his fire and grins at me. His canines are sharp and elongated, the expression on his face nothing short of ecstatic.

Leaning forward, he raises a finger, and *taps*.

The ice between us shatters.

It clatters to the ground in thin shards, leaving a large enough gap for him to step through, the wall now useless and broken. I stumble away from him, forced to tilt my head way up to look in his dark, gleeful eyes.

Fear—all I feel is paralyzing, gripping fear.

"Ice Orean thinks she can beat fire fae?" he asks before his gaze moves behind me and he breathes in through his nose. "Ah, the scent of fear is thick here." He flashes me another taunting smile and then leans in so close that I recoil. "I'm going to enjoy burning every Orean in this city until my flames feed on their bones."

I can see it—this picture he paints. The picture of flaring hatred and blazing death. The picture of ash and despair left behind.

His head dips down and I snap my face to the side just as he drags a hot, disgusting tongue up my cheek, licking off the frost and tears that gathered there. "Mmm. I'll start with *you*."

He leans back and I watch in horror as his mouth opens. At the back of his throat, I can see those harrowing, red-hot flames, ready to be let loose.

Ready to scorch me right here where I stand.

I start to slam my eyes shut so I can look away from Death.

But the shadows have other ideas.

He appears like smoke come to smother the flames.

Dommik is suddenly there, his blade skating across the fae's throat in one quick slice. The red that pours out of the fae isn't fire, but blood instead.

Shock is the last expression he wears before he falls face-first in a gurgle as he bleeds out right at my feet. When the fire fae hits the ground, the army behind him ripples with surprise and fury.

Then, they charge.

The last precious seconds I tried to give Highbell have just run out.

CHAPTER 42

QUEEN MALINA

I stand frozen, my mind reeling as the army hurtles toward us.

"You were supposed to leave!" Dommik shouts at me, just as he leaps over the dead fire fae and snatches up my hand.

The moment the first soldier surges through the broken wall, shadows blast out of Dommik and he whisks us away. The force of his shadow-leaping steals my breath as he vaults us from point to point, so quick and jarring that I nearly pass out.

When he finally stops, I slump, only able to stay upright because his hands are caught beneath my arms.

"Stubborn fucking woman!"

We're in the middle of an empty alleyway, and I lean against the cold stone wall in front of me, letting my forehead rest against it. I can still feel the singe of the fae's flames heating my skin. Can still feel the burn of it against my palms.

Now that I'm still, now that we're away, everything flashes before my eyes, and my entire body shakes, adrenaline pounding through my veins and punching through my chest as black dots start to pollute my vision.

"Breathe, Queenie."

"You breathe!" I gasp out.

He spins me around to face him. His black hair is pulled back, snow and blood speckling his cheek. "For once in your godsdamned life, will you fucking listen to me?"

I shove at his chest, making him growl and release me as I point a finger at his face. "This is your fault!"

"*Mine*?" he asks incredulously. "How is this my fault?"

I tear at my collar, as if it's the source for my strained inhales. Yet it's all over me—this pressure. This suffocating grief.

I let it whip out of me through the lashings of my tongue.

"Because you should have just *killed me*!" I scream at him.

His eyes go wide, and my words seem to blast through the alley and get caught in the air. Trapped in this ugly, tangled net that I have no hope of getting free from.

The longer he stays quiet, the angrier my anguish becomes.

"You should have just killed me, and then I wouldn't have been able to do what I did." I lift my hands to show him the evidence of the slashes that will never heal, though they're bloody and peeling now, the skin gone blue. "If you'd done your damn job, then I wouldn't have been able to get to Seventh Kingdom in the first place. I wouldn't have been able to give my blood and then make *Orea* bleed," I shout scathingly as my fists raise and start hitting him in the chest.

He doesn't try to block my strikes, and that makes me even angrier. "You should have killed me!" I scream as I hit him again and again, though it's my own words that crush me,

512

each one a weight on the ladder of my ribs.

Dommik just continues to watch me while wisps of his shadows curl around us. If I could go back in time, I'd kneel at his feet and welcome his blade.

And the truth of it is, if I *had* died, no one would have cared. No one would have mourned me.

Crystallized tears fall from the corners of my eyes and scrape down my skin.

"Do it," I spit before I reach down and yank up the blade from his holster and shove it into his hands. When he doesn't take it, I push it against him even harder, forcing his fingers around the hilt. "*Do it!*"

I'm demanding it.

I'm *pleading* for it.

For him to strike me down like I deserve.

He doesn't move, and my throat creases with a sob. One that wrings me out and leaves me all twisted up.

"Come on, assassin. Do what you're meant to do," I taunt.

His eyes flash, his expression suddenly transforming as anger rucks up his mouth into a snarl. "*No.*"

My heart pounds through my chest and my fists tighten, making my injured palms sear with pain. "Why not?"

Without warning, his free hand snaps out and clamps around my throat. I suck in a breath of surprise as he holds me hostage against the wall of the building, his body leaning over me. "You don't want to die."

I sneer in his face. "Yes, I do."

His eyes flick back and forth as if he's digging me up and uncovering everything I tried to bury. "You tried to warn them, Malina. Tried to protect them. You did *everything* you could!"

"And I failed!" I spit back. "So I just want you to kill me and be done with it!"

His hold on my throat tightens, and his shadows flick erratically around us as he bears down on me with a dark temper that makes my stomach tighten. "You don't always get what you want in life."

"I want nothing but death."

A cruel smirk curls his lips. "Is that right?"

Heat unfurls low in my belly, but I manage to nod. "Yes."

His thumb presses over my windpipe, straining my breath, making my mind stop spinning and instead holding me right *here*.

"You want death?" he grits out, his challenge lashing against my face and spreading heat with each hit. "*I'm* your fucking death. I will consume you so thoroughly there won't be a wish for any end, because no end will release you from me."

My heart stops. Head hollowing out of everything except his dark vow.

When he leans in even closer, I quiver with need, body flooding with his consuming presence. Instead of blazing panic, instead of frigid grief, there's just this all-encompassing thaw.

"You're *mine*, Malina," he thunders into my ears, the claim raining down and drenching me through. Spreading over me with his unrelenting heat.

"Am I?" I ask in a challenge. Hoping—*begging*—for him to meet it.

His hand flexes around my neck, and he tips my head back, lips coming down to graze across my jaw. "Yes. So you can fucking wish for death all you want, but you won't get it. And right now, I'm going to show you what it's like to be *alive*."

My eyes flare at his words, and then he slams his mouth to mine.

The dagger clatters to the ground.

I meet him desperately, lips parted, tongue searching, moving against him in a frenzy. His kiss is harsh—almost cruel. As if he's punishing me for what I said and proving to me that I really am his.

It's in his biting teeth and the thrust of his tongue, it's the strong grip on my neck, and fingertips digging in hard enough to leave bruises along my pale neck. All of it showing that I don't get to give in. That every sensation belongs to him—to me.

To us.

And I thrill at it all, because he was right. It reminds me that I'm alive. It makes me want to *be* alive.

"More," I order.

He hikes up one of my legs to wrap around his hip and shoves my back against the wall, one hand dropping down. "You're already wet for me, aren't you?"

I turn my head, gasping for air, my entire face flushed. "Yes."

His hand cups me then, and even through the layers of my clothes, it takes my breath away. The heel of his palm grinds, making me shake from want instead of exhaustion, lighting me up with the glare of his hungry eyes.

"I need it," I gasp. "I need you now."

"You want to fuck death? You want to prove to me that you're claiming me right back and come alive beneath my touch?"

His hand continues to stroke against my core, building up these embers between us that've been wanting to be stoked into a scorch.

"Yes!" I fling out with fervency pumping through me.

He bites down on my bottom lip with a satisfied growl. "I'm your assassin. Which means *I'm* in charge of your death. You got that?"

I whimper and nod, trying to grind against him, but he

keeps me pinned.

"Tell me, Queenie."

My gaze lifts to his, binding together. "You're in charge. You're my assassin."

"That's right," he says, beard scouring against my cheek as he drags his lips across, spreading his steady warmth. "And you're my queen. So I will get on my knees and *bow*."

I stare wide-eyed as he kneels before me on the ground and then buries his head beneath my skirt. I clutch at the fabric over his head, trying to wrench him away, trying to wrench him closer, teetering with uncertainty and tightening anticipation.

My noises go high-pitched when he snatches my undergarments to the side and drags his hot, thick tongue over my slit. I flinch, head cracking against the wall when he centers that tongue over my clit and nibbles down on it, sending a shock of pleasurable pain shooting through me.

He licks and laps, faster and faster, making me throb, making me inflate all over. My clit is swollen, my breasts are heavy, and there's a full haziness settling over my mind that knows only brimming bliss.

Then he stuffs two thick fingers inside of me, a wet sound accompanying his pleased growl. I would be embarrassed about how wet I sound if I were still in control, but I'm not, and what an escape it is to hand over my body and let him wring out pleasure. When he moves that growl to my clit, when he wraps his lips around it and *sucks*, I know I will forever be addicted to his reigning passion.

He may be the one on his knees, but I'm the one in complete submission.

My body is ready to explode, ready to fall headfirst over the precipice, when Dommik abruptly pulls away and stands up.

A tortured gasp escapes. "I was almost there," I seethe.

He grins, the expression made more feral by my wetness

that covers his beard. "I'm in charge, remember? So you're going to *get there* with me inside you or not at all."

He reaches down between us and takes out his cock, stroking it a few times, making my mouth water. Then he hikes up my skirts so roughly that they cinch into my waist, but I don't care. I like the bite of pain, just as I like his hold when it returns to my throat.

Because I'm floundering, fumbling, but his authority settles me. His command is a release. His mastery allows me to let go. So I gladly give up my control and gift it to him, because that's what I need, and I trust him to take it. To dominate my thoughts and feelings with his firm grip and hold me together so I don't fall to pieces.

With my thigh hiked up around his waist again, he drags his hard, hot cock against me. Coats himself as he slides his length over my throbbing clit.

"Dommik…"

"Look at me."

My eyes fly up to his and our gazes fit together. Lock into place. Like he's the only one who ever had the key.

Then, he notches his cock at my entrance and starts sliding in. Inch by inch. Feeding himself into me like he's savoring the slow drag and enjoying the way my body stretches to accommodate him.

"Breathe, Queenie."

I hadn't realized I'd stopped, but the moment he voices the command, I gulp in air. At the same exact moment, he shoves the last of himself into me so hard I jolt.

His slow pace is gone now.

He starts thrusting in and out of me, all the way to the hilt every time, and I can't help the moan that comes out as I'm kept pinned to the wall. He's searing hot. His length boiling me from the inside out, filling so much more than just my body.

"You're gushing," he rasps at my ear, unrelenting as his hips punch forward, dick spearing into me with brutal drives that make me scratch against his cloak, nails trying to pierce through. "You're fucking *melting* around me, aren't you?"

"Don't stop," I beg as I clutch him, my palms slick, my cheeks wet. Because if he does, then I'll have to think. I'll have to remember what's happening around us. "Don't stop."

"Never." He grips my ass and starts lifting me up and slamming me back down on his cock, going so deep I cry out. "I'll never be able to stop when it comes to you. You're stuck with me now."

My soul sings at his fierce possessiveness, and I sink my teeth into his neck. He growls with a flinch and fucks me harder, making me bloom with warmth all over. I lick up the border of his dark skin that patches up his neck, just to taste him, just to sip in his claim and quench my deepest thirst.

"Make me come," I tell him as my frost flakes over his shoulders, the white clumps bunching into his cloak. "Make it hard."

A crude chuckle slips out of him. "As my queen wishes."

He yanks me off him, spins me around, and shoves my front against the wall. With my chest scraping against the rough bricks, my hands braced against it, he exposes my ass. I barely take a breath before he grips my hips and thrusts back in from behind.

I grunt from the wicked impact, his length hitting me at an angle that has my eyes rolling to the back of my head. "Gods…"

He wraps one hand around my throat and tips up my head. "*I'm* your god."

His hand drops and he pinches my clit so hard I jerk, though I'm impaled on his dick with nowhere to go. The roughness, the wildness, the way he takes me like he's utterly possessed with the need to have me…it makes me clench harder, makes me keen with the most wanton desire I've ever felt in my life.

With deft fingers, he thrums my clit, and he starts thrusting harder, keeping that perfect pace, hitting into me with merciless impact.

"Get your pleasure, Malina," he says into my ear. "Take it, and remember, we're *alive* because that's the way I want it."

He slams into me so hard my cheek scrapes against the wall, and I come apart. I come *alive*.

Like a jolt of pure lightning striking a lake and dispersing across the entire surface, it blinds me with its force. The moan of release that escapes me is guttural, the intensity of the orgasm all-consuming, full of more pleasure than I have ever felt in my entire life.

He buries himself to the hilt and comes inside me until his searing-hot spend drips down the inside of my thighs and the last of the jolts have faded, leaving me feeling raw and sparkling.

We slump together, both of our breaths labored, and slowly, reality starts to ripple in. I look at him over my shoulder and find that he's already looking at me.

"You're mine," he says gently, and all I can do is nod around the wad that's lodged in my throat.

Tenderly, he pulls out of me, then uses the ends of his cloak to wipe the mess between my legs. I turn around and right my dress, cocking a brow when he does nothing to clean off his cloak.

He flashes me a crooked grin. "Next time, I'll rub it over your skin and leave it there."

I sniff. "You absolutely will do no such thing."

He leans forward and gives me a quick, biting kiss before pulling away. "When it comes to fucking, I'm in charge, and I'll do all sorts of debased things to your body, but you'll enjoy every single one."

A shiver goes down my back, and as we look at each other, we take these last seconds to be in this moment. Just here, in this bubble, where this is all that exists.

Until I take a breath and look down the mouth of the alley, our circumstances darkening my eyes and tensing my shoulders.

As soon as reality comes back to me on the inside, it seems to return on the outside too. Somewhere far off, lightning crackles with a horrific *boom*. I can hear screams rend the air.

My hands tremble.

"The fae breached the city," I whisper, needing to say it aloud.

He tips his head. "Yes."

Guilt rushes in. "We shouldn't have done this right now."

But he shakes his head and brushes his hand over my bottom lip, dusting away the frost that's gathered. "Yes, we should've. Because if we die, we die alive."

I swallow hard, wishing I could block out the distant screams. Wishing he could control this too.

"I…I don't know what to do."

I look down at my peeling, blistered hands. The gashes look angry, scabbed in blue and white. I hear the sound of another boom, while more lightning flashes from the sky in that aberrant hue. Who knows what other magic the fae are capable of? Who knows how much more magic I can give?

"The little girl?" I ask, looking back up at him.

"I got her home."

I wish that meant she was safe, but it doesn't.

"Alright," I say, hands dropping back down to my sides as I take a steadying breath. "I have to try and block them some more. Slow them down. I need you to take me back to the shanties."

"Malina…"

"Just do it. Please."

He sucks a breath between his teeth but reaches out and grips my hand, leaping us away. Leaping us closer.

One second, we're engulfed in his shadows. Another, we're engulfed by screams.

In *mayhem*.

In the middle of the shanties, with its crooked homes stretching above us, the street is flooded with people running away. I have a split second to get my bearings before lightning crashes into the building just to our left, and the whole thing bursts into purple flame. Stone and wood explode out of it and start toppling down toward the crowd.

I don't think, I just react.

Tossing my hands up, ice flings forward, enveloping the stones, freezing them in place on their descent. The people below who would have been crushed drop their cowering arms and look up in awe before everyone's attention turns toward me.

"Get to Pillar Row!" I yell.

They start running, hopefully following my directions, dragging fallen loved ones as they hurry down the filthy street.

Dommik and I run in the opposite direction, going against the flow, toward the danger while people stream past us. At the end of the street, a regiment of fae turn the corner and spot us, raising their bow and arrows.

I shove my magic forward and it comes out like a battering ram, and the solid mallet slams into them. It makes them go flying back from the crushing impact before shattering over them in a rain of sharp shards. Pride fuses to me, confidence flaring.

Dommik leaps to the ones still remaining, moving in a blur of shadows. Mostly invisible, he attacks one after another, leaving a trail of blood and bodies in his wake.

When I see more fae come running from the same corner, I slam up a wall, its sudden existence slicing one of them straight down the middle before settling into place. Blood drips down the barrier, the dead fae pinned in place, as Dommik leaps to the last fae on our side and slices his throat.

The group of fae behind the wall start slashing into it with their blades, but the street is blessedly empty. I turn and start to run back the way we came.

We need to follow my fleeing people, need to defend their way.

"Dommik!" I call over my shoulder. "We need to catch u—"

I slam into someone.

Jolting backwards, I whip my head around just in time to see a massive fae standing over me. Sharp canines gleam with his grin, and his blond hair is clotted with blood. He raises his fist just as I hear Dommik shout my name, and then pain explodes through my skull a second before shadows engulf me. I drop into unconsciousness, or maybe death, but I realize Dommik was right.

I don't want to die.

But if I do, better to die fighting.

Better to die *alive*.

CHAPTER 43

AUREN

Lord Cull's manor sits before us like a gray sun cresting the horizon.

It's three stories tall, made of smooth stone and jutting windows with metal trim. The drive is black gravel and crunches beneath our boots as we pass the pond, its corners perfectly precise and sharp. There are no ripples from swimming fish, no lily pads that float on top. The water is still and dark, just like the house itself.

It looks a bit eerie, though not as eerie as it is seeing my hands swing at my sides in a drab gray color that looks so completely foreign. My hair too, the black strands nothing like my golden locks. The glamour magic Emonie used on me is strange.

Lerana steers us away from the front of the manor, our feet taking us over the cut grass and past the hedges until we walk along the side of the building, passing a row of trees.

"Like Wick said, Lord Cull isn't here, which works to

our benefit, because we wouldn't be able to risk this mission otherwise," Lerana says, speaking quietly while Emonie and I walk on either side of her.

"All I was able to hear was that there are new Oreans here. That's all I know. But Oreans in this manor don't fare well. The ones Cull has on staff all have one thing in common."

"What's that?" I ask.

She turns to me, her teal eyes gone grim. "Their tongues were cut out."

Shock and anger tighten down the curve of my back, snapping my shoulders straight.

"What an *ass*," Emonie hisses under her breath.

I suddenly wish he *were* here, just so I could gild his tongue and make it just as useless. This information spurs me on, making my focus sharpen on what's at stake.

We walk down the length of the manor, but once we reach the back, I frown at the building just behind it, because…it's a *second* manor. It's not another wing—this one is separate and seems much older.

It would be just as austere as the newer building if it weren't for all the damage. The stones are singed and scraped in some areas, the roof looks like it's caving in, and all the windows have been boarded up. Even the ground around it looks like there used to be an old drive here, but they left the grass to take over.

"Two manors?" I ask curiously.

Lerana nods and fixes a few stray hairs, tucking them back into her braid. "Yes, he built a newer one but kept the old. Don't ask me why, because I have no idea. He has his peculiarities just like every noble I've ever met."

At the back of the main, newer manor, there's an overhang with a short wall that hides a narrow back door. It's tucked halfway into the ground by a set of shallow steps.

"Servant's entrance," Lerana says as she leads us toward it. "Now, I'm going to get you working in here for the day, but once you're inside, you'll be on your own. Just keep your head down but your eyes peeled. Like Wick said, this is about gathering information *only*, got it?" she asks sharply.

"Got it," Emonie and I both murmur.

"There you are!"

I jump at the voice spilling out from the tiny window notched into the servant's door. It swings open a second later, revealing a plump fae female with red cheeks and frizzy gray hair pulled back in a bun. "You were supposed to send them at dawn!" she hisses at Lerana as we approach.

"Apologies, Velida," Lerana replies, her voice now much softer, her expression turned timid—nothing like how she was with us before. "My lord would not allow us to leave before luncheon was set. We came as quickly as we could."

The fae takes the lie easily. "Nothing for it now," she says before letting out a blustery sigh, onyx eyes skimming over Emonie and me. "These are your two best workers? They look a bit green."

"They'll serve you very well today, I assure you."

"Fine," she says, waving us forward. "Don't have time to waste. Lord Cull is on his way back."

Lerana goes utterly still. Emonie has stiffened too. My eyes dart around, like I expect him to suddenly pop up in front of me.

"Oh…" Lerana recovers. "Already? I thought he wasn't due to return for a few more days?"

She shrugs and swipes a hand on the front of her apron. "We received word that he'll be here for supper. That's why we need the extra hands today. Half our other staff are…otherwise occupied."

Occupied with the new Oreans perhaps?

Wick would be out of his mind if he knew Cull was

returning, but it's too late for us to back out now. It would look too suspicious. Lerana realizes this too, because after the slightest hesitation, she steps aside. "Of course," she says with a nod. "My lord will just need them sent back for supper."

"Yes, fine," Velida says impatiently.

Lerana turns around, a grave expression tinting her gaze. "Work well," she says quietly before she starts walking away.

Emonie and I share a look.

Then we follow behind Velida as she turns and descends the steps to the servant's door. When we go through, we enter a washroom. The space is uncomfortably hot, with a massive iron stove to our left that's stuffed full of glowing coals in its belly and has pipes leading up from it to the ceiling. Steam and smoke plug the air that instantly makes me flush with heat.

Along the far wall, there's a huge sink where two fae are furiously scrubbing plates and stacking them on a rack above. Neither of them turn around as we walk through, passing another long sink to our right. Velida takes us into the adjoining room, which is a huge kitchen. It's somewhat cooler inside, though not much.

Despite its size, the room manages to feel cramped because of all the counters and stoves eating up the space. There are two cooks, one of whom doesn't bother to pay us any attention from where he's chopping through a pile of vegetables. The other glances up absently for a second and then gets back to stirring a big pot, but I notice with a jolt that she has blunted ears.

Both of them do. Cull's Orean servants.

I find myself stepping closer to them. "Hello," I greet.

They look at me in surprise, but they stay silent, their eyes quickly darting away.

"Don't speak to them. They can't speak back," Velida says, and I can't tell if that's pity in her tone or something else.

But it seems Lerana was right about their tongues.

Velida goes to a large cabinet on the wall beside the cutlery shelves and yanks it open, revealing stacks of linens inside. "Now, there's much to be done. The regular staff have been occupied with other duties, and with Lord Cull's return, it's important the estate be in perfect condition." She snatches up different linens and starts piling them into Emonie's arms. "It displeases him if anything is in disarray."

When the stack is up to Emonie's eyebrows, Velida slams the cabinet shut and bustles over to a small sink, turning on the tap to fill up a bucket. I steal a glance over my shoulder at the cooks again. I know the mission is to find out where the new Oreans are, but I wonder if these two need help as well?

My train of thought is cut off when Velida abruptly shoves a bucket full of soapy water at me. Attention jerking back, I barely manage to grip the handle in time before she lets go, and then she plunks a scrub brush into it, making water splash up into my face.

I blink through the drips, a few strands of my glamoured black hair now stuck to my forehead. Emonie laughs but manages to turn it into a cough.

Velida glares at me, as if daring me to complain. I just plaster on a water-logged smile. "Thank you."

She humphs and spins around. "Come on. I don't have all day. And *pay attention*," she snaps over her shoulder. "I won't be repeating myself to you."

Wow, okay. Velida is kind of a jerk.

Emonie covers her mouth to suppress more laughter, while I wipe the water off my face. Bright side—at least it cooled me down.

We walk through a claustrophobic corridor, up narrow stairs, and into a dining room, which we enter from the back. The door is hidden behind a thick drapery, and Velida pulls it aside as we follow her.

Inside, the floors are black marble with red smears in the stone that make it look like a bloody body was dragged across it. At the center sits the dining table, the dark gray wood filled with knots. There's a chandelier made up of what looks like giant talons. Bigger even than the ones on a timberwing's feet. They're smooth and black and hooked down toward the table, like some invisible creature ready to snatch up whoever might be seated below, while cold candles are held in its grasp.

A stray drop of water drips from my chin to the floor with an audible splat. Velida's onyx eyes flick down to it with obvious irritation. "You scrub the floors," she says to me pointedly before turning to Emonie. "You prepare the linens for dinner service. I'll be back to check on you later. Be sure that you don't screw anything up." She centers her attention on me again. "Especially you."

With that lovely send-off, she turns and walks away, leaving us alone in the otherwise empty room.

As soon as she's gone, Emonie giggles under her breath, magma eyes practically lighting up with glee.

"I don't think she likes me." I frown as I look down at the bucket, and then eye her pile versus mine. "Why do you get table linen duty and I get floor scrubbing duty?"

"It's my superior paying-attention skills and sparkling personality."

"Probably." I look around again to make sure we're alone before I lower my voice. "Those cooks were Oreans—do you think they need our help?"

"I don't know," she says, nibbling on her bottom lip. "But we'll report it to Wick and see what he thinks."

"Okay. Let's take advantage of the fact we're alone right now."

She nods. "Let's do the linens first and then start scrubbing? It'll be the perfect excuse to go through the other rooms."

"Good plan."

Together, the two of us tackle the long table. The linens include about fifty little napkin squares of all different sizes that we have to do…something with.

I just start folding them diagonally. Emonie starts making some weird flowers out of hers.

"I'm not sure Lord Cull is the type of person to appreciate flower napkins."

"Why not?" she replies, folding the fabric into swoops of quick petals.

"The talon chandelier kind of sets an anti-flower tone, don't you think?"

Her eyes flick up. "Hmm. Yeah, you're right." She blows out a breath and shakes out her flower and starts folding it into a half-star instead. "Lord Cull doesn't deserve flower napkins anyway."

Very true.

We quickly place all the napkins around the plates and then adorn the table with a deep red runner that goes down the middle. When we're finished, we hurry to scrub the floors. Emonie sneaks back into the washroom to grab an extra bucket and scrub brush, and together, we move quickly across the dining room.

When we finish, we enter a large hall, with the same bloodied marble swirling across the floor. This grand room is full of sculptures that line the walls like pillars, with more in rows throughout the middle. None of them are simple busts, either. They're all at least my height, if not taller, casting long shadows.

One is a sculpture of an entire castle, each turret and window chiseled into white stone enough to cast its own shadow. There's a dragon sculpture that looks vicious, mouth gaping with rows of razor-sharp teeth. A rabid wolf with its teeth bared. A bow and arrow pointed right at me, ready to pierce me through. A huge spotted feline, its maw bared in a snarl. A woman with blunt ears and tears streaming down her face. A shrouded demon with horns.

And fae. Sculpture after sculpture of terrorizing fae.

One of them is particularly disturbing. The male has a grotesque grimace frozen on his face, and from his back, there's another fae tearing free, dagger clutched in his hand like he used it to slash his way past the fae's spine and out through his skin.

"The lovely decorating extends to this room, I see," I mutter before glancing over at Emonie. I notice the drawn look on her face, the sweat beaded on her brow. "Hey, are you okay?"

She blinks over at me, trying to hide her strain with a smile. "Oh, yes."

"The glamour. It's draining you," I say, worry lacing my tone. If she's already strained, then how will she be able to keep it up?

"I'll be fine," she says dismissively before swiping at the sweat from her hairline. "How about we split up? I can search the rooms on that side, and you take those doorways down there? We can act like we've already washed in here while we search these other rooms."

"Emonie, if you can't hold the magic…"

"I can hold it," she promises as determination settles over her features.

"If you need to drop it, you have to tell me, okay? I don't want you draining yourself, and if my glamour falls away, it could be bad for both of us."

"I know," she says, meeting my gaze. "I promise, I've got you."

"But—"

She cuts me off. "If it becomes too much, I'll tell you."

I study her features. "Okay," I say hesitantly. "Just…don't

put yourself at risk. If we need to go, we'll go."

"I'm the seasoned Vulmi," she says with a teasing smile. "I'm supposed to take care of you, not the other way around."

I shake my head. "Friends take care of each other."

Her expression turns softer, more genuine, and she gives me a real smile. "Yeah. They do." Then she takes a breath and tucks her short hair behind her ears. "Okay, come on. The sooner we gather information, the sooner we can get out of here. And we really *do* need to leave."

"Because of your magic, or because Cull is coming back?"

"Neither. I meant just to get away from the interior decorating," she muses before giving a headless sculpture a disdainful once-over. "It's really awful."

I snort, and Emonie trots off before I can say anything else to her about her magic. So I haul my bucket to the other end of the hall, my nerves wound tighter with the need to rush so she doesn't weaken herself too much.

Going through the first doorway, I find nothing but an empty library, and really, there are more pictures of maps on the walls than actual books inside. Then I enter another room, but it has absolutely nothing useful inside—except maybe the bar full of alcohol.

When I walk back out again, I see Emonie leaving the room across from me. We both shrug, and then turn to look at the stairwell at the same time.

Time to stretch our search.

We make our way toward it, meeting at the bottom steps. The staircase is wide enough for me to lie across, with forged iron handrails in elaborate filigree.

I stare up at its length, heart beating a little faster with trepidation. I hope no one comes to question us.

We're careful not to slosh water everywhere as we ascend with quick but light steps. When we reach the landing, we glance at the corridors on either side of us.

"I'll take the left, you take the right?" I whisper, and Emonie quickly nods.

Both of us haul our heavy buckets room to room, searching for something—*anything*—that might help us figure out where the Oreans are being kept. Every time I open a door, my heart is in my throat, but I keep finding empty bedrooms.

Oddly, despite the size of this manor, I only see one other servant, and she pays me no mind whatsoever as she hurries out of one of the bedchambers with a pail full of ash and a chimney brush in hand.

I desperately want to find the Oreans, want to succeed in this mission, but even though I search every room, I come up with nothing. Frustration twists through me.

I backtrack when I'm done, meeting up with Emonie again at the landing.

She shakes her head when she sees me, disappointment evident in her expression too. "We're not going to find anything up here. Maybe we can try chatting up one of the servants? Get them to talk?"

The thought of trying to *chat up* Velida almost gives me shivers.

"I think we need to check the older manor," I tell her. It's been a niggling thought in the back of my head since I saw it. "Think about it. Cull seems *very* particular. This whole manor is spotless. Why would someone like him keep that old crumbling manor? There's something off about it."

Her eyes widen slightly. "You're right."

"How's your magic?"

"Fine. Honestly," she tells me. "I can hold it for at least another hour. Probably two. I don't want to give up yet."

Her gaze reflects a persistence that I also feel.

"Okay." I pivot toward the stairs. "We'll need to get

outside. Then we can hurry and—"

"What are you two doing up there?"

I nearly jump out of my skin at Velida's voice that cracks across the main hall below. Her expression is lined with irritation as she looks up at us through the designs in the iron railing, her fists poised on her hips.

"Shit," I mutter under my breath before Emonie and I hurry back downstairs.

"You're supposed to clean the dining room, not be up on the second floor!" Velida hisses at us.

"Apologies," Emonie says breathlessly as we stop in front of her.

I barely manage not to spill water over myself in our hurry. "We finished the dining room and the hall. We just went upstairs to see if any of the rooms up there needed scrubbing," I tell her.

"I didn't tell you to do that," she snaps before eyeing the floor, as if she's hoping to find a speck of dirt so she can prove that we lied. When she finds none, she says to Emonie, "You'll come back with me. We have curtains that need dusting." Then her gaze pounces on me. "And *you*. You'll go back to the washroom. There's a load of chamber pots that need washing."

A gurgle of horror gets strangled in my throat, but I bob my head. "Of course."

She yanks the bucket out of Emonie's hand and pushes it toward me and then whisks her out of the room. Emonie sends me an apologetic look over her shoulder before she disappears from view.

With a sigh, I make my way back to the washroom, my steps slow so I don't spill water all over the floors, my arms shaking from the weight. As I pass through the kitchen, I pause when I see one of the Orean cooks at the stove.

I look around to ensure the coast is clear before

venturing over. "Hi there," I say with a smile.

She's wearing a lace cap on her head, keeping her hair out of the way, and she has pale eyebrows and freckles over the bridge of her nose. She stops mid-cut, knife caught in a slab of meat as she looks at me with wariness.

I hesitate, debating what to say.

"Have you worked here long?"

She nods slowly.

"I couldn't help but notice that you're Orean."

The woman goes still, and the knife in her hand clatters against the countertop as she lets go and starts to back away.

I take a step forward, horrified that my simple comment instigated such terror in her. "No, it's okay! I'm sorry, I wasn't trying to—"

She darts out of the room before I can finish my sentence. Buckets in hand, I try to hurry as fast as I can and follow her, but when I get to the washroom where the other two fae workers are still elbow-deep in soap suds, the Orean isn't there.

Dammit.

I hope she didn't run off to Velida or someone else, but I'm even more worried at how fearful she was at just my acknowledgement of her being Orean.

No wonder Wick wanted to take this mission.

I glance around through the steam and the smoke glugging up the air. This room feels even hotter than before. I set the buckets down and my hands scream in relief, while little angry marks are left behind on my cramped fingers. The fae look over at me, both of them pausing their frenzied scrubbing.

I clear my throat, forcing my tone to stay casual. "Did you happen to see one of the other servants come through here?"

They look at me blankly, letting a pause drag out, and

then the one nearest me says, "No."

That's it. Just *no*. Then she turns around and gets back to scrubbing.

Okay, so, not the most helpful.

The other one continues to stare at me, and she has the brightest blue eyes I've ever seen. She cocks a brow when I continue to stand here.

"Velida told me to stack the chamber pots for you," she says, motioning behind me.

I look over my shoulder and...yep. There is indeed a tower of chamber pots.

I can't help but wrinkle my nose. "I thought this manor had plumbing."

"*This* manor does," she says pointedly.

She continues to watch me. Brow arched.

I definitely won't be able to follow the Orean cook now.

"Better get to work." She tosses her black braid behind her before smirking slightly and then gets back to her dishes. "And don't miss any spots."

The other fae laughs beneath her breath.

Rude.

I quickly cross off Emonie's idea of "chatting with the other servants", because clearly, that's not an option with these two.

What *is* an option, however...

I look at the chamber pots again.

She said *this* manor has plumbing. The old one does not or, at least, not anymore—which means that's where these pots came from. Because there's people there who have to use them.

I know damn well Lord Cull isn't squatting over a pot to do his business.

The new Oreans Lord Cull is keeping here *are* in the other manor. I'm sure of it. And the perfect excuse for me to get there just landed in my lap. Not literally, thank Divine, but still.

I take in a deep breath as I walk over to the separate basin and stare down at the teetering pile and at the pair of leather washing gloves left draped over the edge of the sink. The stench wafts up before I have time to plug my nose, and I can see definite…residue left behind.

"Well, shit," I mutter.

Behind me, the two fae laugh again at my expense. But I just tuck my glamoured hair back, yank on the gloves, and get to work.

This isn't exactly how I envisioned my first Vulmin mission would go, but it could be worse. If this stack of chamber pots is all that's between me and finding the Oreans, then I'm going to polish these things to a fucking shine.

What was it Lu told me?

Own your shit.

I guess this is one way to do it.

CHAPTER 44

AUREN

My the time I finish, I'm dripping sweat from the hot room, my fingers feel like they might be permanently shaped like claws after how tightly I was clenching the rag, and I don't know if I'll ever get the stench out of my nose...but the entire stack of chamber pots is clean.

I'm alone, so I take advantage of it and sneak out to see if I can find Emonie. But when I peer into the formal dining room, I find her on a step stool, beating the curtains with a dusting paddle while Velida lords over her.

I don't dare interrupt.

I spin on my heels and quickly retreat. I'll have to go into the old manor alone, but at least I know Velida is occupied for the time being.

In the washroom, I nab a tablecloth from the linen closet and then pile all the clean chamber pots inside of it. I quickly gather up the heap and head outside with my makeshift sack.

As soon as I climb up the shallow steps and onto the grass, I veer to the left toward the old manor. I walk alongside the hedgerows, keeping my eyes peeled while the metal pots clink together with my every step.

I can't help but stare at the old house as I walk its length, gaze hooking onto the cracks in the gray stone, the damage making the peaks of the roof look like a corrugated knife hacked up through the shingles.

Maybe there was a fire and the manor has been falling further into disrepair ever since, but just looking at it makes me hesitant. I have to shrug away the shivers that want to roll down my back, and ignore the wedge in my veins that feels like an invisible stopper pinching my blood flow.

When I get to the front door, I look over my shoulder, but the grounds are empty. The only thing looming over me is the old manor itself, boarded up windows glaring with suspicion. Up close, the singe marks in the wall look more like gouges threatening to tear the place in half.

I move my sack, clasping the corners of the cloth in one hand, and my free hand darts out to grip the knob, but of course, it's locked. Looking around again, I debate what to do, when I hear murmuring from the other side of the door. I freeze, wondering if I should dart away, but with a glance down at my bundled heap, I raise my fist and knock instead.

The murmured voices stop, and my heart pounds for one beat, two, three—

There's a loud *snick* from the lock before the door swings open, revealing two red-and-black-clad guards. At least, I think they're guards, based on the swords strapped to their belts and their generally irritated dispositions.

The one who opened the door has hair with gray and white streaks, and he glares down at me, taking in my apron and frazzled hair. "What?" he growls.

I drop into a curtsy, because I figure that's probably what

servants are supposed to do here. It makes the bundle in my hands clank loudly. "I'm here to deliver these. I was told to come in this way."

The other guard behind him has an impressively long braid of red hair. He narrows his eyes on me. "You're new."

I do my best to keep my expression innocent, keep my heartbeat calm. "I was sent to help for the day. Velida has been giving me instructions."

His eyes drop to my sack. "Give it here," he says, jutting out his hand as he comes forward.

My fingers clutch the bundle so hard my knuckles go white. "Oh, I should deliver it myself, as I was told."

Irritation crosses his face. "This manor is restricted. I'll take it."

I feign indifference and start to pass it over to him. "Of course."

"What is it?" the other one asks.

I smile blandly. "Chamber pots."

Braid snatches back his hand so fast I'm surprised his elbow doesn't crack. "I'm not touching that shit." He looks to his companion.

The second guard shakes his head. "Don't look at me. It's nearly shift change."

They scowl at each other for a moment until Braid opens the door wider and jerks his head to the side. "Take it in," he barks at me.

Relief whooshes through me, but I keep my face demure as I give him a nod. "Whatever you think is best."

As soon as I step inside, he shuts the door behind me and points. "Straight ahead. Be quick about it."

Just for good measure, I curtsy again. "Yes, sir."

I hurry forward, feeling their eyes on my back as I go, making apprehension prick down my tense muscles. I'm in some sort of paneled antechamber, dim from the blocked windows, and the darker lighting deepens my unease.

Forcing my steps to stay unhurried, I head straight like the guard directed, the metal pots shifting with my every step. When I get through the doorway and enter a stubby hallway, finally out of view from the guards, I release a tense breath.

I got inside. Now, I just need to find these Oreans.

The door to my right is boarded up, so I head for the one to the left. As I get closer, my eyes drift to the black handle that swoops up like a sinister grin. For some reason, that pinched feeling in my veins expands and starts pumping furiously instead.

"It's just a creepy entrance," I murmur to myself, but I really wish Emonie was with me so she could play off the nefarious feeling with a joke about the decor.

Gripping the tablecloth's corners in one hand, I force myself to turn the knob and walk inside. As soon as I'm through, the door shuts automatically behind me, and my heart leaps up to my throat when it clicks shut.

I'm left in a dark and narrow space, coming face-to-face with an ominous wall.

It's not original to the house, that much is obvious by the way it affixes awkwardly to the ceiling and the ill-fitting connection to the adjoining walls. It's made of thick stone bricks that should be on the exterior rather than inside here. And as if that weren't strange enough, there's a crisscross of iron strips that stretch across the entire thing, reminding me of the iron cages often bolted over graves to keep robbers at bay.

As I stare at it, my palms go slick with sweat. My heart keeps snagging in my chest, getting caught in the tangle of adrenaline and trepidation, but even so, something draws me forward.

I eat up the short distance until I stand directly in front of it. Goose bumps scatter down my arms, and my ears begin to ring, but when I reach up to let my finger graze over a brick,

I realize my hands aren't sweaty after all. It's gold-touch that's come up to the surface of my skin to slick my palms.

I leave a gold streak against the stone like dripping wax, but it's nearly overrun with rotted lines. They start stretching and rooting around through the liquid in erratic spasms, and my veins thump in response.

Something is wrong here. Strange.

My brow furrows when I see the gilt rot crawl into the crevices of the brick, digging through the clefts, searching and sifting like it's trying to go right through the wall to reach the other side.

I quickly call the magic back to me, but it's slow to react. It seems to grudgingly lift away from the stone in strings before wrapping around my wrist in thin, rigid bracelets. I have to temper the liquid still slicking my palms too, but the rot writhes over them, stretching up off my fingertips like stems reaching for the sun.

Balling my hands into fists, I squeeze tight, my arms shaking with the effort.

The magic doesn't want to go.

It wants to burst out, to stretch back to the wall and delve through the bricks. I'm able to shove it back only because I've practiced so much with it, learned how to deny its seductive call.

But it isn't easy.

I'm not sure I want to know what's on the other side of that wall.

I just want to find the Oreans and get the hell out of here, then tell Wick everything once I get back out.

My gaze lingers for another moment before I turn away.

To my left, I find a staircase rising up, and I hurry over to it. I ascend the carpeted steps with near-silent feet, noticing the worn tread that's turned the runner a muddied gray.

At the top of the stairs, I come to a corridor. The lighting is dusty, the partially boarded windows making everything take on a drab hue that sticks to the walls. There are at least half a dozen doors in front of me, and the corridor veers off into another part of the house at the end.

It's going to take me a very long time to search this whole place by myself, and time is breathing down my neck. Velida is going to be looking for me soon if she isn't already, Emonie needs to be able to drop my glamour, and Lord Cull is going to arrive tonight for dinner.

I have to hurry.

Every room I check is an empty bedroom, just like my search in the other manor. Except here, they're stagnant and dusty from disuse. Left abandoned, some of them stripped of their mattresses or other furniture. I can't help but notice how quiet it is, the tense silence coiling my nerves even tighter.

But the further away I get from the wall, the more my power calms—which makes me even *more* anxious, *more* confused.

I'm just about to turn another door handle when I hear footsteps coming from the corner up ahead. I don't even have time to consider what to do before a servant appears. When she notices me, she falters slightly, her arms laden with a heavy tray.

"Hello," I greet with a smile before I heft up my sack. "I have to deliver these, but I'm not sure where to go. Is it that way?" I ask, motioning toward the corridor she just came from.

Dark eyes flick down to my haul before she nods. Then she quickly passes me by, stealing a look over her shoulder and looking just as twitchy as I feel before she disappears down the stairs.

That's comforting.

Steeling myself, I retrace her steps, cutting to the right at the intersecting corridor. Instead of more doorways, this space opens up to a parlor. What once were stately windows are now boarded-up frames. The carpet is ornate with black and gray swirls, and there's a collection of sofas and chairs around a cold fireplace.

One of these chairs is occupied by a guard. He's got his legs propped up on the footrest, and he's jabbing at his teeth with a wooden pick, looking thoroughly bored. He spots me instantly and huffs out a breath. "Didn't you just leave?"

I pause with a blink. "That was a different servant, sir."

Another huff. "What do you want?"

I lift the sack, letting it clang. "Chamber pots. I was told to deliver them…unless you'd rather?"

His lip curls in a disgusted sneer. "Nice try. I'm not a fuckin' servant. You can do it yourself."

Triumph beats through my chest, though I dip my head meekly. "Of course."

These chamber pots are really effective.

With yet another huff expelling out of him, he slaps his feet to the floor and then heaves himself out of the chair. I follow behind him as he walks across the parlor and through a private antechamber. We stop just in front of a door, and he tugs at a key that's caught on a loop at his belt. As soon as he gets it free, he shoves it into the lock, making anticipation squeeze around me.

Please, please be here…

He shoves open the door. "Make it quick."

I barely remember to nod at him before I plunge into the dark space. As soon as I'm through, he slams the door shut behind me and turns the key.

That would have doused me with panic at one time, but not anymore. Because now, I have power and control. Now, I'm not caged or trapped.

But…someone else is.

Dozens of someones.

And every single one of them has blunt ears.

I found the Oreans.

CHAPTER 45

AUREN

This must've been a grand bedroom at one time. Maybe it was even where Lord Cull himself slept. I'm guessing the large size is why they're keeping the Oreans here—they can fit them all behind one locked door.

Now I know why the mattresses were taken from some of the other bedrooms. The original furnishings in here seem to have been gutted in order to fit the mattresses along the floor from wall to wall. There are no dressers, no chairs or vanities. Just the pilfered mattresses, clumps of blankets, and empty food trays.

While the room is big, it's heavily damaged. To my right, there's a crack in the plaster that reaches all the way to the ceiling, gathering in the corner like a cobweb. Small bits that broke off from the wall lie forgotten on the floor, like loose coins fallen from pockets.

There's hardly any light in here, save for the weak sunshine trying to come in from the lone window that's been buried behind wooden boards. Yet despite the dimness, I can see the curled bodies of the Oreans. Most of them are sleeping, mashed up together, heads tucked down and ears on display.

My blood pumps through my body like a drum.

The smell hits me then, so much worse than just stale air. The odor of dozens of bodies cramped into one space and being forced to do their business with almost no privacy. There's a bathroom to the right, but it's been partially caved in, the wall crumbled down and beams blocking the doorway.

I venture in further, feeling like needles are prickling the back of my neck. My eyes dart around the room, and I try to count all the people I see, but there are dozens of them. Seven huddled on one mattress, eight tucked on another, and there's three more mattresses with even more lumps of bodies on them. I count ten people leaning against the walls and more scattered along the wood floor with balled-up blankets. There's at least forty—no, fifty.

My gaze swings to the person nearest me.

I gently set down the heap of chamber pots, and they clack noisily against the floor, though only a few people stir. I quickly walk over to the man propped in the corner, who's staring at the sliver of window showing through the boards. He has thin gray hair and loose skin hanging from jaw to neck like a rooster's wattle, but his body is buried beneath thick furs, like he's used to living in the cold.

I kneel down in front of him, gaze smoothing over his blunt ears.

"Are you okay?" I ask quietly, not wanting to startle him.

When he doesn't look away from the window, I gently reach out and shake his arm.

The man's head abruptly flops against his shoulder, and then the rest of his body pitches sideways. I jerk backwards as he lands in a heap on the floor, shock coursing through me like a rushing river that roars through my ears and floods my veins.

I stare at him in horror. His eyes are still staring at that window. Neck bent. Body limp. Eyes unblinking.

Dead.

I scramble back, my gaze flying around the room, wondering—but no. I see someone else moving. Hear another person cough. They're not all dead. But…

Maybe they're not all alive, either.

Kneeling down once again, I gently check the man over. There are no marks on him that I can see. No wounds, no obvious reason for his death.

What the hell happened to him?

I straighten up, determined to check everyone else. I start hurrying over to where the people sleep, but as I get closer, I see a man's head turn, eyes locking on to me, and I get a strange feeling. Something about him seems odd.

"It's alright," I tell him. "I'm—"

A loud bang against the door makes me jump. "Let's go!" the guard outside barks.

Dammit!

My gaze swings back to the Orean, to his greasy hair and fur-lined clothes. "I'm so sorry," I say in a rush. "I'm going to try and help get you all out of here. Can you tell me when Cull brought you here? Is he going to force you to be his servants? How many—"

"Wench! Don't make me come in there!" the guard shouts.

I grind my teeth in frustration, but I know I have to go.

I notice that several more of the Oreans have sat up now and are looking at me. "We'll get you out of here," I tell them quietly before I force myself to turn and hurry back. I can't delay any longer or risk being caught.

When I get to the door, I rap my knuckles on the wood,

and the guard instantly swings it open. As soon as I file out, he slams it shut behind me, key turning in place.

"Took you long enough," he says through his scowl. "You having a good look at the traitors?"

My brow dips into a frown before I catch myself. "Traitors?"

"Haven't you heard?" he asks around the pick dangling against his sharp canine. "They left. Now, Lord Cull's got them back. He's gonna break them." His lips pull into a delighted sneer as he sucks on his sliver of wood.

A flash of a memory explodes behind my eyes. Of a Red Raid pirate captain standing in the snow, with cruelty in his gaze and threats on his tongue.

I'm going to use her. Break her.

Hot anger burns down my spine—a tingle that seems to strike against the base of my ribbons.

"Hope I can watch," the guard snickers as he munches on his stick. "I do love when Oreans are reminded that they're inferior to our species."

I don't trust myself to talk—to keep my false subservient tone. So I force myself to dip into a curtsy instead. When I turn to walk away, I skim my hand against his sleeve and leave the disgusting fae behind to delight in his cruelty.

But I can delight in cruelty too.

I'll delight in the little drop of my magic that's now slithering its way up the threads of his shirt. As I walk across the parlor, it dribbles off his collar and starts prowling over his skin, no bigger than a bead of sweat. The thinnest, smallest drip to track up his jaw, slink over his toothpick, and then slip into his mouth.

I glance over my shoulder just as he jabs a stumpy finger against his tongue like he's trying to wipe away the fetid metal he suddenly tastes. But the droplet is already sliding down his throat, already sinking down into his gut. There, the gilt rot will slowly spread over time, eating away the lining with heavy roots that twist and dig.

Just before I turn the corner, his hand jerks down to his stomach, probably feeling the first pinch there, and then, I'm out of sight.

Out of mind.

But my magic won't be out of his body anytime soon.

It'll be slow.

Painful.

Instead of watching someone else break, he can watch his own body spoil from the inside out.

Maybe I should feel regret for that. But I don't. The gold-touch, the rot, the fae *and* Orean heritage that I have—it makes me feel gruesome satisfaction.

Yet that satisfaction is cut short when I suddenly hear rushing footsteps. A lot of footsteps—and heading in this direction. I quickly dart down the corridor and jerk open the first bedroom door I get to and slip inside.

I leave the door cracked, gaze peeking out just in time to see more guards stomping their way down the corridor. "Hurry up," one of them barks.

Four of them pass, heading down the same way I just came. I hold my breath to listen to the muffled voices, but when I can't pick up on their words, I creep out of the bedroom and hurry back to the corner wall and cock my head.

I hear the tail end of the rotten gut guard's words. "Supposed to stay here?"

Someone else answers, his voice clearer. "Yeah. We don't know what he'll want to do with them, so stay at your post for now."

"When's he coming?"

"Just arrived at the other house. Wants them gathered up here."

My heart leaps into my throat.

He's back. Lord Cull is already *here*—

I hear movement, so I quickly dart back into the bedroom, peering through the sliver of the closed door. My pulse pounds hard, a racket that clangs against my hollow bones. I wait seconds.

Minutes.

It sucks the life out of me to have to stay frozen, waiting, when everything in me screams to hurry. To run.

Then, sound picks back up, drowning out my own anxious thrumming, and I go still when I see two of the guards round the corner and head away from me.

Behind them is a stream of hunching, shuffling Oreans being led down the corridor two-by-two.

Fuck.

The guard's voice repeats in my head. *He's going to break them.*

I need to get them out. I need to help them before it's too late.

Belatedly, I wish I'd thought to ask what kind of magic Cull has, so at least I could have the upper hand with that knowledge. But maybe I can just deal with the guards. Maybe I can get the Oreans out before Cull comes into this manor.

Steeling myself, my every muscle goes taut with anticipation as I wait to spring.

I see the last two guards take up the rear of the group, and one of them shoves at an Orean's back. "Hurry up!"

The other guard laughs as the person stumbles.

With lips pressed tight, I dart out from the room and rush up behind them, and then I call to my magic.

It's more than ready to answer.

I reach up, hands splayed behind both of their heads, and ropes of veined gold whip out from my palms and hook around their necks like nooses. The solidifying metal cinches them so tight that the only noises they're able to make are cut-off gasps.

The ropes jerk them back, stealing their voices, their air.

One of them falls to his knees, the worn carpet muffling his fall as he grapples at the rope, though it's already hardening, tightening, his gaze flying around wildly.

My power sings.

The second one topples toward the wall, ready to smack into it, but that'll be far too loud, and I don't want to alert the others.

Quick as a blink, I jerk his noose backwards, making the dangled end behind him bend to catch him. His body doesn't make a sound as the gilded rope slowly lowers him to the floor.

I stand over both guards, panic blotting their eyes, wheezes coming from their constricted throats as their faces turn purple.

Ahead of us, the group still files forward, no one the wiser.

Quietly, I reach out and open the nearest bedroom door. Then, I send another stream pouring from my hands to wrap around the strangled guards' ankles and drag them into the room. I shut the door just as quickly, leaving them to writhe.

Two down.

The Oreans at the end of the line don't even realize there's no one herding their backs anymore. They're also much farther ahead, so I race to catch up without stomping down the corridor.

But before I can reach them, the group veers. Instead of continuing straight down the main stairwell, they're going through a panel in the wall I hadn't noticed before.

A hidden door.

Everyone is heading through it and down the cramped stairs that must've served as a servant's passage at one time.

I hesitate, and then make a split-second decision.

Yanking off my apron, I toss it into the corridor and then follow the Oreans into the enclosed stairwell that spirals down.

When I catch up to the back of the group, I slow my steps and quickly muss my hair to cover my glamoured pointed ears and make it look like I'm as bedraggled as the others.

But with every step I take, I feel that fast thud in my veins return, feel my heart get bloody and beaten as it trills behind the rungs of my chest. High-pitched ringing starts to toll within my skull.

What is happening?

When I reach the bottom and into a tight corridor, I glance down at my slick palms. Rot has overrun my gold almost completely. The usually thin veins are more like a mass of tree roots. It's lifting up and off my palm, stretching, *reaching—*

"Where are the others?"

I jump, head slashing up, and barely stop myself in time before running into the Oreans in front of me. Everyone's halted in the cramped corridor, and the two guards at the front are glaring at me, their gazes tossing over my shoulder, obviously looking for the other two missing guards. I make a show of cowering, chin tucked against my chest. The guards share a look, but then they yank open the door and start shoving the Oreans through.

I nearly stumble as I walk, hands shaking as I contain the writhing rot between my fingers. My pulse races so fast I worry my blood will beat its way right out of my veins and spill onto the floor.

As soon as I'm inside the room, the guard slams the door shut behind me and then shoves me against the wall, but I barely feel it. Because power is swelling beneath my palms, roots lifting, wrapping around my fingers like rings. My whole body feels charged.

The rot is flexing, and there's an excited urgency to it that goes all the way down to my chest. It hisses and prods, like it wants to rip through my body.

When I glance to my right, I see that wall—that iron-clad stone wall.

Except this time, I'm on the other side.

I look around at the grand entry hall, and panic spreads its wings and takes flight, leaving me to be whipped in its back current. Because a magnetism of *wrongness* pounds through me, even as a *rightness* calls me forward.

wrong, right

wrong, right

wrong, right

wrong, right...

The wallpaper is red like blood. Not as bright as the marble floor in the new manor, but a deep, dark red, like a murderous secret done in the dark. But what hooks my attention is the crack in the floor that divides the room, and a broken roof that seems to snarl up at the sky.

Chunks of walls have formed boulders on the floor, and the boarded-up windows are shattered, their glass still littering the stained marble. But...no. It's not stained. It's...

My eyes trace the path, back to the large crack in the floor that spreads and then gapes wide open.

There's a buzzing, a thundering. Or maybe it's only in my ears. Shadows dot my tunneled vision, but I see...*I see...*

A commotion has my eyes jerking upward. To watch someone stalk out from the other side of the room.

And then all the breath steals from my lungs. Ripped out of me like hands clutching my hair and tearing it from my scalp.

My hand flies to my mouth, rot cloying against me as my eyes refuse to blink.

"*Slade...*"

The whisper splits from my lips.

He walks past a pillar, the open doorway spilling in grayed light behind him, making me squint. He's dressed in all black, save for a red wrap of fabric tucked into his collar like blood spilling from a slit throat.

I start to go forward, to get to him, my mouth opening to call his name, because he's here. He's *here*, and he found me somehow and he can help me and—

And.

One heartbeat, I flew.

The next, I plummet.

Or maybe it's the world that crashes around me. Because when he comes into better view, so does everything else.

His stature was similar, but…

He has a slightly different stride. Differences in his muscular frame. His black hair is trimmed so short it's not even half an inch past his scalp, and his beard is thick. The look of threat on his face is familiar though…except the fact that he only has one eye.

The other socket is covered. Leather strap hooked from his forehead to pointed ear, an onyx stone set over the spot where his eye should be. Lines in his pale face disappear beneath the eyepatch, the skin around it a dull gray color.

Not Slade, not Slade, not Slade…

The relief I felt turns into horrible, churning anguish.

Because everything clicks into place with shattering, dizzying, terrifying awareness.

The room. The broken floor. The rumbling noise. The wrongness of it all, and…

"Lord Cull," a guard greets.

The other Oreans are lined up against the tattered wall beside me, the guards at attention, more of them filing in from the opposite end of the room.

Something screams inside of me as all the shattered

pieces of realization swirl like a cyclone.

Can't breathe. Can't blink.

My gaze follows him across the cracked floor that cinches together under his steps, closing the gap without a thought. He walks over it, boots echoing in the broken room that seems to meld around his presence.

But there's one spot that doesn't close.

Doesn't meld.

The widest part of the cracked floor. The part where shadows seem to hover over it.

My eyes snap back to him, but he's staring at one Orean in particular, and when I follow his gaze, my knees threaten to buckle.

There, standing with the rest of the bedraggled Oreans, is a woman.

She has black hair tied loose and crooked over her shoulder. Pale skin. Scared, green eyes. Her petite figure trembles against the wall she cowers against.

Recognition slams through me like a hammer to my gut.

No.

No.

My eyes fly to the other Oreans, all of them dressed in their furs and heavy cloaks. Shaking beneath their wintry clothes.

I want to heave. To scream.

They're all here. *All* of them.

Great Divine...

Every single villager that should be tucked away in Drollard, hidden in their frozen village. They're *here*, in Annwyn.

And that crack in the floor, that rumbling that gurgles out of it, the shadows that hover overhead...

It's the rip.

The rip in the world that tore through the air when Slade

and his father's magic collided. The rip they all got sucked into.

The group we've come to rescue are the villagers from Orea. And the woman that Lord Cull is stalking toward?

Slade's mother.

Because…I'm not just at a random nobleman's house.

And these aren't random Oreans I've come to help save.

My attention locks on to the person stalking toward Elore, and bile rises into my throat.

I thought he was Slade.

But he's not.

Not at all.

Lord Cull is Slade's *father*.

CHAPTER 46

SLADE

The bright morning sun filters in from the window, catching fragments of dust in its glare. I'm behind my desk, while Isalee and Warken are in the middle of the office, sitting across from each other in wingback chairs, talking finances. I toss down a report about the collapsed mine and rub at my aching chest.

It hurts like a son of a bitch.

Even through my shirt, I can feel the raised veins of rot protruding, the swollen shell of my blackened heart.

Probably not fucking good.

When I glance up, I notice Isalee staring at me, so I quickly drop my hand. "I'm fine," I assure her before she can fuss, but there's a frown pulled between her brows that doesn't go away.

There's a frown on my face that doesn't go away either.

Even with all the sleep I was able to get, I couldn't open

a rip. I fucking tried. For hours, despite Ryatt's protests. And now, the spot at the center of my heart that's a sickly brown color has started to spread. It's peeling back in deadened flakes.

I can't heal that, Your Majesty.

A knock at the door yanks me from my thoughts. "Enter."

In strides King Thold. His green viper is draped around the back of his neck, tail hanging down his chest like a scarf. He's not wearing his crown today, but he doesn't have to. His very demeanor screams authority. His gaze sweeps around the room, while two of his guards stand at his back.

"You've been a difficult man to find," he tells me.

"King Thold, how are you today?" Warken greets politely as he and Isalee get to their feet.

"It's been three days, Ravinger," he says, ignoring Warken as he pins me with his stare. "How much longer are you going to make me wait for your answer?"

From the corner of my eye, I see Isalee smirk as her prediction about making Thold wait comes to fruition. Smart woman.

I get to my feet and come around the desk. "We were just finishing our discussion."

He looks between the three of us with impatience. "And?"

"We have decided to accept the treaty of our realliance," I tell him, and I watch relief wash over his face. "But…we have terms."

His snake flicks out its tongue. "What terms?" he grits out.

"The oil in exchange for your food imports," Warken interjects. "It is no longer part of the deal."

Anger fills Thold's eyes. "That is unacceptable. It was part of the agreement."

"And now it's not," I say with a shrug.

His jaw clenches. "I want the oil at the new cost I was quoted by Sir Judd."

"You're not getting it."

I don't tell him it's because the mine collapsed and we *can't* get him the oil.

"This is madness, Ravinger," he says with a jerk of his head. "Your kingdom *needs* my food."

"Yes, and so does your kingdom," I counter. "Consider this my generosity. I am leaving you and yours undisturbed, despite you breaking our previous treaties as well as your participation in the Conflux. I will remind you that I have retaliated against *all* other kingdoms involved."

Thold tenses his hands like he wants to wring my neck. His snake hisses like he wants to sink his fangs in. If it weren't for my magic, he'd probably let it.

"This is our proposed alternative," Isalee says, drawing his attention. "We all know that King Ravinger could very well take First Kingdom under his own rule. Yet despite your broken treaties and the Conflux debacle, all he requests is that you send your imports to Fourth as previously done in the original agreement, as proof to us of your dedication to this alliance. Trust was broken, King Thold," she tells him firmly. "And that takes time to repair. The issue of the oil can be readdressed when we've had that time to mend the fractures between our kingdoms."

He's quiet for a moment, chewing on our proposal, and I'm sure it's a bitter lump to swallow, but swallow it he does. "Fine. But I want the next shipment of oil solely sent to First."

Not like I'm going to be sending any to any of the other kingdoms anyway. Even when we do get our mine up and running again.

I glance at my Premiers, pretending to consider. Warken looks downright pensive before he and Isalee give a nod to me.

"Done," I tell him before reaching out a hand.

Thold eyes it, and the snake hisses. "I think you'll forgive me if I don't shake, King Rot."

I smirk and slip my hands into my pockets. "We'll dine tonight instead," I tell him. "Before you leave Fourth tomorrow."

It's both an invitation and a nudge to get him out of my kingdom. Although, I'm sure he doesn't want to stay here anyway.

"Of course." He gives my Premiers a nod and then turns and walks out, his guards following him.

After the door closes, Isalee sighs. "Well, that's done. With his shipment coming in, plus the extra hands we have to make Fourth start producing more food, we can make up for the losses until we're more self-sustainable."

"We'll still have to ration for a bit longer," Warken adds as he sits back down. "Barley is overseeing that, but we're in a *much* better position than we were before. Even with no further cooperation with the rest of the kingdoms, so long as we have First, plus our own efforts, we should be able to make it work."

"How long until we get the mine fixed?" Isalee asks, gesturing to the report on my desk.

"They're still assessing the extent of the collapse," I say. I can't prove Kaila did it, but I have a fucking hunch that she's behind it. "Do you know how morale is?" I ask Warken, since he was going over the messages from the foreman.

"Better. They've received their higher stipend and were also told they'd be getting a percentage of the oil profits once the mine is up and running again. With that incentive, they're working hard to get it repaired as quickly as they can while ensuring everyone stays safe."

"Good." I look to both my Premiers. "You've handled everything flawlessly. Having you two run this kingdom was the best decision I ever made as a king."

"*Don't*," Isalee retorts, her eyes as cutting as her sharp tone. "You are not to die, so you certainly are not to start speaking your grateful farewells."

"But—"

"Yes, yes," she says, waving a regal hand at me. "Warken and I are quite aware of your potential demise. We came up with a contingency plan as requested, which you can find in that report there on your desk, and that's the end of it."

I barely hold in a snort.

Just then, Judd comes in with a grin on his face and leans against the doorway. When he continues to stare at me, looking giddy, I roll my eyes. "Are you going to tell me what it is, or are you just going to keep standing there with that look on your face?"

"Option three," he replies. "Come see for yourself."

I look to the others, but Warken shrugs. When Judd turns to lead the way, we follow him out. He heads downstairs, through the main entry, and toward the front doors of the castle. Outside, he doesn't stop, boots clopping down the cobblestone drive as he veers past the obelisk statue ahead. But right there on the bridge that leads over the moat, I see a gathering of people. And then—

A roar sounds that makes me jolt to a stop.

Argo.

People rush out of the way as the huge timberwing nearly tramples them in order to get to me. He's in front of me in a flash, his maw pressing against my side, nose chucking up my arm to force me to pet him and nearly knocking me over in the process. I bark out a laugh, my chest swelling with instant relief and happiness.

He continues to nudge my arm, and I scratch him on his favorite spot. "You fucking overgrown hawk, I'm happy to see you. What are you doing here?" I murmur. "Let me get a look at you." I let my hands glide over his feathers, checking for his injuries. It fucking killed me to leave him behind in that desert, broken and bloody. Now, he seems so much better, which I don't understand, considering the gravity of his wounds.

Ryatt comes striding over from where he was gathered with the people on the bridge. He's in full army gear, hair slick with sweat, so I know he was down at the barracks probably running more training exercises. But right now, he's accompanying a girl in her late teens and an even smaller girl who's clutching her hand.

They have short black hair and brown skin with cool undertones, both of their faces carrying a heart shape with a widow's peak right at the center of their hairlines. They're looking around the courtyard nervously, and both are wearing long gray robes—not unlike the religious ones Queen Isolte had worn at the Conflux, which puts me on edge.

My brother notices the look on my face and gives the smallest shake of his head before they come to a stop in front of me. "King Ravinger," he begins. "I'd like you to meet Shea and Wynn. They're sisters from Second Kingdom."

I nod, but I notice that the older one's hands are trembling and she's too frightened to look at me. She bows deeply and then tugs her sister's hand until she bows too.

"Shea was at the docks with her little sister when Argo was brought to the ship. They saw his injuries and offered their services in exchange for passage," Ryatt tells me as both of them straighten back up.

The little girl reaches out and runs her small hand over Argo's feathers, and I blink in surprise as he nudges her with a low purr. He usually doesn't tolerate many people—not even children. The only person I've seen him warm up to other than me is Auren.

"What kind of services?" I ask curiously.

The girl looks up at her sister, and Shea hesitates a moment before answering, "My little sister has healing magic, Your Majesty. She can heal animal's wounds."

My brows jump up, gaze immediately going to the thick wrapping around Argo's wing. I haven't heard of anyone having true healing magic in Orea in a very long time.

"It's all better now," the little girl, Wynn, says. "I healed him every day on the ship. Every time my magic came back." As if to show me, she claps her hands like she's about to play a children's clapping game, but when her hands point out again, they're coated with some sort of fine powder. It would look almost like sand if it weren't for its bright blue hue.

"If she may...?" Shea says softly.

With a nod from me, she reaches forward and gently unwraps the binding around Argo's wing. When the last layer is peeled back, I see the wound is almost completely gone. Only a few missing feathers and a reddened scab area show through his bare skin.

Argo, as if he's well used to this routine, extends his wing and holds it out for Wynn, lowering it slightly so she can reach. I watch as the little girl rubs her palms together, letting the blue powder dust over his wound. The moment it lands on his skin, the powder glows slightly and then sinks in, like a plant sucking up water. Within seconds, the scab is healed over, the skin no longer red.

Amazement travels through everyone around me. Seeing it work in person is extraordinary. The fact that Wynn is so young and yet in control of such a powerful magic is impressive.

Argo trills, and the little girl giggles and pets his head, not seeming to mind a bit that his huge fangs are just inches from her tiny arm. "There, his wing is all better," she says with a grin. "I did his leg first. A little bit every day on the ship. Then I started on the wing. He flew us the rest of the way here. Shea thought it would be better if I showed you the last part of the healing."

"It didn't affect his flying," Shea says nervously. "It's just best to have proof of these things. But as you can see, his leg is also perfectly healed."

That became clear the moment he nearly knocked me over in his rush to get to me.

"I'm in your debt," I say as Argo nudges me again. "Anything you request, tell my Premiers and it shall be paid."

Shea bites her lip, but then says, "Your Majesty, we desire not coin, but permission to stay."

Surprise flashes through me. "To stay in Fourth?"

She nods and wrings her hands. "We...do not adhere to the strict upbringing of Second's faith. We would like to have permission to live permanently in Fourth. And while my sister has this magic and is willing to use it to help others, we ask that it not be announced or exploited. I want her to be allowed to enjoy her childhood. Whatever she has left of it."

I don't like what I see as I read between the lines.

"Is it *only* animals she can heal?" I ask.

Shea shifts on her feet and then starts to nod, but Wynn cuts in. "No," she says matter-of-factly. "I can heal people too."

Shea tosses her a heavy look that tells me she didn't want her to say that. It's clear that these two have been through something and that Wynn was taken advantage of, probably forced to use her magic.

I know what that's like.

"I will grant both requests, as well as making sure you are very well compensated," I promise them, and I don't miss the pure relief that washes over the elder sister's face. "However, I do have a request as well, but it's just that—a *request*, not an order." I kneel down in front of the little girl, and her dark brown eyes peer up at me through her lashes.

"You can say no, and no harm will come to you, and you are still very much welcome here, okay?"

She nods shyly.

"There is a woman here who's in a very bad way. She was wounded, and she hasn't been healing very well. Would you go to her? See if you could help?"

Wynn looks up at her sister, and they exchange a look. I'm not sure what they communicate, but when the girl looks back at me, she nods.

Relief floods through me, though I try not to pressure her and simply smile. "Thank you." I get to my feet and turn to look at my Premiers. "See that they're taken care of—have rooms prepared for them in the castle and bring her to Lady Rissa's room right away."

I hope it's not too fucking late. I hope this little girl has enough magic to help, but I don't know if even this unexpected miracle can save Rissa. Hojat's last report was grim but clear—she's on her deathbed.

A tug on my sleeve has me glancing back down at Wynn. She's looking up at me with wide eyes that suddenly seem sad. When she tugs my sleeve again, I take the hint and lower myself in front of her. "I can feel your pain too," she whispers, and I go still as her hand lifts to my chest. The second she grazes her fingers over my bulbous heart, her eyes widen and she pulls away. "I can't heal that, Your Majesty. There's nothing to heal."

Nothing to heal—because my heart is already dead? Already past the point of returning to normal?

Rot slumps against my neck as if in apology.

Everyone around us has gone quiet and tense. That tension pulls inside of me like a muscle ready to snap, but I don't let it show in my expression.

I clear my throat and straighten back up to my feet. "Don't you worry about me," I say, giving her a smile that doesn't reach my eyes. "They call me King Rot, remember? Rot doesn't need healing."

Wynn looks at me dubiously, and I can feel the others eyeing me too, but I shake my head, letting them know the topic is closed.

I hitch up my chin at the girl. "Make sure you get a good room—you get your pick of the empty ones."

She hesitates for another moment, but then her sister takes her hand.

"Thank you, Your Majesty," Shea says with a curtsy before she leads her sister away, following the Premiers.

Wynn gives Argo a little wave, and he croons after her, looking as forlorn as a lost puppy when he watches her disappear inside the castle.

"Look at you." I shake my head at him with wry amusement. "Hit with *one* measly arrow, and you've gone soft."

He snorts at me, getting snot on my sleeve.

Judd grins. "Ha! Good boy!" He moves to pet Argo on the shoulder, but my timberwing lets off a sudden and ferocious growl at him. Judd stumbles back, nearly falling on his ass.

I smirk while Argo looks on smugly, licking his chops like he's imagining taking a bite out of Judd.

"Rude," Judd grumbles.

"Alright, beast," I tell Argo with a pat to his flank. "Go to the Perch and have a nice long rest."

He flicks his tongue out and then walks far enough away before bolting into the sky. I watch as he flies around the ebony castle, wings spread wide as he veers around a spiked turret before disappearing behind it, heading for the base of the mountain.

"I've never heard of healing magic that powerful before," Ryatt muses, frowning at the door of the castle.

"Sounds to me like they were at that port for a reason," Judd says. "Maybe trying to flee Second Kingdom. Someone probably knew about the girl's ability and was using her."

I nod in agreement. At the Conflux, King Merewen forced his own son to keep up the barrier between us, even as it caused the boy to fit. Any time an adult forces a child to use their power, it transports me right back to Annwyn—to my own father forcing me to train until I was little more than a husk of pain and exhaustion.

My teeth grind with anger.

"We'll make sure no one forces her to use her magic," I say, and I can feel Ryatt's eyes on me. "And, once she's more comfortable, get names. I want to know who used her."

Judd looks at me with glee. "I'm on it."

"Is Os with Rissa?" I ask him.

"Yeah. Hasn't left."

Nodding, I turn and start to make my way back toward the castle. I should be there with him, just in case it doesn't work.

"We'll come too," Ryatt says as he and Judd catch up to walk beside me.

"If this doesn't work..." Judd trails off, his tone taking on a dire tinge.

My lips press thin. "I know."

I fucking know.

I see it in the rare times Osrik comes out of her room. That each time he leaves her, he leaves another piece of himself behind.

"We'll need to—"

A shocking, overwhelming flood of noises suddenly cuts me off. It bolts through the air and punctures through me, jolting my body.

A tenor of voices crowds my ears like I'm standing in the middle of a riot, with hundreds of people shouting all at once.

I look around wildly, my brother and Judd doing the same thing. The guards and castle workers down by the stables and the bridge react much the same way, but I see nothing—don't know where the sounds are coming from.

Is the city rioting?

"What the fuck is that?" Ryatt yells, hand on the hilt of his sword.

He looks like he wants to bolt for the barracks and ready the army. Judd is staring at me with wide eyes. Someone at the bridge is on their knees, curled over, hands desperately covering their ears.

Then the sound comes to a crescendo, blaring so loudly that I see Ryatt and Judd wince. Workers slam their hands against their ears, trying to block it out, the whole courtyard in disarray. But there's no one—no people storming the castle, no source for the sound.

Then, one voice cuts through the rest.

"Please!"

My blood runs cold.

It's Auren screaming—*pleading*—with such raw desperation that it makes me stagger. Feet dug up, yanked from the ground like a weed.

"Please!"

I whirl around frantically, looking for her. Is it a rip? Did I manage to open one and somehow not notice? Maybe a tiny tear that I didn't see, that's been slowly expanding?

The thought of her on the other side screaming for me has me spinning on my heel. My heart is pounding hard, rot and blood pumping through my veins and flooding me with panic.

"Please!"

"Auren!" I shout back, turning, looking. She sounds so anguished, so scared.

Where the fuck is she?

Movement above has my head snapping up, just as figures blast through the clouds. They soar down straight for us, and it suddenly all makes sense.

Queen Kaila.

She's using her magic. Using Auren's voice from the Conflux. Using the sounds of the fleeing crowd.

Rage locks on to my every muscle, my face twisting with pure menace as I watch her descend.

Kaila's timberwing lands on the ebony obelisk, wings spread wide as its talons dig into the statue, making pieces crumble. The castle workers scatter, just as seven more timberwings land behind her, forming a barrier around their queen. Kaila's beast leaps down, landing right in front of me, teeth bared as it roars into my face.

I don't flinch.

Kaila jumps off in a flurry of fury, her magic a cyclone of wisping voices that spin around her, blowing back her black hair, making her appearance look unhinged.

"Where is he?" she snarls, except her magic blasts it at the volume of a thousand voices all at once, making everyone else recoil, my eardrums wanting to burst right out of my head.

My own magic answers in kind.

Rot shoves out and seizes her, flooding up her legs like reaching roots. She staggers, watching as it crawls up her arms, her shoulders, her neck.

Her guards all jump from their timberwings in an instant, but I have them on their knees as soon as their feet touch the cobblestones. They writhe with the rot as it wraps around their bodies and infects their veins.

The black and brown lines slither up to Kaila's mouth and dip inside, staining her lips and gripping her tongue. Her power suddenly cuts off, and all the assaulting sound cuts off with it.

Blessed silence rings out as the magicked voices dissipate at once. Kaila clutches her throat in alarm, dropping to the ground. I stalk forward until I stand over her. My rage bearing down.

"How fucking *dare you*."

My voice sounds like thunder. My vision clouded with fury that's ready to strike.

Her hands are scrabbling at her throat, a wheezing, guttural noise crawling out of her mouth, brown eyes wide. "Where...is...he...?" The words are graveled, like a raw throat scraped over sharp stones, leaving it to bleed past a ruined tongue.

"Your brother?" I ask, leaning over her with malice. "He's fucking rotting in my dungeon as we speak. His body decaying, reeking, while flies feast on his flesh just like *he fucking deserves*."

Her defiant eyes flash, and my hand snaps out to wrap around her neck. The veins in her face start to blacken, little lines shooting through the whites of her eyes as my raging magic infects her. Punishes her.

"You spread lies about Auren. Flamed the fires of distrust and hate. Orchestrated her kidnapping. Led her to an execution." My fingers tighten, her body flailing, breath failing. "You took her from me, *so I took him from you*."

I lean down so she can taste the wrath that seeps out of me. "I will dump you next to him, rotting you from within, making you writhe in fucking *agony*."

Terror flashes across her face.

"But I'll leave your eyes and your ears, so you can watch him slowly die. So you can hear his pitiful screams."

Her magic bursts out of her with one desperate puff of breath. Auren's voice rings so loudly in my ears that I feel a trickle of blood start to seep out of them, scraping down my neck like a gouge.

I wrench her up high in the air, cutting off the last of her air. Her guards are melting into puddles of their own flesh and bubbling blood, while the ground in front of the timberwings crumbles, making them panic and screech, two of them taking to the sky while Kaila's timberwing roars.

I'm going to kill her.

I know it. She knows it.

She must've been a desperate woman to come here herself like this. I could almost respect the lengths to which she's gone to get her brother, if I didn't hate her so viciously.

My magic seeps down, down, ready to infect her with the slowest, most painful poison.

But then, a timberwing suddenly lands at my side.

I whip around in surprise, my rot slipping, just as I see Lu jump from the back of the beast.

Lu? What the hell is she doing here?

She's bloody. Disheveled. Covered in grime. The dark brown skin at her cheeks peeling from the chapping, cloying windchill.

But it's her eyes that fill me with ice.

Because never, in all the years I've known her or had her serve as captain in my army, have I *ever* seen such a look of fear before.

She runs toward me, ignoring the mayhem, ignoring Kaila, gaze locked on mine as she comes to a stop, her breaths panting out in unsustainable gulps. "They're here! They're here and they've slaughtered *everyone*."

My grip slips, and Kaila crumples to the ground as I turn to Lu, my brows pinning down. "*Who?*" I demand.

My heart pounds, ears whooshing as if Kaila's magic is still filling the air, but Lu's next words are far more potent.

"The fae," she says with stricken desperation. "The fae have invaded Orea."

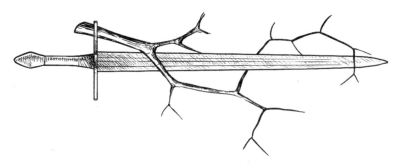

CHAPTER 47

OSRIK

They lit a candle on her bedside table. Like they're holding some mourning vigil for her, even though she hasn't even fucking died.

Yet.

That's what they keep saying. That word—yet. She hasn't passed *yet*, but she will. She hasn't taken her last breath—*yet*. Makes it sound like her death is so final that her surviving isn't even a possibility anymore. Everyone is just waiting for that *yet* to catch up.

The novices keep coming in, wiping wet cloths over her fevered forehead and pressing it to her chapped lips so the water will drip into her mouth. I don't even know what time it is. I drew the curtains over the window hours ago. Blocking out the fucking gods. If they're not going to save her life, then they don't deserve to see her death.

Rissa whines low in her throat, and my hand tightens around her small palm, dread pooling in my stomach. "You're alright, Yellow Bell," I murmur.

Like a fucking liar.

Her inhale is jagged like it's all cut up, leaving behind gashes in her lungs.

"Keep breathing," I tell her.

Maybe I shouldn't. The novices keep giving me sideways glances, but what the fuck do they want from me? I'm not going to just…let her give in. Give up.

"Keep going."

She takes in another labored breath that scratches up her throat with a rough rasp.

Hojat steps up beside me. "Captain, sometimes, our loved ones need to hear that it's okay for them to pass on…"

"It's *not* okay," I tell him.

Tell *her*.

I want her to keep fighting. If that makes me selfish, well, I never fucking said I wasn't.

We fought in life, we can fight in death.

Till the bitter end.

I don't even notice until after he squeezes my shoulder that I didn't correct him when he called her *loved one*. Didn't correct him, because there was nothing to correct.

I love this woman.

And that admission is going to turn past tense before I can even say it to her in the present.

So of course I don't fucking tell her it's okay to pass on. It's not okay.

"You got that, Yellow Bell?" I murmur. "I don't give you permission to die."

I get up from the chair and lean over her, hating the candlelight, hating the way it casts all these shadows over her face. I clasp her cheeks and stroke my thumbs over them. She's still burning hot, but it's better than cold.

"Keep fighting," I tell her doggedly. "Fight me some

more."

But I'm captain of an army. I know what it looks like when the fight's left someone.

Grief latches on to me like a leech, sucking the life right out of me.

"Come on, Rissa Bell. Just a little more fight. A little more time."

We were supposed to have so much more time, but I'll settle for a little. I'll fucking settle for anything other than this. Because this? This is worse than torture—and I would know.

"Captain Osrik?" Hojat says quietly.

I look over at him and see one of the novices handing him a vial. He takes it, looking at me with pity.

Immediately, I stiffen. "What's that?"

His scarred face twists with compassion. "It will help ease her passing. She's in pain."

I snap upright, hands dropping down. "*No.*"

"Captain—"

"I said no!" My body now blocks the bed, as if I can shield her from him. I will, if I have to. "You're not fucking giving her that," I snarl. "She's alive."

"By breath and pain," he tells me as he walks closer, and a firm look melds over his expression. "She's not going to get better, Captain Osrik. She *is* going to die. So we can either let her suffer for several more hours or end her pain and help her pass in peace."

He reaches down and I watch as he places the vial in my hand. "It's the right thing to do."

Right thing.

I stare at the vial. At the swirling concoction inside that we've used on soldiers on the battlefield to put them out of their misery.

It's tiny in my hand but it's the heaviest thing I've ever had to hold.

I want to smash it to the ground. The only reason I don't is because she lets out another whimpering wheeze.

Because she *is* in pain. Because she's still fighting. Because I keep telling her to.

Fuck.

My fingers close around the glass bottle, and I turn around to look at her tense face. My eyes burn like I got too close to a flame. Her agonized expression sucks all the air from the room.

I feel like a stopper suddenly yanks out of me, draining out all my resolve. All my selfish stubbornness.

Carefully, I sit on the edge of her bed. Brush away a strand of her yellow hair and tuck it behind her ear. That flame in my eyes keeps burning.

The candle on her bedside does too.

Her chest rises and falls, raw breath shredding to pieces, making her frown pull down harder. Making her pained whine go higher-pitched.

My throat gets all gummed up, and my vision goes blurry, but I blink it away so I can see her.

Because I won't get to keep seeing her for much longer.

She gives another whined breath, and I close my eyes, head hanging, defeat draping over me. Because I hear Hojat, and I know he's right. I hear her, and I know it's time. I know I have to…let her stop.

The fire in my eyes spreads down to my chest, and I know after this, I'll be scorched to ash. But it's not about me. It's about her. And I need to let her stop fighting.

My murmur is barely audible, but it's only for us. "Okay, Yellow Bell."

Okay.

Glancing down, I thumb off the cork, letting the mouth of the vial gape open. I stare down at the liquid inside. My hand shakes. My stomach feels like it's filled with lead.

But I lift my hand and press the vial to her plush lips, and then I tip.

Watch the liquid start to slip toward her mouth.

Torment slips down mine.

The door to her room suddenly swings open, making me jerk the vial back as I turn to look.

A few people file in, and I frown. "Isalee?" I say in confusion.

The Premier nods to me, clasping her hands in front of her. "Captain Osrik. Hojat," she says next, looking to the mender. "I have someone I'd like you to meet."

My brow furrows deeper as she turns and reveals two girls behind her, one older, maybe late teens, the other one probably not even ten. "This is Wynn and her older sister, Shea."

I see Hojat go pale as he takes in their robes. There's only one kingdom where the people wear robes like that, and he was from there. It's where he got his burns.

Isalee looks down at the younger child. "Wynn, this is Mender Hojat, and that man there is Captain Osrik."

"Like a soldier?" Wynn asks.

"Yes, exactly that."

I just stand here bewildered. Why the fuck would Isalee bring a child into a dying woman's room?

I watch as the girl lets go of her sister's hand and walks closer. She stops in front of me and looks up expectantly. "Excuse me."

My eyes flash up to Isalee, but when she nods, I slowly move. The girl goes right to Rissa's side and studies her for a few seconds. "She's very pretty. I like her yellow hair." She turns to look at me. "What's her name?"

I clear my rough throat. "Rissa."

"What happened to her?"

"She got stabbed."

Wynn's face goes sad. "Oh."

Should I have lied? Fuck, I don't know. I'm not around a lot of kids.

"What do you think, Wynn?" Isalee asks. The little girl glances back at her. "Remember, it is up to you. There is no obligation. No force. You decide."

"Decide what?" I ask, looking between them. "What's going on?"

The older one, Shea, looks at her sister. "What do you think, Wynnie?"

The girl twists a black lock of her short hair and bites her lip. Then, she slowly nods. "I want to."

A look of relief crosses Isalee's face, and she smiles. "Thank you, Wynn."

"What's going on?" I ask again, frustration mounting.

Isalee murmurs something into Hojat's ear, and the mender's eyes go wide. He rushes over to the other side of Rissa's bed. "Miss Wynn, do you need to see the wound?"

The girl nods and Hojat undoes the top button of Rissa's nightdress.

"Someone tell me what the hell is going on *right now*," I demand.

"My sister can help," Shea says.

"Help?" Bafflement clangs through me. "*How?*"

"I fix hurts," Wynn answers, just as Hojat peels back Rissa's nightgown and bandage, revealing the Divine-damned wound beneath. Clustered with infected blood, and swollen, bright red skin clotted with pus.

I hear the older sister suck in a breath, but Wynn reaches out her hand, her small palm covering the worst of it, and I'm so fucking lost that all I can do is stand here and watch.

The girl's black brows pull together, and then she lifts her palm, tongue stuck between her teeth in concentration. She scrubs her hands together then, and a dusting of blue powder somehow starts sifting down from them, landing on Rissa's wound.

It hisses and steams against the inflamed skin. Crackles as it soaks into the stitched slash. My whole body tenses, while Hojat looks on in wonder, and I'm about to fucking *lose it*, but right before my eyes, the wound begins to heal.

It fucking. Starts. To *heal*.

I stagger back. The vial falls from my hand and shatters against the floor.

The startling sound doesn't deter the girl. She just keeps scrubbing her hands. The powder keeps falling down. And the horrible Divine-damned wound, the infection around it…it starts to lessen. The red leeching away. The swelling going down. The puncture itself starting to close up.

I'm so fucking stunned, my stare stuck on the wound, that I don't notice the girl falling until she nearly hits the floor. Luckily, Hojat catches her, while the last of the blue powder sinks into Rissa's chest.

The older sister rushes forward and takes Wynn, hiking her up and propping her small head against her shoulder. "Oh Wynn, I told you, not too much!" The girl's head lolls and her eyes are closed, but I hear her reply. "S'okay. Wanted to help. She looked nice."

I just keep staring.

Blinking. Edge of my boot crushed over slivers of glass.

How.

How how how how…

There's more talking in the background, but I can't comprehend what anyone is saying. I barely notice Isalee gathering the girls and leaving the room. I'm too stunned to pay attention to them. I can't take my eyes off the wound that's now nearly healed. All that's left is scabbed-over flesh and peeled-back stitches.

And…

She's breathing. *Breathing* and not wheezing. The frown on her face is softening too, until her expression turns almost serene.

My eyes jerk up to Hojat. My voice cracks. It doesn't feel real. I almost just fucking fed her that vial to stop her heart. A few seconds more, and I would have.

"*How?*"

Hojat shakes his head, like he's at a loss as much as I am. "Magic."

But he's right.

Because when Rissa's eyes suddenly flutter open, when I see those stormy blue eyes of hers focus on me, that's exactly what it feels like.

Fucking *magic*.

CHAPTER 48

QUEEN MALINA

I come to with clusters of shadows and prisms of light bobbing around me. Instantly, I'm calmed, because I know I'm safe in my assassin's arms. He pulls his magic away, but only slightly. Only enough for me to see him.

Dommik looks down at me, hood pushed back, and I realize he's holding me on his lap. He's...cradling me against his chest. As if I'm precious to him. But as I take in his expression, as I notice the lines of tension around his mouth and the circles beneath his eyes, worry settles in.

"What happened?" My throat is sore, as if I passed out screaming.

I frown, trying to flex my memories, and then they all come tumbling back to me, making me go rigid.

He hesitates as the shadows and light continue to float.

"Dommik, *what happened?*"

"You got a nasty blow to the head," he says, hand

coming up to brush over the sore spot right at my left temple. "You were unconscious for hours."

"Hours?" My mind whirls, dread pooling in my stomach like a puddle of tar. "Highbell?" I croak.

A pained expression crosses his face, but it's the shake of his head that stabs my heart. "I'm sorry."

"Let me see," I tell him.

"They're *everywhere*, Malina. I wasn't even sure where to go. We're on the roof of one of the houses on the outskirts, but they've already swept through."

I push up off his lap and start to stand, but my head spins as soon as I do. Dommik keeps hold of me, gripping my arm, but he doesn't pull the rest of his shadows away.

"Let me see, Dommik."

"Maybe you've seen enough, you ever thought of that?" He lets out a breath of frustration, gripping both arms now as he stands in front of me. "Let me take you away. Wherever you want to go, I can get us there. I can hide us forever if I need to."

The earnest look on his face breaks my heart, because I know he's utterly sincere. He would whisk me away right now. Keep every terrible view out of sight and tuck us into a safe spot inside his bent shadows where no one could find us.

It's a pretty, solitary dream, and a part of me wants to take his offer.

But I'm a Colier. I have always been and will always be a Colier. A captain goes down with his ship, and a queen goes down with her kingdom.

I lift my hand and press it against his warm cheek, and it melts the tiny fragments of ice scabbed to my palm. My nails are startlingly blue as I brush my fingers over his skin. "Thank you."

He blinks in surprise. "For what?"

My throat feels tight, like my emotions have collared it.

582

"For saving me." I swallow hard. "For saving *all* of me."

Not just my life. Not just physically. There are parts of me so ugly, so barren, that I never thought they'd ever be changed—that I'd ever even *want* to change them. There was so much entitlement and bitterness, disappointments and scars. I never thought I could be rid of them. That I could be…better than I was.

His hand comes up to rest over mine. "People don't normally thank their assassins."

A small smile cracks my cheeks. "I don't think the two of us are very normal people."

He nods in agreement before his head dips down to pin me with his stare. "Are you sure you want to see Highbell like this? Wouldn't you rather remember it as it was?"

My father said that to me about my mother. That it was better to remember her in her life rather than in her death.

I shake my head. "How can we deserve to see the delights if we always close our eyes against the horrors?"

He moves his hand to tuck a strand of my white hair behind my ear. "Okay, Queenie."

Breath fills my lungs as I try to prepare myself, and Dommik pulls his shadows away. For a moment, I think we're still in them, but it's only dust and smoke staining the air.

I blink through the murk, though my heart is polluted from the sight.

Devastation.

That's the word that churns through my soul as I look around from this rooftop view at the very edge of the city. Devastation came to Highbell. It swooped in with ravaging thoroughness and brought death to every corner. All while I lay unconscious. I wasn't even *awake* while my people were killed.

The city is bathed in red ruin. From up here, I can see the rows of roads and the buildings that hug them. They should be full of people going about their day. Instead, bodies lie where they were struck down, and blood stains the streets where they've been left.

In the distance, I can count at least six spots that are burning. Other buildings have been struck by lightning, their stones singed, their walls crumbled. The roads themselves are crooked, as if the ground magic cracked the city's core and left the earth to slant.

Up on the mountain, more fae stream up the winding road to the castle. I stare at it, envisioning them going through my hall. Sitting at my table. Someone searching my rooms. Generations of Coliers have lived and died in that castle, and now, an enemy swarms it.

Anger swarms through *me*.

In front of the mountain and arced over the chasm, I can see the bridge into the city. My wall is nothing now except grains of ice trampled beneath thousands of feet. If I follow the line of the traveling army, I can see their path as it winds through the streets of Highbell, going past the shanties just a few streets up from me. They're marching right out of Highbell.

They're marching toward Fifth Kingdom.

Thick dread gathers around me, making it feel like my legs are stuck in it, that it's holding me immobile. Because they're going to do this over and over again. To every city, to every kingdom they reach.

I turn toward Dommik. "We have to warn the rest of Orea."

"Hopefully, Queen Kaila will at least do *that*," he says bitterly.

"We can't count on it. We need to sneak into the city when there aren't so many fae combing the streets. See if we can find a messenger shop. If there are any hawks left, we need to send one to every corner of Orea."

Dommik nods slowly, but I know what we're both thinking. Even if Orea *is* warned, will it even make a difference? And will they even believe me?

The wind batters past us, pulling at my clothes and whipping Dommik's cloak. It's wailing like a widow, or perhaps it's Highbell herself, baying out her agony. Tears fall from my lashes and pelt down my cheeks. "We need to search for survivors."

"They cleared out the entire city, Malina."

"They might not have gotten into every house—"

"They have," he tells me. "I watched. I promise you, they were meticulous."

Frost gathers at my teeth and I crunch down hard, gnawing on the ice while my heart feels like it's being gnawed into dust. But then a thought strikes me, and I turn to look behind us at the forest that borders the city. To where the enormous trees stand tall, warding off the wind and cradling Highbell in its grasp. The forest seems to be the only part not flooded with the fae's march.

"The Pitching Pines," I say with a desperate whisper. "Did anyone escape to the pinewood?"

"I'm not sure."

Hope lurches. "We need to go check."

"There might not be anyone there," he says carefully, as if he wants me to temper my expectations.

"I know," I tell him. "But we have to check. Even if one person made it, we have to see."

"Okay. Just...brace yourself. We might not find anyone down there." He blows out a breath and looks to the trees. "The forest is massive. I'm not sure where to start."

"There's one road that leads into it, off the beaten path. The locals know of it. I'll tell you where to go."

I get my bearings on where we are and then give him detailed instructions on exactly which part of the woods I want to be brought to, just past Pillar Row.

Dommik billows us off the rooftop, and I sway in the shadows, the scent of blood and fire tainting every inhale. I'm glad for the obscurity his magic keeps us in. It's one thing to view it from a rooftop, and another thing entirely to see it up close. The quick and distorted sights I'm able to view are enough to make my stomach twist and my chin tremble. There's scorched buildings, blasted walls, splatters of blood, and dead bodies. So many flashes of dead bodies.

They're everywhere.

Slumped against walls. Face down in the street. Covered in snow, bent, charred, bloodied, piled on top of one another. Alone with no one else around.

When we stop leaping from place to place, I realize the shakiness isn't coming from the magic. It's coming from me.

So much death.

"Hey. Queenie."

I try to brush him off, but Dommik grips my elbow and forces me to face him. His magic is curled around us like a cocoon, keeping us safe within its dark depths.

"They're all dead." It comes out as a whisper, my eyes unseeing as I stare at my feet. "The entire city just...*gone*." My gaze shoots up to his face. "They killed *everyone*, Dommik."

His lips press together, somberness soaked through his eyes. "Not everyone."

"I don't count."

He taps my lips with a finger as if to shush me. "You count, Malina. You always count."

I swallow thickly at the surprisingly tender words.

"Stop it," I breathe. Feeling miserable, feeling grateful. "Don't be nice to me."

He gives me a half-smirk. "You like it."

"I don't *dislike* it," I grumble.

The pad of his thumb strokes my bottom lip as if to reward me. Then he drops his hand and turns. "Ready to search?"

As soon as I nod, he dissolves his shadows and I look around. The entrance to the pinewood is just behind us, the first of the trees scattered around the city. I can see the backs of the buildings on the border, with smoke exhaling into the sky. But in front of me, the massive trees spread out into the forest, and it's like they've made a world of their own.

I start to trudge through the snow, skirts lifted, though the snowfall isn't too deep. The branches hold most of the snow, cradling it like pillows on their boughs. The further we head into the forest and away from the city, the more peaceful it seems. The scent of pine and sweet sap overtakes that of smoke and blood. The sight of stippled brown bark replaces the scorched and busted buildings.

Unlike the destruction in Highbell, in here, there's just...this. Nature, quiet and untouched by the horrors outside its border.

I glance up, taking in the pine needles that hang down like blue and white icicles. Whenever the wind blows through them, they clink together, reminding me of wind chimes. And when they get too heavy, they pitch downward, stabbing into the snow.

The trees get bigger the further we walk. Until soon, they're wider than two, three, even four carriages across. They stretch so high it's impossible to see just where they end their reach above the clouds.

All is still and serene here. As if nothing's wrong, nothing's happened, nothing else exists. What a tempting veil of oblivion nature creates.

As Dommik and I walk past tree after tree, I start to lose hope, because there's no sign of anything outside of this tranquil wood. We don't see traces of a single person.

Until, finally, Dommik stops so quickly that I almost run into him. He veers off sharply, and I hurry to catch up just as he crouches on the ground. He points at indentations in the snow. "Footprints," he says, looking up at me.

Hope fluxes through me, renewed with urgency. "We need to follow them."

He nods, and together, the two of us start rushing, Dommik in the lead as he follows the tracks.

Please, I beg to the magic. To the ether.

Please.

One good thing about living in a climate where snow always coats the ground means that tracking is far easier. Dommik is meticulous about watching the tracks and, luckily, never loses sight of them. Neither of us speaks as he follows the prints, and buoyant expectation rises higher and higher. Because what was a single track of footsteps turns into many.

Heart-pounding minutes pass, and Dommik curls us around a particularly huge pine, and then, there they are.

Huddled around a Pitching Pine that snapped at its base and crashed down onto the forest floor long ago. There are people—at least four or five dozen of them—sitting atop its fallen trunk. When we come into view, they flinch in surprise, yet as soon as they realize we're not fae, the fear leaves their faces.

Then—

"It's Queen Malina."

"It's the Cold Queen!"

They get to their feet, all of them turning around, and I brace myself, ready for their hate—

A woman breaks into sobs, falling off the tree and landing on her knees in the snow. Her dress has spatters of blood at the sleeve, and there's more of it on her face. Her once kohl-lined eyes now drip down her ashen cheeks. But it's the little girl clutched in her arms who fills me with staggering relief. It's the same girl from before—the one Dommik took home. Her leg is now bandaged, and she clings to her mother like she's never going to let her go.

"Thank you," the woman cries, staring up at me with tears streaming down her face as her gaze bounces from me to Dommik. "You both saved her. Saved *us*. And you've come. Our queen has come!" she shouts at the others.

Breath knocks out of my chest.

All the other survivors, every single one, start quietly rejoicing. Whispering out their gratitude for *me*. For *my* presence.

"Our queen has come!"

"Queen Malina, bless you!"

"Thank you!"

"You saved us!"

This display is so foreign, so unexpected, that I'm stuck frozen, unsure what to do. My people have never rejoiced for me. Not since I was a girl. Certainly never as a queen. Yet here they are, with a sacked city and dead loved ones, and they're *thankful*.

I feel so utterly undeserving.

"Please, get up," I rush to say, filling in my stunned pause. I reach to help her to her feet but stop when her eyes widen in surprise. My hands wring in front of me uselessly, snow falling from my fingertips in a nervous scatter. "I am the very reason these fae are here." I look around at everyone where they've gotten up to face me. "I don't deserve your devotion."

I expect my confession to make them turn on me. Instead, the same woman gets up. "You saved us. Built that wall with your cold magic. Tried to warn us." She glances over her shoulder at the others, lifting her hand in their direction. "If it weren't for your orders telling us to retreat here, we would've died with everyone else."

The things I did to help seem so pitifully insignificant. "I couldn't stop them." My words pitch down just like the icicle pine needles, landing at my feet.

But the blood-spattered woman just shakes her head. "Who could, my queen?" she asks softly, lifting her tattered and bloody dress like it's a white flag of defeat. "What are we, compared to fae?"

I thought the same thing. When I first saw them, when I witnessed their magic. When I observed their might. I know that's what they're all thinking. How can we possibly survive, against a force like that?

And yet, here they stand.

Here I stand.

As I look around, I realize what they need. Who they need.

They need *me*.

So I can't fail them.

I draw myself up, hoping I can exude enough confidence for them to draw from. To bolster themselves for the difficult times ahead.

"What are we compared to fae?" I echo, expression indomitable. "We are *Oreans*. That's who we are."

"What can Oreans do against this?" a man calls out forlornly. "Against them?"

I meet his eye. "We can *survive*. If we do that, then the fae have lost. It doesn't matter how many cities they sack, how many kingdoms they take. So long as we survive, we have beaten them."

They exchange looks, wary...but hopeful. Their shoulders lifting just a little bit higher. So I keep the mask on—the one that they need me to wear. The one that tells them I'm strong, determined, undefeated. Because if they see that in me, they'll believe it for themselves too.

"What do we do now, my queen?"

My queen.

Emotion sharpens and pricks the backs of my eyes.

I gesture around at the mighty trees that shelter us. "I will take us somewhere safe." My gaze scans their faces so they can see the sincerity in mine. "*I* will keep you safe."

This pinewood is good at keeping secrets, at keeping the world away. And *I* will keep the fae away. Because I refuse to let anyone here die. I will do whatever I need to so that no more Orean blood is spilled in Highbell.

But if any other blood *is* going to be spilt, I'll make sure it's either fae...

Or mine.

CHAPTER 49

SLADE

"It's impossible." Judd's look of disbelief is countered by the way his fingers fork through his hair and shove it back.

"I'm telling you, it's not."

He stares at Lu like he's waiting for her to crack a smile and yell, "Ha! Got you!"

She doesn't.

Her gaze is solemn and exhausted, her appearance and demeanor hitting us in the gut with the force of a battering ram. I can feel my stomach clenching, my muscles bunching with tension.

We're gathered together in our private breakfast room, except Osrik is still with Rissa. Digby is here, sitting next to Ryatt on the sofa. As soon as Lu made her announcement outside, I had my soldiers drag an unconscious Kaila down to the dungeon. Her importance has grayed in light of Lu's information.

Now, we all look at Lu, trying to make sense of what she witnessed in Sixth. She's slumped forward on a chair next to the dining table, staring at the floor.

"But...*fae*?" Judd goes on. "Here? Fae haven't been able to get to Orea for hundreds of years." His hazel eyes flick to me. "Present company excluded."

"I thought she was lying," Lu mumbles, as if caught up in her own thoughts. "If I'd believed her, I would've been here sooner and maybe been able to help stop the slaughter."

I frown. It's not like Lu to be so scattered when delivering her reports. It's another testament to how shaken she is. "Who are you talking about?"

She braces her forearms on her knees as she looks up at me. "Queen Malina."

Ryatt and I share a look of confusion.

"But Malina..." Ryatt trails off.

"Is dead," Lu supplies. "Yeah, that's what we were told. But it wasn't true. I saw her."

"She was in hiding?"

"She was in Seventh Kingdom."

I rear back, shock widening my eyes. "Seventh? But it was wiped out a long time ago. The land crumbled away into the void."

I've been to Seventh. Flew over it years ago. It was nothing but chasms and splits and a yawning edge.

Lu shakes her head. "I'm only telling you what I heard. Malina was adamant when she returned to Highbell. Nobody believed her, including me. I thought it was just a desperate bid to retake her throne. But she was telling the truth."

The plagued look on her face makes my insides churn. "What happened?"

"Malina went crazy. Started building ice walls all throughout Highbell City."

Ryatt's brows pull together. "Ice walls?"

"With magic."

"Malina doesn't have magic. She never has. It's common knowledge," he says, looking to me as I nod.

"I know," Lu snaps, fist thumping against the table with frustration. "But I'm telling you, she *does*. I saw it with my own eyes. I thought she was walling everyone in—that's what everyone thought she was doing. But then, the fae came." A haunted look glazes over Lu's eyes as she glances at me. "It quickly became clear—Malina wasn't trying to wall everyone in. She was trying to wall the fae *out*."

"Did it work?" Judd asks.

"Not for long. It bought Highbell minutes. But it wasn't enough."

"And Kaila?"

Lu jerks her head. "Fucked off. Left Highbell to fend for itself as soon as she saw the fae coming."

"That's because she doesn't care about Sixth," I say. "Not really. Only about her reach, and only if she could grasp it easily. It doesn't surprise me that she abandoned it."

Lu's lips press together in a hard line. "Doesn't surprise me either, but it pisses me off."

I can only imagine the death that spread through the city. Can only wonder what kind of magic the fae have brought. Kaila could've helped, but instead, she chose to flee.

"What did you do?" Judd asks.

Lu curls her fingers, knocking her knuckles together in an aggravated fidget. "Tried to fucking help," she says, though there's a bitterness to her tone—the kind of bitterness that only comes when the bite of failure is your own. "The massacre went on and on. Felt like ages, but those fae wiped out Highbell within hours." She lifts heavy eyes to me with a gaze that I can feel the weight of. "Men, women, children. Civilians who had no weapon, no fight. They killed them all— either by blade or magic. They just cut them down like stalks of wheat, leaving them in dead heaps on their icy roads. I tried to kill as many of the fuckers as I could, but I couldn't even make a dent. There weren't enough guards. No one was prepared."

Ryatt lets out a thick exhale, while Judd just stares at her, like he's *still* waiting for her to say this is all some twisted joke.

Digby looks as if all the blood has drained from his face. "Everyone?" he asks gruffly.

Lu gives a sharp nod. "Everyone. I found none alive."

His spine hits the back of the sofa as if his body took the brunt of this shock like a punch. Out of all of us, he can understand the true devastation of what Lu speaks. He lived and served in Highbell. Probably knew plenty of people, maybe even had family or friends there.

And now they're all dead.

My hands curl into fists at my sides. I'm fully aware of fae ruthlessness and their prejudice against the Oreans. Fully aware of the level of hate that the fae monarchy bred.

And Oreans hate the fae too.

I've managed to eke by as a fae hidden in plain sight because of time. Enough of it has passed that none of the people here believed a fae could still live amongst them. After hundreds of years, fae almost became mythological creatures to the Oreans, even when the truth of pointed ears and power and spikes stared them in the face. It's amazing what people will turn a blind eye to because of time and surety.

"When it was clear there was nothing else I could do, I flew here as fast as I could. Lost time in a snowstorm that I had to avoid, but that's how I saw the fae marching into Fifth Kingdom. They're going *fast*."

I suck in a breath. "They're still marching? Instead of staying in Highbell?"

Lu runs a hand over her face like she's trying to wipe

away her exhaustion. "They're not stopping."

A knife twists in my gut.

Ryatt looks panicked. "If they get to Fifth's capital, they can easily march right up to our border. They can head for the ports and invade the ships to reach the other kingdoms too. If they get to Ranhold, we're *fucked*."

"I don't understand," Judd says, expression distressed, unable to keep still as he taps his foot against the floor. "How did the fae get here in the first place?"

That question.

It makes the poisoned, blackened organ in my chest suddenly jolt.

Lu's gaze pierces into me. "The bridge of Lemuria."

My ribs close in on my lungs. Heartbeat clustering with an erratic, laden thrum.

The bridge.

The *bridge*.

My thoughts spiral and roil.

It's Digby who looks at me then. Whose voice cuts through the racket that blares in my head. He says aloud what my mind is reeling with. What I should have connected the moment Lu said the fae were here.

"If the bridge is no longer broken, then that means…"

Everything snaps into place. A hope born from horror.

If the bridge isn't broken anymore, then I don't need a rip. If the bridge is linked, I can get into Annwyn. I can find my mother and the villagers.

I can find *Auren*.

During all the time I've been in Orea, I have been at war with myself. Ripped in two, each form wanting to come out—to dominate and thrive. It was a release for me to switch between skins. To be both Rip and Rot. The first, to be the aggressive fae learning to protect me and mine through muscle and rage. The second, to learn to protect in a different way—politically. Magically.

I was able to be the commander and the king. The soldier and the sovereign. I could slake my bloodlust on the battlefield and quench my thirst for control in a throne room. Because of this, I forged the protection of Drollard right along with fear and loyalty of an entire kingdom—an entire realm.

There are two sides to every coin, but there's only one core, and there, I am in complete joined agreement.

Auren.

At my innermost center, where both forms connect, is this seed of her. The golden vine that's grown from the pit of my power of death and decay, and bloomed into gleaming life. When I found her, I knew right then, everything was different.

She is what matters.

If the fae are here, if they truly did get the bridge repaired, then that's my way to get into Annwyn. To get to her.

My mind is spinning. Heart pumping with the need to go. Go *now*.

Everyone's eyes shift to me, but it's my brother who gets to his feet and rushes over, like he knows I'm ready to bolt. "I know what you're thinking, but *wait*. We need to talk this through. We need a plan first," he says, tone vehement.

"*You* plan. You're the commander."

"Slade," he hisses out desperately. "Just... You can't abandon Orea. Think of your kingdom. We have to help. We have to—"

"I'm going to her."

His green eyes ignite, burning everything straight down to the center of his pupils. "You can't just leave Orea to be invaded! This is your responsibility as king. We *need* you. The old laws of Orea were made for this *very* reason. Ensuring that there was always a monarch with magic that could defend against the threat of the fae if they ever returned. And they've *returned*, Slade."

"I made Auren a promise, and I'm not going to keep fucking failing her," I bite out. "And if I can get to her, I can get to our mother too."

All the breath leaves his chest.

"Our *mother*, Ryatt. *Auren*. The villagers."

He opens his mouth, tries to tear at the hair on his head, but it's too short now. I can tell just by looking at him how conflicted he is. "I *know* we need to get them. But Orea's under threat. I swore an oath, Slade. You swore an oath too. Everyone here is our responsibility, and Fourth has the strongest army in all the kingdoms. *You* are the strongest person in all of Orea. You can't abandon them."

"Auren is my priority. Our mother is my priority."

"Don't leave yet." He's pleading with me. Fearful.

"I have to."

"Your power might be the only thing that can stop them. This world needs you."

He doesn't understand.

"If there is ever a choice between her or the world, it's going to be her."

His expression goes stricken, but that's my brother. This is where his loyalty lies. With this kingdom, with Fourth's army, with Orea. Since coming here, this has always been his place.

My place is with her.

Plans are already brewing in my head about how I'll take Argo, what the fastest path toward Seventh is. But Ryatt's pleas keep cutting into my thoughts, leaving them in pieces.

"I'm not asking you to not go to her, to not find them," he says quietly, eyes boring into me. "*Of course* I want that. And I know how badly you need to," he adds, gaze flicking down to my chest for a split second, as if he can see through my shirt to the rotted heart beneath. "I'm just asking for you to give us a chance. Just that, Slade. A chance for Orea.

Please."

My muscles tense. Silence sticks to me, to him, to everyone in the room. Gluey, thick, and viscid, holding us in place as everyone waits to see what I'll say. To see what I'll do.

When I stay silent, his gaze slashes across my face, leaving its mark. "The fae are here, and it's going to take a fae to stop them."

His words settle on my shoulders. Sink into my skin.

Silent seconds seethe by as we look at one another.

It's going to take a fae to stop them.

Fuck.

Without a word, I turn and start to stride from the room.

"Where are you going?" he calls behind me.

I'm going to think, away from prying eyes and his unrelenting pleas. I'm going to plan. I'm going to staunch the spread of torment in my chest as it leeches my energy and tries to collapse my veins, while my fae nature urges me to *go go go*. To hurry and find Auren.

But to them, I just say, "To pack."

Two hours later, everyone is gathered in the formal dining room. I'm wearing army leathers, crown twisting around my head, boots laced up against my shins. My Premiers and Wrath are sitting to my right, and Thold has taken up the spot to my left. I didn't spell out the purpose for this gathering, but we're all watching the woman slumped in the chair at the opposite end of the table.

Queen Kaila's lips are no longer stained with rot, her eyes no longer infested.

It was with great effort that I pulled my magic away, because it was the last fucking thing I wanted to do.

She comes to, head jerking upright, and she blinks around at her surroundings. When she notices the two guards standing behind her, she tries to push to her feet, but they keep her in her chair, a hand on each shoulder.

Kaila's gaze lands on me, her face contorted with both anger and fear. She licks her lips, pulling the bottom one between her teeth, as if to make sure it hasn't rotted away.

"Is it true?" My question is quiet. Abrupt. Like the sudden snap of a twig in the middle of a silent wood.

Her hackles rise. "Is what true?" Her voice is even huskier than usual. Because while I took away the rot, she still has the imprint of my hand on her throat.

"That you fled Sixth Kingdom and left them all to be slaughtered."

I know it is, but I want to make her confess it. At least I'm up-front about where my loyalties lie. Kaila pretends to be the perfect Orean queen, and yet she fled a kingdom the minute there was a threat.

Her nervous, wide eyes shift to the side, but she finds no help from King Thold. He stares at her without giving a single expression away. His viper, however, is coiled on the table in front of him, head raised as it watches her.

She yanks her gaze back to me.

"The city was about to be overrun. There was nothing I could do," she says, lifting her chin.

"Nothing?" Thold asks. "You have magic."

"Voices," she says sharply. "What is that in the face of an army? I'm a queen, not a soldier, and I don't have offensive magic like rot," she adds, giving me a scathing look.

"You used your voice magic offensively enough when you came here," I point out.

"Highbell isn't my responsibility," she says with vehemence.

"Not your *responsibility*?" At the brusque, livid voice,

Kaila's attention shifts to the one person who she probably overlooked. Digby stands against the wall of the dining room, his question pelted at her like the sharpest shards of glass. "You wanted to rule Sixth. You took the responsibility as soon as you took control."

Her mouth curls into a sneer. "This doesn't concern you."

"Actually," I begin smoothly. "It does. Digby served as a guard in Highbell for years. So if anyone can be pissed off that you abandoned the city, it's him."

She tucks away whatever retort she was thinking about flinging.

"So it's all true? You actually saw fae?" Thold asks.

She nods tightly. "Their ears were pointed. They had magic. They were...*other*. You could feel it." A shudder passes over her body. "They were not Orean."

I see Thold swallow her answer like a jagged scrap of metal. "Tell us everything you know about the attack."

"All I know is they marched from the direction of Seventh Kingdom. I left before they breached the city. I saw nothing else."

"And you tried to flee back to your kingdom," he says with derision. "When you must know they'll be marching on your shores next."

"They won't come to Third," she argues with a shake of her head. "They just wanted to gain a foothold in Sixth. I can negotiate with them. I'm persuasive. Third will be fine."

I scoff.

"Don't lie to yourself," King Thold tells her with a harsh edge to his voice. "They're not here for a foothold. They're not here to listen to negotiations. If everything is as you and Ravinger's captain reported, then from those accounts of what happened to Sixth, things are clear. The fae are here to kill and take Orea for their own."

She shakes her head, but she's shaking all over too. "No. No, that's not going to happen."

"It is."

There's mutiny in her eyes—and a hefty dose of denial.

She straightens herself up and glares at me. "I want my brother. Where is he?"

Osrik leans forward, massive biceps braced on the table. "Oh, don't you worry. He's been with me."

Her face seems to pale as she takes in his expression, his huge form, his words. He's not someone you ever want to have on your bad side, and that's the only side she's got.

"What did you do to him?" she asks, and she can no longer keep the tremble from her voice, or the crack of moisture that's split through the seams of her eyes.

It's the only redeeming thing she has going for her—the clear love and loyalty she holds for Manu.

"I want my brother!" she shouts, body leaning forward as she breathes hard, making Thold's snake hiss in her direction.

Osrik and I exchange a look. Then, my gaze flicks to the guard standing at the wall, and I give him the smallest nod. At my direction, he opens the door and in come two more guards. Held between them is Manu.

Kaila slaps a hand over her mouth, eyes gone wide. "Manu!"

This time when she leaps to her feet, I signal for the guards to let her go. She rushes across the room, crouching to her knees where they drop her brother's limp form. She turns him over, sucking in a breath when she sees the state of him.

Rot has seeped through his skin in mottled patches. Pits are bitten into his cheeks, his nose, his neck, his hands, the skin around it blackened with crust. He smells fucking awful.

"You monster!" she screams at me, while tears flood down her cheeks. "He was innocent! It was my order that he was following!"

"Funny you should mention innocent, when Lady Auren was just that," I say, and I'm just enough of a cruel asshole to acknowledge the sense of satisfaction I get from Kaila's suffering. "Manu followed your orders, as you said, which means he wasn't innocent. He was complicit. Worked to kidnap Auren. Had one of our other ladies here stabbed." Kaila's eyes flicker, and I see this is news to her. Osrik glares at her. "Manu deserves everything he's endured. You deserve it as well, and far more."

She bares her teeth at me, chest heaving. "I hope Auren is *dead*. I wish I had killed her myself!" she shouts, cheeks high with color.

"*Careful*," I growl as I slowly get to my feet, fists braced on the table so she can see the rot writhing through my skin.

She swallows hard.

We stare at each other. Full of bitter fury. Full of hot hate.

I let her stew in it. Let her sweat.

Then, I give a flick of my hand, and she flinches. But nothing happens. At least, not to her.

Her attention drops down, and she gasps so loudly it echoes through the room. She watches with pure disbelief as the rot on Manu's face fades as I start to draw it away from him.

Her head jolts up. "What is this?"

As I get to my feet, the rest of the table follows suit. I yank my collar away from the writhing lines at my neck, nearly spitting with anger at what I'm about to do.

"It's a choice."

She goes utterly still.

"I'll give him back to you," I tell her.

Shock contorts her features, pulling at her black brows as she looks from him to me. "*Why?*" she asks in disbelief.

She *should* be in disbelief. Because in no other scenario

would I ever fucking let her walk away. Everyone else is surprised too, their attention riveted on me.

"Because there's *one* opportunity to stop the bleed before it spreads," I say, lifting a finger. "We must go to Fifth and rally their army. Cut the fae off before they can overrun Ranhold like they did Highbell. Stop them before they can reach the shores. I will let you and your brother live, and in return, you will ready your army. You will also take an elite force and fly to Fifth as soon as possible."

Her hands tremble where she clutches her brother, dragging his head into her lap. "We have no hope against fighting them," she argues. "We three may have magic, and a scattering of other Oreans throughout the kingdoms, but it'll be *nothing* compared to the abilities or numbers that they have."

"We do not roll over and show our bellies in the face of attack!" Thold shouts at her, making her flinch from his ire. "We bare our teeth and bite back!"

"Unless biting gets us put down that much faster," she lobs. Then her sharp gaze stabs into me. "Besides, *you* murdered King and Queen Merewen. *You* cast out your rot around Third Kingdom and spread fear to every corner. You weakened us right when we needed to be strong and united! You're no hero."

I don't deny it. She's right.

I'm no hero.

But it's the consequences of *her* actions that pushed me to be the villain I warned I would be.

"Whose fault is that?" I ask in a deadly quiet tone.

She blanches.

That's what I fucking thought.

"Time is running out, Kaila," Thold tells her. "Orea's only hope against this threat is to band together right now, before it's too late."

That's why she's still breathing.

Because her kingdom is devoted to her, and her army is loyal. Orea needs that army.

If she helps, then I'll wait for my vengeance. I'll bide my time.

If she runs, I'll have every right to hunt her down and not feel an ounce of fucking guilt on Orea's behalf.

It goes against my every instinct to let her and Manu walk away from this, but letting them live, letting her rally her army while bringing four kingdoms together is Orea's best chance.

And that's what my brother asked for. A chance.

So as difficult as it is, that's what I'm offering.

"If the fae truly want to take Orea, then it doesn't matter if we band together," she argues bitterly. "We're dead." Her gaze flicks around the room. "You're all fools if you think you can stand against the fae."

"You're the biggest fool of all if you think lying down is better," Ryatt seethes.

Her eyes narrow on him, but she keeps her mouth shut.

"A choice," I repeat, holding her gaze. "It's the only one you'll get, and far more than you deserve."

Kaila's face twists with loathing.

She tries to hold steady beneath my glare, but she can't stop the tremble in her hands. I want to kill her. Want to fucking rot her through and stake her head to a spike on one of my turrets for the hawks to peck at. A tear falls and she clutches Manu tighter, as if she can hear my thoughts.

My rot pinches against my hands, wanting to burst out, but I hold it back.

Give us a chance.

"What's it going to be?" I ask, my tone dark.

The tension thickens, spreading through the air between us.

"Die here and now... Or rally your army. Fly your fiercest, most powerful elite to Ranhold as soon as possible. That is your choice."

She swallows hard, and silence saturates the tension, soaking up every inch of it, weighing down the air even more and making her shoulders hunch.

"Fine," she finally says. "Third will fight. Now take the rest of your revolting magic away from my brother," she demands through her teeth.

I arch a brow. "Say please."

Fury flames in her eyes. I watch her squirm until she grits out the pride-crushing appeal. "*Please.*"

I smirk, just because I know it will madden her. And in that smirk is a taunting threat.

With a flick of my wrist, I tug the last of the rot away from Manu. Within seconds, he starts to cough and gag. Kaila jerks him onto his side just before he starts vomiting up thick black poison that spews out of him in a putrid slop.

"Manu!" she cries.

When his stomach is emptied, he slumps and catches his breath. Already, his skin is starting to return to a healthier hue, his breathing evening out.

When he sees all of us, he gasps and looks around wildly. When he notices Osrik, I see him flinch. Kaila breaks his attention as she throws her arms around his neck and hugs him.

When she pulls away, he takes in her tearstained face like he's still trying to piece together how she got here. "Kaila, what's happening?"

"Your sister just saved your life," I tell him, tone flat. My eyes flick to Kaila. "Now take him and get the fuck out of my kingdom."

She doesn't hesitate. Kaila quickly gets up and tugs Manu to his feet. He sways slightly but she instantly bolsters him, pinning her shoulder beneath his arm to keep him upright.

When she starts shuffling him away, she stops and looks at me. "How do I know your magic hasn't taken root inside of him? That you aren't tricking me?"

"You don't," I reply with a shrug. "So you'd better show up at Ranhold."

She pauses for a second and then turns and drags Manu out of the room.

Nobody speaks for several moments, though I know all of them are thinking the same thing that Thold says aloud when he finally breaks the silence. "Will she come?" he asks, letting his serpent hang over his shoulder.

"Maybe," I say.

"Maybe not," he says.

And I nod, because he's right. Maybe not.

Kaila's heart isn't for Orea, it's for her brother. And as much as I hate her, as much as I want to kill her and Manu both, in this, we are alike.

Because my heart isn't for Orea either.

"We need her," Thold says. "But we'll fight regardless."

He's a far better king than me.

"I can have my elite reach Ranhold within the week. What's your plan, Ravinger?"

What is my plan?

Everyone waits to see what I'll say. I feel them all. Feel Ryatt.

Give us a chance.

"We'll leave at first light," I tell him, and I hear my brother let out a breath.

Looking at me, Thold holds out his hand. Surprise flashes through me, but I reach forward and shake it.

"For Orea," he rumbles.

A far, far better king than me.

After Thold and his guards leave, Ryatt comes over to stand beside me. "Thank you," he murmurs.

I turn to him. "We have Thold and his soldiers, and when we get to Ranhold, we'll have Fifth's. And if Kaila actually shows, we'll have her forces as well," I list off. "You asked me to give Orea a chance, and this is it. I've brought four kingdoms together as best I could. But know this. I'm going to Ranhold because it's on the way to Seventh. I will help set up the defense against the arrival of the fae, and I will use my power as much as I can, but then I will be leaving," I warn him. "Auren is my priority."

Like Kaila said, I'm no hero.

Now that I know there's a way to get to Auren, nothing is going to stand in my way. So I'll give them this chance, but if it's not enough, then so be it.

Because I'm going to that bridge whether Orea stands…

Or falls.

CHAPTER 50

AUREN

Lord Cull.
Slade's father.
The Orean villagers.
Elore.

As the truth of everything slams into place, I see it all with new eyes.

The two manors. Why Lord Cull kept the old one and erected the stone wall. Why this room looks the way it does. Why the Oreans are all in heavy winter clothing.

Why I've had such a bad feeling since the moment I entered this place.

The crack in the floor isn't any mere damage. The space above it isn't just shadows. This is the *rip*. The one Slade and his father made when their powers collided.

Except unlike the one back at Deadwell, or even the one at the Conflux, this rip fills the air with inherent *wrongness*. It looks nothing like those other ones. This one is…faded. As if it combusted and lost its connection, and all that's left now is a churning cloud of shallow shadows. Whatever happened to this rip, the result is clear, there is no world on the other side of it.

It's broken.

When movement catches my eye, I look down, realizing that what I thought were stains on the floor are actually old rot lines infested through the marble.

My attention pulls away when I suddenly feel a trickling sensation.

Like water sluicing over me.

I gasp, the breath getting glued to my ribs as I look down at my palms. My gray, glamoured palms that are now blooming with patches of my true gilt-colored skin.

Shit. Emonie.

The footsteps echoing through the hall make my head jerk back up, and I curl my hands into fists, as if trying to contain the fading glamour and the writhing rot.

Slade's father stalks forward.

Stanton Cull.

Cull, not Ravinger as I assumed, because Slade must've taken his mother's—

My gaze hooks on to Elore as he stalks toward her like a demon ready to drag her to hell. Terror claws down my back, but the intense rage claws even harder.

I won't let him fucking touch her.

I take a step forward, but when the guard next to me lurches like he's going to shove me back, I react on pure instinct.

With a swing of my arm, a whip of gold slings from my hand and slaps into his chest, sending him flying across the room. He lands with a crack, and I feel the eyes of everyone suddenly land on me.

Then the metal grate of swords being drawn rings

through the air as the other guards start rushing toward me. Magic pours out of my palms like a fountain, drenching my boots and pooling onto the floor.

"What the fuck is this?" Cull's voice cuts through the room, his steps stalled in their track toward Elore.

But I know his reputation. I know what he's done. I know what they call him.

The Breaker.

So I know I have to get Elore and all the other Oreans away from here—away from *him*. I can't risk them getting hurt, can't put Slade's mother in danger. The last thing I can let happen is for any of these people to get caught between Cull and me.

I act quickly.

The gold that I've accumulated at my feet surges forward as fast as I can push it. He has a breath to realize that it's coming for him, and he raises his hand and snaps his fingers. A piece of the floor breaks and wrenches upward, and my gold knocks into his stony barrier, smashing it to pieces. Debris from the impact sends him falling back, his head cracking loudly against the tile.

The guards lunge, but I punch another wave of magic toward them before they can reach me. My molten gold thrusts out, hardening into fists that ram into their torsos, sending them flying.

Before they even land, the ground breaks beneath my feet like a beast come up from the earth's core, with jagged pieces of marbled teeth to snatch me from below.

Instead of panicking, instead of startling, my body reacts without thought or emotion. Only pure fae instinct. I pitch myself to the side before the crack can devour me in its widening mouth, pushing two Oreans out of the way just as I fall.

The second I hit the floor, I lift my hand, shoving the

liquid gold at Cull—whatever I already have at my disposal, whatever I can use the fastest.

A cord flings into him, snagging around his waist, filling me with vicious satisfaction. It yanks on his body, trying to topple him again, but the guards are back up, coming for me. I use my other hand to direct more gold to slap into them, to pin them down—

Cull snaps his fingers.

Pain *erupts* in my arm.

Agony strips me of breath, of movement, freezing me into incapacitation.

Broken. My arm is *broken*. It hangs at an odd angle. The bone in my forearm split, my limb useless, pain imploding throughout my body.

Through blurred eyes, I notice that more of my gold skin has started to bloom up my arms like blotting ink. The glamour bleeding away in growing splotches.

Cull snaps his fingers again.

I flinch, ready for him to break another bone or snap my neck and kill me, but instead, the roof breaks even more than it already was. Surprise runs through me, but I have to brace myself as the gap widens and sends pieces of ceiling careening down, aiming right for me.

I roll out of the way, the movement tearing a scream from my throat, though it's drowned out by the blaring crash of falling debris. Pieces fall right where I was a second ago, and Oreans shriek in fear, scrabbling away, trying to avoid being crushed. I see Elore crouched and being barraged with small pieces, arms covering her head as dust rains down.

Fear and anxiety pounce on me like a predator, crushing me with its weight.

I need to get Elore out. I need to get everyone *out.*

Tears stain my vision, but I grit my teeth and try to yank at my magic. I feel it swell inside my chest like a full breath.

It writhes and roils with my fury, but when I lift my good arm to try and blow it all out, it falters.

The pain makes my gold-touch stutter, rising up only to fall again like a person stumbling from exhaustion or drunkenness. It's like being tortured by Queen Isolte all over again.

"Fuck," I hiss as I struggle to my feet. "Push through it, Auren."

Shaking all over, I try again, my heart beating so wildly I worry it's going to hammer right past my ribs and roll onto the floor. But that thump in my chest is obliterated when more of the ceiling breaks.

I manage to send a whip of gold to lash out at Cull, but when the stream curls around his fist, he abruptly goes still. He stares at his hand, perhaps really *looking* at the gold for the first time. That one remaining eye of his runs over the black veins that writhe through the liquid metal…and then that gaze drops to the floor.

Mine follows.

My eyes widen as I see the decades-old rot slithering through the tile, like it's come to life again.

And all of it is moving toward *me*.

The roots thread through the floor in slow movements, making the tile crack and groan as it starts to circle me in a protective ring. As if in response, the rot in my palms sprouts up, reaching for the rot in the floor like it wants to reunite.

Goose bumps erupt over my entire body, and I gasp as I feel the full-body shiver of a cold tide receding. My eyes flush with tears, my ears twinge, and when I look down, I see the rest of the glamour washing away like letters drawn into the sand, erased by the drag of the tide. My hands, arms, hair, the fake coloring all pulls away until my true skin gleams.

Please let Emonie be okay…

When my true self shows, the Oreans gape at me. My

eyes meet Elore's, and she stares in horror, hand cupped over her mute mouth in recognition.

Cull's eye goes wide, drinking in my real appearance.

I take advantage of his surprise, gritting my teeth against the pain as I make the gold around his hand tighten. But before it can fully cement in place, he breaks it in half, freeing himself.

Dammit.

Panting and clutching my arm against my chest, I manage to make both pieces rejoin, before winding them together to form a rope. It shoots out to wrap around his ankle, and with one tug, I yank his feet out from under him, making him crash to the floor.

I try to immediately make a new stream pour from my hand, but it drips slowly instead. When I attempt to make the small pieces shoot toward him, to enter his mouth or nose or eye, it's too sluggish, too imprecise.

The rest of my gold is still keeping the guards at bay, but barely. It stretches around them like desperate fingers, holding them against the wall. So I call to the rot in the floor instead, trying to get it to attack Cull, to pollute him with decay, but it doesn't quite answer to me. Sweat starts tracking down my brow as I urge it on, as I try to ignore the pounding in my arm.

Come on.

Instead of attacking him, the rot deteriorates the floor beneath him. It might not putrefy his ass, but it does make him fall through the collapsing tile as it abruptly gives way.

Arms flinging out, he manages to catch himself before the ground can swallow him up. Gold drips from my hands in clumsy sloshes, but I meld it together and toss it toward him. The thin stream hardens and sharpens mid-air, ready to pierce through his chest as it shoots forward, and I hold my breath...

But his power shatters mine into pieces.

The tiny spear I formed explodes like a star, sending bits

flying. The blow against my magic is intense enough that it sends me rocking back on my heels as though I've just been punched in the chest.

Cull hauls himself up the rest of the way as I fuse my gold back together again. I send it for the fucker's throat, but he dives out of the way just in time. Then he turns and snaps his fingers, making the wall right next to me release a violent *crack.*

Jerking my head around, I see the wall start to tilt, and I react.

I call for my arm cuffs, my belt, my buckles, for every bit of gold I'm wearing that I've reserved as a last resort. Because the way I keep pulling more new gold out of me is taking its toll, and the pain is draining me so much faster.

In a blink, every bit of gold liquifies and pours off of me, and I toss up my hands just as the wall breaks open and falls. Before it can crush me, my gold splays out like a net, catching the chunk and stopping its trajectory.

My head swims with the effort, but I hold it, sweat dripping down my spine and soaking into my ribbons as my arms shake.

I need to get the Oreans out of here.

"Run!" I shout at them.

Now that the broken wall has created a gap to the outside, they have a chance. My good hand lashes out, grabbing the first Orean I can reach, and I pull him toward it. "Go!"

Everyone else starts to rush toward me, running as fast as they can, but some of them seem weakened, slow.

Cull snaps his fingers, trying to mend the wall and close the break before they can leave.

"Oh no, you fucking don't," I growl.

I use the net, flinging it forward like a slingshot, tossing the chunk of wall at him to cut off his attention. Gratification curls through me when he doesn't move fast enough and the rubble knocks him in the shoulder. The rest of it smashes to the ground in a deafening blast, but I take advantage of the moment to call the gold to me, and I fling it toward the gap in the wall.

I form an arch there like a protective, reinforced doorway. It ripples, holding back the groaning walls that are trying to mold back together. I shake, feeling my very muscles tremble from the strain, but I don't let go.

More Oreans race through it, and I watch them sprint away from the manor. And there, ahead in the grass, I see Emonie stumbling to a stop, eyes wide as the first Orean nearly collapses at her feet.

Thank Divine.

The walls slam together above my arch, and I can physically feel it bearing down on the top as if the weight were on my back. I grit my teeth so hard my jaw cracks, but I don't let go. I can see Cull out of the corner of my eye, straining, furious as he tries to overpower me.

One of the Oreans accidentally stumbles and bumps into my arm as they race for the archway. A gurgled scream gets caught in my throat, pain blacking out my vision for a moment, and I nearly lose hold of my magic, the arch dropping a foot before I catch it again.

Push through it. Shove down fucking weakness.

I heave, but I swallow down the bile and force myself not to pass out, to stay standing.

Then the pressure on the arch suddenly lifts, so quickly that the absence of the strain has me flinching. My glassy eyes lift to look around, I see two more Oreans sprint out, and then there's no one left except...

Elore.

I turn, my blood running cold as I see Cull with his hand squeezed around her throat. Her face is turning red from lack of breath.

I can't breathe either.

He squeezes harder, making her eyes bulge, fingers scrabbling at his grip.

Rotten gold pools in my palm.

"You use your magic, and I'll snap her neck," he threatens viciously.

I've seen this scene play out before—when it was my neck on the line. It was another controlling, cruel person who eked out the threat and tried to force control. To force submission.

Fuck that.

Cull looks down at her with evil victory, while tears slip down her cheeks.

The sight of her makes my pain become secondary. My rage overpowers it, cutting through it in the same way lightning blasts through fog.

"Leave her alone!"

With a flick of my wrist, a small puddle of molten gold vaults toward him in a thousand tiny drops that harden into thin needles.

He's focused on Elore, saying something in her ear, so he doesn't notice what I'm doing until he's suddenly stabbed in the neck, every shard embedding into his skin. He lurches back, causing both of them to fall to the floor.

He rolls to the side, neck bleeding from countless pinprick punctures, the golden splinters sticking out of him like needles on a pine tree. Blood drips down his collar, disappearing into the red cloth stuffed at his throat.

I push the rest of my gold to stream toward Elore. It loops around her back, helping her to her feet, and starts pulling her toward me.

At the same time, I start bending the little slivers in Cull's neck, making them meld together so I can choke him out, but he breaks it with his magic and tosses it away.

Shaking, I clench my teeth and make the golden shards fly up and stab into the open wounds at his throat. I make them delve deeper, ready to send them into his bloodstream and straight to his heart, to stab every organ, ready to fucking kill—

Suddenly, the broken bones in my arm *grind*.

My scream shreds the air.

My hold on my magic sputters out like a snuffed candle, my gold going liquid and dribbling out of Cull. It all sloshes down in a useless puddle, making Elore stagger with its sudden absence, the thick liquid tripping up her feet.

Bile swarms my mouth, and one look at my arm makes the pain a hundred times worse. I can *see* it. See Cull using his break power to make the two pieces of bone scrape together, pulling the skin sickeningly as they move. Agony clots my vision like stains of ink, and I sway on my feet, my body giving out.

Just as my knees buckle, someone's arms come up behind me before I can crash to the floor. I blink, thrashing to get out of their hold, but when I look up, it's Wick who has me.

He immediately hauls me out of the manor, pulling me beneath the arch. Cull drags Elore up too, keeping hold of her arm as he pursues us. Outside, I can see the Oreans running for the trees.

When Cull breaches the gap in the wall too, Wick picks me up and starts sprinting us away from the manor, making the pain so much worse. My vision topples dangerously, and I know I'm going to pass out, but I try to force myself not to.

Stay awake.

Ignore the pain.

Stay. Fucking. Awake.

grind—grind—grind—grind

"Here! Escape here!"

Ludo's shout causes the Oreans to run for him, probably only trusting him because they see he's fighting off two of Cull's guards. Beside him, Emonie is fighting too, a dagger in hand as she spins and twists. She's deflecting blows from the guard she's fighting against, keeping him away from the fleeing Oreans. Brennur is behind them both, and there's a lush fairy ring at his feet, its flowers and grass in a perfect circle, much bigger and taller than the one we used before.

A group of three Oreans stagger into the ring and instantly disappear. Then another group goes through, and another, and another, filling me with tense hope.

We can get away. We can get everyone out of here, safe.

Ludo and Emonie continue to fight, but in my peripheral, I see more guards rushing toward them. Every running step that Wick takes as we hurry toward the ring jostles my arm, making it nearly impossible to talk, to think.

"Wait." My voice comes out as nothing more than a raw croak. I don't even think Wick heard me.

One look back shows Cull scanning the yard as he follows us. He spots Brennur and the ring, sees his guards fighting Ludo and Emonie, and then his eyes land back on me. He doesn't run, doesn't rush. He just strides after us with the promise of death in his eyes while hauling Elore with him.

I have to get her.

"Wait!" I push against Wick, and this time, my voice comes out loud enough for him to hear. His head jerks down to look at me as I struggle to get out of his arms. He releases me, and we both stagger, my ankle nearly twisting as I land.

"What are you doing?" he shouts as he reaches for me again.

I wrench away from him. "I can't leave without her!"

"Auren—" His eyes suddenly go over my shoulder, and then he shoves me out of the way.

I stumble, just as the sword that had been aiming for me swings down and slices into him instead. I gasp as it cuts deep into his bicep, and Wick shouts out in pain.

His sleeve slashes open, and blood bursts from the wound.

But I stare in shock because the blood…it's not red.

It's *gold*.

CHAPTER 51

AUREN

Shock stiffens my body. All my thoughts cinch.

My eyes widen, heartbeat going more erratic as I stare and stare. Gaze caught on the gold blood that gushes from Wick's gash.

Estelia's voice buzzes in my head. *Every Turley ever born had some part of them that was gold.*

Wick's face swarms in my memory, of how he looked at me when we first met in the field.

You really are her…

The startling truth runs rampant, stampeding through my ears with a deafening charge. Shock, disbelief, and outrage scatter, pulling me every which way. I feel like someone has knocked the wind out of me, barging into me again and again as I try to breathe.

Our eyes meet for a split second, his gold blood saturated between us, flooding me with newfound realization.

His expression is…

Regretful.

Guilt-ridden.

Soaked through with a begrudging acknowledgement that drenches us both, raining down the past and the present.

Wick is a Turley.

It's all I hear. All I think.

Until our connection is abruptly cut off when Wick turns to face the guard who tried to attack me. Time hurtles out of its pause, like a door flinging open.

Wick moves with impressive speed. With one hand, he reaches forward and grips the guard by his face, and then *blows*.

A cloud of gold ash suddenly erupts out. It's thick and cloying, bursting right into the guard's forced-open mouth, filling past his lips, weighing down his tongue. The guard starts choking as more glinting ash piles in, a cloud of thick powder surrounding his head, obscuring him from view.

His hands claw, trying to scoop the ash out of his mouth to clear his airway, but it doesn't work. He collapses to the ground, and Wick spins, yanking a hidden dagger free just in time to fight off another guard.

Movement in the corner of my eye has me whirling, and a guard rushes at me, blade raised. Before he can swing, his spine suddenly cracks in half, like a tree trunk snapping. He pitches forward, dead before he hits the ground. Eyes staring, unseeing.

"No one touches her!" Cull yells as he stalks forward, Elore's feet dragging in the grass as he wrenches her along.

I clutch my aching arm against my chest and face him, thoughts racing.

Behind me, the last of the Oreans are trying to get to the ring. Ludo is fighting. Emonie is fighting. Wick is fighting. There are more guards running this way, surrounding us from all sides.

"Retreat!" Wick shouts. "To the ring! Hurry!"

My focus is on Elore—on the terrified look on her face. I can see all the years of abuse and degradation in her eyes. All of it centered on the man who has hold of her.

"Auren!" Wick calls behind me. "We have to go!"

"I'm not leaving her!" I toss back over my shoulder.

I shovel magic out of myself, forcing it past my pain and scooping it past my palms. Sluggish, thick clots drop onto the grass.

Cull sneers at my pathetic attempt. "Why did the rot move to you?"

When I don't answer him, he tightens his fist, and his magic intensifies.

grind—grind—grind

I'm shaking all over. With anger. With determination. Trying to concentrate on my magic even through the debilitating pain.

"Fuck. You."

I send the clotted gold zipping forward. Make it sharpen. It stabs into his hand where he grips Elore, forcing him to let go. Blood oozes from the hits, but he lifts that very same hand and snaps his fingers.

Pure, piercing, agony explodes through me.

I look down at where he's just broken one of my ribs.

Trying to inhale is torture.

My legs give way, knees slamming hard into the ground. I pitch forward, barely catching myself from collapsing by bracing my good hand in front of me. My arm shakes as I try to hold myself up. To keep from falling face-first. Sweat and bile and tears are ready to pour out of me. The grass in my vision spins. The breath in my lungs tightens.

But the spot in my chest—the seed of rot left behind...

It *seethes*.

"Why did the rot move to you?"

I bite my tongue to keep from screaming.

Gold congeals against the grass.

"Tell me!"

I lift my head, glaring with defiance. With fury. With threat.

His eyes harden. His hand lifts.

The Breaker keeps breaking. But not me.

Snap.

Behind me, I hear Ludo shout.

Snap.

Emonie screams.

Snap.

Wick cries out.

My stomach heaves, strained neck barely able to look back, to see them sprawled on the ground, clutching broken bones, panic and hate and desperation slamming through me, and I have to *do* something. Have to stop this. Have to save everyone.

"I'll keep breaking their bones one by one unless you tell me what I want to know," Cull shouts. "Why did that rot magic come toward you? Why is it seeking *you* out?"

So that's why he isn't just killing me. He wants answers.

"I don't know."

My voice comes out like a whisper. My gold curdles and cools. But the rot that runs through it writhes. The spot in my chest burns.

Thrums.

My ears pound, not from the pain, but the drumming of the rot. Not just the rot that's intertwined with my magic either, but the rot from inside the house.

His rot. *His* magic.

It's thumping. Pulsing. Like veins from a heart. Beating through me in a way I've never felt before.

My fingers curl into the grass.

GOLD

I wake up the fae beast inside of me, make it open both eyes.

Slade's magic is singing its seductive song, baying out like a wolf howling at the moon.

The song of power calls to my beast.

So I set it free from the cage of my ribs.

And I let it sing *back*.

And as soon as I do, that rot in my chest starts burning hotter.

Hotter.

"Tell me what connection you have with my son!" Cull demands, voice cutting through the air.

His son.

My head lifts, eyes spearing him with glittering fury. "He's not *your* anything," I snarl.

He's my everything.

Protective possessiveness flares up from within. Slade is mine. Not his.

Mine.

I claim him—my heart, mind, body, beast, my soul claims him.

Cull's eyes gleam with thirst. "So you *do* know him. Is he here? Did he send you? Tell me!"

I feel my stomach pitch and sway. Squeeze in on itself as bile burns my throat and waters my tongue.

My hand digs deeper into the grass. Into the soil beneath. My beast leaps up, talons latched into my torso. I feel it reach up and close its mouth around that seed of rot.

I suck in a breath.

Then the beast swallows that seed of power whole, and my entire body shudders. My entire world *twists*. Something at the deepest part of my being shifts.

Melds.

Cull doesn't see. Doesn't see behind him. Doesn't feel

what I feel. Unaware of Slade's magic swimming beneath his very feet, stretching toward me—reaching to my own rot.

Like Slade himself is holding out his hand, and I'm reaching right back.

Nearly touching.

Nearly there.

I can feel him as surely as I can feel my own skin. Can sense his very soul as if it's intertwining through mine.

Weaving and weaving and *weaving*…

Cull's brown eyebrows slam together at my continued silence. He doesn't hear how loud my roaring song is. Doesn't hear the violence screaming through the roots in the ground.

"I will break *everyone* until you tell me what I want to know," he threatens as he yanks Elore over to him by her hair. "Including her."

Her.

Our eyes lock.

My gold ones.

Her green ones.

The same exact shade as Slade's—like he's the one looking out at me.

The ground rumbles—I rumble.

Fury is hot. It's wild. It's beastly.

It's rot.

Cull lifts his hand. His finger poised against thumb. Ready to snap. Ready to break.

Instead…

I break

open.

Slade's rot smashes into mine, and I rupture from within.

Time tilts.

Distance thins.

And something…collides.

AUREN

I gasp.
Breathe.
The air of Annwyn. The air of Orea.
I pitch backwards.
The beast and the seed surge.
Combine.
My back heats.
Rot delves. Not with death, but rebirth. *Life* tears free.
Two souls reach out. Clasp. My ears echo with two heartbeats.
With a bonded song.
My aura flares.
Changes.
I can feel him.

I can feel her.
Changes.
My aura pulses.
A roar sounds in my ear. Souls tether.
was my dying heart.
Scales erupt over my chest, bursting from what I thought
My two sides...they *mend*. Something else tears free.
Something shifts.
Bursts.
My rotting heart suddenly swells.
My knees buckle.
Her warmth. It consumes me.
I can scent her.
I gasp.

SLADE

CHAPTER 52

AUREN

Time snaps back into place.

Cull is frozen, standing there gaping at me. Elore's eyes have gone wide.

It feels like a star as hot and bright as the sun has suddenly burst out of me, roots as dark and poisoned as death streaming in.

Confusion, elation, and something unnamed—but its essence feeling so utterly fitting—sweeps through me. I look down, my whole body shaking, a gasp tearing from my throat.

I've only seen one aura before, and that was Slade's while in his Rip form. Dark, coiling black emanating around him like smoke and shadow. An aura that pulsed with his essence.

He said my own aura shone like the glowing sun.

And that's what I see.

Light has exploded over my body in luminous warmth. But…there are now shadows of black curling through it.

Like our auras combined.

Inside, I convulse with a wave of heat and tepidity, with light and dark, life and death.

Black and gold.

There's this connection I can't quite explain but somehow understand intrinsically. Like two hearts beating as one.

Breathlessly, I watch the glowing gold and wisps of coiled black slowly sink back into my skin until the flare of colors is gone. But while I can't see it anymore, I can still feel it. Can still feel Slade's presence. Gently. Softly. Like the quiet moments right before waking, when I can sense him lying next to me. Like when he enters a room and I know he's there, even before I turn to look.

A cruel bark of laughter startles me, wrenching me away from my inner reflections. I jerk my head up and see Cull's eye gleam, his teeth flashing with a menacing grin.

"Well, that explains everything, doesn't it?" he says, his gaze cruelly mocking. "*Päyur.*"

My brow furrows.

That word…spoken with the old fae lilt. I recognize that word… How do I recognize that word?

Then I remember.

I remember me, back in Ranhold. A dark library. A cover made of elderwood, stitched with red leather. A forbidden book of the fae that I slipped into my pocket.

I remember peeling it open and seeing an illustration inside of it.

Of a woman with flaxen hair that gleamed gold. Of a fae male beside her with wings. There was a haze that enveloped them both as they embraced. Almost like…

Joined auras.

And that word, just below them.

Päyur.

My heartbeat rumbles. Resonates.

"That explains the rot," Cull says, his expression arrogant. Ecstatic. "Tell me, how long were you able to see my son's aura? How long have you known you were fated to be a bonded pair?"

Bonded pair…

My vision tunnels.

One sharp memory suddenly shoves forward. As if it's been waiting to burst in all along.

My mind's eye sees it so clearly. A frigid night, out on a balcony, beneath snow and stars. Beneath demanding want and debilitating confliction.

Beneath a set of black eyes.

I look up, letting snow fall onto my lashes, and when I turn to glance at Rip, I find he's already looking at me.

"So, still angry at me?" he asks with a wry tinge to his tone. I leap at it, relieved to end the silence, to move past the rebuttal on the stairwell.

"Furious."

Rip tips his head down, as if he expected nothing less.

"You?" I ask him.

"Livid."

Our mouths twitch in synchronicity, shared smirks tipping up at the corners.

He leans back in his chair, the spikes along his back disappearing beneath his leathers. "We're quite the pair, you and I."

At his words, chills scatter over my arms, even though I'm wrapped beneath the blanket. "What do you mean?"

There's an enigmatic look on his face that I can't decipher, and he opens his mouth to answer, but appears to reconsider, going silent once more. Flakes of snow land on his black hair, soaking into the inky locks while he considers me with that intensity I've grown so accustomed to.

"It's remarkable, you know."

"What is?" I ask.

"We might be the last two fae in the entire world, and somehow, our paths crossed that night."

His words from before, about how my aura was a beacon that he followed, make a lump appear in my throat. "Fate does funny things."

"It does."

It does.

My mind is a cyclone. Twisting and twisting. My emotions are in chaos.

And still, his words echo.

We're quite the pair, you and I.

Quite the pair, you and I.

Pair, you and I.

Päyur, you and I.

CHAPTER 53

AUREN

He knew.
That's the thought that chokes up and lodges in my throat. I can taste the truth of it at the back of my tongue.

I only ever had a vague inclination about auras. As a little girl, I can remember them abstractly. So when I first saw Rip that night in the Barrens, I knew he was fae. I'd never seen an Orean have an aura before, so the black haze that always clung to him like smoke and shadow, plus his slightly tipped ears obscured behind his hair and helmet? I knew what he was. I could sense the *otherness* in him.

Except I never knew that only fated bonded pairs could see them. I never knew what it truly meant. How would I? I was five when I left Annwyn.

But Slade knew.

Emonie's previous words come back to me.

"You can see his aura? Not many fae get to. No wonder

you're dying to get back to each other."

I didn't think about it. Didn't stop and consider why, when I returned to Annwyn, I didn't see any other auras. I've been too wrapped up in trying to find him, trying to manage my power...

And his.

I glance down at my palms, watching the twisting lines across them.

"Where is he?"

My eyes shoot up. Cull is closer now. Elore is too.

He sees my attention on her and tightens his hold on the back of her neck. "Look at this, Elore. A true Päyur right in our midst. Not that you'd care much, would you? It's not as if you're one of the very rare Oreans to even be capable of bonding with fae. But here she is. Bonded to our son." He glances back at me. "And my son, nowhere in sight." His expression is full of sadistic promise. "But I have you, don't I?"

"No," I snarl. "You don't."

I fist my hand, and Slade's magic that flooded in now answers my call. The amassed rot explodes out of the ground, shooting up in a violent upsurge that cracks the earth.

It rises like serpentine roots, thick and sinister and towering.

A breath. That's all they have, and then it slashes at every guard, hurling them away.

And because I acted too suddenly, without warning, the biggest root of all slams into Cull, the abrupt appearance of the magic and strength taking him by surprise. He goes flying.

"Auren!" Wick calls.

Time to go.

With my good hand, I snatch hold of Elore. Together, we start racing toward the fairy ring where Wick, Emonie, and Ludogar are already gathered. Wick's shoulder looks shattered. Emonie is clutching a broken hand, and Ludogar had to crawl to the ring, his leg snapped. My own broken bones jolt in torment, stealing my ability to breathe, but I push through it.

Miraculously, none of the guards have gotten to Brennur. None of them were able to cut off our only escape.

Behind me, the poisoned roots grow and grow, looming over the grounds, thickening like the most treacherous brambles. But then I hear the roots start snapping. Breaking.

"Go!"

We all shove our way in at once. Clustered together, bodies bulging inside the ring, the five of us plaster against one another. My feet are on tiptoes, good hand clutching Elore, Wick beside me, still bleeding, breathing hard, Emonie shouldering Ludogar to keep him upright.

And we disappear.

The world crumples like paper, tossing away, tossing us with it. Disbelief fills me, the chasm of my surprise slowly filling me with elation. We got out. We got *away*.

But revulsion sinks through my stomach too as we travel through Brennur's magic. I don't know why I hate the fairy ring so much, don't know why I have such an aversion to it, but I do. A cold sweat breaks over my skin, and I want *out*—

We land. Everything smoothes.

I grip Elore's hand, squeezing tight, tears of relief starting to pool around me. "We made it. Everything's alright, we're—"

The world comes into view, and I instantly realize that I'm wrong. Everything isn't alright.

In fact, it's very, very wrong.

The fairy ring we're huddled in is at the mouth of a castle.

Towering over us, the white structure drips with swooping stone and stained glass, every pane lit up with the reflection of the setting sun. We're just before the castle's front steps, a short, wide stair thrusting out from the huge double doors like a tongue that spat us into the courtyard.

And surrounding us are at least a hundred Stone Swords.

My blood runs cold. My heart trips. Because every single Orean villager I'd thought had gotten away from danger is here, on their knees with a blade at their throats and dismay on their faces.

A king stands before them. Dressed all in gray with a regal mantle lined with fur. He has taupe skin and a hard expression, and on his head sits a gray crown with sharp spires hewn from rock.

King Carrick.

Alarm blares in my ears and reverberates down my limbs, making me shake with it.

"What's happening?" I breathe as I look around wildly, trying to understand. "Where are we?"

"We're in Lydia, but we shouldn't be," Wick says, confusion clear in his tone. "We should—"

The fairy ring suddenly gives us a big *shove*.

All five of us get pushed out. Wick is only barely able to keep hold of Ludogar before he goes sprawling. Emonie stumbles but manages to right herself and presses up against me, while Elore clutches my arm so tightly that her nails indent into my skin.

As soon as we're clear of the circle, there's the sound of a fierce wind. The grass and flowers blow through the ring, though I don't feel the breeze. I barely have time to glance back at it and see people start to appear inside the ring before—

grind—grind—grind—grind

I'm on my knees, buckled from the agony of my arm and rib. My ears are ringing so loudly I don't even realize the others are screaming until I have the wherewithal to look around and see Emonie, Wick, and Ludogar all on the ground, obviously going through the same bone-breaking agony as I am.

Their pain kills me. Floods me with panic.

Elore crouches down in front of me, pale hands grasping my cheeks, her expression frenzied and terrified. Even through the horror of this moment, the fact that Slade's mother is trying to comfort me makes me want to cry.

The Breaker stands over us, glaring around like we're rodents in a trap. But I'm not looking at him. I'm looking at Brennur. Beside me, so is Wick.

"What the fuck did you do?" Wick yells at him, his voice hoarse. "What the fuck have you done?"

The old fae's eyes shift away. Grayish skin mottled at the cheeks.

Betrayed. We were *betrayed.*

Brennur opened up the fairy ring here, instead of safety. Here, in Annwyn's capital...

Whipping gusts of fury blast into me, but my body and mind are too dazed to move.

Wick is on the ground, clutching his shoulder, blood still soaking through his shirt, looking like he got stained with smears of my gold-touch. But even so, he tries to use that ashen magic of his, tries to blow a stream of it out. It barely sputters, like dust in a feeble puff, before Wick is screaming, laid out on his back.

grind—grind—grind—grind

I'm going to pass out, and maybe I would have if it weren't for the fact that Brennur moves closer to me. If it weren't for the fact that I catch another whiff of the leather from his vest. An undertone to it like it was soaked in...bark.

Oak bark.

My head hollows out. My heart does too.

I'm not here, at the fae's castle. I'm there, in Bryol, when

I was five years old. When a leather gag that tasted of oak bark was pressed into my mouth. When I was stolen from my guards, separated from the other children and taken into Orea.

Orea…where old fairy rings used to dot across the lands when fae had lived there.

Bile heaves up my throat and spews from my mouth, making my broken rib stab me with horrible pain. The acid burns, but my eyes burn hotter.

"You," I breathe, staring at Brennur as I wipe my mouth against my sleeve. "It was you, wasn't it? You took me to—"

I don't even see his cane before it slams into my face.

Pain explodes across my cheek, making my vision collapse and my body go sprawling back onto the ground. I think I might've passed out for at least several seconds, because when I come to, the royal guard has Elore, Wick, Emonie, and Ludo on their knees by point of sword.

Hate and fury flare hot in my gut, molten and burning.

The fae king looms over me, right alongside Cull. Side by side, the two of them are backed by the glaring castle, their expressions monstrous. Victorious.

"So it's true. *Auren Turley*." The king bites out my name with a gravelly voice. There's so much loathing in his granite eyes that my hackles rise. "You're supposed to be dead."

"You fucking will be," I spit out.

Gold and rot rush out of my palms and slam into the king, Cull, Brennur, knocking them back, nearly skidding them into the guards…

The Breaker snaps another rib.

Agony staggers my power, rips it away. My liquid metal sloshes to the ground in an ineffectual heap, like wind torn out of the sail of a boat.

"Enough of that," I hear the king say distantly, even as Wick and Emonie also scream my name. I can't see them through the tears blurring my eyes.

"I need her alive, but I need her useful," Cull says.

"A useful Turley?" King Carrick laughs but rubs at his chin in thought before glancing at someone out of view. "Bring Una."

I pant against the grass. The battle with Cull, how much I've used my gold-touch and Slade's rot, it's taken a toll, hacked into me again and again, like the swing of an ax against a trunk. The pain, every break Cull inflicts, it's like the last cut before the tree falls.

The king looks back at me, at the defiance flashing through my sweat-slicked face. He raises a brow and then glances at his guards. "Start killing the Oreans."

"No!" I wrench up, black dots clouding my vision, but I see the first Orean fall, a bloom of blood weeping from the man's throat.

Then another.

Another.

grind—grind

More Orean bodies fall.

"Stop!" I scream again and again, trying to claw my way forward, gold staining the grass with my drag.

stop stop stop stop stop

The pain, the death, the heart-stopping realizations, I need it all to *stop*.

"I'm doing them a favor," the king intones. "Dying here in my courtyard is much quicker than the ones who are dying in Orea."

What?

I drag my eyes up to the king's hard face.

"Oh, didn't you know?" he asks before looking around at Wick and the others. "I've finally made it happen. The bridge of Lemuria has been unbroken. My army marches on Orea as we speak, killing everyone in its path. Soon, *every* Orean will be dead."

Wick shouts. Struggles. The villagers wail.

But my ears have latched on to one thing.

The bridge of Lemuria has been unbroken.

Slade.

I can get to *Slade*.

This thought is the only thing powerful enough to cut through the agony, and the drain, and the vulnerability.

The king has miscalculated. He thought his words would only bring me despair and panic, and they do...but they also bring vicious, surging hope.

I don't wait. Using this burst of power, I shove everything I have at Cull and the king. The blundering puddle on the grass suddenly sloshes together, lifting like a thick limb. With a grunt, I make it arc toward the two fae, ready to gild them solid, ready to fucking kill them all because I can *finally* get back to Slade—

Hands behind me suddenly clap over my ears.

There's instant, intense pressure, like I've been dumped into the bottom of the sea. Plunging down its depths far too fast.

My magic tumbles out of my grip.

It feels like my eardrums are about to blow out, my eyes ready to burst from their sockets. I scream from the pressure, trying to wrench away the hands, but then, something *digs in*.

Tunneling down my ear canals, probing into me, making me scream even louder, though I can't hear it. There's a clicking that peals through, encompassing everything else. My gold splashes to the ground, my body slumps.

Something burrows

burrows

burrows

into my ear, into my *brain*.

Like a caterpillar chomping through a leaf, a mouse tunneling through the dirt. I go rigid when it suddenly hits something in my mind. Delves in.

Goes deeper.

The fight, the fear, the anger, it all just stops. It's scooped out, leaving holes and pits in their wake.

And I...

I?

I blink.

My head feels light. My ears sound hollow. Something chomps...

"How long will it take?" I hear someone ask.

Who?

What?

I'm very far away. Or very close. I'm watching myself from above in a disconnected dream.

But wait...there was something I needed to do...someone I needed to get to.

A stranger comes up beside me, wiping her hands off, blue striped eyes looking at me with contemplation.

She smiles. "Not long."

People scream. When I look around, there are so many faces looking at me in horror. In devastation.

"What did you do to her?" the fae with a wound on his arm shouts.

I frown...

But a hand on my arm tugs me away.

I feel my memories, my *self*, tugging away too.

And away

And a w a y

And a   w   a   y

Because this is what it feels like...

to forget.

THREE QUEENS
PART TWO

There once were three queens,
inside two different lands.
Past, present, and void,
to whom destiny hands.

Three queens were declared, but only one born.
She was the ice that looked on in scorn.

The other was brought, through a bridge, she was made.
When her fate fell, the goddesses bayed.

The last was a vine, who reached through the split.
Gilt come to rain, Fates come to knit.

Together they were, apart they would be.
But these different queens, heard the song of the Three.

And that ballad, it played, like a whisper or drum.
It sang in their ears, with a pulse and a thrum.

The stars above, they watched and they waited.
Divine gripped the bridge and fed snow into Jaded.
Then tipped back the sun, and out hatched the gold-plated.

That is how the Three were then fated.

There once were three queens.
But one thing about them, the same.
These three were reborn.

And with magic…
they claimed.

ACKNOWLEDGEMENTS

Writing this book during postpartum with a baby was no easy feat. I gave everything I could to creating these pages, and I don't think I'd ever be able to adequately describe all the emotions I went through. But the only reason I was able to write a single sentence this year was because of my family and friends.

I'm thankful for my husband, for getting me through every dark day. My oldest daughter, for always being my little sun. And for my brand new daughter, for bringing so much new love into our lives.

To my parents and sister, sometimes I feel like I couldn't breathe without you. You helped me so much, healing me again from the inside out, helping me through postpartum and this deadline. You were here for weeks at a time, helping in any way you could, and I am so grateful for how much you rallied me and made me feel like I could do it. To my niece, thank you for dropping everything and coming out to help.

And thank the goddesses for postpartum doulas. Without their help, my anxiety would have been so much worse, my healing so much slower.
My life went through a major transformation while writing this book, and *Gold* itself transformed too.

For the better.

There were growing pains, but I've never worked so hard or for so long on a single book like I did with *Gold*. Now that it's written, I'm so happy with what it became.

And the only reason it became anything of worth, the only reason I was able to finish the damn thing at all, was because of the amazing people who helped get me through each chapter.

Sarah A Parker, Ivy Asher, and Ann Denton, I don't even know how many messages we exchanged over the course of this book. Probably thousands. I always say I couldn't create a book without you, but this time, I mean it on such a deeper level. Because through so much of this, I was struggling to find my way with a new baby, while also trying to navigate these characters. I have never been more stressed, more pressured, or more emotional than I was while writing Gold. But you three helped get me through each day, helped me polish every single sentence, dove in time and time again, dropping everything else just so you could read for me or encourage me to keep going. You're my best friends, you're amazing women, incredibly talented writers, and I am so damn grateful for you. Thank you for seeing me through to the end and talking me off all the ledges. You didn't just make Auren stronger. You made me stronger too.

To Helayna, you're such an intrinsic part of my process, and I'd feel lost without you. Thank you for being here for me during the wait and the rush, and for all the time you spent on polishing this book, right down to the tiniest detail.

To my agent, Kim, thank you for cheering me on, for all of your support, and for your continuous hard work on this series, taking it far beyond anything I could've dreamed. You are a freaking superstar.

To Rebecca and everyone on the Plated Prisoner team at Penguin Michael Joseph, thank you so much for taking on this series and believing in me and in Auren's journey. Thank you for helping me shape what Gold became, and for all of your patience and advice.

To Aubrey, thank you for making such gorgeous covers. I love your beautiful brain.

To CR Jane, Rachel, and Candice, thank you for taking the time to read and for all your feedback. And Rachel, for also managing my social media, especially while I just wasn't in the headspace to be able to do it. You are amazing and have the perfect eye, and I'm always so grateful for your help.

To my formatter, Amy, thank you for making *Gold* truly shine.

And a BIG, HUGE, GINORMOUS thank you to the readers.

I am in constant awe of your continued support. I see all the posts, tags, BookTok videos, cosplays, artwork, and comments, and I just want to let you know how thankful I am. I feel like I empty a part of myself every time I write, but then your kind words and enthusiasm fill me back up again. I wouldn't be doing any of this without you. Thank you for loving this series and taking the time in your own busy lives to fall into this world with me.

And for anyone going through a dark time, just remember a new dawn always rises. One day at a time. One step. You are strong, just like Auren, and you shine just like her too.

—RK